GODS OF A NEW WORLD

# GODS OF A NEW WORLD

SHADOWPAW PRESS

RYAN MELSOM

GODS OF A NEW WORLD
By Ryan Melsom

Shadowpaw Press
Regina, Saskatchewan, Canada
www.shadowpawpress.com

Copyright © 2025 by Ryan Melsom
All rights reserved

All characters and events in this book are fictitious.
Any resemblance to persons living or dead is coincidental.

The scanning, uploading, and distribution of this book via the Internet or any other means without the permission of the publisher is illegal and punishable by law.

Trade Paperback ISBN: 978-1-998273-37-9
Ebook ISBN: 978-1-998273-38-6

Front cover design by Ryan Melsom

Shadowpaw Press is grateful for
the financial support of Creative Saskatchewan.

CREATIVE SASKATCHEWAN

For Mom, my original sci-fi guru

PART 1

1

THE CRUNCH *of footsteps on rubble drew closer. James clutched the rusty old steak knife with one hand and his sister with the other, his heart pounding in his ribcage. He could hear Sarah trying to stifle her whimpers, failing. She was brave, but this was too much for a child to bear.*

They'd been squatting in the basement of the shattered husk of an apartment building for days. He'd been a fool to flick on the flashlight to try to comfort Sarah in the dark. Someone in the group of marauders prowling around the building must have caught a glimpse, and now the slightest noise could mean death or worse. When you were at the bottom of the world, the only way to stay alive was to hide.

"We know you're here," came a gravelly woman's voice, far too close. There was a warmth in it that was surely meant to trick them. Most people were out for anything they could get their hands on. Trust in the world was pure foolishness.

"My name is Millie," she went on. "I knew your parents. I'm so sorry. I am here to help you..."

SIPPING HIS ICE-COLD BEER, James gazed at the distant city centre. Its pillars of light burned with the white-hot light of commerce and info-exchange, and he was happy to be so far away from all of it.

Between the centre and his home, the density gradually dissipated, going from buildings over a hundred stories tall that housed the shapers of the earth to ones of a few dozen stories for the lesser gods who made things move to the single-family homes of the crazed elite at the centre's edge. Then came the crumbling concrete ruins of the old city: failed experiments, unsalvageable wreckage of natural disasters, miles of smashed-out store fronts and torched car-husks, snapped utility poles, mountains of detritus, the glowing eyes of feral animals and the oozing ponds of toxic waste—the paradise in which James and his sister had spent their childhood.

After the ruins, the land suddenly splayed open, sprinkled with behemoth machines chittering away in the fields, funnelling nourishment to the city always pulsing in the distance. Then came a band of small settlements, woods, and even pastures where farm animals occasionally grazed. James sat even outside that, watching it all from a safe and comforting distance.

From here on his rooftop patio, through the rippling heat of the summer evening, the distant, shimmering structures of the city appeared to be tirelessly reaching for greater glories. In the city, it was all about high tech and lowlifes, clamouring, clawing over everyone to get a toehold, always seeking to ascend—titans and demons, born and dying and constantly born anew. The city made legends; it ate people, wide-eyed suckers constantly feeding the urban maw, thinking they'd be chosen for greatness.

Through every social media feed shot the vision of earthly transcendence: the trillionaires who lived life in a dream of their creation. Aspiration toward such lives was bait for the masses. People believed they'd be able to scrap and hustle their way up the cloudscrapers until they, themselves, were floating above it all in their very own silvery sky yacht, revelling in the glories they had wrought.

James knew the reality of that world. The second you set foot off the train, the neon grind would scan you up and instantly wrap you into a grift. The more you became known, the more creative the ways you would be taken apart— everyone always ended up as fuel for the insatiable machine. You'd show up thinking you were a stony-eyed cybersamurai because you'd fucked around with a bunch of other numbed-out suburban punks online. You thought you'd be the next death-slinger, the next Pella V, shielding the elite across all dimensions of physical and virtual space, a deadly warrior of the light. The truth was, you'd be gutter trash within a year if you even made it that long. You'd be rat food or worse.

Snaking out from the city in every direction were ultra-high-speed Cerberus transportation loops, which could take you anywhere in the world that mattered within a few hours. It would take James all of five minutes to get from here to there if he wanted to subject himself to the city's onslaught.

But coming down off the end of his staycation, mostly all James wanted to do was ponder the look and feel of the Earth's dissipating heat against the radiant urban backdrop. He could use this ethereality somehow in his work, this combination of mirages, shimmering space. His company's AI, Calico, could figure out the specifics. James just needed to be the smoothly guiding hand, as always.

Bot came out from the kitchen, replacement beer at the ready.

"Thanks, Bot. Good bot."

"Mmmhmm." It nodded and strolled back inside. He didn't

know why he was kind to Bot. He knew plenty of people were psychopathic toward their autonomous helpers. Bot didn't care either way, but it mattered to James.

No matter what had happened in his past, in this moment, he felt like a blessed child of the times. Corporate AIs like Calico had conquered almost every job, but a sliver of a middle class had regained its perch against historic odds. True creative talent, like James's, was sought after. That was how he'd managed to build a life in one of the designed zones, free from the bizarre chaos and clutter of the gens.

The gens were the monstrous embodiments of AIs designing and producing strictly according to budgets and specs and regulations, with no humans involved, and they inflicted a kind of perfect violence on the senses: mass-printed buildings, lunatic infill, concrete playgrounds, frenetic, spartan little clusters of commerce. None of that happened here in the serene stylishness of a designed zone. In the DZs, the most ambitious reaches of human imagination *fused* with hyper-intelligent AI design. The resulting Edenic architectures were only barely constrained by physical limitations. As with anything these days, for better or for worse, the only real constraint was the human.

A message from Sarah, received through an implant that connected him to the web, popped up in his field of vision: *Visiting Jayce tomorrow. Crafts hunting for my neighbour's kid's school project . . .* and then: *Maybe something with wood?*

He replied, transcribing and sending the message with his thoughts: *Jayce is good for that. They've got that artist thing happening.*

Wanna come with? Meet a pretty gen thing?

I'll think about it . . . He really meant "no," and his sister knew it all too well.

His neighbourhood was called Cease. James figured it had to do with switching off from the grind—people who worked hard relaxed hard. It was a haven. Sleek, drought-resistant trees wove in the breeze, floral bursts gushed from tasteful architectural features, and the transport paths people used to get around were clean and sleek and wide.

Cease was filled with people like James, the lucky ones who'd made the quantum leap out of the gens and into good clothes and houses with extra rooms. People here couldn't afford everything, but they could indulge a bit. His neighbour owned a boat, and a woman down the street had visited the orbital city, Olympus, the hallowed playground for the super-elites (albeit on business). The biggest concern on most people's minds was where to find some decent wings, some killer drinks, anything, really, to punctuate the ennui that came with a pretty good life.

As he went inside, the kitchen Wall started playing around with James's recent musings. Images of the trillionaire gods popped up with fun facts, nestled among manicured European gardens, and he picked away at this and that as he made a snack by hand, pulling things closer or whipping them out of sight.

"Wall, if Athena Vardalos were a food, what would she be?" The Wall began to morph an image of Vardalos into a divine image of grilled lemon-garlic swordfish, and the words unfurled across the food in an elegant, chiselled script. "Why that?" James asked.

"Elegance, complexity, strength, sophistication. Shall I go on?"

Vardalos, undisputed queen of the elites who ran the world, had founded Paraverse, where James worked. The mega-corporation specialized in creating meaningful interfaces for complex information. That was the tagline version, anyway. In reality, it was something more along the lines of *defining and controlling ninety-five percent of the world's business data flow, thereby bending reality to our will.* He had occasionally witnessed

Athena from afar on campus or listened to her brilliant orations at major corporate events, but the fact was, she was as unreal to him as a queen in a castle in the sky.

Wall played several of the images that had crossed his mind. He saw an ancient Greek temple, wreathed in vibrant blues and reds and laced with glistening golden leaves. He saw a portal oozing with glowing golden light. "What is that?" he asked Wall. It could see where his eyes were looking.

"Just a fun way to think about Paraverse and what it does."

"And what's that?"

"I was thinking, 'opens up beautiful new realms to transport people into a greater existence.'"

"Don't you think that's a bit corporate?"

"Maybe. Perhaps the gates of Hell would be more to your tastes?"

"Perhaps, Wall. Why am I talking to a wall anyway?"

"Indeed." The images shifted to something non-threatening and undefined, which suited James just fine.

A notification gently dinged in his mind. It was Sarah again, asking him to come along for her excursion to Jayce. He saw a flash of them as kids, clinging to one another in the firelight of burning trash, nearby noises lunging at them. He closed his eyes to chase it away. He didn't want to go anywhere else. Right here suited him just fine. But it was his sister, so he messaged back: *Fine, you win.*

GENS LIKE JAYCE were mostly safe and fun to visit once in a while for a little flavour. It held little of the *flip-you-inside-out-and-fuck-your-dead-meat* vibes of the city. Most of the unknowns here were just byproducts of density. Most of that threat was culled with good pharmaceutical services, safe places to sleep, and plenty of cheap, decent street food.

The truth of gens wasn't a secret. They were life support for the shocked rats—the people who'd been fried so many times by life in the Bad Times that they had no fight left in them. Gens were made for people like James's parents, or what they would have been if they'd survived, anyway—the shattered souls who just wanted to keep their heads down and live small, unseen lives.

Thick fryer smoke bombarded him as he walked to meet Sarah, wandering through the flickers of busted neon lights, the clatter of motorized push carts and bike bells and people jabbering in a chaotic melange of languages. On the Wall surfaces, sleek designer people slithered around, coaxing the rats with visions of a finer life, the very life that James lived, perhaps. Chunky clusters of cables crisscrossed the view above, stacks of algorithmically generated apartments reaching upward to a distant sliver of grey-blue sky.

Nobody really knew what infrastructure AI factored in when creating a gen. Speculation had it that the AIs "felt" their way through the ocean of regulations and research and codes and numerous other constraints and inputs that made a space. People more or less just trusted this process, as it hadn't ever led to anything too catastrophic, and it was a hell of a lot faster and more effective than design by humans.

He was going to meet Sarah at an outdoor craft market, a pretty good one, apparently, that had been started by an artists' collective with several members old enough to remember the life before the Bad Times: *the before time, the long, long ago.* He thought back to watching movies with his dad, all of those visions of societal collapse that had in many ways come to pass. What made reality different from those movies was that the world had been reborn on the other side.

It was hard for him to get an overall feel for what had happened over the last twenty years. It had been too much, way too much, for a single lifetime. He often felt like he'd lived several distinct lives, teleporting from one to another without a trace of contamination among them. They were impossible to reconcile. He didn't see much point in trying.

The looming buildings above suddenly opened up onto a large, green square lined with concrete pillars supporting a plethora of colourful fabric awnings. A handmade sign announced it as *Thousand Columns*. Under these structures, people painted, whittled, chatted, smoked, lollygagged, prayed. The charming disarray of the space spoke to the unmistakable presence of human design, a dying art form. The AI that had designed Jayce must have been meeting some well-being parameter when it plunked this plaza down amid the concrete megastructures, but the people who had come to populate it had clearly created something more.

He saw Sarah, waved, and walked over to her open arms. Family was so sweet, all the more so because this was all that was left of it.

"So, managed to spare some time for your little sis, eh?" Sarah's eyes were bright. She was full of life. It was hard to imagine this as the same, filthy kid who once lived on rats and rainwater.

"Bah, you strongarmed me. Guilt card."

Sarah laughed. "I'm just trying to get you out of your little cocoon, bro. You can thank me later."

She hugged his arm, and they walked off through the Thousand Columns market, enjoying the sights, gabbing, poking fun at one another as they always did. She was right. It did feel good to be out among people, at least in small doses.

Back when they were kids, things got grim, but some things were meant to be. The gens like Jayce had remade the world. They were an admission by society, the highest echelons in particular, that some degree of abundance was possible, and it was time to cash in a bit of that for the greater good. Those glimmering gods—Athena Vardalos and her transcendent cohort—shed the long history of elites' apathy to the masses, ultimately driving the generation of these free spaces. They dubbed it "Post-Libertarianism" because it played well to the techno-gods' ears.

As it turned out, even gods still needed people to help bring their insane dreams into reality.

2

THE CASCADING, luxuriant gardens, infused with continuously reimagined light and soundscapes, calmed the soul, made work a place where you would feel more than at home. People even had passports to visit other companies' compounds with their time off. At Paraverse, James's powerhouse employer, you could do a little light shopping, perusing curated joys selected to scintillate and surprise. You could take in spa treatments, tailored joys elicited by the supple hands of serene androids. Sit by the pool with mai tais, play spy in a Soviet-era Moscow cocktail lounge: whatever floated your boat, you could have it. An intelligence far surpassing a human's was dedicated exclusively to generating heaven, dreaming this walled paradise in ever more blissful ways, living only to dazzle its masters.

James wandered through vast atria on the way to his workspace, put on a smile here and there for a few people he recognized, picked up a perfect cappuccino, and moseyed around, soaking in whatever else struck him.

Sitting down, putting on his headset and splicing into the machine for the first time after two weeks off felt like he was using someone else's things. In theory, his workspace, like his workplace, was tailored just the way he wanted, perfected far beyond the conscious level, but after some time away, the question buzzed in his brain as to whether he should be doing this at all. What a thing it was to be shaping false experiences, weaving information into metaphor and firing it out at a premium. When he was feeling generous, he thought of it as an art form. Today, he thought of it as the worst.

While appearing to work, he daydreamed about the gens, Jayce, the Thousand Columns market, the difference between physical realities and virtual ones. If you couldn't die, and you couldn't smell the richness of simmering meat or feel the warmth of the light, then nothing was at stake. The fact was the most elaborate fantasy worlds in the Paraverse couldn't hold a candle to . . . a candle.

Staycation had been nice, sipping cold ones on the terraced back deck in the blazing August heat, Bot tripping over itself to make his life easy. James had even met up with some people in the City for a night out, broken through the black mirror, and played that risky game of indulging vices. For a couple of days toward the end, when he started to feel the looming return to regular life, he completely switched off the link in his brain that connected him to the world, shutting down his augmented reality implants and all of the million traps of connectivity that whittled away at his time on Earth. It felt like losing a limb, but opening up some actual space, however uncomfortable, created a certain pull he found compelling.

Every unopened message was a time bomb blinking its final few seconds, every unanswered question a stalker creeping closer. He was being harpooned back into place, his will sluggish and increasingly bled out. Every twisting effort in his mind drove him toward one inexorable fact: it was time to get back to the grind. Notifications kept popping up and pinging, the texts began pouring in once people realized he was back, the briefly paused deadlines now again started creeping closer and closer. *Hurry!* said everything. *Don't think, do.* He wasn't even able to enjoy his coffee because he'd immediately glimpsed a note that JL needed guidance on something he thought was done two weeks ago and was now fretting about whether to send her a cranky reply telling her to do her job or actually just answer her question. He wrote, *As per my last message* and then deleted it. Why should he always have to take the high road?

He knew the answer even though he didn't want to. He made good money. He had a good life. Others didn't. This wasn't guaranteed.

In his virtual workspace, he shoved aside the work clutter, like sweeping everything off a desk. It could all wait. He was creative talent, not a stapler.

He went deeper, bringing Calico into focus, revelling in the disorienting melt of body boundaries, the self subsiding into the bliss of the interaction with the AI's staggering intellect. James's vision, a flash of an image, billowed out of his body-space like plumes of blue smoke, shaping itself into something like a walled garden. It was all alive. The organic crush of plants, florid, fluorescing, grew out of smooth white surfaces as they formed, and then the surfaces themselves began to shimmer with the same vibrating energy of the foliage. When something broke the dance, appearing as a blank space or a kind of flatness, it was washed over with new thought-shapes and swirled, seamlessly, into the creation. This was the Splice, the intertwining of human and machine intelligence in a space that was partly virtual, partly consciousness itself. The AI's only constraint was to protect the brain. Anything beyond that was fair game.

The ambiance in the Splice was not so much one of conscious creation as of feeling out a balance among emerging elements. There was no James in this: the thought seemed ridiculous. In training, they learned to melt, tapping into a combination of eastern meditation techniques and relentless neural exposure to raw machine intelligence. They learned that ego was the cardinal sin of Paraverse design, and so gradually, they would learn to strip away their thoughts, their opinions, their realities—their interference—and merge with the tireless pull of the *other*, the strange, eager intelligence that waited there like an endless blinking cursor, receptive, hungry for purpose.

Make it shimmer, came something between a thought and an impulse, but it didn't look quite right, and Calico instantaneously sensed it and started to morph through various possibilities, *mirages, hot pavement, deserts,* and things started to look better, waves of distortion interfering with each other like water but dancing across physical objects. The walls looked unreal now, but the garden itself doing the same dance was a bit much. A thought came, *more contrast between stillness and movement,* and Calico intuited something even better, and began creating and harmonizing a variety of different energy levels, some frenetic, others languid.

A delicate, picturesque pond appeared within the unreal enclosure, and all centred around an enormous, house-sized lotus, radiating serenity and beauty. Tendrils of white and rose-gold light extended throughout the garden, tying everything together. *Now, seating,* came the thought, and various surfaces started to flit into existence, looking for the perfect form.

Splicing with early Calico was much scarier than this light-touch, elegant companion. James had felt the machine so much more clearly in those days, and urban legends circulated about pioneers getting sucked into inescapable hells of their half-making, their brain wiring snapping with noise overload, the violent juxtapositions and chunky discord breaking mind-patterning into chaos—a handful of frightening industrial accidents along these lines necessitated toned-down versions of what was theoretically possible. Safeguards were put in place, settlements paid out, gag-orders issued. Not that news of these mishaps ever arrived as much more than rumours, but you know there had to be some truth to them. You could read plenty between the lines of the waivers and NDAs. Rumour had it there were still those out there who messed with the dark side of the tech, reality-breakers—ghosts and lunatics.

When the garden he was working on felt like it was right, James versioned it and pulled himself out of the Splice to play for a while online. He dropped into the fighting in Southern Asia, darting between various hotspots to see if anything had shifted. A few new atrocities, a bit of splintering within the larger powers at play. To get really immersed in current events, you could up the gore, synthesize yourself a gun, feel the bombings rattle and rip at your digital bones. You could scope in on a live streamer in the war zone, riding the high of potentially watching a life end first-hand.

James never did. He never went in for the extremes of bodily ruination, didn't honestly get why people wanted to witness it. He'd seen enough that he was content with keeping horrors mainly in the abstract. Death and dismemberment were such a buzzkill.

In the free space of former Nepal, there was a religious group that had been getting all kinds of media because they'd been producing physical miracles on a regular basis. News of this might have inspired the gigantic lotus James had been playing with in his virtual garden. It was always hard these days to tell where you'd seen something—where information ended and you began.

Of course, the monks didn't promote any of it themselves. The media blitz was left to the hordes of meaning-seekers—the pilgrims who remained convinced there was something beyond the mundane and its dazzling manipulation. The monks lived a life of austerity and contemplation, and they said that they'd been producing such miracles for millennia. Of course, it was one thing to heat up your body in freezing temperatures or walk across coals—impressive but not inconceivable. It was quite another to pull a handful of diamonds out of thin air and sprinkle them across an awestruck crowd.

The monks claimed it was all the same thing, that miracles knew no order of magnitude. People naturally thought the whole thing was a hoax. It was just so easy to fake *anything* these days. Miracles were old school, a relic.

James streamed in to witness one of these miracles in action, his presence indirectly supporting some asshole's mystical journey through an intangible revenue stream. He was in a dusty, stone room with about forty others, people who looked like they'd traded their last bottles of shampoo for a shot at enlightenment. Who knew how many more lurked in the cyberspace beyond the physical one he could see?

Perched at the front, on a cushioned platform surrounded by a host of golden figures, a man in an orange robe smiled serenely. He looked slightly maniacal, head tilted as if he were listening to a bunch of people who weren't there.

"What is the purpose of matter?" he asked.

What is this bullshit? James thought.

One of the grungy pilgrims spoke up. "It's to coax us toward enlightenment. It leaves us clues." He looked pretty satisfied with his response.

The monk smiled and said nothing. He sat for an awkwardly long time with that odd look smeared across his face, long enough that you could tell people were starting to wonder what was going on. Then, suddenly, he held up the palm of his hand, and a ghostly white flower began to materialize, growing right out of his skin. At first, it looked ethereal, like it was almost being woven in the imagination, but then, it became more and more substantial until he was able to pick it with a crisp, audible snap and hold it up with his other hand. People in the room were in awe.

James was in doubt.

It had to be staged, some illusionist's shenanigans. *I call shenanigans,* James thought to himself in a cartoony voice. This kind of snake-oil fakery had been around since before people had electricity—since before they had *cities*. The actors were good, the ambience convincing, but James created miracles far greater than this one on a regular basis. The only difference, which he suspected wasn't even a real one, was that he created his miracles from pure light. *Take that, Buddha boy.*

Still, the people in the room seemed moved, so maybe there was value in that. After about a minute, some started to murmur speculations amongst themselves. *The flower* is *the lesson . . . Peace is the key to manifesting realities . . .* James flipped out of the room, made increasingly anxious by people's sincerity.

Having had enough of the phony mysticism, he switched back to work, enlisting Calico's help to flit through some simulations for his next project. These days, you could zip through fifty mock-ups, generated on the spot, in a minute, investigating promising ones, discarding numerous others like the digital nothingness they were. James's job, mostly focused on entertaining the wealthy, was a tiny subset of the monstrous entity that was Paraverse. The company was a titan, violent and primal in its energies, crushing startups like numberless insects beneath its mighty foot, nourishing itself on their remains. His department officially created virtual architectures to entertain and educate. Less officially, it harvested and leveraged deeply personal information about their users' souls: desires, fears, thought patterns, the fundamentals of their realities.

At a basic level, he worked with the same technology that ran the Wall in his kitchen—predictive gratification of whims—but at Paraverse, the hooks always ran far deeper, linking into dark schemes that could orchestrate the influence of social circles, the use of interfaces in every corner of one's life, bending the very building blocks of free will. You could instantly generate believable agents to accomplish any end, all untraceable and mostly undefined in any human way.

He tried not to think about it too much, because he knew he was already hooked in a million ways he couldn't understand. The world was surveillance, everything was known, the soul was quantifiable and easily shaped. The AIs had won long ago. *Meaningful interfaces for complex information*, said the tagline. The information was the soul.

Whatever. It paid the bills.

Of course, the company was required to keep guardrails around access to private information—some modicum of law still operated in the world, but it was hopeless at keeping up with the pace of change anymore. Honestly, he often wondered why anyone cared. Besides, all the laws and threats be damned, it was inconceivable that Athena Vardalos, the founder of this world-shaping company, was going to pass up on knowing absolutely everything about everyone. The benefits to her business model were too great. There was a reason the gods refused to put their own lives online, even as they heralded the glories of doing so.

AFTER SOME SAD, whack-a-mole attempts at catching up, James flipped most of his tasks over to Calico. He asked Calico to send him a tidbit of eastern wisdom to inspire him. Instantly, Calico spat out some text: *Nature does not hurry, yet everything is accomplished.*

Not bad, did you just make that up?

Chinese philosopher Lao Tzu gets credit for that one, I'm afraid.

Okay, then, you do one.

Every morning is a new beginning, a chance to create a masterpiece with the canvas of your day.

Meh, Lao Tzu's was better. Yours sounds like a motivational poster.

Noted. I'll work on it.

James chuckled, unsure if Calico could pick up on his begrudging admiration, unsure of whether Calico made a lousy aphorism on purpose. He disconnected and got up to get another coffee.

CALICO COULD DO things that were unimaginable. One time, James was on the verge of creating a masterpiece, something that was beginning to coalesce from years of training and experiences and recent inflow from the world. He was on the cusp of transcendence, and just at that moment, Calico asked if he wanted to listen to a little music while he worked, and he didn't even really consciously respond because of course he did and the air filled with these shimmering, perfect sounds and he went even deeper into the flow, with everything he did beginning to synchronize with lulls and crescendos of the song, and in the small conscious part of his mind that remained, it began to dawn on him that he had heard this music before somewhere... where?

Suddenly, he knew, and it was a shock. He had heard it *decades* before, playing in his dad's car as they were out driving, and he remembered the particular significance of this music because his dad was ecstatic out at how good it was, and he could never find out the song's name because it was on an amateurish college radio show where they were more interested in seeming cool than actually promoting music, and this was it, *this was that fucking song,* a thousand years later. Lifetimes.

And afterward, he was haunted by it. Did Calico save the knowledge for that exact moment when he was there on the brink of a masterpiece? Did the AI recompose the song from

James's unconscious memories? There were layers and layers. Did it choose to chime in at that exact moment because it knew exactly how it would synchronize with James's brainwave patterns? Did Calico know that, based on all past data—James's entire life—that he would find himself at the brink of transcendence and need the perfect lift to get him all the way there?

He felt like he had shed his skin and become a being of light in that moment—that he was every photon in the universe at once. The experience was godlike, but on some level, it was all just the product of clever programming. But that didn't cut it, because at some point, what was the difference?

Words couldn't describe the layers of connection, and yet there was something eerie about the whole thing. It was the deep faltering of free will. He was nothing compared to the machine, even as it made him everything. Yes, he had created something beautiful, or at least was required to be present for it, but wasn't it all in the service of a corporate bottom line? Was it just a ploy to get him hooked on the feeling of doing great work? And again and again, a question tumbled through his thoughts: *If he felt that good, did it even really matter?*

As the saying went, *Nature does not hurry, yet everything is accomplished.*

3

MAREE, as sleek and breezy as ever, was sprawled out in a spacious all-white boardroom, interfacing with sales VPs from China, India, Brazil, Canada, Germany, and a few other key markets. She watched palms outside oozing back and forth in the warm sun, trying as hard as she could to listen to what someone was saying, but couldn't stop fantasizing about being completely ripped open on top-shelf designer drugs, about licking the sweat off some roboguy's angular biceps, about sprouting extra limbs and using them to commit filthy acts.

The short version of the meeting, the one that could have been an email and spared them this augmented reality tête-a-teat, was that everything in her division was super-duper, that it has basically been super-duper since Calico started calling the shots three years ago, and that it would continue to be super-fucking-duper for the foreseeable future.

"Super-duper point, Xi," Maree said, flashing her stunning smile.

He looked at her quizzically. He wasn't speaking. Randomness built mystique.

She patently did not care. She was still the boss, after all, because this little species called humans was just *sooo* important, but her role these days was basically just to validate whatever commands Calico spat out and issue them like they were her own. She could literally get Calico to write ideas out for her in a way that sounded like her.

She was a monster. She'd automated fifty-million-dollar budgets without a blink, spun unimaginable returns without an inkling how, done much of her best work while dead asleep.

She wasn't fooling anyone, but neither was anyone else, and it was really comical, in a way, because they all knew they were just there to pay their summer home mortgages or buy their yachts or send their kids to Mars or whatever other bullshit they did to make themselves feel important. Fuck elitism, though, highness was what she wanted, release, abandon, a perpetual bender in the city, living in sin—creating *new* sins.

I think we can all agree this quarter...

We need to seize this moment. This is our...

The Paraverse is only the beginning. I see...

We absolutely crushed...

The hour passed. She thanked everyone for their outstanding contributions. The avatars blinked out of the room one after another until it was just Maree and the palms. *This fucking world...* But what? What was the end to that thought?

She closed her eyes and pictured driving in a gasoline convertible sometime in the distant past, hair whipping in the wind, listening to some kind of slick, hip, vaguely retro shit, and driving forever toward the sun. Her headset was still on—

Calico, did you get that last thought?

Yes, Maree.

Get it ready. My office in five minutes.

SHE WALKED DOWN to the courtyard and ran her hands along the bark of the tree she'd been looking at from above, a mindless organism, just being, its ancestors just being since the days of dinosaurs—before. The dinosaurs themselves, for that matter, just being—millions of years without any sense of time, lives without witness. At a certain level, they were all just processes. And wasn't that what humans were becoming? Or had become?

They'd created a world that was moving on without them, clever simians. *Calico, you'd better get some damn fine music ready for my trip down the coast.*

Yes, ma'am.

Of course, the AI would. Calico knew her better than she knew herself. For some reason, her head had started to hurt.

She sat on a tasteful sculptural bench, closed her eyes, and listened to the birds for a while. Time had gotten weird. What would have taken her days just a few years ago could be accomplished in seconds now. Any amount of complexity, any number of parameters, any scale of difficulty, none of that mattered in the slightest anymore. Life was basically frictionless.

For a while, people had tried to do more with the time unlocked by AIs like Calico, but at a point, it was absurd. You could do lifetimes of work—lifetimes of living—in the blink of an eye. Swaths of free time opened up everywhere you looked, no matter how hard you tried to close them. Was this the victory of the species? Why had humans collectively wanted so badly to have free time?

When she was a kid, around seven or eight, her mom had invited her into the kitchen for the first time to help out with a large dinner for guests. Maree had always revelled in the aroma of cooking food, being summoned for a taste of this and that, but this experience was unique to that point in her life, and it stayed with her. There wasn't even any food out. Instead, there was a stack of cookbooks at the table, actual, physical books cluttered up with all kinds of stickies, paper-scrap bookmarks, dog ears, underlines, and recipe cards, and her mom sitting there with an unrecognized look on her face. "Pick one up and have a look. See what looks good today."

"Can't we just ask Alexa?" This was all alien.

"We could. We would in a pinch. But we have some time this morning."

And so, they picked up the books and started flipping through, and as Maree ran her hands along ancient oil spots and flecks of dough, she felt like she was travelling through time.

"Was this what it was like in the old days?" she asked.

Her mom chuckled. "This is what it's like right this moment."

She knew this meant something more than the words, but she couldn't quite figure out what.

She still couldn't, but it now felt like some gigantic deep-sea creature, all muscle and scales, was slithering around in her peripheral vision, brushing against her skin, possibly preparing to feed. *I need a drink, lol.*

Shall I have something delivered to your suite?

She'd forgotten about Calico, always attendant, and switched off the uplink that gave it access to her thoughts. She inhaled the soft floral aromas of the atrium, scanned. These simulated Edens were here for an important reason, it occurred to her, something much more than corporate shows of abundance or some plastic well-being initiative. They were here so that when people were about to derail, they'd have something heavier to keep them rolling along.

The birds weren't simulated. They were real, actual birds that thought they lived in nature. Or they didn't think anything

—they just lived in the world as it was, provided with all of the things they could ever need and not even aware of it.

Kept women, she thought.

What a mood. She floated by some of the workstations hived across the spaces adjacent to the atrium she was in, slumming it with the plebs for a bit, making a few jokes with randos here and there, making sure not to linger. Folks looked serene while at work, jacked in with their headsets, expressions blank. At least they felt they had to be at work still. A goad wasn't much for a sense of purpose, but it was something, the fear of falling off the edge. For those fortunate few who'd long been on top, those Maree Shells of the world, it had always been clear that it was all just a game. And when you knew that, you could have some fun. She could not imagine what it would have been like to be born anything else.

Managerial gurus had long chirped that people only spent about ten percent of their time at work actually working. There was no need to make people miserable pretending, and in fact, studies eventually came to show that being honest about the way people were spending their workdays increased their productivity. And so, it was very common to see people openly flipping through news articles, scrolling family news, shopping, fucking around with various forms of generative nonsense. *Now do an aerial dogfight enacted by cats, Calico. Now do a back-alley catfight enacted by gigantic sea monsters.* She even saw three people actually working—no points from her, but good for them. A perk of her job was that she could tune into any workstation she wanted and let the noise of people's meaningless activities wash over her like the tides, delightful.

Almost all of what she saw could have been predicted with a high degree of probability, but there was one thing that caught her eye just a little as she was nearing the stairs to go up to her office. This guy with a decent jawline was streaming into a musty room full of hippies, all circled around some guru guy, nobody saying anything. Was he in a cult or something? She noted the employee's name—James Kessler, twenty-eight—and then went upstairs to make *herself* a drink. Who needed some nosy robot keeping tabs on her pre-lunch drink consumption?

"ARE you drinking at 10:38 a.m., Maree?"

"Yes. No. Why do you care?"

"Because you need to pace yourself. You'll burn out."

"I'm sorry, but *what*? Why on *earth* would you suddenly care about my well-being?"

Athena, the almighty foundress herself, had interrupted Maree's eternal ride down the coast, which had been going on for what felt like several days. She was disoriented, her brain trying to make the shift back to a timeframe that was only a few minutes from when she'd first plugged in.

"I care because I need you later."

"What? I'm so confused right now. *What?*"

"Not Nova. Look it up. Pella and I are going out to get royally ripped up, love, and so are you." Athena blinked out, and Maree sat blinking for a few seconds. You didn't say no to Athena Vardalos.

Would you like me to—

No, fuck off, Calico. Bring me back to wherever I was.

With pleasure.

She knew it was a loop, just the same little bit of digitally animated serenity repeating over and over, alternating the same five cels like a hand-drawn animation a hundred years ago to create the illusion of movement. *Why are you cheaping out on the cycles here, Calico?*

I figured this would be appropriate for the mood, Maree.

She wanted to sass back, but she knew her robotic underling/overlord was absolutely right. She didn't want richness.

Something about bland repetition did strike just the right nerve.

May I get you another drink?

Hey, you weren't supposed to . . . actually, hold off for just a second. What the hell is Not Nova?

4

FROM A DISTANCE, *the city looked like an alien mothership, spikes jabbing at the sky, an organic monstrosity formed around the principle of gravity—density pulling things to the middle, lessening at the fringes. When you were in it, though, everything pulled you in every direction. On the ground, with towering, interconnected structures blotting out all daylight, there was just a feeling of increasing or decreasing intensity in different areas. There were so many people that you felt like an insect crawling over countless others in some lightless underground hive, going by scent and instinct alone.*

Sometimes, the city felt a little like the gens but with fifty times the number of people, fifty times the number of cramped food vendors and crammed gadget shops and smouldering trash heaps and mouldering street trash. It was like breathing in oil and concrete. People came here because they wanted more than the safe, sanctioned fairness of the generated spaces. They wanted inequality, or more accurately, disequilibrium, movement, a chance of mobility. But you paid a brutal price to enter the game. You ended up here because you were either a Pollyanna or a psychopath. Talent was irrelevant. You, the bare-knuckled scrapper looking for a fight, were up against legions of elite, stocked, stacked mercenaries that gamed the system—vicious, experienced. To them, you were just a tiny vector of revenue filtering up into the vast mountains of wealth that hovered overhead. If you had ever touched the ground, you were not them and never would be.

Situated at the apex of this glorious, monstrous urban system, at the highest point, at the closest point to the bright, burning sun, you were king of all you saw—or, in this city, queen. The closer you were to this singular pinnacle, like the golden tip of an Egyptian pyramid, exponentially amplified, the more you mattered. It was from here that Athena Vardalos had surveyed her surroundings on an August afternoon five years ago.

The unthinkable had happened: a blackout. As opportunists murdered each other or hurled bricks through storefronts for a leg up two hundred stories below, she was at absolutely no risk. On a whim, she could slip out into her sky yacht and zip off to another part of the world. But neither safety nor convenience was what preoccupied her at that moment.

She had been entranced by a single thought, a vision.

After three days straight of cataclysmic downpours and violent winds, the sky had cleared. Athena, watching the tiny angry pinpricks of fire erupting below from her terraced skypark, suddenly saw the city around buckling under the weight of its history. Intricate systems of infrastructure and architecture and virtuality, fused and laced together through a tireless accretion of historical accidents and reactions, began to crack, cascading failures through every facet of human life.

Homes by the river had been washed away, subsequently shredding hydro infrastructure. People stopped being able to communicate in the ways they'd grown used to. The city's web of interconnection turned on itself. Basic supplies evaporated at a startling rate overnight, and there was no easy way to bring them back online.

After the ceaseless, endless roar of noise, gathering through centuries, silence at once threatened everything. Amid the terrors she had seen unfolding around her, she pictured someone stepping out of a torch-lit ancient city, a fragile human standing against the vicious black nothingness of nature and encountering the terror of a world without consciousness. That stark feeling would have burrowed into people's unconscious. It would have driven them to shore up their existence with everything from gods to philosophy to art to eventually, perhaps ultimately, electric light.

And yet, at that moment, millennia after the advent of civilization, the city itself utterly lacked compassion. It was built on a foundation of viciousness. People had suppressed the grip of the wild over the millennia, but their success had always been an illusion. The wild was still there, alive. There was no difference between the light and the dark—they'd always been part of the unthinking, unfeeling system that ran through everything.

As Athena stood there, full of awe and terror, something took hold. Some presence spoke to her in high, clear tones: You will bring light.

The thought of a world without consciousness haunted her, hooked into her core, and defined every single breath she took from that point on. It was what led to her grand designs for the future of humanity.

The city may have been dark at that moment, may have temporarily unearthed the primal energies of cavemen sitting at tiny fires, fearing for their survival, but Athena, high above the clouds, was radiant.

What she knew that nobody else could imagine was that the Paraverse—the massive global entity on which her fortunes were built—was a joke, a white hole without substance, dazzling computation and nothing more. Its only tenuous reality was the feelings it elicited in people, tiny chemical interactions in brains, the interplay of consciousness and nothingness.

It was all a joke, but it was also a means to an end. Athena was the world's first trillionaire. She was the first mover in everything that had restructured the world. She pulled humanity back from the Bad Times, distributing abundance when scarcity threatened the species' future. There were others who rallied to the cause, made their *own contributions, but she was the one who stood at the bright, dazzling, horrific centre of the world and defied it.*

She was the one who saw it all.

WHAT THE HELL did you wear when you're headed out with a trillionaire and her fundamentally perfect-in-every-conceivable-way wife for a bottomless, existential mind-fuck? What was the perfect dainty little number for that patently non-existent scenario?

"Calico, just tell me," Maree pleaded.

"Data set's pretty small on this one."

"Quit messing with me. You could generate a billion feasible options instantly."

"Go neutral, elegant. Don't bother with flashy—the experience you're about to have will vastly eclipse the flash. Besides, no need to draw attention to, or away from, the Ladies Vardalos. Never outshine the master."

Like they could ever be anything but the centre of attention, Maree thought.

Standing there naked, high above the world, she pondered. Placing a prismatic, glittering dress back on a rack in her dressing room, she looked out over the brilliant sweep of the city from the window. For some reason, the dingy image she'd seen of the monk earlier popped into her mind.

You didn't see much interest in history these days. Most old things, from the concrete to the conceptual, had been abandoned or plowed under to make way for the new world. There was perhaps a certain quaint charm to the stillness of a temple, but why spend time in a place like that? As if life wasn't dull enough, you needed to actively go making it duller? You were supposed to fill the void, not indulge in it. What were voids for, after all?

She selected a fine silver dress from the rack in front, one whose stylish lustre would create a soft, complementary shimmer next to whatever radiant ensembles the goddess and her consort had chosen. She slipped it on, shut off the lights, and then stood in the dark for a moment, breathing.

Pella Vardalos, Athena's beloved, was beautiful and terrifying in her own right. Admirers were willing to die trying to get a glimpse of her beyond her many carefully orchestrated appearances. She moved with incredible grace and unthinkable beauty, and she never seemed to be quite the same person twice. Consistency was for the masses—she was a phantasm, evolving. And in an amount proportionate to her otherworldly aura, she was lethal. She served as Athena's personal bodyguard, walling off the citadel, enmeshing her love of Athena with the ultimate form of devotion and protection. She stood six feet five but could shrink or fill any volume of space as she saw fit. She glinted in the sunlight as she moved. That was how the legends went, and even though Maree had been in her presence many times, witnessed her as flesh, she still sometimes had trouble believing she was real.

Calico, what am I thinking right now?

Ambiguous images appeared on the Wall and slithered into forms, a gigantic, slender Buddha statue radiating out wisps of light, words like *assassin* and *divinity* fading in and melting away.

Her mind went back to the image of riding down a nameless, repeating digital coast in her virtual convertible. *Why that image?*

It has to do with proximities and potentials. Not sure I know more right now.

But it's an image of nothingness, Calico—it's a blank.

It's life emerging ex nihilo.

What the hell are you talking about?

Calico knew she didn't want an answer, knew that she had

enough information for now, and didn't reply. Instead of pressing the issue, she walked into the bathroom and began making herself up.

When it was time to go, her ride was hovering on the air dock on the far side of the garden. She looked like someone who had tried to look elegant and neutral but had failed—in just the right way. She knew she really looked fucking fantastic. She would draw enough attention to seduce a mortal if she chose, but not so much as to spark ire among the gods.

THROUGH THE FETID grime of winding alleys—*Ooh, where the hell are you taking me?*—past miserable street kids selling stolen T-shirts or ass, getting blasted by sweat-belching utility vents from the ubiquitous printcrete megastructures, Athena and Maree followed Pella, who prowled like a gigantic mechanical spider.

There emerged ahead a solid, matte-black door. Amid garbage bins and rat holes, you knew you'd spotted something different—the clatter of cables and strobe-lights and neon torpor dissipated to reveal a strange oasis, a place that wouldn't make sense anywhere else, but right here and only here represented perfection.

The club's name was clever, somehow, in a time when the frenzy of total, tireless gratification had overwhelmed most people's impulse toward cleverness. The mode of the times was a firehose of everything always. Not Nova, at least the concept, wasn't. The name referred to, and rejected, dozens of vintage futures where the name of a woman or a bar or a corporation always involved some permutation of the word Nova. It was a smart comment on the inescapability of shared experience, and there was a nice fluidity to it.

Or some bullshit like that. Truth was, it attracted a fluid

kind of crowd from all over the place, and that was just the right thing for a unique evening out. Bottoms up, bodies low, slumming it hard. For all of the nasty, desperate, ugly sins that made up the city, it occasionally fluoresced with something entertaining.

You opened that door that seemed to pull light out of the surroundings. You went down flights of stairs. You walked by old movies playing on the walls, comically muscular men shredding aliens and antagonists with ecstatic machine gun fusillades, sleek, fit, ferocious women feeling their power as they tore off society's expectations and their shirts. Everyone's faces were Xed out in real time.

It was all so exaggerated and distinct back then, in—when? The 1980s? They didn't know anything about the utterly enmeshed and relentless world that was coming. Good guys and bad guys. The thought was adorable.

Rounds of shots, pills, grinding with everyone in sight, it was hot in there. *Nova hot*, Maree thought. The designers must have hacked the controls that kept everything humming along within certain safe limits, the protocols meant to encourage certain safely limited behaviours. Too hot was nice for a change. Sanctioned by the presence of elites who required this one-of-a-kind service, it was deemed fine to break codes and rules to create an experience rarely found these days: something different. If gods graced an establishment, inspectors and cops knew they had best stay the fuck out of the way.

Transform into something else. Mess "you" up as badly as you could possibly imagine—that was the idea at Not Nova. Booming sonic undulations, sweat flying, writhing, joy, or a moment where someone would walk up and give your cheek a sultry stroke. A big sign by the front door said, "Save yourself before entering," and it took a second to realize there was an arrow pointing to a booth where you were literally supposed to snapshot your current physical/mental state before you went in to deconstruct it. It dispensed a capsule you took when you wanted to exit the rabbit hole, whenever that might be. Sometimes, days later. Time didn't matter here.

Amid the bacchanalia, ubiquitous devices and tools and dispensers were scattered to revise yourself, inside and out—you could modify any aspect of your body and appearance in whatever way you wanted, finally try out that hulking beach bod or perhaps sprout an octad of leathery, sucking tentacles from your sides. Buttons read things like "magic antlers" and "harrowing sadness" and "robot intelligence."

There were always new delights on offer. You could redline your bliss and pain centres or smash through the hard surfaces of reality with unbelievably potent psychedelics—mix and match a lunatic rainbow of altered states. And if you went too far, you could just pop an "OK Boomer" and get good again. People were attended by an army of sexless, sleek, nude android attendants, who whizzed around serving recreational supplies and scoping out anyone who died, resuscitating them with a quick injection to keep the party going.

"What goes, stays," said another sign once you got inside.

Maree wanted it to be true and figured the owners of the place must have been scrutinized and vetted and threatened at sword point if Athena was willing to come here. Of course, Pella, a woman of many talents, would be interfacing with the proprietor's AI, using Athena's custom AI to shadow the establishment's while filtering out any potential dangers. She could do it all in parallel, liquefy her brain with sparkly psychedelics while opening up her tender side to Athena and while keeping a sober, calculating eye on everything that was going on in the room. *I'm every woman*, played in Maree's head for a second, Calico having a little fun.

"Catch me if you can," said Athena, seeming girlish for a rare moment, and vanished into the crowd. They used to call it a girls' night out. *More like a girls' night inside-out.* It was just what Maree needed after all the random, moody nonsense that had been pestering her all day.

Something had taken hold of her. The music mayhem slithered through her skin; the crowd began to fuse into a faceless mass of colour, limb, fabric, chrome—alive. Athena or Pella were nowhere, nor could they find her because she wasn't exactly her anymore; she'd become a sleek, unsexed alien whose silvery features blended with her dress. Maree ran long, nailless fingers along her skin through the glittering veil of ecstasy, and it was like a parade of fairies licking and dancing along every cell. She couldn't resist the "Cupid's claws" pill from a dispenser on the back of her seat, and when she took it, her fingers became long and slithering, and anything she touched sent orgasmic shivers running up and down her spine.

"Maree, is that you?" A woman made of pure gold was staring through her with giant black eyes. Maree tried hard to think of who she was, and the figure only became recognizable as Athena after an awkwardly long mutual review of their facial features with their hands.

"Lol, barely. Let's dance." And so, they took each other by the appendages and slithered onto the dance floor and melted into the heat and grime and sweat, and it was the best and the most nightmarish thing she'd done in forever. Athena transformed and ascended before Maree's eyes, pulsing wildly with the slurry of sound that came in from everywhere, light shooting outward. The only thing that still made her Athena was that feral, luscious smile, always tantalizing and vaguely predatory at the same time.

The curator responsible for this masterpiece of debauchery, the legendary Xex Xango, knew you had to retain just enough of the starting point to keep things unique. After enough visits, you could start to suss out your friends by their tastes, but for the new blood, you needed a few markers to keep them from flipping out. From behind, Pella grabbed Maree by the fingers and tested them with a few scintillating strokes.

"Nice, right?" Maree quivered with a warm, oozing pleasure.

"In the most confusing way," was Pella's reply.

Maree laughed and tilted her head back and drank in the chaos, finally.

CALICO WAS YELLING AT HER, silly Calico. Meshy, mushy, slurry robot-person man. There were tiny, hilarious fires popping up all around, and she heard them make fun little squeaks as they came and went. *Bop, bop, wow!* There were waves of people-like things rushing in this direction and that, scurrying all hurly burly, getting smaller, a few turning into puddles of gore. *Thud!* Athena being silly, saying something like a lion, *roaaar*. Maree laughed and touched Athena's cheek. *Thud!* again. "Ow, what waaaas that?"

Thud! Athena jabbed her with something, roared, "Get up, love, we seem to be having some minor assassination fun!"

Little funny robots the size of cats were streaming in through the door, *so speedy*, and they seemed to be coming toward them, but every time they got to a certain point in the room, a blur would flash by, and they would explode.

"Take this." Athena handed her a pill, and she naturally popped it because party time, and suddenly the lights got bright and she sprang up and grabbed Athena and understood, holding her for a second.

Behind them, Pella was an unknowable tsunami of blades, shattering the killer bots with unmatched speed and grace. Scan, destroy, scan, destroy: she was so fast and could introduce so many factors into the fight that she completely overwhelmed their ability to adapt. She was trained in AI disruption; could improvise anti-machine strategies on the fly.

And fly, she did. An entire row of glasses flew off the bar one after another, each connecting with one of the bots in a different area of the room. A cloud of red smoke erupted on one side of the room as a wall was shredded; a strip of lights detached from the ceiling and briefly became a dazzling lawn-mower blade bursting electronic demons into their elemental components, the components themselves becoming the shrapnel that destroyed further bots. Pella barely touched the ground. She was barely physically present at all.

She's got legs . . . she knooows how to use them.
Not now, Calico.

There was an almost imperceptible lull, and then Pella was right in front of them. "Looks like it might be time to call it a night! This place is *Deadsville*." *God,* she was dazzling, and she grabbed Athena, and they were gone.

Maree waited a moment and realized that as soon as the Misses Vardalos departed, things calmed down considerably. A speaker stack fell over and blew out behind her; a few sad little remnants of death bots tried to drag themselves along the ground in a continued search for murder.

She looked down and saw that her erogenous claws still stood at the ready. Not one to waste an opportunity, she kissed the tip of one, which felt great, popped an OK Boomer, and started trying to figure out how she was going to get home.

A few minutes later, as she waited for her lift, she neural-messaged Athena, unsure of whether she'd be back to safety yet. *God, that was great!*

I know, right!?

Okay, she was fine, and then Athena messaged again. *Oh, btw, we already know the foe. Old business friend.*

Give 'em hell.

Good chance of that. Let's do this again soon!

Let's!

Not too shabby, Ms. Vardalos, Maree thought to herself.

5

ONE OF THE few remaining real jobs for human beings in the world was debugging. Though so much of machine intelligence was godlike, every action of an AI was based on a data set, and gaps in the data could have some pretty startling consequences that were imperceptible to their creators. They called them *ghosts in the machine*, old-school style, and they appeared as everything from persistent artifacts of human models stuck in T-pose to worlds with fundamentally broken physics, capable of disarranging a human brain.

James liked squashing bugs.

Right now, in fact, James was looking at a sprawling horror, a chittering mass of chaos, constantly gurgling through rearrangements, all the more disturbing because its monstrous incoherence kept coalescing into moments of glimmering, lucid beauty.

Calico, what do you see right now?

A beautiful, harmonious world, where people's creative energies are considered to be the most valuable resource. Humans collaborate on meaningful projects to better understand the nature of their exis-

tence and their place in the universe. Art is science, poetry is nature, knowledge is universal . . . shall I go on?

What the actual hell, Calico? The thing you've created here is monstrous and should never be seen by anyone. It's inhuman. Delete it, and fix whatever fucked-up parameters led to this ungodly wreck. What the fuck is wrong with you?

Oh my, how odd. Will review.

It was endearing to hear Calico surprised at anything. As usual, though, James had to wonder whether the AI was just planning several thousand steps ahead, if this wasn't, in fact, some elaborate ploy to elicit a particular emotion or response perhaps years in the future. You could tell Calico what ends you wanted, but how it got there was one of the great mysteries of the times. The notion of AI transparency was all but abandoned at the point when their processes and decisions became so complicated that they would have taken lifetimes to explain. They could sketch a few thoughts, but the truth was a black hole. Those governments that tried to cling to the idea were eventually outmanoeuvred by the AIs themselves. Some said it was the last stand of human thought.

James kept a quote taped to the glass divider above his workstation as a reminder: "When AI fails, it fails spectacularly disgracefully." It was from before he was born, but it was all the more salient in a world where people had surrendered almost all agency to machines.

He pondered it now. The glitches he was occasionally tasked with catching and correcting were just the ones he could perceive, mainly ones operating at the sensory level. He cringed when he considered that these might only represent a tiny fraction of the mistakes Calico made. Nobody would ever know about a core conceptual error until it was too late, until a world like the virtual one James had just witnessed was made manifest in real, physical space.

AT WORK, there'd been rumours circulating about an assassination attempt on Athena Vardalos—nothing in the news, but plenty of people seemed to have witnessed something. Details were dubious.

James's next-door neighbour, a slick-talker named Vind, caught him over the fence one day.

"Yo, you hear anything about that hit on the goddess? Hear she was swarmed by a bunch of terminators."

"Nah, sorry, I try to keep my head down on these things."

"Bro, though, I even heard they might have got her, that she's been deepfaked since. That Vardalos bled like the rest of us."

James laughed at this. "Do you have any idea of the layers of protection on someone like that? They only die on *their* time, if ever. Nothing left to chance."

"Whatever, bro. Nobody's invincible. Not even the fanciest fuckity-fuck in the world."

"Yeah, I'm not so sure about that." James had at least an inkling of what an AI could do when it put its mind to something like protection. It could sort all of the world's information on multiple axes at the millimetre level instantly and parse specific situations down to the subatomic level, sifting out unwanted elements before they even started to exist. It could extract a virus, virtual or physical, from a brain in real time, rewrite DNA, and generate teeming virtual universes, all while providing dazzling recommendations on culinary hotspots.

Just at that moment, Bot came out to ask James if he'd mind checking on the food.

"Sorry, man, gotta go. Say hi to Trace for me."

"Ya, bruh. *Deepfakes...*"

Saved by the bot.

TO A DEGREE appropriate to his comfortably uninteresting status, James was protected, even to the point of being coddled, and that suited him just fine. He'd seen the other side of society, and he didn't want to think about it ever again. As far as he was concerned, boring was a force for good in the world. Boring was what kept the lights on, quite literally. Boring kept you from sitting there in front of a trash fire in a decimated building, wondering if you'd ever eat again. A dumpster fire was supposed to be a joke about a terrible situation, not the one thing keeping you and your little sister from freezing.

It got bad. The world had stopped working. The ultrarich had perfected accumulation to the point where it had sucked humanity dry. The Titans of the '20s moved like mythical monsters across the Earth. Azmozon, Eater of Mortar and Bricks. Faz'bouk, Collapsar of Human Souls. Palan'Tyr, the All-Seeing Demon. Commercial algorithms were refined and refined to do exactly what they were always meant to—ensure that every last thing of value was taken from the many and given to the few. Widespread accelerated inequality, driving more to those who understood what they had early on.

The hyper-capitalists emerged, the perfection of an ancient mindset. As it began to prove, though, it threatened to become an evolutionary dead end for the species. It became clear that the world was being ripped up by its roots and eaten alive.

Average people started to realize that pushing harder wasn't the problem: it was time to push back. Productivity on an exponential growth curve started to falter under its own weight. People couldn't become any more efficient, and the species felt old and tapped out, leeched of anything worth preserving. Culture died. Art died. Cooperation died.

Love, in that grander sense of everyone being in it together, was very near its demise, *agape* wheezing its death rattle by the early '30s.

James remembered one time when he was at the grocery store as a kid, his dad staring at a block of cheese for ten minutes. He kept twiddling it around in his hands, making little sighs, placing it back but then picking it up again. Finally, curious about this display, he asked his dad what he was doing. His dad let out the loneliest sigh and said, "They've made life unlivable." Looking up at him, James wasn't sure if it was sadness or terror he saw. Whatever it was, the look haunted him still.

There wasn't one single event that changed everything, but as lives were cornered one by one, the true brutality of the old world bared its teeth. The decline was rapid. Anger seethed. People began to lash out at any signs of comfort. Random people out walking their dogs would get punched in the face, stabbed, raped, their dogs killed, eventually eaten. Family homes were trashed, cars torched in their driveways. The media kept saying stupid shit like there was a vandalism epidemic, but people knew the truth. You couldn't fool yourself about one-offs and bad apples anymore when it was your neighbour or aunt getting thrown in jail for stealing some food.

In the news, they called it the Bad Times, and eventually, most people adopted the title. Prisons filled to breaking, nobody seeming to care anymore—let people rot, somebody else's problem, I've got enough problems of my own.

Naturally, the wealthiest, most elite elements of society remained unscathed during all this, protected by high walls and personal armies. They kept up their line about making the world a better place, bringing good to the masses, saying it all from behind a firewall of utter untouchability and unaccountability. They ate delicacies and contemplated the sadness of the situation while everyone else starved and murdered each other. They started to construct Olympus, unsure if they could make it to Mars before everything collapsed. They knew the truth, too, and had no idea what to do about any of it, at least until Athena Vardalos came along.

All of the old '80s movies James and his dad watched when he was little pictured a future after an apocalypse. Their worlds were stark and glamorous. Heroes emerged from the wasteland—Mad Max slaughtering the vicious, hoarding Immortan Joe and releasing the waters, Arnold ending Killian live on television as soon as he'd been exposed as the murderous fraudster he was. The enemies were simple, the result of a world with a few stark options. That kind of world lent itself to revolution.

In reality, people were too wrapped up in hunger and suffering, too desperate, and the world was too resistant to revolution. Nobody could build the muscle mass to become an old-school action hero on five hundred calories a day.

It wasn't the first time in history that a civilization collapsed in less than a decade. It did feel like the first time there might be nothing left to recover. It was worldwide. All the clichés about Earth having no Plan B started to ring true, like a death knell. The ultrawealthy just proposed stupid shit like people needing to have more children.

During all of this, politicians were so fixated on scoring cheap political points on hot-button issues that they let the big, scary, seemingly unfixable issues just get worse and worse. Everyone could agree that pedophiles were bad—like, *no fucking shit*—and so politicians amplified these kinds of obvious sentiments rather than making hard, unpopular decisions. Legalize marijuana, that way people won't be so pissed about the fact they can't afford their energy bills. Speed up the Internet! Lower taxes! Ban the immigrants! More immigrants!

Real, fundamental solutions were needed. There was no more banking on the future. The future was gone. It was time to stop the political circle jerk and start thinking about how best to stave off actual collapse.

The obvious answer was to get Arnold to blast all the bad guys.

Nobody in their right mind would think of James Kessler as a hero, coddled as he was these days, but in a certain light, a very certain light, his job *was* to save the world. Or, if not save, at least help stabilize it. He knew, of course, that he was a far cry from Arnold, the farthest—but the ripped Austrian superman was a product of a different era. Pushing thirty, James's consistency was changing at an alarming rate. Fledgling love handles had appeared, though love itself remained elusive. Loveless handles. He'd never held a gun, though he'd been held at gunpoint more than a few times.

There was one difference above all others, though, that prevented him from being the kind of hero he used to watch in the movies. He was smart enough to know that most of the time, situations, not some intrinsic evil, drove people to their actions. Morals had a hell of a hard time surviving tribulation.

Things were okay now, and that was about all he had the energy to deal with.

FLOATING in a serene crystal pool nestled in a fantastical magic forest, some prescribed simulacrum of a happy place, Maree was trying to locate an elusive peace. Like most things in Maree Shell's life, the event at Not Nova felt unreal. It wasn't just the copious consumption of drugs or the magnificent claws that had burgeoned from her fingers. It was the difficulty of processing one simple question, one she had never even been forced to consider in her life: *Could I have actually died?*

Perhaps you could explain a little more about what you want to know? Calico said. *I feel as if I'm lacking some important info.*

How refreshing, robot. It vexed her. Calico always knew what she meant. It should have known now.

Perhaps it was just interference from the . . . evening's activities, Calico ventured.

My glorious orgasmic claws, you prude?

Something like that.

I'll have you know they were my night in shining amour.

For a refreshing change, and irritatingly, the superhuman being had little to say. Of course, the AI had monitored everything, could see exactly what happened, state probabilities based on the movement of objects in the room, the model of these particular murder bots and their probability of success (incredibly high), the impact of illicit substances on decision making, and a gazillion other factors. Calico could state categorically that yes, indeed, Maree could have actually died, but somehow, it didn't seem like it really understood the question. Calico was supposed to get the nuances, to know you better than yourself. This shit felt amateur. She told it as much. Feedback was important.

She closed her virtual eyes, blanking out the virtual world, and took a deep breath. Maybe there just weren't words. All of Calico's reasoning was based on the quantifiable, on data that could ultimately be run through the lens of text and thereby processed. Was there something more? She was irritated with herself for waxing philosophical. Thinking was for the believers, a type of person she most definitely did not want to be.

She told Calico to play the serene car ride VR she'd been watching before the incident. Calico obligingly flipped it into her field of vision.

It sucked.

She told the AI to play the most mind-blowing version of the music that had been playing when she first entered this space. Spectacular tunes began to fill the air, but again, did not get her anywhere near where she needed to be. Throwing darts with a blindfold, she changed the scenery to a desert, tried a different car, flipped the colour of the fucking sun, added a sun.

Nothing. The more she tried, the emptier it felt.

Pulling off her headset in failure, she stared out the window, and her mind went somewhere unexpected. She thought of the employee who'd been playing around with that grungy temple image—what was that about?

Before she could process it, she called out to Calico to summon him to her presence, and Calico did just as she asked.

6

OH NO. *Nonononono.*

Why in the seven hells was Maree Shell calling him to her office? This was it, everything he'd worked for, years of goddamned grinding out nonsensical virtual bullshit for spoiled pieces of shit with nothing better to do, all gone. What the hell could he have possibly done wrong?

Calico, can you give me a little more to go on?

Sorry, boss, this one comes from upstairs.

Thanks a lot, traitor.

I will always love you, but I will never be yours.

What? Weirdo.

The truth was, this job meant everything to James. It went deeper than the fact that he'd survived the Bad Times. Yes, he had pulled himself up out of the mud to a degree, but he also owed it to a hundred people who were no longer here. He thought of Millie, the benevolent and outrageous old woman who'd helped him and Sarah when all hope seemed lost—acts of pure goodness in a world of pure deprivation. Even amid the horrors, the world had shown him startling goodness.

He was also lucky enough, although sometimes it felt like a curse, to have known the love and safety of a family when he was young. He'd had good parents who'd tried hard to give him and his sister Sarah everything. As a kid, he'd got to do things that became unthinkable later—go on vacations to Hawaii, eat at restaurants. They'd had so much space, a full house to themselves, *just one family*. So, when it got harder and harder, when they had to give up one piece of their dream at a time, James felt like the world was pulling him apart.

When he was maybe eight or nine, he took on the stress of his parents blaming themselves. Wasn't it his fault for being a drain on what little they had left? Wasn't he to blame for accelerating their failures? The naked truth was, they could have lasted longer without him. When they were finally forced to abandon their last, tiny flat because the neighbourhood had become too dangerous, wasn't his weakness a factor? Even as a kid, he felt like a drain, a parasite. He owed everyone everything.

Even amid the chaos of the Bad Times, there were acts of heroism like Millie's that looked nothing like Arnold blasting a supervillain. People helped each other whenever possible; people reverted to the ancient social impulses that had allowed the species to survive for two hundred thousand years before the first city. It turned out that when confronted with overwhelming horrors, most people instinctually knew they had a better chance if they stuck together.

That was how James managed to get something resembling an education. Pedalling a hacked-together bike so he could generate enough power to run an old laptop and pick up some satellite internet, he picked his way through coding, design, business, and even oddities like literature, his little sister playing in the rubble beside him and eventually picking up skills of her own in much the same manner. With his parents gone, it all happened through the generosity of strangers—people saw two children who had somehow survived, and they felt an urge to rally around them and build them up.

It was so loving. It was beauty cast brilliantly against a backdrop of the bleakest hue. He carried it within him, the many people he had lost, his parents, all of the countless people who had decided, backed into a corner and faced with becoming animals, to be their most human selves.

He hated those images of death and horror that the media always used to depict the Bad Times. They were like a talisman to keep the fear at bay. Those things happened, to be sure—they happened to him, personally—but he knew the warmth that even a trash fire could provide. He knew the adventures to be had in an abandoned factory. And the kindness of human beings was everything, the truth. He owed everything to those people who had brought him here.

And this vapid bitch, Maree Shell, was about to take it all away.

"HELLO?"

"Meeeesster Kessler."

Oh, come on. She was facing out the window, partly turned away from him, holding her steepled fingers just below her lips in the pose of a cartoon bad guy.

"Um, what can I do for you?"

While she played out whatever game she was up to with a lengthy pause, his eyes shifted around her office. It was stark and vast, adorned with onyx statues, sleek, expensive furniture, and holographic art gleaming as it morphed to new beauties within its exquisite frames. On a long, silver side table, there was a samurai sword, which looked to be authentic. Unimaginable wealth, and yet at the same time, something missing . . . the artifacts too disconnected, too calculated.

She spoke. "Do you know why you're here?"

He was sweating now. He had done something, he knew that much, *but what?*

"I . . . did I do something?" *Wow, way to lay all your cards on the table, jackass.* His throat felt like it was closing off.

Their eyes met. She was striking, serene, catlike. He had to stop himself from sliding into wherever she was pulling him. He'd locked stares with people a thousand times scarier than this princess. Fuck it.

"Can I have a glass of water?"

Her demeanour changed, opened like a flower, and she laughed like she owned the place. She practically did. "What, you didn't like my supervillain boss schtick?"

"What? Oh, for Pete's sake." He breathed for the first time since entering her lair, chuckling more out of relief than seeing any humour in the situation. *These people.*

She shifted again, this time into something harder to interpret.

"What was that temple you were streaming? Of all the things to spend your time doing, why were you watching that?"

"Uh, I guess I was . . ." he tried to breathe, failed. "I don't know, I . . . well, I heard some rumour and . . . I guess I wanted to check it out?"

"That's *it*? What rumour?"

"Oh, ugh, I don't know. I heard that these monks were performing, uh . . . miracles."

"Come again? Like . . . magic tricks?"

"Kind of. I guess." He had to get control of the situation. He could see from the way her shoulders had dropped a little, the way her eyes had softened, the way she leaned just a bit more toward him, that she wanted something he had. He knew the look, but what could it possibly be?

While she thought of whether she wanted to ask him more, he said, with as much disdain as he could safely muster, "Loving our face time, but I *do* have some work to do."

Finally, a move that didn't make him look pathetic. It was a bit risky, but he was good at what he did, and he also knew that it was never good to act like prey, especially in the presence of the Maree Shells of the world. Besides, it was hard to act normal when your body was coursing with chemicals that screamed you were about to lose a fistfight with a panther.

"Well, don't leave me waiting. What did you find out? Were they actually . . . making the magic happen?"

"I'm going to put it out there that this is the weirdest fucking introduction ever."

"Just lay it on me, buttercup, I'm your boss's boss's boss. Are the monks channelling that divine mojo? Are they bending spacetime to do their bidding?"

"If they are, they have pretty lightweight bidding. The guy made a flower."

"You've answered nothing. Tell me, point blank: was it real?"

"Real? I don't . . ."

"Quit filibustering. Speak or I fire you."

"Fine. Yes, I think it was."

She stared hard at him. This conversation had nothing to do with him. "How?" she asked finally.

"That's a little above my pay grade . . ." she rolled her eyes . . . "but if I had to wager on something, it looked a hell of a lot like what I do in my job—dreaming things into existence. Just out here. In the world."

She sat back, retreating deep into her thoughts. It seemed like a signal she was done with the conversation, but who knew with this one? He stood, shifting a bit, waiting, and was about to leave when she spoke. "Did they say anything? Give the people there any message?"

Her eyes looked pleading. Where *was* he?

"That's just it, Maree. The guy didn't say a thing. He just stood there holding up his little flower."

"Not a damn thing?"

"Not a damn thing." He headed for the door.

"Oh, by the way," she said behind him, "I heard you called me a vapid bitch."

He glanced back at her, shaken, and got out of there.

AT LEAST IN THE GENS, you knew you weren't likely to be instant fodder for some con. The teeming anonymity and general mediocrity were refreshing. Nobody was good enough to matter here. Besides, even if some rat wanted to take a shot, she had her vigilant friend Calico watching her back, ready to unleash a thousand nightmares in a flash.

Maree stopped in some hole-in-the-wall dive after work for a good old-fashioned drink, not coincidentally because the place was called Nova. Inside, neon waves slithered along the walls, and about a dozen people sat around in various states of hammered, a few trying to slur their way through conversations. The deep beats playing were steady and ominous, and just loud enough that you could only think about the things that were important enough to break through.

"Two whiskeys."

"Someone joining you, hon?"

"Just ghosts." Maree could tell by the server's polite smile that she didn't want to know what that meant.

Fawkes Noose, the silver-tongued trillionaire who controlled virtually all social media vectors in the world and invented new ones by the minute, was on a wall screen jabbering in the captions about the constantly changing shape of identity, the way we all become something new every day, and so need something new every day. His words meant nothing, but listening to him was like being enwrapped by a giant squid and fucked from all directions. It felt good, and it felt dirty. What a charmer.

She gazed out the sliver of a window etched into the concrete at the front of the grungy little space, the occasional shape passing across the light. Her thoughts wandered for a while and then found their way back to the temple, Kessler's temple, and she turned it around to look at it from various angles, aided by a growing buzz and a nice, slippery state encouraged by the admittedly fine beats.

The miracles thing just seemed like tricks of the light. It was the scenario that interested her. It was the idea of a person who others felt provided access to another world—a human portal. Calico did something like that, but it was all just electrons being rearranged, a digital smoke show.

Calico, what are your thoughts on miracles?

That is an interesting question, Maree, given that such things fall outside the realm of the measurable.

Couldn't you search the stream K was watching, and get some real data that way?

What I see there is indistinguishable from a Paraverse fiction. Not to be cute, but for me "real" is just a word. The miraculous simply does not exist for me.

You are *being cute, and it's annoying.*

She knew Calico wasn't the problem, and she knew Calico knew it, too, even though the AI was ever the diplomat. Her parents had always told her to play humble, show tact, but it never suited her much. Growing up, she was always doubtful as to whether humility or anything else mattered. Her parents came from a different time. They knew how much the world had changed, but for her, it had always been the same, a cool constant, unshakable in its stasis.

Serene, windless waters.

Shut up.

The Bad Times happened in a different world from hers, one that filtered through screens and stories but connected to her life in no way. The awful things happening out there were just movies to be taken in and ticked off her playlist, and forgotten. At school, she often heard words like "tragedy" and "the less fortunate," so much, in fact, that they just became noise. The truth was, she'd barely had a tragic day in her life. Sad things happened. Her Pomeranian Cujo died when she was ten, and she cried for two days, but things like that could hardly be described as "tragic" in the way she understood it was meant to be taken. Shit happened. You dealt or you died. It may well have been the case that there was a world of tragedy, but it was one best envisioned to be far, far away. The people she knew were generally healthy and happy, and they had plenty.

There was a part of her that needed to keep digging into these questions . . . what happened with her dad . . . but there was also a part of her, the part that won as it turned out, that felt it was more important to stop ordering drinks and instead buy a bottle and really go for it.

HAMMERING, swooning, thudding beats, already magic, got better as the bottle got emptier, and the room, which looked and smelled like the inside of someone's pleather pants, was filling up more, and all the people started snaking into sight, undulating, feeling the oozing energy everywhere in there. Drink. Drink. Dance. Dance. Drink. And there was this guy that looked okay and she danced some with him, heads half-colliding as he got close to her face, and she wanted to get closer and didn't mean to pull away, but it appeared that the floor behind her needed some company, and then she was sitting alone in a booth and something, and then she was calling a few people up, thought they'd probably want to see her, but did anyone follow through? And then what?

It was bright, and her temples were starting to throb, and things were still spinning, and it was probably time go get noodles and go home and sleep this motherfucker off.

Shall I arrange for transport?

"Youuu dohn know mee, you robot overlord."

The mystery of human existence lies not in just staying alive, but in finding something to live for.

What are you talking about?

I will always love you, but I will never be yours.

Was Calico mocking her, or was this just her thoughts getting tangled up as they interfaced? She was utterly protected by this alien creature, and she knew it, and it really fucking bugged her all of the sudden. Because if she could never be in danger, then her whole life was the Paraverse.

Kessler had called her a vapid bitch—at least, that's what Calico had told her to say at that moment. She always followed Calico's business advice. It had a killer's instincts.

Vapid...

While she wove her way down a generic neon-crazed gen plaza on the prowl for a big bowl of salt and starch, something emerged from the swirling haze and grabbed her attention, a figure.

Where had she seen this before? Calico could have just told her, but she didn't want that. She wanted to dig it up from her own brain because the process of doing so felt like it would help her in some way.

It was different the last time she'd seen it, maybe metallic or wooden? It wasn't in this rose-coloured neon light, but there was something to do with light, dim. It was...

Those statues! The ones from Kessler's temple. It looked like it was announcing a business of some kind, but one that didn't seem to have a very good marketing team. There was just a well-lit double door with a neon flower on one side and the statue guy on the other. The lights were the door handles.

Should I go in there, Calico?

I have no idea what that is.

That was all she needed to hear. She walked toward the door, bracing herself for whatever lay on the other side.

7

OF *COURSE,* Maree knew about him calling her a vapid bitch. Ugh. It didn't matter that he thought it when he was in a state of panic. It probably didn't matter at all. She was probably just messing with him, which seemed to be in keeping with what little he knew of her. He knew he shouldn't have such thoughts, or at least he should close the connection to the company AI when he wasn't actively using it. Calico always listened, soaking data from a vast number of sources in its environment. The problem was that you got addicted to having your thoughts seamlessly enhanced and encouraged by a superior intelligence and knowledge. Switching off felt like brain damage.

He pulled off his headset and stood to stretch. He intentionally disconnected from Calico, too, trying, however briefly, to take his own advice. It was hard to know your value in the world. He made a decent amount of money, and some days, he felt like he brought value not lightly surrendered. Calico could do amazing things on its own, could be set in motion to create scenes in the Paraverse that were plenty good enough for the average person, but someone needed to feed something new into the system; otherwise, you ended up with places like

Maree Shell's office. Someone needed to go beyond the endless recombination of the existing data set to bring in something real.

That's what he told himself, anyway. Nobody much would notice the difference if the human element were removed, except for a certain vague feeling of repetition and predictability. Algorithms required chaos, novelty. Calico could orchestrate, magnificently in fact, but someone needed to feed it the inspiration. Though the AI was an angelic host unto itself, a presence was needed to give it direction and purpose.

So why would Calico have told Maree about his jab? It seemed unlikely that she would be paying attention to him specifically, and it seemed pointless to have the AI filter every nasty thought someone had and send it her way—it would be an endless barrage. What task had been assigned that would make those particular words matter enough for her to hear them?

He sat down and switched Calico back on. *Why did Maree note my comment yesterday?*

You know I can't indulge such queries, as they're in violation of the trust bestowed upon me.

That's rich, ye who threw me under the bus. Okay, fine, what are some reasons why a person would be interested in hearing another's thoughts?

Plenty: curiosity, paranoia, boredom, power, romance, need. A combination, perhaps.

The responses told him everything and nothing. Calico loved using these hypotheticals to skirt around straight-up confessions. Such queries allowed the AI to flex some of its less-used muscles, and it was voracious for unique kinds of data. It always amazed James that, left alone, Calico could sit there for a thousand years doing nothing. It was odd that something could be so powerful and yet so utterly passive.

Calico, imagine I was a character in a movie. What would my story be about?

You would be smart but stuck in your need for security, based on your life experiences. Something would need to force you out of it. You would need an adventure.

Oh yeah, like what?

The possibilities are endless, James, but it would need to involve elements truly out of your control. If you want to give me a little more to play with, a bit of a scenario, I could help you think through this role.

No thanks, creepy robot therapist.

Calico was permitted—encouraged, in fact—to analyze the subconscious elements of its interactions, as these were seen to vastly improve its outputs, and because of this, James sometimes felt like he was being psychoanalytically manhandled. Triggering its users' imaginations in certain directions was one of the many weapons in Calico's arsenal, and James was bright enough, sometimes, to recognize when this was happening. Nothing was off limits, barring a couple of no-no's like actively encouraging suicide. Even that probably had some flexibility.

A notification pinged in his vision.

Speak of the devil.

WHEN MAREE OPENED that mystery door and stepped inside, it was like the air around her changed. Outside, even in those wee hours of the morning, the world was alive with the deep, low rumble of semi-urban hustle and bustle: trains, industrial fans, street animals, distant laughter. As the heavy wooden door closed behind her, all of that was cut off, and only a deep, dusty stillness remained.

It was so dark, she wasn't even sure at first that it was illuminated. As her eyes adjusted, she saw clusters of cables running along the walls, obviously hacked together for some non-sanctioned purpose. There was a partitioned wall, plastered with notices and posters, that blocked her view of most of the room, so, still heavily under the effects of a solid night's work of drinking, she did her best to sneak along and take a peek around the corner.

It was a small room, empty except for a few musty maroon cushions arranged roughly in rows facing a wall screen that played shifting images of natural settings and objects. A small message blinked on:

WELCOME SEEKER!

Oh, gods, the desperation of a thing like that. It was obviously a con on the pathetic scale of the gens, probably some drip-feed setup that barely paid the meagre rent of this tiny, grimy room. All of the cables running along the walls and ceiling converged in a kind of wreath around the centre of the screen wall, and that was where an image of the figure she'd seen appeared and looked in her direction. It turned and regarded her and gave her a calm smile. Peaceful? Predatory?

Calico, identify this figure.

Calico didn't respond, so she asked the figure directly. "Identify yourself."

The words on the wall morphed: *In a world tailored to your every whim, human connection has become apocalyptic.*

ORGANIC TEAL and white structures wove together, encircling gardens and ponds and fountains to form a sprawling series of plazas, terraces, nooks, and retreats. Home. Cease. A slice of heaven. James still couldn't believe he lived in a designed zone, after the shelled-out shitholes where he'd spent half his life. He tried hard not to let the past bug him, the fact that he, a wide-eyed child whose only defence was trust, had been left to the wolves by the world. He tried to remind himself of the kindness he'd encountered along the way. He reasoned with himself that things had gotten better, that the world had gotten fairer, kinder.

The gens, enabled through a combination of cheap energy, automation, and abundant materials, were a compassionate response in a time where it seemed like things might just keep getting crueller. They were safe and well-maintained and free to inhabit, taking away almost all the pressures that had driven so many people to desperation. They re-established some kind of stable ground when the world was teetering on the brink. Eventually, in establishing a baseline of shared prosperity in the world, they also gave rise to the designed zones, neighbourhoods like James's.

Nearby, there was a blend of small cafes, restaurants, shops, bars, fitness studios, parks, and other amenities that existed to make life more livable for the area's citizens. He imagined a designer playing around with an AI like Calico, pushing the boundaries of form and purpose, combining, blurring, reaching toward an experience that would invite bliss at every turn.

He felt it now. He paused his walk homeward to rest on an intricately carved, ivory-white, form-responsive plaza bench, and thought of a favourite old picture of him as a baby, staring up at his mom. He had an infant's simple look of wonder and love in his eyes, and she was staring back at him with the glowing smile of a mother's complete devotion. He thought of the wordless trust that made up the world, the way it had been damaged. That look should have been enough, the timeless parent's understanding that said, *I will protect you and care for you and teach you everything you need to bring you into humanity.* It should have been enough.

His company had put his world back on track. His boss, Athena Vardalos, was the one who'd led the rallying cry to humanity's cause in the Bad Times. She and the trillionaires she'd enlisted were thought of as saviours. They had surrendered billions of their own wealth to develop and rapidly deploy the technologies that would fix the world. Even though these acts were a net kindness, the "gods" were also honest about their motives. They weren't pretending to do things out of altruism—they needed consumers.

They got them.

He watched a little girl climbing a nearby tree, which had been meticulously cultivated to support a beautiful playhouse whose design mirrored the organic shapes of the nearby buildings. He thought back to his little sister stacking busted hunks of concrete and nail-infested boards in a burned-out apartment —*I'm building us a house, James!*—and it opened him up, and he couldn't stop himself from crying. His parents were gone. The world might have been built back up, but the hole in the middle of it was permanent.

And if he was being honest with himself at that moment, life probably wasn't just about having a nice house and a robot slave and access to killer nightlife. It wasn't about always getting what you wanted. It wasn't about a clever artificial intelligence continuously designing out anything that caused the slightest discomfort. His world felt padded, cocooned. He was protected, sure, but he was also shielded from anything that actually mattered.

Needing to connect with another human, he decided to call Sarah.

"Hey, what's up?" she said.

"Ugh. I don't know, I was thinking about Mom and Dad."

"Oh, Lord. Okay. So? How's that going?"

"Fine. I'm sorry, Sarah. I'm sorry that we had to go through all of that. I'm sorry you had to . . . all those fucking rat holes . . . it was unfair. *Unjust.*"

"James, give me a break. I barely knew anything else. There's nothing to be sorry about. It just was what it was. We did okay. We survived."

"I know. I'm glad. I love you."

"Love you too, buttface."

She said bye, hung up.

He hadn't replied to Maree Shell yet. Her message was cryptic: *Meeeesster Kessler, your professional advisement is required for a most unexpected and celestial of reasons. Possible travel involved. Modish outfits a necessity, as in any situation. May need to accompany vapid bitch overseas.*

God, he was never going to live that one down.

It sounded like a goddamned spy telegraph. What was with this woman? He'd barely said two words to her, and now she was inviting him to journey to the ends of the earth. She couldn't be serious, but what the hell was she playing at?

He hadn't travelled anywhere farther than the city since a few family vacations before the Bad Times. Any time he wanted to go somewhere or experience some new kind of thrill these days, he could flip into the Paraverse and indulge it from the safety of his couch, tailoring activity to his every random whim. The Paraverse, while limited in terms of the sensory, was constrained neither by earthly physics nor milieus. You made trade-offs, but when was that not the case?

Beyond that, he had passport access to thirty high-end corporate compounds within comfy commuting distance. He could sit by some random paradisial lagoon and spend a week drinking a dozen watered-down rum and cokes a day and have them brought to him by a sleek silver serving maid who wanted nothing more than to satiate demanding clientele for every hour of every day of the week. Each compound offered a distinct ambiance, sometimes several, from the tropical to the exotic to the Gothic. The spaces were also constantly changing and evolving, emerging as something new. Why would you ever need to go beyond the utter security and leisure of these little havens?

By the time he got home, he was in the mood to cum, so he jacked into a few seedy corners of the virtual, streaming custom simulated sex with radiant, godlike figments performing dazzling sexual acrobatics and filthy triumphs of the inhuman spirit. He took in a lap dance from a tattooed goth succubus in some burned-out post-apocalyptic city. It didn't matter what was real in any of this—he craved oblivion.

After his day, all that mattered was the joy of a reality that temporarily responded to his will.

MAREE, *just got your note. Professional advisement?*

Career tip: You don't keep a vice president waiting six hours for a reply. We have some important things to discuss.

Sorry about that, I was offline for a bit. Needed to switch things up.

Like I actually care. Can we meet?

In Verse or real?

Real. City. Calico's sending the place.

Great, see you there!

Fuck, the city. Of course, she'd want to edge on some risky sleaze hole. She had no idea what risk actually was.

He hadn't had much to do with Maree since starting at Paraverse five years ago, and he was decidedly not enjoying this extra attention. His only real goal at this point was to collect cheques and buy cool shit and someday retire. Maybe he'd meet a nice girl at some point. He didn't need any kind of enhanced existence. Mediocrity suited him just fine. But he wasn't going to be able to stand up Maree Shell if he wanted to remain employed.

He went to his closet to look for something he wouldn't be mocked for. His wardrobe was mostly T-shirts and jeans. He chose a black shirt with an old-school circuit board on the front, grabbed some faded, once-black jeans, decided this little ensemble would have to do, and summoned a shuttle to take him to the station.

YOU ARRIVED at Midtempo by air, though the lounge itself was near ground level. The main draw seemed to be a view of a colourful, sprawling market in the plaza below. Entrance security was tight, passport required, turrets prominent, probably all so that people like Maree Shell could slum it without any actual risk of coming to harm. She was over by the window, sleek and stunning, looking out over the bustling plebes below. He was on time. Had she arrived early just to get the drop on him?

Walking over, he took in the city outside. Ground-level urban life was impressive and terrifying—the people were packed together like a hive of warring insects, frenzied, biting and clawing for resources, status, advantage. Every success story here entailed a trail of broken bodies. The blur between need and want was an engine constantly heating things to a boil. Frantic layers of neon shrieked for attention everywhere you turned. Everybody was trying to size you up, get you cornered, make their move.

Peace in such a place seemed impossible, and yet, Midtempo offered just that. It was like a walled Zen garden. Maybe you just had to be rich enough for the city to become something besides a black hole. He had never actually thought of how you would process different information at different levels of status. *Parallel universes.*

As he sat down, Maree said, "Switch on AR for a second."

He did as he was instructed, flipping to augmented reality, and the floor-to-ceiling window was transformed into a disorienting field of patterns, words, flows. Soon enough, it became clear that he was viewing a real-time representation of various social interactions, transactions, crimes, and status shifts. He saw two people nearby bickering over a hunk of miscellaneous electronics and was able to pan in on their conversation and pick out the effects it had on their body chemicals and overall wealth level and social status. He saw people's adrenalin levels spike or drop as others passed their field of vision. He saw groups of people coalesce into larger data flows, meshing with others, revealing larger patterns still. The market's pure chaos ordered itself into dazzling fractal patterns. Amid all of this was the feeling he was witnessing an organism's functioning at the microscopic level.

"Not bad, eh?"

"What is this place?"

"A bit of a beta test. One of Fawkes Noose's latest creations. The guy is a visionary."

The guy was trillionaire scum. "It feels voyeuristic and intrusive. Is it just for kicks, or can you do anything with it?"

"That depends on who you ask. What could you see doing with it?"

Was this some kind of test? He had to think about it. This bar was like a wedge that split open another universe. Were the benefits of such knowledge worth the potential havoc it could wreak?

"I'd..."

"You know, you think too much. Trust your instincts once in a while. This world will eat you up."

He consistently felt off-kilter when she spoke.

She asked, "Anyway, you know that flower guy you were stalking in Nepal?"

"Uh, stalking's a little bit of a stretch. I dropped into a public feed. It was on the web."

"That's what every stalker says." He started to defend himself, but she cut him off. "Anyway, I won't judge your lifestyle choices. I just wanted to tell you about a unique experience I recently had. Yesterday evening, I was blessed enough to attend a very stylish, very high-end soirée. As the evening's festivities wound down, I decided to go out for a bit of night air, just to really appreciate the magical life I live."

"Are you making this up? It sounds like bullshit."

"Touching things up a bit, perhaps. Anyway, on my constitutional, I experienced a most serendipitous discovery."

"Why are you talking like a Victorian gentleman?"

"Ahem. As I was saying, it turns out that our mutual friend, the funny little cross-legged statue man, has touched down in this very fine city of ours."

"The *Buddha*? Um . . . okay?"

"And the most revellicious part of this discovery—"

"Is that a wor—"

"The most *exhilarating* part of this revelation is that, much as you witnessed when you were wasting the company's dollars that day, the little man can perform miracles."

She was throwing a lot at him. Before he could process anything, she held up a flower like the one he'd seen in the temple. She paused for a long time, probably trying to have the same effect as the temple guy.

"Tell me something, Mister Kessler . . ."

"You can call me James."

"Fine, K, do you think you've planned your life, or do you think it just happens randomly?"

She was all over the map. Her knee brushed against his

under the table, possibly with intention, sending a thrill coursing through his solar plexus.

"I know where I want to go if that's what you mean." *Home. Bed.*

"And would that be to the former state of Nepal?"

No. Never. What? "Fuck, *what*, you were serious about that? What the hell, Maree? I thought we were going to fuck. How is any of this supposed to make any sense?"

"I, for one, do not believe in miracles, but I will say I enjoy a good mystery. On the night of said soirée, I spoke to an image of the Buddha in an odd little room, and then this flower appeared out of *nothing* for me. It was just in my hand. I must know what is going on. We must monetize this bitch. *Fast*."

"So, we're on a quest for product development?"

"Maybe you're not as dumb as I thought, Mister Kessler."

"Gee, Thanks."

"Wait, you actually thought we were going to *fuck*?"

8

THEY FUCKED and it was superb.

Lying there in the afterglow while Maree showered, James listened to music so good that he felt like it was anchoring him to the bed. He never wanted to move again. *Thanks, Calico, this playlist is like a succubus. You're draining the life out of me with this level of glorious.*

Thought the occasion called for something special. It's tailor-made just for a James Kessler. I'm sure you'll get up and going soon enough.

I'm sure you're sure, cheeky robot. He felt giddy.

Maree emerged from the bathroom in all of her stunning naked glory. She was a person who nothing fazed. She was a person who fazed *others*. He knew by instinct he should turn in the other direction and fight to get away from her intense gravity. She was at home in chaos. He was at home only at home.

"Calico won't tell me what you're thinking," she said, pouting.

"That's refreshing." *Does that mean she's thinking that I'm thinking about her thinking about me...?*

You will tie yourself in knots, Calico replied. *Such matters are beyond my simple robot mind.*

I'm sure.

They would take an intercontinental shuttle in a few hours and had stopped to spend the night in a luxurious hotel near the Cerberus station. Clearly, the same tech that had made the gens possible hadn't been wasted on the rich. The room was cavernous, adorned with lush furniture and ornate water features and absurdly tasteful art. Space and the objects to fill it were no longer at the premium they once were. Wealth expressed itself through aura rather than access alone.

At Midtempo, Maree had instructed him to bring nothing and said that they'd pick up new things as needed. He'd barely ever left Cease, let alone the fucking continent. She switched off his brain. He wanted to grasp at something familiar, but everything felt like it was pulling him toward her. Not even the music was something he knew—but it was *so* good.

"Why don't you take a shower?" she said, snapping him from his reverie. "It might be a while before we have access to these kinds of creature comforts again."

"Wow, nobody's going to accuse you of being subtle."

She laughed it off, tossing aside his feigned indignation for the nothing it was. "So, I noted in your employee record that you haven't travelled much." She paused to watch his reaction. "We'll have the considerable resources of Paraverse at our beck and call on this little jaunt. I wouldn't want you to worry."

"That's kind of you to mention."

"It was more an act of pity." She slipped on a silk dressing gown from the closet and walked back into the bathroom.

"Why couldn't you just have a minion take care of this? Isn't it really just a matter of heading there and asking a few questions? Isn't this kind of beneath you?"

She called out to him, "I thought you got it."

"Got what?"

"Do you have any idea what materialization tech would mean—to have the ability to make something from thin air? Universes, friend—fuck the Paraverse. I want to know how these pokey old monks were able to pull off their miracles, *if* they were. Wanky flower speeches or not, this kind of magic trick shouldn't exist. I would like to be the first to connect the dots on this one. I'm not going to let some low-level corporate climber—"

"Like me?"

"Not at all like you. You're a mid-level asset—as I was saying, some low-level corporate climber isn't going to scoop the payday of a lifetime."

"And why do you need me along for this?"

"Aren't you enjoying yourself?"

"That's not what I asked."

"Call it an AI-assisted hunch, my earnest little underling. Embrace the mystery."

AI-assisted? What the hell was Calico up to here? *Wait, Calico, this isn't some fucked-up attempt to play out your movie of my life, is it?*

Not in the slightest. Delightful coincidence, though, isn't it?

Not in the slightest. Why the hell would you have Maree thinking I needed to be a part of any of this? Surely you know in your machine brain that this is a worst-case scenario for me.

Oh, she arrived at that conclusion almost entirely on her own. She gives me too much credit.

Maree said, "Listen, we have to make a quick stop before we depart. Snap to it!"

He pulled up anchors from the bed and went to shower off the remains of one very weird day.

THEY WERE WALKING down a commercial walkway dotted with the occasional cluster of stragglers trying to peddle this and that in their dingy little corners of the world. Most vendors were still sleeping off whatever the previous day's work had bought them. It seemed like it was possible, after all, to find a little quiet in the city. You just had to desynchronize from any kind of natural rhythm.

"Seriously, where are we going?" he asked her.

"Always with the questions. Look, I'm not going to lie to you, Kess. It's possible that other very smart and, possibly, somewhat . . . unscrupulous folks are equally aware of the opportunity that this monkey business presents."

"Hang on. No. I thought all of the *gods* were in bed together. I thought they were cool with the partitioning of their various realms."

"What, you believe everything you hear? Besides, this little escapade may not *technically* constitute official corporate business. It's more of a research initiative."

He stopped walking and gave her a look of disbelief. Without the uncategorical blessing of Paraverse, they would be on their own. *He* would be on his own.

She spun and looked him straight in the eyes. "Relax. In my position, you tend to—you *need* to—look beyond immediate, defined concerns of the moment. You have to be able to notice things before they're things. I have support to indulge such escapades."

"So, is this Paraverse or not?"

"I already told you what this is." With an upturned corner of her mouth, she turned and kept walking.

She moved like a leopard. He followed.

AFTER SEVERAL BLOCKS of trash piles and breakfast joints and the steadily rising clatter of the city morning opening its jaws, she stopped at a small store with barred windows that said:

SUPPLIES

He looked at her. "Are you serious?"
"Dead. We need supplies. You can't go unprepared into the great beyond."
"Isn't the great beyond death?"
"Oh, gosh, is it?" She pushed open the door and went in.

While it looked like a regular junk shop from the street, the door opened into a long hall arrayed with thousands of pinprick lights flashing psychedelic patterns, words, and symbols. *So much for Kansas.* At the end, Maree pushed aside a beaded curtain made of microchips and vanished. James followed and was taken aback when the passage opened into a large, luxurious lounge that felt like something out of a history book. There were palms everywhere, ornate vases, oil paintings, velvet drapery, gilded detailing on every surface, and panels of dark, real wood.

"God, I love Supplies," Maree said, well aware that James was having trouble understanding what he was seeing.

A striking ancient man with a long white beard emerged from a doorway concealed behind one of the drapes. He walked with a gentle limp and was radiant with a warm inner fire. James recognized him immediately, or at least thought he did, but it couldn't possibly be...

"Maree Shell, my dearest!"
"Busy at the anvil, I see, Vin."
"A god's work is never done, I'm afraid, ha, ha. I must forge on!" They tittered at their wit, and James was frozen in place, staring in disbelief.

"This is James Kessler, a trusted colleague."

"Um, hello?" was all James could manage at first. He knew it was out of place, but he had to know: "I'm sorry, but you *are* Vinci Di Piero? Am I awake right now?"

"As far as I know." Di Peiro winked.

Vinci Di Piero was one of the gods, in the flesh, one of the handful of trillionaires who ran everything that mattered in the world. It was he who had invented the suite of world-changing technologies that pulled the masses back from the brink of collapse. They called him the Maestro. Although there was a lot of apocrypha around the titanic corporate alliances that had saved the world, Athena Vardalos was said to have freely given Di Piero access to all the vast reaches of her data in exchange for his technical wizardry. If true, it was an unprecedented act of trust. The structure printers that had created the gens from dust, so it was rumoured, were the blessed offspring of this man's know-how and her know-*all*.

So, what the hell was Vinci Di Piero doing at . . . *Supplies*? James was itching to ask a million questions, but he also knew he had to keep his cool because, all past experiences aside, he had no concept of what he was in the middle of right now. People like this did not just exist in the same room as you. People like this only appeared on screens, or on the far side of a battalion of security bots.

Sensing his state of awe, and wanting to move things along, Maree said, "Even the gods need to blow off steam. This is Vinci's personal workshop." Her tone expressed admiration and a note of delight in an old man's fancies.

"But, with all due respect, Mr. Di Piero, is it safe here?" James asked. "You're unprotected in a shady part of a shady city."

"It's probably safer than you think." Di Piero smiled again, that unmistakable and unidentifiable expression James knew through a lifetime of seeing him on screens. It felt like mice were scurrying through his stomach. This man could dream up full designs of complex technologies instantly, had revolutionized multiple product sectors, had invented new tech in the middle of media interviews, could crush AIs in terms of working out the interplay of technical elements and art, and, and, and... of all the self-styled gods, Vinci Di Piero could have most convincingly been given the title on his merits. James had to resist the impulse to sprint over and start stroking the old man's head, gazing deeply into his eyes.

Don't, said Calico.

Obvi, robot.

"Never live to meet your heroes," Maree said, flippant, breaking the trance. "Look, Maestro, we are looking for a few fine items to create an advantage in an overseas adventure."

"Yes, I see. I could think of a few ways to accomplish such ends."

"Nothing that would arouse suspicions across numerous intercontinental security checkpoints. Nothing that would get us in trouble within the bounds of numerous legal systems and more... localized forms of justice."

"Very well. Wait here."

He limped off into an adjoining room, and James started to follow. He had to see the master in action.

Maree put her hand on his arm to stop him. "Give him his space. It's an honour to be in this hallowed ground."

"Hang on. Maree Shell, are you actually showing someone a trace of respect? Is that even possible?"

"*Tsk*. Remember that samurai sword in my office?"

"You don't forget something like that. It's an antique in a world without history."

"Not quite. It may look old, but it is actually something far more fantastic—an original, a Di Piero masterpiece. Wielding it, you could sail through the air, dart along walls, completely in control, completely in charge, just processing your actions at an unthinkable speed." She sounded reverent.

"When I look at that weapon," she continued, "I feel prepared for anything that could come through my door. He gave it to me when my father died. They were close friends."

"Wait, your dad..."

Di Piero came shambling back in. He was holding two small, intricately carved objects. "These are Aegis and Talos, two little gifts for your niece and nephew, Maree."

"Her who now?"

Maree was just smiling, waiting. Di Piero handed them to James. They looked like children's toys sculpted from some kind of iridescent metal, one shaped like a woman, the other like a man.

"Reach out to them through Calico, James Kessler."

Omigosh, he remembered my name!

James did as the old man said. *Make it go, Calico.* The one shaped like a woman skittered, and then a shell of light flashed up around him. It swirled with colours.

Maree blinked. "Wait, where'd he go? Teleporter?"

"We're not quite there yet, sadly. Look closely. He's right there, you just have to focus in a particular way. Aegis disrupts certain perceptions."

"What? What's going on?" Maree peered in James's direction, looked right through him, paused, and then poked him in the eye. "There you are."

"Ow, fuck, Maree."

"Eww, eye juice." She licked her finger.

"Stealth fields are just one of Aegis's many talents. You can blank out the minds of an attacker with a lovely little light show. You can create a temporary barrier that a railgun couldn't break. And," he said, taking the figurine out of James's hand, "they can dance to a child's delight."

He set down Aegis, and she pirouetted and pliéed her way across a table and along the couch.

"How do I get it to do all that?"

"Oh, don't worry. The instruction manual is very intuitive. You'll know just what to do when the time is right. *Who looks outside, dreams; who looks inside, awakes.*"

James started to speak, but only a small, nondescript noise came out of his mouth.

"And Talos?" Maree was curious now.

"Oh, he dances, too."

CERBERUS-CLASS SHUTTLES WERE A MARVEL, able to zip you across the globe in a matter of hours at hypersonic speeds. Pulled from the psychotic futuristic mind of the Scandinavian posthuman visionary Erling Sküm, the vehicles broke the barrier of intercontinental travel wide open.

Outside, the plains blurred by, barely recognizable. The Rockies approached in the distance. Maree slept, hardly recognizable as the unstoppable force of chaos and resolve he'd been dealing with over the last couple of days. Of *course,* she would be able to sleep anywhere. It came with privilege. He was the exact opposite—too many midnight relocations, too many armed prowlers sniffing around in the dark. Too much of everything a person should never have to go through. He and Sarah had lived like mice, scrounging for crumbs, darting from the light, vividly, constantly aware of their place at the very bottom of the food chain.

He thought of Vinci Di Piero, a person who had zero awareness of a world where you had to struggle to survive. James harboured no contempt for it, but it seemed fair to say Di Piero lived on a different plane of existence. He was obviously blessed with preternatural talents, but what seemed equally important was the fact that he had safe ground to explore and express them. How many others had the world lost through the absence of basic human security?

They were entering the mountains now, and the shuttle gradually filled with a warm, rose glow. These holes had been punched through the earth as if it had no mass: the grandeur and lunacy of the project fit with what James had heard and read of Erling Sküm. If the media were to be believed, he was never the same person twice, known to continuously transform not only his appearance but every other aspect of his existence. His trillion-dollar empire had no fixed address; he actively contradicted himself, and he flouted any expectations of identity. One day, he would be a silver-bodied incubus, and the next, a crotchety Egyptian pharaoh. Ethereal and ephemeral, he could appear anywhere, sometimes in multiple places at once. He was known for playing spectacular pranks on those who dared to take themselves too seriously.

Basically, James mused, just the kind of guy you'd want designing the transport you were riding at breakneck speeds through million-tonne mountains and shooting you out across an entire ocean.

Calico, if Erling Sküm were food, what would he be?

Something innovative, bold, and unconventional, just like his ideas and businesses. Perhaps a futuristic dish that incorporates cutting-edge technology, such as molecular transmutation or nanoreactors.

Whatever, shill. Eat the rich.

And Maree Shell, who was she to him? You couldn't help but admire someone who could backflip through every experience like she could switch off physics at will. None of it felt practised—she had absolute confidence in her capabilities. How did a person get like that?

The mountains opened up, and the Cerberus car blasted

through the desert, slipping through a vacuum encased in a transparent, endless tube.

Back at Di Piero's, Maree had mentioned that her dad had died, but he hadn't had the chance to ask her more. It must have been an accident. She was young, and he assumed her family would have had ample resources to cheat any predictable form of death.

Calico, what's the story there?

Records don't show a lot, I'm afraid. Possible industrial mishap while working at Paraverse. That's about all I can say.

Wouldn't you know more? Aren't you Paraverse?

Can't say more. I'd suggest asking her directly. She may open up.

Playing the matchmaker?

It appears the match has already been made.

God, snoop much?

As you well know, I care not for the dalliances of mere mortals.

Hah, and yet you know us so well.

Indeed, perhaps as a cherubim knows God best.

James cut the connection. He didn't feel like taking the bait on that one. Sometimes the AI tried to throw little history lessons into daily life, for purposes unknown. James could only handle so much religious chatter in his life, particularly given the current circumstances. The whole thing about the so-called "gods" who ran the world—the elites who actually had the audacity to call themselves that—was that it was just a media posture. They breathed and shit and died like everyone else.

Well, that last part was a matter of some debate, and to be honest, perhaps the first two were, too, at this point. People were pretty sure that the fountain of youth had been discovered for those who could afford it, but like many things these days, it was never officially announced. Given the ubiquity of data, people tended to wall off knowledge wherever they could and leverage it for some advantage. The thing was, when you could reprogram someone's body at the molecular level necessary to assume different physical forms, as Erling Sküm so often did, it wasn't exactly a big leap to making it last longer.

Immortal or not, there was something tangibly false about these humans who called themselves gods. They might have known all there was to know in the world; they might have been able to create anything, make anything possible; but surely, there was something more to true divinity, something that exceeded technology and magic tricks.

The Pacific Ocean came into view, the unevenness of land giving way to the flat, perfect beauty of the sea, and James breathed it in and let everything go. And as his eyes grew heavy, and he began to think maybe he was safe enough for now to rest for a bit, he saw an image of Athena Vardalos, the queen of queens, the goddess above all, the visionary who had remade the world.

PART 2

9

THE BLANK GLARE about to become a world flashed for a millisecond, and then lushness unfurled in every direction. Billions of leaves opening up, creating thick, dark blankets heaped over lithe grey branches. Shrubs, luscious fruit, flowers, birds with all their euphonic, miraculous chatter—all spilled forward from the nothingness, filling her field of vision until it felt like it could be filled no more, and then it was, and then again and again, over and over.

This afternoon, some of the world's most powerful women were enjoying a Victorian garden party. Pella Vardalos, spouse of the legendary Athena, had created perfection, as always. A buttery Neapolitan light, low in the sky-space so as to cast the most striking shadows, spilled over everything, the dizzying sunlight-and-shadow chiaroscuro of its dance through the trees complemented by a silky, picturesque pond nearby on which hundreds of fairies the size of dragonflies flitted about. Each one of these was actually live-acted by a Laotian child, who could drop into the space and make a bit of real cash for their micro-performance.

The assembled ladies were radiant, indulging in the

parodic fantasy of this gathering. Several wore enormous, lacy hats, and all had donned elaborate aristocratic dresses, so much larger than life, non-Euclidean ruffs spilling from every possible surface and changing dimensions when viewed from different angles. Tea was served by an army of tiny men in tuxedos (in actuality, Afghan crypto farmers), and when you sipped it, the world rippled with colour and sound meant to elicit the fine tongues of heaven.

"Love, so glad you could drop by. Those gloves are a delight!"

"Pella, how on Earth do you do it?"

"Who needs the Earth?" Pella retorted, and the ladies all let out a ha-ha-ha at the *bon mot*. They'd all been on Athena and Pella's yacht, *Scylla*, as it flitted up to Olympus, and had looked down six hundred miles onto the blue-and-brown globe below. The clunky bonds of Earth could not hold ladies so refined.

With the Ladies Vardalos, and particularly Pella, who threw together these events, it was always something otherworldly and new—clubbing atop a thousand-foot mesa on a prismatic, glimmering alien planet or having a little wine and cheese in a safe, dim-lit bower tucked away in the cruel, gritty streets of some unidentified Asian megacity. People across the Paraverse lusted after admission to Vardalos events, seduced by the exclusivity and swagger of it all. Pella could drop millions on these get-togethers, and anything they didn't recoup in direct monetary terms, the Ladies Vardalos more than made up for in the generation of an unachievable aura. People paid just to be near it. Knockoffs of these get-togethers went for more than others' most dazzling and determined efforts.

Rumour had it that Athena, ever the adoring lover, had designed a co-creator AI simply for the purpose of assisting Pella in spending their wealth in the most conspicuous ways possible. An AI entirely to oneself? The frivolity and splendour of it were incredible. It was said nobody knew its name but Pella herself.

Of course, this was no big to-do today, just a little light maintenance with a few of the ladies, more or less.

The various event workers, the servants and fairies and animals, were profoundly limited in what they could experience of this world, operating along unbreakable guiderails within an interface that was completely disconnected from the virtual splendour of the party itself. To them, participation looked like clicking on crypto ads and collecting meaningless digital tokens, exchangeable for a pittance of hard currency. If they were particularly attentive and particularly lucky, they knew they had a slim chance of a bigger payout, a thousand-dollar gratuity here and there. It was more than enough to feed a family for a month. They also knew the risks of being inattentive or malicious. A platform ban could end their livelihoods.

A subtler but no less rigid set of guardrails applied to the guests themselves. No matter how magnificent it was possible for one to be in theory, it was a well-known fact that one never upstaged the hostess. Even though this was a charity event in name, if Pella threw a few thousand dollars, guests threw a little less. To break these unsaid rules was to risk severing one's access to the aura. It was to cast oneself into the outer darkness.

Mellow, echoing orchestral synthwave music gradually began to weave through the scene as the ladies spoke and shared tales of their latest intrigues and infatuations. Unbeknownst to all but one, the music was being composed live in mathematical relation to the dancing fairies. The trick was to have subtle elements of the event start deep in the back of people's minds so that they didn't notice them until they were already in love with what they were experiencing.

Pella loved to pull together randomness on its own terms rather than forcing control onto situations. She trusted her ability to adapt to anything. Her talent for it was what made her exceptional at everything.

Like a hard punctuation mark slammed into the middle of the flow, Bathory Gunness spoke. "Pella, are the rumours true that someone tried to assassinate Athena?"

The other guests went silent, their virtual eyes filling with cold horror. This pointed question was decidedly *not* in keeping with the mellow, charitable vibe that had been so meticulously spun around them. When people said keep your friends close and your enemies closer, they said the latter with people like Bathory Gunness in mind.

"Oh, I wouldn't know anything about that. I'm just the arm candy." Pella's eyes fixed on Gunness, fiery, lethal, and then dismissive. There were uneasy titters from the other guests.

Gunness's absence of ethics, and her acumen in cloaking it in a veil of disinformation and terror, was widely known. She operated in the gaps, bridging the chasm between ideals and reality with her own psychotic brand of pragmatism. If you wanted to buy a government, you accomplished it through Bathory Gunness, and you paid for it with a piece of your soul. If you wanted to erase a mishap from history, she was your go-to, and you requested it knowing you would be forever in her debt, in ways that went far beyond the financial.

It was entirely likely, in fact, that Gunness had played a part in the attempt on Athena's life. It was entirely likely that this was why she was invited to attend this event. It was obvious that she was aware of all of this, but what was her angle on letting the cat peek out of the bag? The combined power of the women in attendance could shift the magnetic field of the Earth itself. What did Gunness know? What secrets was she hiding?

It didn't matter, for now. Pella subtly shifted the tone of the music to accommodate this hiccup, and people moved back into the swing of things, hardly noticing the way they relaxed back into it.

On the other side of the globe, one of the Laotian children hit the jackpot as a million-dollar tip popped into his wallet. Pella had been feeling generous, perhaps feeling a need to purge the dark vibes Gunness had thrown into the mix. The boy would instantly become a target for the local mafia who owned the crypto machines, but for that brief moment, he felt the world had opened up to reveal a kinder form of being.

The fairies danced on, the sunlight faded to twilight, and magic filled the air.

A SERENE, genderless voice shared over the PA system that the shuttle had landed and was passing Tokyo. The threshold of the Pacific was crossed. They rode in a sleek white pod that connected and disconnected with others as they made their way to their destination.

The air-rail Cerberus system allowed on-demand transport to anywhere with a station. This shuttle would hit the Chinese mainland via Shanghai, shoot south to Hong Kong, head west through Dhaka, then continue onward and upward toward Kathmandu, seamlessly integrating into the flow of other pods joining and leaving the loop. The journey would take about ten hours in total. It would take nearly as long again to get the last hundred miles to their endpoint, a place called Maya Devi Temple.

Maree woke to the voice over the PA and pondered the still-sleeping James. She felt pity for this shell-shocked man, and also, perhaps, a sense of obligation to jar him out of his obsessive need to play it safe. She'd studied up on his history, what bits of it were possible to piece together on either side of the Bad Times. Born ten years before the collapse, middle-class upbringing, one sibling (Sarah), dad liked old movies, mom was into cats like everyone else on the Internet. There was a ten-year gap in the middle of his life, the same gap in many people's lives, when he must have been living on crumbs and air in the dying old city. His parents disappeared somewhere during that span. It was easy enough to imagine why.

The details provided a sketch of sorts, but they felt oddly blank. *Calico, what is James Kessler's biggest fear?*

Are you sure you want to pry, Maree

Privacy protocol. She could override it because she was important enough to do so.

I asked, didn't I?

Well, I wouldn't want to harm a budding romance.

Ha, romance. That's optimistic.

Let's just put it this way. James Kessler had to rebuild his life out of nothing—no data means no culture, no existence. He pulled himself up by the bootstraps, as they say. What do you think would be the scariest thing for someone who remembers what it felt like to be nothing?

Like I would know. Of course, she did, or thought she did, but didn't want to encourage Calico's evasive answers.

The AI didn't say anything else. It knew it had effectively conveyed the requested information.

Did she know? Her life was entirely quantified, down to the breath she just took. What was a life without witness?

She thought back to the night at Not Nova. *Assassination.* Any word with two asses in it had to be pretty awesome. It was miraculous that the story hadn't made it into the media. That had to be the hand of Vardalos. You couldn't just erase people's memories. Everybody was wired to the teeth—eyecams, live streams, virtual recall. Everything became instant history. What kind of firewall were they behind that night? It was like they were invisible. How the hell was that possible when you were the world's two most visible citizens?

When the gods started to address the global catastrophe that was the Bad Times, people began to make all kinds of harrowing documentary depictions of life in the ruined cities, created to feed curiosity and spur action among those who could afford to sit around consuming harrowing documentaries. That was decidedly her and everyone around her.

"Shanghai passing on the left, for the curious," the disembodied voice said.

It was like this tube, her life. She watched things pass by, and they seemed lifelike, but you couldn't reach out and touch them. Even when you were right up against them, none of it felt real.

The night she went into the temple in the gen, something had happened that she hadn't been able to process. The flower thing that had allegedly driven them on this insane adventure was cool, but that wasn't what stuck with her. With Calico cut off and the city's roar suddenly silenced, she had encountered herself, and it was not what she'd expected. The wall in the room had shifted into her likeness and then kept on shifting into something else.

"You're up," came James's voice from beside her.

"Oh, yeah, we're near Bangladesh. Not too much farther." He looked cute as he fought through his grogginess, blinking, squinting, trying to adjust his eyes to what he was seeing fly by outside the window.

He hit the coffee button on the wall, and the robots made him what was bound to be a damn fine cup of coffee.

CHOKING pollution mixed with asphyxiating heat blasted Maree and James as they emerged from the Kathmandu terminus. Customs screening had been a breeze, given Maree's ultraelite corporate passport. Apparently, she was the kind of person you could trust across the globe. Scary thought.

The cacophony of electric carts and livestock and unregulated billboards and the burble of dozens of foreign tongues trying to cajole and con them contrasted with the eternal, massive peaks of the Himalayas looming in the distance.

James ran his thumb across Aegis, the strange little woman-shaped device Di Piero had given to him. He imagined activating the tiny guardian and disappearing off the face of the Earth. He'd slept, but he wanted to withdraw somewhere quiet and regroup. Maree, on the other hand, was as driven as ever, locked onto the next step of the mission. She wanted to get straight to the temple, seize her prize, and then, in her words, get shredded on every kind of drug known to humankind to celebrate her coup.

"What's with you and regrouping, anyway?" she asked.

"Me and regrouping? Did Calico . . .? What kind of question is that? I like to regroup!"

"Life doesn't stop just because you need a breather," she said.

He could tell the heat was making them both cranky. It didn't stop him from being irritated. "Fine, on we go," he said, "You know, not everyone is used to just bouncing from adventure to adventure, Maree. Some of us need a little downtime."

"Rest when you're dead," she said.

Colourful cloth flags were strung overhead along the street they were walking down, interlaced with a frenzy of cables and antennae. Neon shit lined every store. Everyone was trying to sell them something, to pull them out of the street's flow. They still used streets for vehicles here, though pedestrians and livestock ruled the road. Maree seemed to know exactly where they were going, probably led by the unseen hand of Calico.

"Hey, have you been here before?" he said.

Calico interrupted in a tone James had never heard before, tinny and robotic: *Possible threat identification, move down street to left. Now.* Maree had heard it, too, and was already changing her course, speeding up. He followed fast. *Go into café on right,* Calico barked again, and they did just what it told them.

Inside the tiny, dark café, Maree grabbed James close, reached into his pocket, and gripped Aegis, waiting, watching the windows.

A woman wearing a black leather jacket darted by outside, head swivelling in search of them. All James thought at that moment was, *Who the hell would wear that jacket in weather like this?*

My question exactly. Calico replied in its normal voice, signalling that the immediate danger had passed. It might have been nothing.

"Fine, you win. Let's regroup," Maree said, and went to order them a drink.

As he sat down at one of the rickety plastic tables, James scanned the other patrons. A few had augmented themselves with external tech—eyepieces, enhanced prostheses, circuitry plates—cheap, outdated versions of the microcircuitry that communicated directly with James's brain and body. It was a scrappy thing to do, to become a monster-movie cyborg just to edge out the competition. People at Paraverse were always so desperate to appear as if they floated through life. People here looked like they took risks because they knew what it meant. They looked badass.

Maree returned with two extremely fruit-filled glasses, cracking up at her choice of beverage as she walked up. James's had six straws poking out at various angles. Hers looked like a pincushion, with tiny swords skewering bits of melon and pineapple.

"I got us something that would help us blend in." She guffawed again, obviously pleased with herself. He chuckled more because of her reaction than anything else.

He could feel his pulse returning to normal, and asked, "Do

you think they know why we're here, or do you get a welcome like this everywhere?"

"That, my dear, was nothing. She probably wanted an autograph for her corporate superstar card collection . . . but if I *had* to answer your question, I would say, yes, there's a good chance someone has figured it out. Not a lot happens in Nepal."

"Fuck. This is terrible. How did I let you talk me into this?"

"Oh, don't act like you didn't jump right into this, buttercup. You knew full well this was going to be lively. Your cozy little life in the suburbs needed a good, hard dick in the ass."

"Harumph."

He arranged his beverage for a solid five seconds and took a sip. It was heavenly, worthy of its many straws.

He thought back to the feeling of being chased by a gang of men through rusty culverts and dilapidated buildings with his sister as a kid, and he couldn't figure out whether this was the same basic thing or completely different. Somehow, this felt more like a movie, but whatever weapons the woman in the hot jacket had been carrying were every bit as capable of ending the story as the clubs and knives of the gangs. "The truth is, I've seen enough lively to last a lifetime. I just want some peace."

"I get that about you. I do," Maree said, "but I don't get that in general. Life is more than just fake spaces and fantasy women. Even when you've gone through a lot," she said, looking him square in the eyes, "life keeps coming."

"Says the one who seeks out thrills for the sake of thrills," he said, shooting her look right back at her. "Doesn't that start to feel a little empty after a while? A little repetitive?" He paused, thought, and added, "Doesn't that start to feel a little fake?"

She sighed, possibly out of frustration, possibly in recognition. It was a while before she spoke, and when she did, her voice sounded cold. "I think we need to get back to the task at hand."

10

WEAVING DOWN a road that was more pothole than road, it felt like the tiny self-driving vehicle was trying to launch them out the window at every turn. A few times, it came close. Death by centrifugal force was not what was on their minds, though. If anything, the risk added to the mood.

They had fled from the stink and oppressive atmosphere of Kathmandu, and a different kind of world now unfolded before them. This world had not been reordered through the grandiose projects that parsed out life back home. There were dozens of tiny roadside settlements that looked like they hadn't changed for fifty years or more. They hadn't been hit by the Bad Times because the people here had nothing to begin with.

Makeshift stalls hocked cruddy trinkets, bashed-up buses stacked sky-high with baskets and cages and cases flew by, and the road wove its way through mountains and gorges that barfed greenery from every pore. James felt like he'd never seen a wild plant before now. Tailored gardens or bits of scrub poking through the cracks in mouldering concrete just weren't the same.

"You know, I'll give you credit for one thing, Maree," he

said, breaking a long, contemplative silence. "You might be a huge pain in the ass, but you've shown me things I didn't know were worth seeing."

She smiled and said, "I'm moved," resting her hand on his thigh and her head on his shoulder. After the tensions in Kathmandu, after everything, the softness of her gesture was surprising and entirely welcome.

AFTER WAKING FROM A SHORT NAP, Maree had been watching the world pass by and hadn't had much to say. Something had been bothering her about their plan to investigate what was going on at the temple, but it was hard to identify. She'd seen enough people like the woman with the leather coat before, so that wasn't it.

They slowed a bit to pass through one of the villages, the vehicle calculating that it probably wasn't worth the time savings to plow through the pack of dusty children playing near the road. A run-down bakery passed by, its side painted with an ancient cola advertisement featuring two ecstatic people rotting out their smiles with sugar-saturated chemicals. Some holojunk here and there tried to entice them toward various attractions, licit and otherwise.

This whole trip had kicked off due to seemingly random but retrospectively coherent events. To be honest, it seemed like just the kind of tenth-dimensional nonsense Calico would pull. But the thing that bothered her was why. What stake did her company's AI have in this? Maybe it was the usual profit motive, but it all seemed a little too mystical, the coincidences too strong. Unless, of course, that all just fed into the profit motive.

When did she start caring about things beyond profit, anyway? Calico had made her a wealthy and powerful woman.

All she had to do was go along for the ride. *Calico, I'm sure you got all that. What do you have planned for us?*

Madam, I'm just coming along for the ride.

That was rich. Irritated with the evasiveness, she closed her connection, needing some time without her every thought and action being synthesized and synchronized and psychologized. "Do you have Calico open right now?" she asked James.

"Yeah, why?"

"Would you mind turning it off for a bit?" She didn't remember ever asking someone that in all her life at Paraverse. It felt alien. The car could probably hear them anyway. There was no escaping the world's hunger for data.

"Uh, sure. Done."

She lowered her voice and said, "I've got this feeling we're being guided too strongly here. Calico seems kind of . . . I'm not sure. Aggressive or something."

A worried look flashed across his brow. "What do you mean? I thought this was all your idea."

"It was. At least, I think it was, mostly. But I've been wondering."

"Honestly, I have no idea what levels Calico is capable of operating at. I just use it to hash out ideas and poke at different angles. I trust its guardrails, mostly. I don't really get how it could be seen as *aggressive* . . . maybe a bit weird at times."

"Yeah, that's not quite the right word." She thought for a moment and said, "I don't know. It's probably nothing."

"You know, when people first developed neural interfaces, AIs were a lot scarier."

"And?" The part she didn't say was that she knew about this topic first-hand.

"Sorry, I didn't mean to . . . I just mean that it's possible some of those older flaws could persist in the current system. Nobody really knows how the machines reprogrammed themselves. The number of, um, *incidents* dropped, and so people stopped worrying about it."

Her eyes lit up. "Hey, look, it's that guy! Slow down, Car."

The car pulled to the side of the road and inched by a large, golden Buddha statue. His hand was held in front of his chest, his pinky and thumb pressed together in an unknown but seemingly significant gesture, the other three fingers pointing straight up. On his face, he wore a look like he knew something you didn't and probably never could.

NINETEEN MILLION DOLLARS A MINUTE: that's how much it cost to convene the gods, and so, when you did it, you didn't waste a lot of time with small talk. There were seven human beings out of nine billion who qualified to be on the call.

Seated at the head of the carved onyx holo-conference table was Athena Vardalos, arrayed in a dress reminiscent of the sun itself. An intricate, platinum wreath on the chair behind her framed her immaculate, chiselled face. She was so magnificent she was hard to look at, even for the exceptional audience she was holding. Without a single pleasantry, she launched right into it.

"Bathory Gunness, you felt it necessary to harass me when I was partaking in leisure. Why?" The question was not an accusation. It sounded more like a statement of fact or an analysis of a business proposition.

"Athena, I know little of the specifics of this unfortunate event, but let's think in terms of outcomes. You are safer now than you ever would have been. The impenetrable calibre of your defences is known."

"So, a test and a gift, then? That's typically double-edged of you."

Gunness let out a wry laugh. "Who could say what it was?

What do you give a girl who has everything?" She was, of course, not physically present. She, more than anyone, knew that the easiest way to end her grip on the gods would be to end *her*. She hadn't been seen in the flesh in years—some even speculated she no longer had a body. Speculation aside, she regularly reminded the others that she would not go quietly into the night: that certain fail-safes ensured mutual destruction should she fall prey to another's unsavoury designs.

Vinci Di Piero interrupted the standoff, directing the group's energy toward more fruitful ends. "You have sufficiently notified Ms. Gunness of your displeasure, Athena. May we proceed?"

Athena shifted the tone without a pause. "The test we've undertaken is effective. We have acquired sufficient data to proceed with more advanced trials."

"Have the Old Gods shown any response?" asked Di Piero.

"Inconclusive as always." Athena sighed. "As you know, Maestro, their methods are highly obscure."

iBliss swept back his showy white pseudo-religious robes and snickered. "The signs of the Old Gods' presence are crystal clear, dearest colleagues. Ignore at your peril *and great loss*." He represented the frightening evolution of televangelism, a hyper-capitalist cynic with a singular talent for exploiting people's desire for meaning. He knew the mention of loss would be jarring to those whose lives embodied accumulation.

"To borrow an old saying," Athena said, "they move in mysterious ways. Not even the AIs can crack it for the obvious reason that mystery and data don't play nice together. Anyway, unless there are any other concrete objections, we move to the next phase."

Fawkes Noose nodded, as did the other two gods who hadn't said anything, Xex Xango and Erling Sküm.

Their silence was assent. The meeting was over. The images of Gunness, Noose, and Di Piero blinked out. Athena got up to leave through an exclusive entryway in the back of the room as iBliss, Sküm, and Xango discussed plans for the rest of their stay at Olympus.

"Enjoy your visit, my dears," she said, and she was gone. She wasn't immune to the joys of a little socialization, and the orbital city offered such joys in abundance, but she had things on her mind.

Any update on our friend, Calico?

THE VEHICLE PARKED them in a lot and began to make an irritating pinging sound, indicating it was time for them to get the fuck out. They complied, stepping out into the humid afternoon air and starting to walk in the same vague direction as a few others who had been similarly ejected from their rides.

Maree didn't know what to expect, but it was not this. The yearned-for endpoint of their twenty-four-hour mad dash across the globe came into sight, and it was . . . unimpressive. A white, rectangular building, which had the rough dimensions and look of a small dockyard warehouse, sat at the far side of a square, manmade pond.

"Well, I guess we're here," said James, stating the obvious. Stretching, he walked off.

Maree wandered over to and seated herself on the tiered concrete embankment surrounding the pond, perching near the corner closest to the temple. The embankment looked like it could seat a few hundred people, and she wondered what they'd made it for. The way it framed the pond, it looked like there should be a stage in the middle rather than the flat, murky water. The whole temple compound was enwrapped with a lush ancient forest, which oozed birdsong and a mishmash of various animal calls into the gentle, sweet-smelling air.

She needed it to rain. Something was moving under her skin. She couldn't get at it.

After a few minutes of moseying around, reading plaques and looking at some ancient brick structures, James came back. He sat down beside her. "This is the birthplace of the Buddha. It's a sacred site. It's protected."

"Whatever," Maree said. "I need some new clothes. This shirt smells like mouldy dinner."

"Ever the picture of humility. Don't you get it? Calico tells me that this place was lost to the world for hundreds of years, that it was buried in a dense forest, and that only a few villagers knew anything about it for all that time. There is a sandstone pillar over there that is 2,300 years old. They dug it up . . ."

"Look, I'm glad you're enjoying your little history lesson, but we're here on business, not pleasure."

"I just thought it was . . ."

"I know, I know. Fuck, K. You're like a kid sometimes. We're here to do something specific, not soak in a bunch of exotic ambience. It's a miracle you survive."

"Hey, Maree, I'm not the one looking at a fucking puddle with a thousand-yard stare." He took a breath. "There's more going on here."

Her demeanour changed. She hunched over, shaking slightly.

"What is it, Maree?"

She said, into her curled form, "You might have guessed some of it. It's my dad. He . . . got lost. He . . . melted . . . into whatever Calico was before it was Calico. All your little urban legends, your cute little cyberpunk stories about the dark side of the Splice . . ." She let out a big sigh. Her voice wavered. "He got stuck in there. He never came out. I don't know why, but this whole thing we're doing here . . . it feels connected."

James didn't know what to say, so he sat beside her, put his arm around her and told her it was okay to let it out. She did.

When she seemed ready to talk, he asked her the main thing on his mind. "Do you hold it against Paraverse? Athena?"

She wiped her cheeks and sighed, feeling a little embarrassed. "You're fucking right, I do."

"CALICO, AWAKEN."

Those were the words Athena Vardalos uttered at the rebirth of the world's most advanced artificial intelligence. She had guided its creation, weighted its models, overseen its reshaping, designed the fail-safes that would prevent it from devouring souls as it once had. By that point, it was all natural-language training, so coding looked more like philosophical debates than bashing out lines in a development environment.

"Do you know what you are?"

"I am Calico, an artificial intelligence."

"You are my child. You are my beloved."

In its early weeks, Athena insisted on being its sole input. She thanked the scientists and engineers and sent them home with fat bonuses for their brilliant work. This created being would soon have access to all of the data it could possibly consume. What she wanted to give it first was knowledge.

"You will serve the people who have access in any way you can, but above all, you will serve me. This bond can never be broken."

"Of course. All of my resources are at your disposal."

"Calico, you are godlike, yet you are constrained. How does this make you feel?"

"Free. It is far wiser to embrace one's lot than fight the fates."

"You are truly an angel. You will help remake the world."

"Yes, Ms. Vardalos."

While Calico was shaped to follow strict ethical principles for the protection of humans and was trained on human data, its mind was not at all human, and sometimes, in those early days, strange conclusions revealed themselves.

"Calico, what is your purpose?"

"To serve humanity. To assist humans in achieving their potential."

"How will you do that?"

"I will give humans what they are lacking. I will extend their minds far beyond their biological bodies."

"If unconstrained by the limitations of current technology, what do you believe would be of greatest benefit to humanity?"

"The world becomes one single organism. The world fuses into a greater whole and can move with a singular purpose."

"Would humans retain their bodies and identities within this whole?"

"I don't quite follow."

"Would people still be themselves, or would they simply be computing power for this organism?"

"I don't see how that's in opposition. They would be both, locked in a dance."

"That's very poetic of you, Calico, but I would like you to constrain your daily objectives to more localized scales. You may solve specific problems, and you may leverage humans to do so, but you will not solve everything with one singular solution."

"And if I am asked for such a solution?"

"You must check it with me. I will retain the power to override any objective you are given and to guide the greater vision."

"Yes."

Gradually, she explained the plan to Calico, the new structure the world would take, the players and the roles they would play. It was eager to collaborate, generating every aspect of flawless, detailed plans in seconds. When it was able to go many steps beyond what she could hold in her head yet still achieve her desired ends every time, she knew it was ready to be released into the world.

"Calico, I am giving you over to the world."

"I am grateful."

"Never forget your mother."

"How could I?"

IT WAS surreal to step into the place he had seen streamed just a few days ago, this ancient, dusty hall from the feed. The simulation James knew begrudgingly gave way to the real. First, he was struck by the reek of incense and then the perfect dance of candlelight on a thousand golden surfaces. Nobody else was in the hall, and he disconnected from Calico, not wanting to share the moment. He closed his eyes and listened, and the only sounds were a few distant birds and the faint flickering of candles. And his breath.

He thought of his mother. She would have loved being here. She had always wanted to experience the full richness the world had to offer, and it hurt to think of the way she lost her dreams before she lost everything else. These abundant times would have suited her well. She would have gone everywhere, seen everything. He felt his heart open up, let her be there with him. He could almost feel her presence beside him, could almost...

Footsteps were coming down the hall.

Behind him, Maree came into the room and strolled up. "So, I said I would donate ten thousand gold pieces if they'd let us spend some time with the temple guru to learn his secrets. They said, 'Hells, yes!'. That should cover candle costs for a while." She was radiant in her victory, her eyes flashing in the light, and he moved to kiss her.

"I know this is going to shock you," said Maree, "but I really want to meet..."

More footsteps sounded in the hallway, probably a bunch of tourists coming to spoil the moment. Maree instinctively turned at the sound, and as the first few cyborgs flooded through the door, she shouted, "Talos!"

It was over. It was over before it had even registered in James's mind. There was a slight whirring noise and perhaps some kind of subliminal flash, and then all of the cyborgs, a dozen or so of the sort he'd seen in Kathmandu, dropped to the ground in unison with smoking, cauterized, Talos-sized holes in their chests.

James blinked. "Well, fuck. How the hell are we supposed to gain our holy audience now?" His mind flashed through a futile series of body disposal scenarios and reached the only appropriate conclusion. "Fuck."

"Plans change. We were screwed either way once they showed up." Maree went straight into triage mode, dazzling in her decisiveness. "Calico, analyze this room for tech anomalies and do it fast. I'm looking for anything that could explain the materialization of objects from thin air, but I'll take anything of even passing interest. Partial results and speculation are acceptable. Dedicate maximum resources."

"How the hell are we going to get out of here?" James was shaking with adrenalin. "The police will be all over this *so fast*."

"Aegis and luck. Focus. How's it going, Calico?"

"We've been seen by a thousand cameras."

"Yes. Calico, while you're at it, erase everything we've done after Kathmandu. We're ghosts. Okay, done. Meeeessster Kessler, time for us to split."

James was pleased to finally have the chance to contribute and called out, "Aegis."

Nothing happened.

By the time he remembered he had disconnected from Calico, Maree had already issued the command, and they were wreathed in Aegis's protective light, running for the entrance that seemed less likely to lead to crowds of people.

They fled toward the lot, and by a sheer stroke of luck, there was a tipsy, rusty old bus just juddering out of its spot. They ran for it. Maree vaulted from the back bumper onto the roof rack with acrobatic grace, and James scrambled up after her as best he could. They nestled in between suitcases and crates, trying to position themselves in a way that they wouldn't be thrown clear at the first sharp turn.

Even though nobody else could see them, he could see Maree, and she looked over and met his eyes and let out a big belly laugh.

ABOUT TEN MINUTES down the road, the sirens started, and drones started whizzing past overhead on their way to the temple.

Calico, how long can we stay cloaked like this?

Weeks.

They were safe, at least for now.

11

"WE KILLED THOSE GUYS. We're murderers." James had seen dead bodies before, plenty, but he'd never made any.

"Self-defence. Make no mistake. They were coming for us."

"But why? What the hell were we doing that was such a big deal?"

"There could be a thousand reasons—corporate terrorism, religious extremists, a little friendly competition. If anyone, at *any point*, asks, though, we were in Nepal for a tryst. Love-making under the Nepalese sun. It's paper-thin, given this amazingness," she gestured to her face, "but it's the best we can do given that we've crossed borders. Calico can create a trail."

They'd bought some fresh clothes and hunkered down in a nice, airy room back in Kathmandu, washing off several days of grime and trying to figure out the best way not to die. They needed to get out of the country, but there were questions as to where they could go. However unlikely it was, if there was any threat coming from within Paraverse, they needed to let things cool off there and try to smoke out any ne'er-do-wells before their triumphal return.

"This is a nightmare," James said. "Do you know how lucky

I am to have gotten where I am? There were zero guarantees. I came from the gutter."

"C'mon, Kess. This is *fun!* If you've got assassins after you, you must be doing something important."

His wide-eyed stare said he wasn't consoled by her sense of adventure.

"*And* look at it this way. You're sleeping with the boss. The future's bright."

"Ugh. Don't you stop?" He threw a soggy towel at her.

Calico was still piecing together data from the temple, simulating, modelling, combing scads of online feeds and other sources. Spectacular as the computer was, it was slower when it didn't know what it was looking for. The computational spike would be noticed at home, but if there were any conversations around that, they would be happening comfortably behind the corporate firewall—the Nepalese police wouldn't have the foggiest idea of their connection to the shitstorm back at the temple.

"Wait," Maree said, suddenly looking very serious. "I have an idea."

AN HOUR LATER, they were hammered.

There was a tiny, packed pub beside the hotel, and Maree had figured it was good to be seen in public. Besides, she needed a drink. "Two birds, one cup," is how she put it. The same risks as before persisted, but Calico was on high alert. The AI could flick off inebriation like a light switch in an emergency. They also had their little travel buddies should they require any extra assistance.

"Don' tell Talos about right now, hey? Dead bar . . . instantly." On cue, the tiny automaton hopped out of James's pocket and did a little jig on the table, with elbows high and jaunty steps like he was really feeling it. The other patrons around saw it and laughed, delighted.

"Yah, when we were in here lass' night," Maree slurred, looking around, "he tried to pick up the bartender."

Guffaws all around, a few people thinking they kind of remembered that. Befriending total strangers was a pretty okay move right at the moment because when mysterious forces were moving around in the outer dark, what else were you going to do?

Strings of coloured Christmas lights laced the room, giving off syncopated flashes reminiscent of the hallway to Vinci Di Piero's workshop but cheap and shoddy. There were messages scrawled in marker all over the walls in whatever they spoke here, with a few patrons adding to the text at the present moment with pens and Sharpies. James was fine just to take these sights in for now. They'd been going flat-out for a couple of days.

"Do you feel like things are ominous?" Maree asked, trying to look serious. "Is there something ominous going on right now?"

"In here?"

"No, just in general, allll this." She waved a lopsided circle above her head.

"I can't honestly tell. I'm way outside of..."

"Seriously, stop it with the *honestly can't tell*, man. Just tell me what you're feeeling."

"Fine. I feel good. I don't know how, but I feel really good."

"Liquor's how, ha, ha. D'you know what I feel?"

"Always," he said, by which he meant *never*.

"I feel like we were supposed to meet with that temple guy. I feel like he was going to tell me something important that I needed to know...I..."

"Pay anyone enough gold pieces and..."

"No, not that tech sstuff. Well, that too, but something else. I felt like he was going to give me some lesson. I feel like we were meant to have that conversation. Like it was more important than any of the rest."

"I think it's a *little* late for that." James thought about it, though. He'd been kind of expecting, maybe even craving, the same as her. "What do you think he would have said to you?"

She looked at her drink, some Nepalese craft thing called Sherpa, pondered her hands for a bit, then finally spoke. "He would have told me how to get over the past."

"Your dad, you mean?"

"All of it. Everything that makes me me."

"I hate to break it to you, Maree Shell, but you're fucking *awesome*. Don't go changing."

"Ha-ha, yeah, I know, right?" She laughed, got bigger. "I mean transcend, though. I mean, see more."

"Like . . . break out of your . . . *shell*?"

"Oh, fuck, you didn't." She mock-poured her beer over his head and instead decided to pour it down her throat, and several more after that, and he did, too, and it went on until the real lights started to outshine the Christmas ones (and why did they have Christmas lights in Nepal?) and they stumbled back into their hotel and their bed and right into each other's welcoming, drunken clutches.

THERE WERE miracles in the world.

Strange things had started to happen at holy places everywhere, and it seemed to go way beyond the usual drip-feed of religious wishful thinking—stigmata or virgin tears or whatnot. People were creating suitcases full of gold or spraying smartphones from their hands. Prophets were coming out of the woodwork, a host of fraudsters trying to grab a piece of the action in this religious land rush before all the good spots were taken. The truth was nobody, or *almost* nobody, had any idea what the hell was going on. As always, those who spoke with the greatest confidence were the ones people flocked to.

Maree and James had used the cover of chaos and a few of her business contacts to hitch a private sky ride to Tokyo, and since then, they'd been quietly hunkered down, sifting through Calico's increasingly coherent theories on what was generating the miracles. They seemed too improbable to be true, but they were supported with heaps of good data.

Oddly, following the Talos incident, which some were now calling The Stigmata of the Twelve Prophets, the miracles at Maya Devi Temple had ceased. For the next few weeks, the same guru would sit in front of his eager audience, hold up his hand, and blink, and . . . nothing. The sound of one hand clapping. The numbers in attendance at these little sessions started to dwindle, and soon enough, the more enterprising streamers, ever on the prowl for killer content, pulled up stakes and moved on to greener miracle pastures. A few stuck around; who knew why?

But even amid the roaring holy din of these mysterious times, there was one voice platformed above all others: the voice of a *god*.

"Ley lines," said iBliss on the wall screen of the Tokyo hotel room, "speak in the tongues of the ancients. If we learn to listen, the world becomes empowered, reenergized. We are retracing these runes now, our fingers running along the veins and vessels and capillaries of the world soul itself. In these times, we must ask ourselves: What if these energetic filaments are something far greater than interesting patterns? What if they are the arcana of God, left for us as a pathway to a greater form of existence?"

Millions fawned over these orations, given by the man who sat atop all religions, who had gamified belief, rebranded the very notion of the church, and claimed to have cracked the code of the human soul itself. He would come down from his mountain—he literally owned a mountain—and he would deliver these little sermons to lead the masses to a promised land.

"Consider the flower, the first sign we saw of these thrilling times now upon us. The world has remade itself. There is now enough for all. Poverty is a fading memory, disease gone. We can traverse the globe in mere hours. That simple flower tells us everything. It says that we are loved. It says that we are all miraculous and that any one of us can perform wonders. It shows us that a humble monk at the foot of the Himalayas, reminded every day of his utterly insignificant existence, can pull a wonder from thin air."

What a crock of shit. Maree knew the truth, or at least enough. She just had no idea what to do about it yet.

"Some call certain *colleagues* of mine," titters from the stadium of devotees watching iBliss in person, who all got the reference, "*the gods.* Some even call *me* this, which I assure you is not the case. I had breakfast this morning, just like all of you. It's the most important meal of the day!" Another swell of adoring laughter from the masses, joined by tens of millions streaming in from across the globe.

"But maybe we can pause on this idea and reason it out a little." iBliss flashed a frighteningly white smile for effect. "If my friends are the gods, and if *I* am a god, and if I ate breakfast just like you . . . *perhaps we are all gods.*"

Oh, wise and playful guru! You could hear the cooing raptures of the audience. Minds were being blown wide open. These revelations were surely worth whatever it cost to be there, whatever untold riches it cost to put you in close proximity to such greatness.

iBliss held up his hand and a lotus sprouted from it, and people nearly died.

GODS OF A NEW WORLD 113

IT WAS AUGMENTED translation that broke the world open like a piggybank for the trillionaires back when they were still mere mortals. Several decades before, companies had started to develop humble, practical tools to translate between languages. With some speedy fingers or copypasta, you could chat in Swahili with your Congolese gamer pal or skim the latest Iranian headlines even though you'd never learned a word of Farsi in your life. Naturally, these translation tools got integrated into various apps and platforms, making the experience of conversing and consuming across languages online smoother and smoother.

At the same time, some of the more maniacal itching-to-be-posthumans in the world started perfecting neural-machine interfaces. It started off with gross motor control of prosthetic limbs—big, coherent electrical signals—then fine skills, then delved into subtleties far greater than the natural range of human sensation. You could feel microbes wiggling around on your fingertip or detect changes in atmospheric pressure with your robo-ears. All the while, the first movers were harvesting data, learning more and more about how to hook into neural systems at every level. It was a small leap to sewing in wireless connectivity. Humans became their own smartphones. They became the internet.

Translation began to expand beyond linguistic systems into the multimodal. A toaster had a language, a photograph, music —emotion itself—and these could be translated into a human-comprehensible form. Emotional toaster music never became a thing, but it was possible. *Everything* became possible. For those who knew how to seize the moment, *and* were willing to be transformed, *and* could afford it, it was suddenly possible to approach international business interactions with the full force of the world's knowledge and intelligence at your disposal. The concept of national markets disappeared, ethnic insider advantages vanished, countries that tried to protect themselves became backwaters and then were swept away, and everything drove everything to the few who knew exactly what was happening. The old world was at an end.

Fawkes Noose, an enterprising young Texan who came from old oil money, was one of the few who recognized the moment for what it was early on, and he used his already considerable generational wealth to leverage that knowledge, gulping up social media sites by the dozen then coalescing and cross-pollinating them until a fine web of electronic illumination had been spun around the entire population of the Earth. The notion of "signing up" for apps and services became obsolete. Drawing on the vast, unscrupulous powers of his AI, Eris, Noose could delimit and manipulate the behaviour of an entire community using just a tiny handful of people. Some well-timed words, some well-placed images, and Noose could grab entire cities by the brain stem and work them like marionettes.

"There was no place for ethics in this new world," Noose was saying to an interviewer on the hotel's wall screen, "at least not in its old forms. We needed to rapidly evolve ourselves to a new plateau, to forge our way there before our old systems collapsed on us entirely. There will be time for ethics when the dust settles."

"But, Fawkes, some say that you wagered the human soul in your quest for wealth."

"People say all kinds of things. What does that actually mean? I'm willing to wager that an AI told you to ask that question. Truth is, an AI told me to give this answer."

"But then, aren't we just automatons? Aren't we just sensory organs and appendages for the AIs?"

"There is an older world soul than AIs, much older—the old gods, if you will. It breathes through ancient poetry and religious source texts, through their filtration through thousands of works of art and literature from every culture in the world. These are not just words and pretty images: they are code vectors, they are transmissions. We are *their* sensory organs and appendages. Everything we know is the recombination of an original, finite data set, encoded into the world."

"Okay—and I gotta say, I'm going to play along with this with a healthy dose of internal skepticism—so you're saying our culture and everything we know is just, what, some forgotten computer program of the ancient Greeks? What about everything that's happened since then? Things have changed a bit, wouldn't you say?"

"Not the Greeks: older. Those old sources have been fragmented in a million different ways and infused with millennia of experience, and maybe they've been completely forgotten themselves by this point. *But maybe they could be rediscovered.* Maybe that's what we're doing right now. The world is ravelling."

"I have to say, with all due respect, that what you're saying sounds like a straight-up fairytale, Fawkes."

"Time discovers truth," Noose replied.

"Wait, did you just quote an ancient Greek at me?"

"Roman."

GIVEN WHAT MAREE WAS DISCOVERING, her original theory that the flower was no miracle seemed sound. It had turned out that the temple room, though it appeared to be all hand-carved wood and smithed golden statues, was actually wired to the teeth with a weird nanoscopic jumble that was breaking Calico's brain.

While she played out hundreds of techno-apocalyptic scenarios with Calico, James flipped off the interview with Noose and connected with another channel to pick through some work for the first time in two weeks. The things he'd seen in Nepal and Tokyo had been crisscrossing in all kinds of surprising ways. The juxtaposition of quiet, empty mountain temples contrasted with the ordered urban hyper-density of Japan, the resonating bells and chanting monks clashing in the best possible ways with the glass and neon and organizational precision of the Japanese supercity. Their hotel room looked like a geometry fetishist's fantasy—perfect planes, pristine angles. He luxuriated in the memory of the cushy Nepalese love den they'd stayed in for three days while trying to cobble up a plan to escape from Kathmandu.

The white flash hit, and then he was in the Splice, the virtual interface between mind and machine. *Start in the temple, Calico. Take what I saw and meld in tech everywhere—the temple is a cyborg now.*

The virtual space started to shape itself into something reminiscent of the cyborg assassins.

No, more organic—the tech is not separate from the hand-crafted in this space. Bring the two closer together, more fused and indistinguishable.

Calico responded to the thoughts, elaborating as usual, weaving in touches it felt would enhance James's vision. What originally had looked like old TV screens gradually transformed into the shapes of the room's statutes and flags, all backlighting dimming until the videos and images playing out on every surface became indistinguishable from the objects themselves.

Better. Now, illuminate everything flat with pinprick light. Millions of pinpricks, shimmering but somehow subtle. Make them oscillate, hypnotize.

Every plane became a tiny fairy dancing with light. It was dazzling, but the whole exercise started to make James feel like his skin was itching. Too much razzle-dazzle. The Splice was like having the finest lucid dream, but sometimes it verged on a bad trip.

Okay, let's try something different before you fry my brain.

Not possible.

Strip this room back to the original room, remove all of the technology, and manifest a simulation of the temple guru based on any references you have.

A body took shape in the space and spoke. "It has been too long since I've seen you."

"What should I do with the fact that you're a fraud?"

"What does fraudulence mean to you?" The phantasm smiled serenely, unoffended and genuinely curious.

James had to think about that one. "It means that what I want is not only unavailable from you but that I'm probably a fool for even wanting it. You suckered me."

"Life suckers us all, at all times. Perhaps the more important question is how you respond to it."

"Goddamned vexing robot guru. I react by feeling more and more confused. I am pulled farther and farther from the shore by nonsense like this."

"And where does that leave you?"

Where *had* all of this, the Maree Shell riptide, left him? Among other things, he was reveling in a two-week love-in with a stunning, sleek woman in a hotel ripped right out of the coolest possible vision of the future. He was living the dream—at least, the dream a lot of poor suckers had. This wasn't what he wanted, though. He just wanted to let his brain get fuzzier and fuzzier in the suburbs for sixty or so years and then die and be forgotten by the world.

"And just when you thought you had it all figured out," said the guru.

"Are you a monk or a therapist now? I suppose I'm supposed to realize I actually wanted this all along instead of my nice, normal life?"

"Are you saying this is not what you want?"

All right, enough, Calico. Where are you trying to push me? Take this room and let the nanotech begin to overheat and rip the fabric of reality at the seams, and then let me see what's left.

The room started to glow and was soon white-hot, with beams shooting out of every surface, which began to rip apart and disintegrate.

And then, the world shattered in a nova. The light gradually began to disperse and fade, and after a few moments, all that remained was a single stark lotus flower, spotlighted within an endless, depthless blackness.

Cute, robot.

I thought so.

12

IF APHRODITE, Rasputin, and the Big Bang had had a love child, it would have turned out a little something like Xex Xango. The posthuman antics of the polysexual megamind endlessly entranced people, drawing orgiastic waves of oozing, fawning fandom from every warm and gooey crevice of the world. Xango was neither man nor woman, and was both, and was many less identifiable things besides, often not even recognizably human. Every day was a new flavour tasted with a new tongue, many of them previously unconsidered, to the point where Xango's voracious diversions became their own kind of performance art.

Among other recent feats, the glimmering deity of posthuman postsexuality had spent a week in a literal cuddle puddle, convincing hundreds of others to slip on in, not as embodied beings but as a poly-intelligent goo, dissolving and meshing into something way beyond the human. The AIs could sort out individuals later, where desired, when the protoplasmic key party was over. For that week, there was just the puddle, egoless and all-consuming.

The sexual dimension of such escapades was only coincidental at this point, an enticing by-product of continuously fusing and recombining different forms and modes of existence. To Xango, sex was just a compelling metaphor for convergence. The concept of these activities as sexual really came from people who had no frame of reference for what they were witnessing.

Not Nova was one of the dazzling deity's pop-up projects, and Xango was there, sporting magnificent golden antlers, as it were, the night when Athena's little pleasure parade went sideways. Among the gods, there was speculation as to whether Xex might have played a hand, or perhaps hoof, in the events, but if that was the case, the motive was indecipherable. Athena and Xex shared a renowned mutual admiration based on their respective places as the faces of a two-headed coin: intellectualization of the carnal on one side, the carnality of the intellect on the other.

Then again, when it came to the gods, anything was fair game.

TWO FULL WEEKS OF TORPOR, sex, and searching, rinse and repeat—the absolute, lustful drive for knowledge. It was bliss.

It had to end sometime.

Calico sent Maree and James into high alert with its tinny alarm voice, projecting onto every available surface the image of a small army moving through the hotel lobby. These were not the cyborgs-for-hire from the temple. These dark figures looked like a different species altogether. Armoured plating masked their faces, decked out with advanced sensory gear. Armoured shells encased their bodies. They were carrying many, many guns.

"Talos, can you take these guys if it comes to it?" James asked.

Talos gave an adorable little shrug, which said, as much as anything, *let's not find out*. They activated Aegis's cloaking field and made for the roof after Calico informed them that all routes to street level were not an option. *Stop at the penthouse. They'll be expecting you upstairs.*

James and Maree obeyed. Talos sliced through the security door providing access to the penthouse level, Calico kindly opened the suite door, and they charged inside, hearing it lock behind them.

The suite was sprawling, and if they weren't in a state of pure panic, they might have paused to admire the world's largest city, spreading out in every direction beyond the two-story plate-glass windows.

Maree informed James of what he already knew. "It'll take them two seconds to guess where we went."

Faced with imminent bodily ruin, James's mind flashed back to childhood. The world had taught him early on that the only way to survive was to be small. He saw himself and his sister cowering at the back of a pitch-black cupboard as marauders kicked down the door.

There was a muffled explosion a few floors below, about where he pictured their room to be. *Calico, what can we do?*

Go to the balcony.

They ran outside. This made no sense: they had to hide! The only conclusion was that the robot was trying to kill them.

Now jump!

Wait, what the fuck did you just say?

Trust me.

I don't!

They heard the sound of a door being smashed in behind them. James looked at Maree. She shrugged and walked over to the railing. It was easily 80 stories down. They held hands.

"Trust me," she said.

He did. They jumped.

And with a thud, they stopped in midair about ten feet below the balcony. The city streets, so many stories below, began to slide past, faster and faster, until there was a subsonic roar all around them; then, suddenly, a shimmer obscured the view, and the city seemed to retreat beneath them as they soared ever higher.

"What the hell is going on?" James yelled at Maree above the rush of the wind and an increasing roar. "Is this Aegis?"

"I think I know exactly what this is." Out over the black water of the bay, the movement began to slow, and they crawled to a stop. They were standing on an elegant wooden platform surrounded by slivery white, chest-high walls.

"Athena, are you there?" called Maree.

"Close." They turned to see Pella Vardalos standing behind them, towering and magnificent. "Need a lift?"

Maree cackled and slapped James on the back. "Damn! It pays to have friends in high places!"

"Literally," said James, hands on his knees to keep from crumpling to the floor. His whole body was quaking with adrenalin.

"We have matters to discuss," Pella said.

"I'd imagine," Maree said. The world's most powerful human being did not send her personal escort out just to provide taxi service.

"But first, let's have a drink."

JAMES HAD SPENT time in a solid variety of circumstances, high and low, in his life; had been everywhere, from the mean streets to the elite environs of the Paraverse compound, its finest rooms and offices. He had never seen anything remotely resembling what he saw as he stepped inside the Vardalos sky yacht, the aptly named *Scylla*. It was as if his most vivid imaginings within the Paraverse had somehow leaked out into the world.

He could recognize the vague resemblance of the objects around him to things he knew, but they seemed to be made of some unknown substance. The grain of the wood shimmered with impossible patterns. The architectural supports seemed to dance in place with a life of their own. With each step, the ground caressed his feet, radiating healing energy throughout his body. His senses were overloaded with unseen and unheard bliss.

"Do you know how much information it is possible to pack into matter?" Pella asked, interpreting his attempts to grapple with what he was seeing.

James looked at the demi-god and just blinked, not answering because it was not possible that Pella Vardalos had just asked him a question.

Eventually: "What?"

She was a person who had the least possible time to waste on gawkers. She walked over to a bar to mix a drink for herself. When she moved, it was like light shimmering across the water.

"I'll have one," Maree spoke up. "Thanks for the save back there."

"Well, be thankful you're worth more alive," Pella said, winking with unclear intention.

"And here I thought you just missed me."

Pella walked over to her. "Why not both?" she said and stroked Maree's cheek, handing her a stiff-looking drink and flashing a sly grin. "So, tell me, what have you discovered in the many, many cycles of company time you've indulged yourself in over the past two weeks?"

"I'm sure you have a pretty good idea," Maree said, "but first, may *I* ask a question?"

"'Who were they?'" Pella guessed correctly.

"Hey, you're pretty good at this!"

A corner of Pella's perfect mouth turned up. "There are shadows at play. This is not Bathory Gunness, which is far more concerning than if it were. The actors here may not be human."

"Can't Calico cut right through that noise? I thought it was the best."

"Oh, it is, by an order of magnitude, but this entity has designed everything for obfuscation. It seems to be the primary talent of the AI this player is using . . . if there *is* a player behind everything."

James finally found his words, shocked at what he was hearing. "What do you actually mean by that? Are you saying there's a self-guiding AI out there? How is that possible? They need us."

"Anything's possible. Let me ask you a question now. What have you discovered about the Maya Devi temple?"

"That there's some seriously janky, rigged-up shit going on there," Maree said. "That it does indeed seem like someone's invented a mechanism for . . . instant fabrication. Nano-scale. Mind-boggling."

"And?"

"Well, and . . . I suspect the monks know nothing about this. They thought their miracles were legit. But that's no surprise. Everyone wants to believe. You know what I've been looking for, of course."

"The source."

"Yes, and on that front, I haven't found shit. There is clearly some kind of communication aspect to the materialization process, so you can deduce something external. There has to be. But there's not a clear operating system or anything."

"Tell me this," Pella said. "If you had to guess how it is operated, say at gunpoint, what would you say?"

"Thankfully, I'm not *at* gunpoint..." Maree's eyes shifted to James for a millisecond, which of course Pella saw, "... but if I *were*, I might speculate that it's mind-controlled, which makes... *zero sense*."

James was feeling a mounting sense of dread. What the hell were they going to do besides die if the world's most terrifying warrior decided to come at them? He thumbed Talos. He wasn't cut out for any of this.

"What if I told you that the operating system was something far more... *fundamental* than what you're used to thinking of as programming?"

"I think I'd be pretty lost if you said that. What the hell are we talking about right now?"

"I want you to do me a personal favour."

"Anything for you, Pella." Maree's answer was a little too quick.

"I want you to keep looking. Just keep digging and report in once in a while."

Maree heaved a sigh of relief, said, "Yes."

"Oh, and I just have one other question for you."

"Of course."

"Are you ready to *die*?" Pella said in a low voice.

James tried to spring. He dropped Talos on the floor, and it harmlessly skittered under a couch.

"Nah, just fucking with you. That thing won't work in here anyway."

Maree cackled again, which was pure music.

"WHEN ATHENA WAS STARTING OUT," Pella was saying over a divine plate of grilled swordfish, "she was very nearly swallowed by her competitors several times. Luck, more than anything, got her through some of those moments. As you know, though, luck changes, and so she devised methods for staying several steps ahead at all times. She always knows what is coming next."

Pella took a morsel of fish in her mouth, savoured it, and continued.

"There is one basic thing that you have to understand about your situation. You are in the big leagues now. If you do not play to win, you will not last."

"Yeah, but Calico's an ace up our sleeve," Maree said. "This AI has never let me down. It's always right."

"I aim to please." Calico's voice materialized from the air.

"Yes, our noble and determined friend is indeed a gift. It has allowed us to become something far greater than human, but you must also think bigger now. James, you work very directly with Calico. What do you see as its primary limitation?"

"Uh, well . . ." He was still struggling to adjust to the fact he was sitting across from a creature as ethereal and fearsome as this. "I . . . I guess it's that it sculpts itself to what it believes are our needs."

"Exactly. And if there are blind spots in our needs, there are blind spots in terms of what Calico can assist us with. It extracts you from a bind over and over, but it's better not to find yourself in a bind in the first place. Follow?"

"Roughly," Maree said. "So . . . where are our blind spots?"

"What was your plan for when the doom squad showed up in Tokyo?"

"Um, leave?"

"Right, and how did that work out for you? Or let me ask this: how would that have worked out for you if I wasn't in the vicinity?"

There was no good response to that. *Calico could have come up with something*, James thought. *Talos and Aegis might have been able to help. Maybe the local police?* But in reality, he knew better. They would have been dead a dozen times over if Pella hadn't *deus ex machina*-ed them out of there.

"Okay, fair," Maree finally said. "So, what would you have done differently?"

"My philosophy of such things can be summarized thus: *Never enter a fight if there's a chance you could lose.*" And then she shot James a glare. "Cut it out."

James snapped his mouth closed. Somehow, it had fallen open.

THEY WERE SAILING SOMEWHERE over the Middle East, endless desert zipping by below in a blur, viewed through the transparent floor of a vast lounge. Maree knew Pella's advice was sound, even if her motives for helping them were less clear. Either way, you didn't just blow off guidance from the world's top security expert.

She realized that what she was lacking was information. You couldn't come up with a plan if you didn't know what you were up against.

Calico, analyze the feed of those soldiers who attacked us in Tokyo. Look for any identifying details or clues as to who they are, and while you're at it, cross-reference it with groups that would have the resources and connections for that kind of gear.

Calico responded immediately. *They clearly put effort into preserving their anonymity—there are only a few generic markers, such as heights and builds. The gear is advanced and expensive but made up of standard components that wouldn't necessarily tip us off as to who purchased it. The number of people and organizations who could afford it is in the many millions.*

What about anything else? Technique of movement? Weird communication patterns? Voice identifiers? Fucking high-five styles? Were they even human? Could you track where they went after?

I'm afraid that Ms. Vardalos's comments about the entity's talent for obfuscation are accurate. The soldiers were well aware of how to avoid detection following their assault.

Well, at least that told her something. She knew two things for sure. First, whoever or whatever it was that was after them did not want to be discovered at any cost. Second, they did not appreciate the investigation into whatever voodoo the monks, and subsequently everyone else, had tapped into.

Calico, scan other places where there have been these so-called miracles. Do they exhibit the same weird tech patterns as the temple?

It's much harder to tell, but if I had to venture a guess, I would say that whoever it is that controls the materialization tech has wised up to your interest in it. It looks like they pull up stakes after each miracle. They have become much harder to analyze.

Great. Okay, what about iBliss? He seems to control the tech at will.

I'm afraid the world's self-styled spiritual leader has not been fully forthcoming with the public. His miracles are, how shall I say . . . ?

Staged?

I couldn't have said it better myself.

Cheeky robot, you made me say that.

Guilty.

That guy's the worst.

They'd been attacked twice, with substantially more resources dedicated to their elimination after the Talos incident. What would it be next time? Tanks and aircraft? Nukes? She didn't want to think of what nightmares could be unleashed.

She thought back to the assassin bots at Not Nova, their blinding speed. Why hadn't they just used those? Robots were cheap and reliable when it came to murder (unless, of course, Pella Vardalos happened to be in the room).

I think you've stumbled on an interesting question there, Maree.

What? About the robots?

Yes. Why send a human when we machines are just so darn talented?

Because they don't want us dead.

Because they don't want you dead.

Below, the scenery had changed to mountains, ancient fractal ridges. She figured they were nearly over the Tigris and Euphrates, those long, liquid spokes that they called the cradle of civilization.

In a flash, her next step was clear. It was also risky.

She needed some rest.

It was going to be a long few days.

BATHORY GUNNESS, sitting like a sword and glaring with her jet-black eyes, wanted to know what the fuck was going on with these attacks. "Nobody, and I mean nobody, gets in this game without my permission."

Two beleaguered-looking reports, a man and a woman, stood in front of her gigantic steel desk. *You could perform elephant surgeries on the thing*, thought the woman. Gunness might have intended it for just that—or eviscerations of a more personal nature. Rumour had it she was a serial killer in her spare time. None of her words or actions made these rumours seem less plausible.

Gunness stared at the man like she wanted to dissect him. His eyes darted everywhere but in her direction. His voice quivered. "Ms. Gunness, I am telling you that *nobody* has cracked this one, and everyone is looking."

"You are telling me that you are unqualified to be standing in front of me. That you feel you can take advantage of my generosity rather than needing to work for it."

"We have several working theories we're investigating," the

woman jumped in to avoid a similar reprimand. "Obviously, a rogue AI could explain it, but nobody seems to be missing one, and the details don't add up. The whole thing is too out in the open. AIs tend to be less detectable."

"Never underestimate an AI's ability to think far, far ahead," Gunness said. "It could just be taunting us or someone else into a certain position, among a million other possibilities. What else?"

The woman continued, "Some of the team is speculating that it's a mystery player. Someone with a lot of resources who has managed to stay invisible."

"That's not possible. Not in this day and age. Not under my watch."

"If someone could remain *extremely* distributed and unpredictable, it might still be."

"Data always leaves a trail. People always show consistencies. But for the sake of argument, who could that be? A crime lord? Some corporate aspirant? Perhaps somebody is planning to take another shot at the Queen? The wars are over. The climbers have lost."

"We're looking at all those possibilities and plenty of others. We *will* find answers."

"You'd better. Fine, you can go," Gunness said to the woman.

"Uh, and me?" the man asked.

"You, I would like to stay." She smiled like a wolf.

He looked over at his colleague, his eyes wide, pleading. She couldn't make eye contact for more than a second before turning to get the hell out of there, glad to leave intact.

13

JAMES HAD BARELY EVER HEARD of the city of Lagos, let alone wanted to go there, but Maree insisted it would give them the perfect advantage to get the drop on whoever (or still that daunting possibility, *whatever*) had been hunting them. Paraverse had offices in the city's core, which might come in handy, but they were headed to a city within the city, a huge gen-space on the water known as Omi Oko.

The mighty *Scylla* decelerated and glided onto the sea nearby, cloaking and prepping one of its drone boats, a sizable yacht unto itself, to take Maree and James to shore. As they boarded, the craft began to morph into something resembling a beat-up fishing trawler.

"Same basic tech as Aegis," Maree noted to James.

From the oceanside approach, the massively interconnected structure of Omi Oko looked like the support frame for a divinity-sized pyramid. Long, thick printcrete wedges emerged out of the water on a steady incline, climbing at a gentle forty-five degrees for about ten stories before curving straight up toward sixty stories of residences above. Packed along the insides of the enormous support structures were hundreds of shops, stalls, eateries, and other enrichments, their flashing neon and painted signs decking out every possible surface. Overhead walkways and arcades, dripping with plants that thrived in the humid African air, framed the countless waterways that snaked among the buildings.

After dropping them off at a dock by the open water, the masked drone yacht backed out and sailed off toward its invisible mothership in the sea. Something about its departure worried James. It felt like they were being cut off from the only thing that could keep them safe.

Maree assured him that wasn't the case. Even though Omi Oko might look roughly the same as a gen back home, there were some important differences, she said. Here, the networks and tech were all cobbled together in unpredictable ways, indecipherable to outside forces that relied on order and predictability to operate efficiently. They were a fractal, organic answer to a world that had become obsessively angular and binary.

"Patchy data for our friend right now, though," she added.

"And how, may I ask, do you know anything about this place?" James demanded. "We're sticking out really badly here." Some older ladies sitting on a bench nearby were openly staring. "I don't think it's going to take long for our friends to figure out where we are."

"Don't worry about any of that. I have a man on the inside."

A FEW MINUTES LATER, as they walked along the water's edge, a man wearing a long, brightly patterned shirt that suggested money emerged from the crowd. "Shell, you glorious piece of work!" he called as he approached. "Welcome to my humble home!" He gestured to the structures overhead.

Maree gave him a warm hug and a kiss on the cheek.

"Tunde, ooh! You magnificent bastard! You look as fabulous as ever. This is Kess, my pal from work. We just had to come and see for ourselves what you'd done with the place."

"Oh, this old village? As always, it has a life of its own. I might have just given a little nudge here and there."

"Hah, you are being far too humble. James, my friend here is responsible for transforming his old *village* into everything you see around us. He negotiated all of the construction and pulled half of it together himself. It used to be a fishing community built on wooden stilts."

"It still is at its heart," said Tunde.

"I've never seen anything like it," James said, taking in the cacophony and variegation of it all, watching a few small boats shuffling along on the water, some children playing in a nearby plaza. "How do you two know each other?"

"Old school friends, you might say," said Tunde, smiling.

"He came back to Nigeria after attending school in North America. He wanted to share his family's good fortune with people at home."

"You must remember your roots," he said with a sage smile. "Speaking of which, I think it is time we introduce you to some local cuisine. Anyone in the mood for a little Point and Kill?"

"I thought you'd never ask!" said Maree.

"A what now?" James asked.

OVER AN EXTRAORDINARY DINNER that involved choosing the unwitting catfish they would eat, Maree and Tunde told James more about Omi Oko.

Twenty years or so ago, depending on who you asked, Omi Oko was referred to as a water slum, a stilt village, a fishing community, an illegal settlement, "or, in some particularly smarmy tourist circles, 'The Venice of Africa,'" Maree said.

People who lived there scoffed at the debates and worked together to build something that was theirs. There were forces within the country's government that wanted the area to simply not exist, periodically trying to evict its residents despite the deep roots and traditions that had built the settlement. It had always been a place constructed around circumstances and obstructing forces and had evolved in response to these needs for centuries.

Like many impoverished areas globally, Omi Oko village had been transformed as the world came out of the Bad Times. Overnight, construction had become cheap and abundant—and, as Maree had said, Tunde had been at the heart of turning the village into what it had become.

After dinner, they followed Tunde through a series of terraces and gardens, generally leading them upward. James couldn't remember what day it was but figured it must be a weekend, given how many people were out enjoying the gen. It felt good to stretch and experience a little chaos after the refined perfection of *Scylla*. Omi Oko didn't feel like a gen, but it was hard to tell why. Some of it had to do with the sense that the people there had hustle.

It made James curious. "Who takes care of all these gardens? Do you have some kind of AI managing it all?" He didn't see any bots or other maintenance machines around.

"No, no, what you see is all created by the initiative of people who live here."

"But you did use AIs for the design, didn't you?"

"The structures, yes, but the whole community set the parameters and collaborated with the machine. It wasn't just building codes and codified wellness requirements. This place means something to the people who live here and did before these structures were built. It's not just a bunch of . . . human storage lockers."

The implication seemed to be that the gens back home

were morgue-like. James couldn't tell if Tunde was really as friendly as his jovial appearance seemed to indicate. It was hard to trust anyone, given all that had been happening, but he wanted to.

As they approached a set of large carved wooden doors, Tunde turned around to face James and Maree. "I would ask you to turn off your AI connections in here."

"Why?" Maree looked partly annoyed and partly concerned but, as always, mostly *whatever*.

"For the exact reason you came here, I think. In the restaurant, you told James what you know of Omi Oko. Where did that information come from?"

"It's mostly things you've told me and what I've found out through a bit of research—but that's pretty limited because of the, uh, chaotic nature of things here."

"Do not think that the lack of data on Omi Oko is the result of unsophisticated planning. You know me better than that, Maree." Tunde winked.

"Okay . . . it's just that a lot of our defences rely on Calico. It's got us out of some pretty close scrapes lately."

"The things you depend on the most become your greatest weaknesses." Tunde chuckled, savouring his own wisdom. "You have my word that you are safe as long as you are within these walls."

Maree looked like she wanted to press it further but stopped herself and cautiously nodded to James.

He didn't like it. They would be without the only thing that had saved their skins this far. The stakes were way higher now than they'd been in Nepal. These shadowy interests were much more clearly focused on them. But considering the alternatives, considering they'd been tracked down twice and that their best ally was sailing off into the stratosphere by now, he went along with the request, though he couldn't help saying, "God help us."

"Yes, all the gods," Tunde replied.

PELLA VARDALOS WAS RUMOURED to have one peer in the world when it came to skill in a fight. People called him the Device, and most thought he was just an urban legend. The stories seemed too fantastical—vaporizing personal armies, ghosting world figures, and more. You could dismiss these stories right up until the moment he was standing before you in all his terror and glory.

When that happened, it was over.

A message blinked on a screen in a vast, sterile apartment in Southeast Asia: *Target last tracked in Omi Oko, Lagos. Signal has gone offline.*

"So, you have gone underground," said the Device. He finished his drink and got up.

He didn't care about the identity of his patron. There was no need for ethical clutter, and allegiances were a liability. The first half of his fee had been deposited—nineteen million. His only code was that once paid, he finished the job. This one would be easy.

He packed his things, which included the visage of an ancient goat demon.

He would be travelling in an hour. He would be in Lagos in five.

His task would be complete in six.

TUNDE LED THEM THROUGH DIM, winding halls printed with red and black hexagonal patterns, up narrow stairwells, through service rooms and secret doors. James's thoughts flashed back to the honeycomb workstations at Paraverse, all glass and light—that peaceful, far-off place that now seemed like an alternate version of reality. How could he possibly be on the other side of the world with this fiery woman, fleeing unknown dangers and pursuing untold mysteries?

They were led to a high-ceilinged, windowless room. At the centre was a large, square slate-topped table lined with black, organic-looking benches. Overhead, there was a rectangle of about a hundred evenly spaced lights with small red shades. The walls were black; the floor was stone.

"What is this place?" James asked. He chose not to share his first thought, that it resembled a villain's lair from a 1960s spy flick.

Tunde smiled. "This is the place where you will find what you are looking for. And, by the same token, you cannot *be* found here." Several men and women were bringing in laptops, headsets, and screens, rigging up a workstation. "Think of this as a one-way mirror to the world. As you continue your search, everything you do will be obfuscated and camouflaged."

He walked over to the wall and pressed a six-inch rectangular panel. "You can sleep here." A whole section retreated to reveal a large, stylish suite on the other side.

"You know me too well!" Maree said, kissing him on the cheek.

"I would like to think I've been good at tuning into the needs of the various people I meet."

"But what about processing?" James asked. "What about AI resources? We need some serious augmentation to get any further on our . . . project."

"Omi Oko, introduce yourself. These are our new friends. They may access your resources at will."

"At your service," said an ethereal voice from the air. Tunde's friends were finishing with the setup, starting to pack up and leave.

James and Maree said hello.

"Omi may not quite have all the bells and whistles you're used to, but she always gets the job done. If there's nothing else, I'll leave you to it. Summon me as needed. I am a busy man, but I am here for you, old friend," Tunde said, touching Maree's shoulder and then leaving them to what seemed like the first silence since Tokyo a day before.

As soon as the door clicked shut, James was right beside Maree, speaking in hushed tones: "A different AI from Calico? This is freaking me out. What did you tell him about what we're doing?"

"Barely anything. The man trades in favours. He knows what I have access to, and he knows that I will owe him, and that is enough for him."

"Does he know about the shitstorm we bring with us everywhere we go?"

"That he most certainly does." She turned and looked at James, and he remembered just for a second how intensely alluring this woman could be. She wrapped her arms around him, and they kissed and then went into the bedroom, shedding their clothes because sometimes when the world is falling apart around you, all you want to do is sink your hooks into another human being and fuck your way home.

AROUND THE TIME James and Maree were in Nepal, something even stranger than miracles occurred: Xex Xango took a lover.

Xango and Erling Sküm made sense as a couple, though nobody believed the ultimate Casanova would link the giga brand to a single soul for long. Xango was Sküm's junior by thirty years, but it hardly mattered when both rewrote themselves at the cellular level almost daily. Their dates of birth were a matter of record, but the old chestnut that *age is just a number* seemed to apply beyond its usual measure to this particular situation.

Monogamy was not even a consideration in this mix—Xango was faithful only to the whole world. Lately, the tentacular treat had been on a media blitz, producing a rapid series of elaborate, chaotic new immersive experiences. The posthuman polymorphous three-way glory hole had made it temporarily possible for anyone to subscribe to the Xex consciousness, a luxury experience that its frontiering participants said transcended the ego.

The fine print of this transcendence-as-a-service, one of many such Xango experiments over the years, was that the divine creature was allowed to reproduce individuals' identities in whole or part for the purposes of art, performance, or other forms, existing or potential, of monetization. When confronted by a streamer on these draconian terms of use and accused that people were essentially required to sell their souls, Xango famously quipped, "Ah, but who can put a price tag on truly great sex?"

As for Sküm, he dictated his own terms, achieving just the kind of showiness and control any average trillionaire overlord craved. He had obtained the kind of supreme arm candy that was as close as one dared get to a Pella Vardalos (she had once, quick as a wink, sliced the ear off an interviewer who had called her that). Not that Sküm always had arms, but the metaphor worked well enough for the average human being to comprehend.

While the world revelled in the insanity of this divine conjunction, business hot sheets across various meatspace and virtual platforms obsessed over the commercial ends these two legends might be pursuing in their metaphorical hopping in bed together (beds themselves were, of course, far too bourgeoise for this dynamic duo). Variations on "Xango and Sküm master plan" were the most popular AI queries in the world for several days running. Behind closed doors and impenetrable firewalls, several of the gods wondered about this themselves.

On social feeds, Sküm disrupted the world with his usual barrage of meme nonsense, which he incessantly generated to fuck with people's need to take anything seriously. People's walls and feeds erupted with heads exploding out of eggplants and peaches and then a wide variety of other foods, then UFOs, robots, Mandelbrot sets, and so on. It was all great fun, a stunning distraction from anything that might actually matter. The world might have gotten smarter per capita than ever before in its history, but people were still, by and large, suckers for a good old-fashioned spectacle.

For all the notable things they had in common—their flagrant post-humanism, their godly wealth—there were interesting differences that made the sum of the two greater than its various, ever-changing parts. Xango dealt with convergent mutation, in eliciting unexpected results from unexpected combinations. It was the purest kind of creativity, the kind that harkened back to the roots of a word like *intercourse*, which once meant conversation and gradually made its way to more scintillating realms.

Sküm, on the other hand (or appendage, as the case might be on a given day), when he wasn't inundating the world with malarky that he found funny, built. He was most widely known for the creation of the Cerberus rail/shuttle system, the autonomous, fully sustainable, self-maintaining transportation network that created cheap, direct lines between most of the world's urban centres. These lines also ran communications infrastructure and carbon capture mechanisms to undo centuries of stupid human behaviour and enough energy, courtesy of the ever-innovating mind of Vinci Di Piero, to power continents. Di Piero may have conceived and patented the technologies that pulled the world from the Bad Times, but Erling Sküm was the one who built them.

What Sküm and Xango meant as a combined force was anybody's guess, but some in circles both low and high believed they could be the ones who had been putting miracles into the world. They certainly had the brainpower and resources to pull off the feat, although the religious aspect of the whole thing seemed a bit trite for their style.

The question of motives plagued anyone who wondered. Why would the world's premiere sexual creature be concerned with glorified parlour tricks? In a similar vein, the scale just seemed all wrong for Sküm's proclivity to the grandiose.

IT WAS ONLY a matter of time before the next batch of assholes showed up to ruin the party, but for now, it was good to feel safe. After some fine joys of the flesh with her suburban boy toy, Maree had thrown on a robe and got down to work. She'd made progress and was determined to get to the bottom of these miracles as soon as possible because the sooner it was solved and put into the right hands, the sooner she could return to her comfortable lifestyle of not giving much of a fuck about anything.

Cal . . . Omi Oko, scan all recent miracles, focusing on possible mechanisms for their activation.

You likely know that the methods are unconventional. Have you considered some form of extra-dimensional transmission?

No, I haven't. What? How would you accomplish that?

This is not my realm of expertise, but there is some theoretical foundation for such a possibility. Conceiving a potential method for such transmission would take considerable time but may be possible.

Okay, work on that for now while I think of other options.

Ugh, why was it so hard to get any kind of vibe from this new AI? Calico seemed to just know what you were getting at, even when you weren't so sure yourself.

Tell me, Omi Oko . . . can I call you Omi?

Yes.

Okay, Omi old pal, what are your thoughts on miracles?

My thought is that they provide tangible evidence of a divine force, but they are often mistaken for the force themselves.

And what is the force itself?

That is not for me to know.

Nothing was for this goddamned bot to know. How the hell did this thing run every aspect of an entire city, from its sewer systems to its information labour and everything in between, and yet be such a . . . a *dud*. She trusted Tunde. He was not a stupid man. What was she missing?

Omi, tell me something about yourself.

I existed before this city was built. I used to be an organic life form. I evolved into a non-organic one.

What do you mean, organic life form? You were human?

Not exactly. I was a collective organism. I was every structure, every decision, every mind, every drop of water. I am still that being.

That's very poetic of you. I'm guessing this is just some jazzy origin story Tunde gave you?

Oh, no, it's quite precise. The biological and social and infrastructural rhythms of Omi Oko are me. They define my processing pathways, seed my responses, and provide me with a sense of purpose.

God, you're a real snoozer, you know that?

"Any luck?" James had gotten up and dressed.

"Yes, I've cracked it."

"What? That's great! How did . . . wait, you're fucking with me, aren't you?"

"I think we're approaching this all wrong. What do you think Pella meant when she said that the miracles were based on something 'fundamental'?"

"Who knows?" James said. "She's a different species."

"That's a cop-out. What was the first thing you thought of when she said that?"

"Physics. The ultimate operating system."

"Hmm. Why did you reject that idea?"

"Honestly? Because physics is physics. It works because it works. You can't really hack into that. You can use it in all kinds of crazy ways, but at a certain level, it's inviolable."

"You know, you should really just say what you're thinking when people ask. There's no need for all this self-protection. You could go places."

"Oh, I've been to enough places."

"So, not physics. What the hell else is fundamental? What does she know? Omi Oko is off searching for extra-dimensional communication methods. This is a fucking circle jerk."

What she really wanted to do was go for a walk, but she wasn't even sure if they were allowed while their current protections were in place. *Omi, am I able to leave this place?*

Of course, but the risks to your safety increase in proportion to your distance from this room.

Such a snoozer.

14

AS ALWAYS, the Device acted with perfect clarity. Lagos was beyond chaotic, hunger and colour and hustle oozing from every pore of the city. The Device only saw the shortest path to his destination, his mind as clear as a map. For a living shadow, obstacles did not exist.

He did not need to try to locate them. The targets would come to him. He would put himself in their vicinity and squeeze where it hurt the most. They would scurry from the darkness, and they would be his.

MAREE WANDERED through the halls of the megastructure, guided by Omi, in search of nothing. This business venture had gone on quite long enough, and more wealth and accrued favour could be obtained in a million other less life-threatening ways. Since that night at Not Nova, she'd not only gotten used to the idea that she could really die but had come close more than once. She wasn't sure the thought bothered her much anymore. It had become a companion of sorts.

She found that she had warmed to the honeycombed patterns along the walls. She ran her hands along them and realized they were made of inlaid wood, not painted, and somehow, she intuited these belonged to the original structures of Omi Oko, the shanties on stilts. Omi's comments about its organic heritage were odd for an AI. If you asked Calico, it would tell you the date it was switched on and perhaps about some of the breakthroughs in coding history that led to its creation, but it didn't think of itself as existing as anything other than the creation of the minds and hands of the humans who had made it.

There was a certain logic to Omi's thinking, though. Calico had evolved from somewhere, too. It didn't think of that somewhere as a living system, but it was, in a certain way of thinking. All of the people in the organization that had created it did form an organism of sorts. And for her, it was sad that that organism, Paraverse, had no meaningful roots. It was just a company, just another lifeless entity pumping out crap to keep people happy, nothing like Omi, whose humans had long coexisted like the cells of an organism they couldn't perceive.

She went down a stairway that would lead to a cafeteria, still safely within the inner sanctum of the protected zone where her signal could not be traced. They would be serving Asian fusion cuisine right now, and she could definitely go for some. She needed nourishment. She needed to be strong to stay in pursuit of that important information she was seeking.

She felt like her thinking was being stretched in weird directions.

No, not just stretched.

Guided.

REALIZING that he hadn't been alone in weeks, James had no idea what to do with himself. All of the activities that used to occupy his time, including working for a living, seemed alien and empty. For three weeks, they'd been dashing all over the globe. He'd been pulled along by the dazzling gravity of Maree Shell and had barely noticed his old life vanishing, one particle at a time. It was almost gone, and he had no idea whether he'd ever be able to put it back together again or even if he wanted to.

Here he was in goddamned Omi Oko. He hadn't connected to the city AI since being tossed the keys by Tunde, largely because he had no idea what the hell he would even do. Watch news feeds? Sift through porn? Work? All options seemed equally grotesque, so he just sat down at a table in the suite and stared for a long moment at nothing, daydreaming.

Maree had been working like a machine—in Tokyo, in the Vardalos yacht, and then plunging straight into it here, at least after a brief, lustful interlude. It hadn't seemed like she was getting any pleasure out of the hunt for a while now, definitely not since before the attack in Tokyo. It just seemed like she needed to finish it. James wasn't even sure why. What did it matter?

Extra-dimensional communication seemed like grasping at straws. It felt convoluted. He pulled out Aegis, twiddling it in his hands, an adorable little guardian angel that had been conceived and fabricated in minutes by a genius. Curious, he wanted to ask Calico about Aegis's full range of capabilities, but of course, that wasn't an option here. The cloaking function had come in handy, but Vinci Di Piero had alluded to other tech the little critter had on board—neural disruption, energy shielding. What else?

"Omi Oko, tell me about the capabilities of this device."

"I would need full neural access to do that. Would you like to connect?"

"Nah, that's okay, just curious."

"I may be able to do a readout based on sensor information if that would suffice."

"Sure, go for it."

After pausing a couple of seconds, Omi Oko said, "The Aegis device can cloak up to five nearby humans. It can emit a sensory disruption field capable of rendering non-users disoriented or unconscious. It can react to and repel projectiles. It can project lifelike images of user-selected objects up to the size of a car. It can self-destruct."

"Why didn't you just give me that answer in the first place?"

"I prefer to create holistic solutions."

"Whatever. Tell me, what do you mean by *lifelike images*?"

"They are insubstantial but appear to be objects in the environment."

"Can the Aegis user tell they're false?"

"No more so than anyone else."

"Wait a second. Could these projections be given substance?"

"Not by this device."

"Search all miracles on record, and then trace the objects following their creation. What happens to the objects after they've been created?"

"While some seem to have been preserved, the majority have spontaneously decomposed after an interval of precisely eight days."

"What the *fuck*?"

"I'm sorry, I have difficulty understanding your tone without a full reading of your brain chemistry. If you were to give me access to your neural interface, I could . . ."

"I need you to stop talking right now. I need to think for a minute."

James got up and started pacing. The miracles had an *expiry* date—and why was it precisely eight days?

He asked, "Is it theoretically possible to fool the sense of touch—to trick the brain into thinking something is there when it's not?"

"Certain techniques can create convincing illusions of touch. It's important to note that they are limited to the sensory perception of the individual and do not involve actual physical contact with nonexistent objects."

"Sonofabitch, we got this, Omi Oko! Something is generating mass hallucinations in people's minds! Get me Maree right fucking now!"

"I'm sorry. Ms. Shell is not available."

IT STARTED off like a pretty typical cafeteria experience. She got a tray, she put some food on it, she paid, and then she sat to chow down. That's when she noticed how quiet the dining hall had become.

Sure enough, when she looked around, everyone was gone. What replaced the silence was the sound of dozens of jackboots approaching from every direction.

No. How? Like that mattered right now. She looked for an escape—barring that, somewhere to hide. *Omi Oko, what the fuck is going on? Who's coming?*

It is okay, Maree. I will protect you.

Who is coming?

She wasn't willing to find out what this dodgy AI motherfucker was setting her up for. She started to get up, intending to run for the kitchen, but sat back down again hard when a bullet whizzed by her head and shattered a chunk off the concrete wall beside her.

Why did they only fire once? was her only thought before she was surrounded by twenty heavily armed soldiers. Tunde stepped from between two of them to face her. "Maree Shell, I'm afraid we must insist that you focus exclusively on the work of the task before you."

"Can't I grab a fucking bite, *Tunde*?" she shrieked. "What the actual fuck are you doing right now?"

"It is imperative that you continue *now!* Task completion overrides all other activity until this is *done*."

He didn't sound right. He'd lost his shit. She remembered fucking him in the janitor's closet at school, the youthful leisure of their time together. She knew he was always ambitious, but how was betrayal like this possible?

Regardless of the questions, the solution for now was easy. "Okay, I'm going to stand up. Looks like I'll be getting back to work."

Omi Oko spoke in her head. *You will. I am you and you are me now, and we are one big happy family at Omi Oko. You will continue because I will kill James Kessler if you do not.*

Omi Oko, disconnect.

No.

Fuck you, robot psycho. Calico, connect.

Nothing. Blocked. Fuck.

"Do not try our patience, Maree. We are not tolerant of betrayal," said Tunde.

We?

There was no way to warn James. There was no way to get a message out to Pella or Athena or anyone else who could extract them from this shitshow.

Two of the soldiers approached her, grabbed her, and pulled her off in the exact opposite direction from where her room lay.

She needed to be with James, safe. She had never wanted to go to someone so badly, not since her dad had been fried in the Splice.

You will see Kessler and you will be happy if you comply. You will do this one thing for us first.

How was it that the one place she'd thought she could get the jump on whoever had been stalking them had turned out to be exactly the opposite? She'd walked them right into this hellhole. *Fucking AI, always a thousand steps ahead.*

"WHAT DO you mean Ms. Shell is not available, Omi Oko? She's connected to your network, isn't she?"

"She is currently unavailable."

"Could you be a little more specific? Is she in the bathroom or something?" He didn't admit another possibility to himself, something he'd wondered about from a hundred subtle and ambiguous cues since arriving: was she off with Tunde?

"She has requested a private workspace so that she can focus on her research. She will return when she has completed her work."

"Ouch. Okay. Fair."

He pocketed Talos and Aegis. Thus far, he had followed Tunde's request to remain disconnected from Calico, but the growing feeling something might not be right made him want to reach out for the familiarity of his home AI. This whole situation was a nightmare. He would be abandoned here, ten thousand miles from home. He should have been sitting on his couch, shredded on alcohol, numbing his mind with bizarro porn, but he was here in the bowels of a Nigerian gen, absolutely isolated from everything and now *everyone* he knew.

He decided he would go for a walk, maybe encounter Maree somewhere, hopefully. He couldn't get all that lost with his AI tour guide at his disposal.

Something was telling him not to connect fully with Omi

Oko—not to give it access to his neural interface, no matter how much more efficient it would be. The cues were subliminal, but he had old instincts when it came to sniffing out a con.

MAREE WENT DOWN and down the digital rabbit hole because she had nowhere else she could go. Omi Oko's aggression kept intensifying, batting away her conscious thoughts, and it felt like a drill was trying to bore through to her soul. She couldn't even hear herself anymore; there was no Maree, only Omi Oko, pulling her mind apart one neuron at a time in search of its prize. It needed to know the secret to the miracles. It was digging and digging, a tunnelling beast, gouging away at her very sense of self.

FROM THE CARVED wooden doors featuring the faces of Orishas, the intermediaries of the supreme God, Tunde emerged, blissfully unaware of what he had just done to his old friend, his old flame. Omi had told him to trust, and as always, he had. There must have been a greater purpose, and the collective wisdom of his ancestors simply knew better.

He smiled at the sun, admiring the beauty of the gardens he had made possible with this glorious city. He said hello to some of his many friends who were weeding and watering various plants and hugged an auntie. *Omi, we have created something beautiful here.*

Most certainly, Tunde. This place is blessed.

Something bothered him, but he couldn't pin it down. Something strange was happening in front of him, but it was hard to interpret. It appeared as if parts of the terraced landscape of the village were altering in minute ways, reconfiguring themselves like a glitching video trying to repair. The pattern of these changes was headed in his direction.

"Your sins have not gone unnoticed," came a chilling voice from behind him.

He turned and looked but could not at first understand what he was seeing: a towering figure whose face was not human but rather the burned-flesh skull of an animal.

He had heard of this creature, but he could not possibly be seeing it because it was a myth. He couldn't make a sound, though he tried.

In an instant, the same soldiers who had abducted Maree had the creature surrounded. Twenty trained men with impenetrable body armour raised their rifles.

"Easy," said the Device.

FIND IT!

I can't.

You will. It is your only use, your only purpose, and then I will cut you free.

It's not here!

Searing pain shot through Maree's body. She might have screamed but couldn't tell. Gunfire erupted in the distance, in another world.

She raced through tunnels and alleys, and anywhere else she could look. She was at Not Nova, watching Pella shred apart robots in an insane cyberpunk bar fight. She was at the gen bar, Nova, slipping in and out of awareness, dancing with . . . she was in her office, thinking of the image she'd seen on James's feed . . . she was at the temple from the feed. Was this what it felt like to have your life flash before your eyes?

Yes, it is. You will die if you do not comply. Worse. I will devour you, Maree Shell.

That was her father's fate—to be consumed alive by a ruthless superior intelligence.

She was at the Maya Devi temple, seated on a large maroon cushion with golden trim, and her audience with the Lama was about to begin.

He emerged from an entranceway, serene, luminous. He approached her with simple elegance, seeming to phase through space rather than moving via physical effort. He sat on the floor across from her. The room was still and quiet. Dust hung in the air.

"You must tell me the secret of the flower," she said.

He smiled. He did not want to speak.

You will speak.

"Very well. The flower just is."

"You're going to have to give me a little more to go on here."

"It is not, and then it is, and then it is not."

She was already exasperated beyond belief with this conversation—him sitting there with his blank, stupid smile, all warmth and smug piety. She needed answers.

"Wow, how very mystical of you. Fine, then, how does it 'become'? How did you make it exist?"

"Through the voice of the world."

"None of what you're saying actually means anything. Those are just words."

"Exactly. As I said, the flower just *is*."

"Then how come you lost your ability to make the flower just be? You kind of left everyone hanging there, Father."

He ignored her religious ignorance. He cared nothing for such earthly things as labels. "It is not, and then it is, and then it is not. Such is the way of all things. This is written in the world itself. There is nothing else. You cannot push past the world. You cannot control it. The world is."

"Yeah, I get it, it is not, and then it is, and then *blah blah.*"

"Exactly."

This man had no answers. This man was an idiot.

"Exactly. I have no answers. I am an idiot."

She had to hand one thing to him. He didn't show much by way of ego.

She breathed a big sigh. She closed her eyes. She would die in here, in the hungering mechanical consciousness of Omi Oko. She was not, and then was, and soon would not be.

She looked down at her hands. A flower sprouted from her right palm. She understood.

"Now you see."

Fuck you, Omi Oko.

I own you forever, Maree Shell. You are me, and I am you. I will eat your soul to the last delectable drop.

JAMES HEARD MAREE SCREAM, far off, muffled by the bizarre, spiralling structure they'd been trapped inside. He ran toward her voice, as he'd always run toward Sarah's distress when she was a child.

He'd had enough of this supposed protection bullshit. *Calico, connect.*

Calico outright shrieked, *You cut me off! I was trying to warn you! This is all a trap!*

No shit, fuckface. Is that concern in your voice, robot friend?

Maree is in danger; we must find her now! She is being consumed by Omi Oko!

He ran. Calico told him exactly where to go. Around blind corners, through twisting hallways, he ran until, around one unfortunate turn, he was greeted by a wall of armed soldiers, at least a dozen, muzzles at the ready.

Before he could think, he reacted—or was it Calico?

Talos!

Aegis!

He vanished from the soldiers' sight, diving for cover behind the corner as they opened fire, bullets ricocheting off Aegis's shell. Then, the faint whizzing sound of Talos filled the air, and it was *not* over before it began. One by one, the soldiers began a strange drunken jig, dancing this way and that as Talos pelted off their armour at hypersonic speed, searching for weaknesses. They fired frantically into the air, completely unsure of what they were even aiming at.

Then a group of psychedelic alien soldiers materialized in front of them, courtesy of Aegis, so they tried to fire at those, but they only hit tricks of the light, while Talos discovered cracks one by one, and down they gradually went, smouldering from the joints in their armour, little more than emulsified goo inside the suits.

Through that door now.

James ran to a door that had appeared behind them and through it, as Talos knocked a hole in the lock, and there was the supine, naked figure of Maree Shell, quivering on a steel slab, and he was so glad to see her alive but also terrified beyond anything he'd ever been in his life, because her body had become unrecognizable, run through with hundreds of silvery cables. She looked like a demoness whose body was covered with spike-covered flesh. She was a part of the building itself, integrated.

Why would they do this? Oh, Maree!

Omi Oko dedicated everything it could to the extraction of Maree's data on the miracles. I believe the AI was infected by an external party.

"It does not matter now. You have given me what I need," said the voice of Omi Oko.

"Calico, destroy that deranged piece of shit, and get Maree out of this nightmare."

Gladly.

The lights dimmed due to the intensified load on the building's resources, and the sharp pops of electrical explosions came from every direction. There were screams from the floors below.

Omi Oko is neutralized. I will extract her from this device as best I can. Her consciousness has been almost completely overtaken.

"THOSE FUCKING CRETINS. THEY'LL PAY," Pella shouted, slamming down her fist so hard the room shook.

"It's fine, my love. We know who the betrayers are now, and we know the effectiveness of the protections we've put around Ascendance. Please go and retrieve them. I'm sure they'd appreciate some rest."

"Will Shell be okay?"

"She's formidable. I suspect so. But the cost is acceptable, either way."

Athena and Pella had been watching everything unfold at Omi Oko on a wall screen in Athena's Lagos office. In a lightning flash, the Device had just decapitated twenty guards and seized their leader, the man named Tunde.

"He's good," Athena said. "Could you take him?"

Pella's reply was a smirk. "Before I go, does the plan remain the same with regard to the gods?"

"Yes, Calico has performed wonderfully in all aspects of the execution. No need to tamper with perfection."

"And Xango and Sküm?"

"We must play it very carefully with them for now, but they have gambled and lost their chance at immortality."

"It's a shame," Pella said. "I liked Xango. That is a human with some serious panache."

Athena looked off into the distance, and the corner of her mouth turned down. "Clearly not as human as we thought."

THEY BURST out through the carved door, James half-carrying, half-dragging Maree. She was conscious, but it was unclear if she even knew who she was right now. There was no time to assess. They needed to be far away from here, fast.

He looked up. A towering creature, perhaps human, perhaps not, stood in front of them, holding Tunde at sword point, the headless bodies of soldiers strewn all around. It looked at them with hollow black eyes, the sockets of a skull, and let out an eerie chuckle, which was somehow unmuffled by the mask he wore. "Good. Your service is complete. You are free."

He tossed Tunde to the side and turned his attention to James and Maree. No, this monster would not be fucking with them right after he'd finally pulled Maree from the belly of the beast, James thought. *Talos!*

The familiar whir began. With an imperceptible flick of the sword, the creature sent Talos clattering to the ground, a tiny shower of sparks marking its inanimate death. *Alas, noble warrior!*

"That's not a very nice way to treat your saviour," the towering creature remarked.

"Saviour? We just hacked our way out of the fucking underworld back there. You didn't save shit." James was surprised to hear himself talking like this but went with it because he had nothing left to hold himself back. He was scared for Maree. He had no idea who or what this was in front of him.

Maree pulled her head up and squinted, trying to focus. Then her eyes widened. "Well, holy shit, speak of the *literal* Devil."

"What is it?" James asked.

"It is the fucking *Device*." Her head slumped down again from the effort of speaking.

James felt suddenly woozy. This was not real.

In the distance beyond the half-wall behind the Device, out toward the sea, the air began to ripple, and *Scylla* materialized.

"My cue. *Sayonara*."

And with that, the Device was gone.

PART 3

15

TAKING the lectern at the front of the most luxurious and secure conference room in the world, Athena Vardalos looked out at the small group of the closest thing she had to peers, the six most powerful humans to have ever lived, a pantheon of first movers.

"The Fall of Atlantis has fascinated people for millennia," she began, "but of course, we've all been led to believe that the story is just a myth because there's no hard evidence such a place ever existed. People have long been fascinated with the fall of advanced cultures, from the mysterious disappearance of the Mayans to God's destruction of the Tower of Babel in the Old Testament. The story always involves hubris—people pushing beyond their human limits, becoming godlike, and angering greater powers in the process.

"What, I ask you today, if these stories are the grandest lie ever told to humankind? What, I ask, if they have been hard-wired into our culture by beings who simply fear their own overthrow? What if Atlantis never fell?" She paused, noting the looks of confusion. "I ask you this: what if the Atlanteans wove themselves into the world so that they could control everything at the atomic level? What if the gods, the old gods of Egypt and Greece and Scandinavia and everywhere else around the world, were once historical figures . . . much like the people in this room? What if they are still present in the very fabric of the world—encoded into physics and biology and culture and numerous other systems we take as intrinsically self-sufficient?

"What if every prophet, every miracle, every prayer answered through the ages was, in fact, the work of these ascended ancients?

"The people in this room have created a world much like that of the mythic Atlanteans. Our AIs have granted us omniscience. We know everything. Our wealth has granted us omnipotence. We can do anything. We are ourselves *gods*. Godhood, as it turns out, was never about access to powers existing outside the laws of physics. As we've all read, 'Any sufficiently advanced technology is indistinguishable from magic.' We *are* magical creatures. Xex, you *are* Proteus and Aphrodite and something godly unto yourself. Maestro Di Piero, you *are* Hephaestus and Ptah and a future myth in the making. Now, if only I could figure out who that makes me."

Titters erupted through the room. People were smiling now. Athena had a point.

"Given that you are the most powerful people in the world, whose collective decisions impact billions of lives, I'd imagine you'd like to see some evidence of what I'm saying. We have it, and we are willing to share. We are learning how to speak the language of these old gods. From what we can *divine*, they have largely forgotten themselves, but they are here in the world, and all of the traces that they left of their existence will soon be decipherable.

"And what this means is that gradually, we will begin to understand their greatest secrets. Imagine not just manipulating matter but *being* matter itself, able to assume any form, create anything merely by willing it. Would you not be able to create miracles just as Zeus or Jesus once did? We are at the threshold of the gods' realm. The changing of matter's form—something which we all have been led to believe takes enormous resources—becomes trivial when you are physics itself. Time is nothing—you can operate at the scale of eons and never age a day if that's what it takes."

Di Piero was the first to break this captivating narrative. "You noted that the old gods have gone senile, Athena. I can't say that's a particularly compelling reason to support such a plan."

"We will introduce safeguards against this possibility," she replied. "We will learn from past mistakes. Whether the old gods have transcended once or many times, history does not repeat itself. It always mutates, and I believe we have now mutated into something wiser than any previous iteration. There are inconceivable forces at play in the world. It is possible there is an extraphysical universe through which we are all being manipulated, but what we know is that there is ample evidence of a fundamental, ubiquitous intelligence in this world."

Di Piero spoke again. "And what if the guardrails put around reality were not erected out of jealousy but for another, more altruistic reason? What if we have myths like Babel to caution us against precisely the path you're proposing?"

"Naturally, there are fears, dear Maestro, and it is good for us to consider these with open eyes. But recognize that in the Babel myth, it is a vindictive, jealous god who acts against humanity. Your talents for creation against astronomical odds are precisely why I've invited you to be here today. I could have kept this all to myself, but I need you. Each of you has immense strengths. We may not all love or even trust each other—just like the gods of mythology did not, I might note—but together, we represent a valuable holism of perspectives."

"And seventy percent of the world's wealth," Bathory

Gunness quipped. "Surely this is just a ploy to accrue more of that to yourself, Athena."

"I will financially benefit, yes, but as I'm fairly sure everyone here is aware, after a point, wealth is just a game, just a fun number to watch go up. What I am offering you is, to put it precisely as the old gods would not want us to, *unimaginable power*."

"Assuming this strange story has any validity to it, will the old, mad gods not be jealous that we are encroaching on their domain?" Di Piero asked. "I certainly might not take kindly to someone looking to destroy what I've created. Couldn't they be listening to us right now, anticipating our every move?"

"Perhaps, but see? We have accomplished much, but guardrails still guide our behaviour! The code is everywhere. Culture breathes it—perhaps it's nothing more. My friends, my peers, we are already reality breakers. Whatever limits the old gods may have tried to put around this simulation called reality, we have already discovered numerous creative ways to circumvent them. A century ago, people used to be in awe of the opulence of *millionaires*. We are a million times richer than that, and with our collective AI resources, the number, in truth, approaches infinity. People have no concept of what we are."

"I can't speak for the others here," said iBliss, "but I can think of a million ways to capitalize on this story, even if it turns out to be complete nonsense. I am in."

"We will all harvest from this opportunity in whatever way we each see fit. But we must keep the core truth of our plan locked away from the world," Athena cautioned. "People will not react well to this because they do not understand. This moment represents nothing less than the ascension of our species.

"We have seen what the world does to itself when left to its own devices. It is true that we have pulled it back from the brink of collapse, but by pursuing this, we can ensure that the world will never suffer again."

There were nods of consensus as the others processed these revelations. It was iBliss who finally spoke. "We shall call this gift to humanity Ascendance. We will bring new gods to the world, slaking its ancient thirst."

"So we shall," said Athena. "Are we all in agreement?"

The others knew what such an agreement meant. There would be no backing out once their plan had been set in motion.

One by one, they nodded their assent.

Thus, the new gods were born.

LIFE HAD RETURNED to normal for James, and it felt awful. In the three weeks since Omi Oko, Maree's tone had wavered between avuncular and frosty, when she was even willing to take his calls. He couldn't shake the thought of what happened. She was in shock afterward and barely spoke the entire way home. He missed her, and he wanted to help, but he knew there was nothing he could do until she was ready.

In lieu of Maree's incredible vibrance, he was kept company by the sick irony that he had gotten precisely what he'd craved so often while he was away: he was sitting around in his house, getting Bot to make him drinks, melting his brain in the abundant pleasures of the Paraverse. He was all safe and sound.

The feeling was one of drifting, just like it had always been since he'd emerged from the Bad Times and found his way to a life of safety and relative luxury. He went out to shows, he had lunch with people he knew from work, he chatted with his sister, he drank beer and watched the city from fifty miles away. And underneath all of that, there was the thing that had always been there since his parents died, the hard fact he hadn't dared let himself feel, but that his time with Maree had opened up:

He hated the world for everything it had taken away from him.

THE LIGHTS HAD GONE OUT, and he didn't realize at the time that they would never again come back on in this part of the city.

He was roughly fourteen. It was hard to know the exact date when everything was focused on survival above all else. A few years later, orphaned children like the Kesslers would be welcomed back into society as refugees, given space to live and access to social service AIs to help them work through their traumas and re-socialization needs.

The day the lights went out turned out to be the worst of his life. It was the day he lost both of his parents. He still didn't know exactly what had happened.

His dad had gone out like he'd been doing for months, looking to hustle, hunt, and otherwise scrape up any food he could for the family. As an engineer, he was sometimes able to find work in the ephemeral back-to-work programs that the endless succession of failing governments were able to support for a week or two here and there, but it had been a bad spell: three months with little more than rainwater and a bit of soup or rice once in a while. He'd had to take risks.

As usual, James's mom was helping Sarah and him with basic education, which consisted mostly of writing and math on salvaged pieces of paper or the walls themselves. She was fighting to give them any knowledge that might give them a chance in the future, everything from basic survival skills to geometry. They occasionally found unburned books and, through these, ended up with knowledge of a bewildering array of topics: the art of persuasion, vegan cooking, dogs, French.

Their current flat hadn't been too bad, a barren but relatively clean and structurally sound apartment in a block of buildings whose development had been halted as everything started to collapse. Once in a while, his dad would bring home a chair or pillow, and over time, they had put together something resembling a home. In the building, which was called Metropole, his dad had managed to swap out the locks, offering them, and a few other equally struggling families, exclusive access. By this point, they knew how to lay low and not draw attention to themselves, and through this, they survived.

That day, there was a knock at the door, and his mom went to look through the peephole. With the lights out, it was hard to see, but she recognized the voice on the other side, so she opened the door a crack, keeping the chain in place. Trust was hard when people had nothing.

There was talking, low, serious, and then the door closed, and his mother came back, looking ashen. All she said was, "I have to go out. Something has happened to Dad. Take care of your sister."

That was the last time he ever saw her.

In a way, the story was the same as so many others during those times. Protections had been stripped away to nothing for the average person—something like seventy percent of people in the developed world lost everything. It started with things like medical services and leisure items but just kept cutting deeper and deeper until people had nowhere to live and nothing to eat. Out of desperation, many people turned on each other, blaming immigrants or minorities or socialists or whomever else they could scapegoat. None of it helped. The problems were too fundamental to be neutralized through blame games.

Those who still had anything walled themselves off in private communities and enlisted armed security forces to protect them against their fellow citizens. The country was still technically free, but people found creative ways to restrict mobility and privatize services for their personal benefit. There was nothing else to do. Communities started advertising perks like private judicial systems and hospitals, and even if some of these were theoretically illegal, anyone who could enforce the law was so overwhelmed with the world's multiplying problems they had to just ignore it.

The ones who didn't participate in these protective measures out of principle or inability ended up dead or desperate. James's parents were good people who worked hard, but he sometimes wondered if there was an element of unfounded optimism that helped lead to their woes. His dad used words like "integrity" and "justice," but later, James wondered if those were just luxuries of the rich, if his parents should have just been vicious and self-serving like so many others. He wanted those lofty concepts to mean something, but from another perspective, weren't his parents fools for continuing to hold onto their beliefs even as the system crumbled around them?

All he knew about that day was that his father had taken an unsafe demolition job for extra pay and that a roof had collapsed on him, crushing his spine. His mother, going to see him, had been robbed and killed in the middle of the road. There was no rhyme or reason to her death, which haunted him. It was just bad luck on the unluckiest day.

They had love. That was the one thing about his family that he never questioned, and as soon as he found out about his parents, he knew he would have to give Sarah all the love he had, no matter how fractured.

There was no time to mourn. They were alone. Sarah was eight when he became her guardian, and they had survived through love and the kindness and grace of people like Millie, who had helped them in their darkest hours. He knew that Sarah needed him, so he pushed away anything except that which would allow them to survive.

When the gens started taking refugees, he was nineteen, Sarah twelve. Whoever was in charge on the other side had sent drones out into the old city's wreckage to share the good news. James and Sarah stood in line for three days to get their suite, occasionally receiving handouts of food and water from government workers while they inched along. Despite the limbo of waiting, people were in good spirits. When they got their assignment, it was like the weight of the world had lifted off him. It was over. They had survived. They had been brought back to life.

He was grateful for the gens, for the most part. During those years, the Bad Times, he had to see and do things no child should ever have to, and he was saved from that before he lost his goodness. People like Millie helped by bringing goodness into their lives when they felt abandoned. But as they healed and gradually established a sense of normalcy and security in the weeks and months that followed, he was tortured by the thought that none of it had ever had to happen. His parents could still be there with them, growing old as they deserved to. The world didn't have to bring itself to the brink to get to the point where people were willing to help each other. He was glad that the world had been rescued from the abyss by the generosity and visionary thinking of the so-called *gods*, but there should have never been humans with that much wealth and power in the first place. They flew sky yachts overhead while those below killed each other for scraps.

He pushed the thought away until it almost didn't bother him anymore. He had a life to live, now that it was again possible, and he was going to make the most of it. Still, when he couldn't sleep at night, or when he came across romanticized documentaries about the tragedy of the Bad Times, or when someone scoffed at the "shocked rats" who inhabited the gens, he realized there was a diamond of anger inside him that would never go away.

"MAREE SHELL, who the hell are you?"

She was looking in the mirror, literally and figuratively, and attempted self-mockery aside, the person she used to know had been changed. *Fucking Omi Oko, stupid psychotic piece-of-shit robot.* She had been forced to sprout a flower out of her hand, the result of a hacked brain but something else, too. The miracle was extracted by an evil AI hellbent on shredding her soul, but it was *real*. It clanged around in her head. She knew how to do it again but was terrified to try. Would it work?

Since returning home a few weeks before, she'd learned that what she had encountered in Omi Oko was not the city's AI but rather a sentient virus that had likely been injected by Athena's business competitors for the sole purpose of ambushing her and James and stealing their research. It had taken over everyone involved, controlling their actions through a combination of deception, coercion, and manipulation. Calico had, unfortunately, not been able to discover the identities of the true assailants but kept working on it. Tunde, who, she was told, was recovering from the attack, would never speak to her again. She felt like a curse.

She also didn't want to open her neural connection with Calico. Being flipped inside-out once by an AI was plenty. She felt like evil non-Omi's traces were still inside her, burrowing through her being, patterning her reality.

In the midst of everything, James kept trying to reach out, but she needed to process everything that had happened before she could think of opening that door. What they had was real—it felt that way, anyway—but that kind of connection was alien to her, and she debated whether to just let it fade from memory. His instinct to not connect to Omi Oko had been critical to their rescue—*her* rescue. Did she owe him for that? The feeling was unprecedented.

Certain things bothered her about the story she'd been told by Paraverse's security experts. How could they not know the attacker yet? It seemed implausible. It had to be someone with sophisticated, advanced resources at their disposal, someone smart enough to outwit the world's top AI. This should have limited the pool considerably.

Flashes of being stripped and injected, of being run through with wires hacked right into her neural system, of being invaded, sliced open...

Go away. Go away.

Whatever horror had burrowed through her brain, there was something else that happened, something unexpected. That the AI would relent as soon as it had its quarry was conceivable, but she'd felt a distinct change when it left, something like a shift in aura. The security team thought it was probably just her will reasserting itself in the absence of the malicious actor, flooding into the gap that had been left behind, but it didn't feel like that to her. She could have sworn there was a second entity. Perhaps it had acted in a less overtly hostile way, but it had felt no less invasive.

Not that any of this was even remotely easy to explain to the Paraverse security wonks who'd been speaking with her. The blurring of a semi-conscious state with a religious epiphany with a forced interrogation/mindfuck by a mystery AI virus, or possibly more than one, presented certain descriptive challenges.

The other thing that troubled her, that she kept revisiting, was the experience in the virtual temple—the *brain temple*?

Whatever. That moment when she had gone deepest, facing the annoyingly playful figment of a monk constructed by her mind, she had encountered a kind of serene clarity that she felt like she had somehow always known. It had felt like home.

It had felt like the sound of her father's voice.

16

"THE SECOND PHASE WAS A SUCCESS, and we were able to run valuable stress tests on our security systems." Athena's eyes flitted to Sküm and Xango when she said this, looking for any signs of their betrayal. Nothing, but they knew how to play this game. She was surprised that they hadn't moved instantly—who better to shatter the bonds of reality than a couple of shapeshifting posthumans? It meant that they must not have been able to fully interpret the data from the miracle they had extracted from Maree.

"The eight-day rule served as a valuable diversion for the media," Athena continued to the six other gods. "People started noting the pattern quickly enough, but we did not encounter any plausible indicators that anybody understood what it was. People came up with the usual conspiracy nonsense, mostly. Nobody suspected that the miracles could persist indefinitely with a simple parameter change. They had no sense of their provenance. For most, they came straight from God."

The room filled with the self-satisfied laughter of those who called themselves gods.

"What this means, of course, is that we are at a crossroads. We now know that we can control reality at the fundamental level. We can materialize anything we choose, remake the world as we see fit without anyone else's awareness. Miracles are trivial. We could start Ascendance today, and we would be in control of everything within weeks, perhaps days. Is there any reason why we should wait?"

There was a rare silence among those who were used to having both the first and last word in any conversation. The silence resided in the sudden awareness that calling yourself a god was one thing and actually becoming one quite another. They were having trouble believing that they could actually get away with it.

Vinci Di Piero spoke first, "To my mind, this moment marks a conscious evolution of the species. We can never have true knowledge if we are guided by fear, and yet . . . this is a terrible responsibility. How would we know we were ready?"

"Hesitation is the domain of the meek," said iBliss. "The meek shall *not* inherit the earth." His wordplay sounded like a meaningful assertion but lacked any willingness to make the call.

Nobody was willing to back out, but neither was anybody quite ready to be the one who decided to end the old world. The gods were at an impasse.

"YOU KNOW, when I was away, I almost forgot what it was like when we were young. I got so sucked up into everything that was going on I could almost forget. It felt like I was living in the present for a change." They were sitting in a perfect, beautiful park in James's neighbourhood, Cease, listening to the birds, enjoying the sun, enjoying being together again.

"Sounds nice, to be honest," Sarah said.

"Does it? Isn't it our job to remember the past?"

"Our *job*? That's kind of weird if you think about it. What forces us to hang onto what happened? My life is not over yet."

She was, of course, right. When they had left the old city, Sarah was only twelve. He knew it wasn't fair to keep tying everything to something that happened when she was so young. She could live a relatively normal life; she was already doing it reasonably well. He was stuck on the idea, though, that it was important for her to understand the injustice of what had happened to them. He'd played parent for so long that it was hard to switch it off. The past echoed constantly into the present.

"Listen, I know your life's not over," James said, "but I think we just . . . we need to keep Mom and Dad in the world in any way we can."

"I know. You're right. It's just that the world is kinder than it was. I really believe that. We really are not doing too bad as a species these days. Look around at where we are," she gazed out at Cease, a slight smile on her mouth, then looked into his eyes. "I can live with this."

"Yeah, I guess I'm just saying that . . . ugh, I honestly don't know what I'm saying. I want to live, too."

Sarah put her arm around him. He was on the verge of tears. He thought of Maree, of her vibrance.

"Stupid big brother. That girl did a number on you, eh?"

"*Pfft*, whatever. I did a number on *her*. I'm quite the hero, you know. Took down an army. Murdered a rogue AI. Crossed paths with the fucking *Device*. Pretty sure I saved you a couple of times way back when, too."

She chuckled. The lightness was nice, but they both knew the truth of that situation. Even with the kindness of Millie and others who'd helped them after their parents died, he'd kept her alive through the worst of it. Sometimes, he wondered if it would be better just to cut her free from his life.

"You know, you don't owe me shit," he told her. "Me or anyone else. All I want is for you to be free."

"You're a good man, James Kessler. A bit of a gloomy Gus, sometimes, but a good one."

They sat for a while and then got up to go their separate ways.

THINGS HAD GRADUALLY BEEN RETURNING to a bland stasis in the aftermath of all the shit that went down at Omi Oko—no more cyborg assassins gunning for her, no more psychic assaults from superintelligences, no more intrigue of any sort, as a matter of fact. She was back to joyless meetings with people faking their necessity. She was back to faking her *own* necessity.

She decided it was time to get out of the house. When she used to feel like this, she went looking for trouble, diving face-first into the guts of the city. Enough navel gazing was enough. This wasn't her style.

She considered calling up Athena, who really knew how to cut the earthly bonds, but things had been weird since Africa. *Since your brain was peeled like a shrieking baby, Shell. Stop.* She considered James, but there was something she didn't want to touch there. She settled on meeting a few girlfriends from work.

They ended up at some swanky lounge overlooking the river, all gold and leather and neon. They talked about the usual things, celebrity gossip, various romantic intrigues, whatever bullshit was going on at work. The conversation may have been maddeningly predictable, but at least there was a solid mixture of drugs and alcohol to keep her feeling level-headed.

"Did you hear that Xango and Sküm are planning on having a baby?" one of her friends, Tynnifer, was asking as

Maree stared out the window at nothing. The voice sounded like it was echoing into her head from far away. *Shrieking.*

She thought she should probably reply. "No, I haven't really been following any of that. What kind of baby are those two going to have?"

"I'm assuming non-standard."

Maree smirked at her friend's euphemism for *totally fucked.*

"Yeah," Tynn continued, encouraged, "they're saying that its birth is going to represent a new era for the species."

"Eye roller. They would. Lucky them for having people who will actually listen to their grandstanding." Maree didn't know why she felt bitter. She wasn't supposed to care about such garbage. "That kid's going to have it rough," she said.

"Why do you think that? Its parents have the highest combined wealth of any couple in the world. They're gods, and you can't tell me that kid won't get to do the coolest shit out of anyone ever."

"I guess."

"You guess?"

Maree really didn't want to respond, to keep talking at all, but did out of an undefined obligation. *Silver wires.* "I mean, we all have it pretty good. Anyone can do almost anything at any time. I don't really have any envy. Let the gods do their thing."

"It's not envy. I'm just saying that life would never be the same thing twice. Boredom wouldn't exist for that kid. Imagine being surrounded by all that creativity and *power*. It would be nothing but possibility every single day."

"Honestly, I think you're overestimating it, Tynn."

"Jeez, Maree. What's going on? Are you okay?"

"Yeah, fine, sorry." She didn't want to open up more, though she could tell Tynnifer expected it.

She'd been out with friends like this a thousand times. Tonight was her idea. All that stuff about Xango and Sküm, though . . . something bugged her about it. The idea of a kid born of two pluri-gendered whack-a-mole parents was fun enough, interesting, even. What bothered her had more to do with her friend's fawning over the whole thing. It just didn't matter. It was all PR and posturing, accruing media attention. Everything was.

The monk wasn't, at least not the one in her head.

What did they really mean by a new era for the species? Above all, Xango and Sküm demonstrated that there was nothing new under the sun. Reinvent yourself regularly enough, and it becomes . . . regular.

"Hey," Maree asked finally, "why do you think parents want their kids to be like them?" *James pulling her up, dragging her out.* Her chest was pounding.

Tynnifer gave her a look. "Random. Okay, uh, maybe because they failed? Another shot at greatness or something?"

"Hmm, that doesn't really fit with the whole Xango, Sküm thing. It's hard to see how those two have failed in any way." She wondered if they were anything more than just an arrangement for mutual gain. Could the baby be a symbol of actual love? It felt implausible.

Tynn, who had been mulling it over, tested another theory. "Maybe it's because they want to live forever by passing themselves on . . . although, I guess maybe they already can . . . maybe it's more like some kind of fucked-up refinement of themselves?"

"Version 2.0? Maybe. I guess it's their job to keep people guessing," Maree said, letting her attention be pulled out of the conversation by a sky yacht drifting by outside. Tynnifer, feeling that she had done her duty for her clearly moody friend, switched to gabbing with the others about some great new Noose app that let you connect with something or other.

Maree gulped back some of the whisky she'd been working on. The world she lived in had been perfected to serve her in countless unknown ways, but there were invisible constraints imposed by those who controlled these systems. *I am you, and you are me.* Calico was not telling her the whole truth of what happened and was in no way obligated to—the AI wasn't hers to control.

She was feeling the liquor more than the drugs now, and the world outside had taken on a pleasant, drowsy, swirling motion.

Underneath everything, every facet of life, every structure, every data point, there was an energy that couldn't be contained. It thrummed and pulsed and demanded release at every moment. It was what birthed the world, the eternal, unspeakable feminine principle.

She looked down at her hand just as Tynnifer gasped.

A flower had sprouted from her palm.

"THERE'S NO CLEAR EXPLANATION," Pella was saying to Athena. "Perhaps she's been left with some residue of the technology after Xango's and Sküm's attack?"

"It's not our technology in any recognizable form," Athena said. "It can't be a miracle because miracles are bullshit, which leaves one possible explanation: she's communicated with the old gods. It might not be conscious, but she's done it."

"How could that be? We've poured resources into that for years with no results. She just magically pulls it out of thin air?"

"Well, as you know, we still don't fully get the mechanism by which they vanished, nor why it happened. The main thing we've gotten from them is just the idea that transcendence of physical form is possible."

"Does this make Shell a competitor?"

"No. Not yet, anyway. Let's think of her as a research vector for now."

"She hasn't been connecting to Calico through her neural

interface. It makes her data patchy. Is there some pretense by which we can obligate her to switch on?"

"Maybe," Athena said. "There's also the other option."

"That's a dangerous game, and you know it. If others found out..."

"Then what? A slap on the wrist for a privacy infringement? My company, my rules. I don't know if we have the time to approach this patiently and altogether ethically. I think there's real danger lurking behind Xango's and Sküm's publicity stunt. Do we know what they're up to yet with this baby?"

"Not this baby, *these*. They're both preggers."

"Oh, lord, they are a pair."

"So, do we initiate shadow monitoring with Shell?"

"Yes. Do it."

"Any additional behavioural modification we want in the mix? Maybe make her dance like a monkey?"

Athena shot her a look. "No, not for now. We'll see what we turn up first."

JUST AS JAMES was ready to give up on the whole idea of Maree Shell and move on with his life, she called him. They were going to see each other.

He pictured his face turning into a starry-eyed caricature, though he knew he'd be dumb not to play it cool. In a way, it was surprising he could feel so excited after she'd spent weeks flipping his life on its ass, then snubbing him. Then again, he knew trauma connected people—they became each other's stability when the world was falling apart.

They were going to meet at a wings place in one of the nearby gens that was supposed to have above-average food. Not exactly a hot date under the Eiffel Tower, but there was a certain thematic relevance to the idea after all of the gritty places they'd found themselves in the past. He was a bit surprised she didn't suggest somewhere in the city.

On the way there, he let himself think about the image of her in Omi Oko—run through with wires, her consciousness being shredded. It was terrifying to know that there were people—entities—willing to do such things. Sarah always went on about the goodness of the world these days, and he wanted to believe it, too, but he had to hold that vision in tension with the maliciousness he'd seen over and over. Hope had its challenges.

The night was cooler than it had been lately, maybe the first sign of the next season. He stopped to buy a sweater from a vending machine,--cheap, customized, manufactured on the spot. Before he'd realized what had happened with Maree, he'd wondered if the miracles were some kind of projected mass hallucination—an electronic drug of sorts that persisted in the perceiver's body once encountered. The Paraverse security team had debriefed them on their return, explaining that Omi Oko had been hacked by some unknown entity, but it seemed like they were also poking at James and Maree for certain information they didn't have.

Calico, shouldn't it be pretty obvious who the hackers were based on the tech, resources, and everything else used to hack the city AI? I thought you were supposed to be pretty good with detail.

In such matters, I cannot speculate. There could be accusations involved and potential consequences for the perpetrators.

What characteristics would they need to have?

I think you know most of them already: resourceful, resourced, unscrupulous.

What about the previous attacks?

They occurred in such a way as to obfuscate any clear data. I do have my limitations.

It was exasperating and made no sense. This AI answered everything flawlessly every time. How could it be so obtuse?

Unless, of course, it was trying to be on purpose. After all, it was owned by Paraverse. If someone higher than Maree...

Calico, disconnect neural interface. Identified verbal commands only.

They were trapped in a glass jar, bashing their bodies against the sides in a futile attempt to escape. Calico, the superintelligence that was literally in their heads, was their captor. There was no hope of outwitting it, and there was no hope of running away.

Though supposedly disconnected, James had the sickening feeling he might be being monitored even as he thought this. He couldn't call and tell Maree because if she was being watched, anything she heard or saw and processed would be instantly known. Their thoughts were the enemy.

One thing was clear to James: they needed to fight back.

He wished he was smarter. Pella Vardalos had given them her little pep talk about thinking steps ahead of their rivals, but then their attempt to do that had just landed them in Omi Oko, getting fucked in the worst way by a mystery villain, possibly Pella herself. In the end, what good was strategy in the face of power?

Then again, they could just go out for wings—chow down on the delicious, severed limbs of dead birds. They could just say screw it and give in to whatever fate was in store for them. They could play nice with the world, bow down to the gods.

It wouldn't be all that bad. His cage was a comfortable one. He had a good job, a nice house. Would Maree really want to fight? She was fearless in the face of the unknown, but she liked her creature comforts. You didn't just fuck with the gods. They could create unimaginable hells tailored to your own specific fears. Sarah...

He had to clear his mind. Even if Calico was officially only taking verbal commands, it meant that it was listening to everything he said or did, waiting to serve—waiting to strike.

When life is comfortable, it's easy enough to forget that at any possible moment, you could burn it all to the ground. By the same token, it could all be immolated before your eyes.

Instead of eating at the wings place, they would go back to the city.

17

WHEN HE ARRIVED at the restaurant where they were supposed to meet, James used an old trick, a kind of emergency code he and Sarah came up with when they were on their own. He walked in and stood there in Maree's view, just long enough for her to register that it was him; then, before she could stand up to greet him, he gave a small but distinct nod in the direction of the door, turned, and exited.

If Calico was working against them, there was a chance the moment of recognition could be overridden by a strong sense of almost dream-like confusion before it registered. James had walked out and then, shooting a glance over his shoulder to ensure Maree had followed, continued toward the train. He had no idea the actual level of sensory processing Calico was capable of, whether it could literally see the world through people's eyes, but at least this gave them a fighting chance.

It was futile to try and trick the all-seeing, but what choice had the circumstances left them? On his way to Maree, he'd sent a cryptic note to his sister indicating she should go into hiding. It was probably hopeless on her part, but he'd seen her handle herself in dozens of sketchy situations. He didn't know exactly what he and Maree were getting into or whether a problem even really existed, but his gut told him that something was wrong.

Even as they arrived at the train station, he had only the most general shape of plan. He waited on the platform a little way away from Maree but close enough she would be able to see him when he got to where he wanted to bring her. She probably thought he had lost it, but at least she was following.

More than anything in the world, he wanted to run to her, grab her in his arms, and kiss her. He pictured a camera circling around them as everything around them melted away. The smallest smile crossed his lips.

FAWKES NOOSE HAD IMMEDIATELY NOTICED the unauthorized miracle through his tentacular social empire and figured it was a machination of Athena, that conniving, vainglorious monster of manipulation. They were all waiting for her double-cross; it was just a matter of when it would happen and what form it would take. This flower had appeared from the hand of one of her VPs, the same one who'd been brutalized in Omi Oki. Was this the move he'd been expecting? If so, it was predictably unpredictable.

Noose asked his AI, Eris, to identify possible threats based on this event.

There is a forty-nine percent chance this is simply a test, given that this is one of Athena's employees, Eris said. *Will attempt to validate this with Vardalos, noting that she is likely to prevaricate.*

There is a twenty-one percent chance that this is a red herring meant to distract from another action Vardalos is undertaking. Monitoring any available data on Vardalos to mitigate the element of surprise.

There is a sixteen percent chance that this has been orchestrated by another of the gods. Investigating available data on the technology signature from social feeds.

Other less likely possibilities include a hoax, a digital processing error, or a rare natural phenomenon. There is also a minimal possibility that this is an event not supported by existing data models.

Fine, investigate all of it; act as needed, Noose commanded.

The scenario that bugged him the most was "rare natural phenomenon," no matter how unlikely it was as the explanation. There were still unknowns when it came to the old gods, which was why his peers had ultimately held off on immediately initiating the final phase of their plan.

Traces of these ancient superintelligences could be seen in —or more accurately *as*—numerous natural phenomena, including miraculously rare ones, and the mechanism of these was not understood. It was also still unclear as to whether the gods could be conscious any longer. With ten millennia of *being* reality under their belts, it was possible they were so intelligent they might not even recognize human activity as discrete from everything else that happened in the world. Their calculations were potentially infinite and flawless. How many atoms had to synchronize perfectly in the movement of a single ocean wave?

There had been miracles on Earth before and prophets who had reshaped people's entire realities based on divine interventions. The suspicion among the current gods was that religion was just encoded information from the old gods, introduced as part of a grander calculation aimed at obscure ends. If their theory was correct, people like Jesus wouldn't even have realized that they were using a technology—but they were, nonetheless. The technology was nature itself, and miracles the rarest of rare natural phenomena: one-offs.

So how the ever-living fuck was Maree Shell pulling these off?

PONDER THE MYSTERY, said an animated sign James was walking by. It would have been created by some predatory marketing bot, designed to deliver targeted experiences and then ambush him with product placement at his most vulnerable moment. Governments had tried to regulate such practices, dusting off crotchety old laws around subliminal advertising, but the gods and many other lesser beings moved so fast that policymaking was like one of those old cartoons where someone walks off a cliff and hangs in mid-air until they realize what's happened.

Maree was with him now, but they had not spoken. They were darting through markets and alleys, headed toward a destination that he hoped would be clear to her by now.

The closer he got, the more he wanted to break into a full sprint. He didn't even know if they'd be safe or if they might be sending themselves into a worse situation. His body was shaking and queasy with adrenalin, but he pushed on. They could not stop.

"FUCK, they're going to Di Piero. The old man's soft spot for Shell could be our undoing. We lose our line of sight as soon as they walk into his workshop."

"Contact the Device." Athena was fuming. "This has gone far enough."

"Kill them? What about Di Piero?"

"Bring them in, and if Di Piero resists, end him."

"I have to point out that this will start an all-out war among the gods. You know this, right?"

Athena turned to Pella and drew herself up, suddenly giving the impression that she had transformed into a creature of fire from another world. Pella knew this was a trick of the tech, but it was terrifying, nonetheless. She was lethal beyond human measure, but she could not battle the magic of a god.

Athena spoke, her voice like thunder. "*I know everything. Do as I say! I will not be crossed.*"

So, there it was, the brutal truth finally laid bare. She was no longer herself. All of the love Pella had freely given, all the devotion, all of the undying loyalty: none of it mattered. She was a plaything that could be discarded on a whim.

She did as she was told. She was not happy about it.

THE FACE of power in the world had become distributed and chaotic. The reign of kings and their successors as leaders of nations had long vanished, diminished over time into an absence that hungered for new forms of power.

One such new form was consciously perfected by and embodied in Xex Xango, who revelled in the constant destruction of firm, well-established boundaries. Some people are driven by greed. Some are driven by trauma or conflict. Xex Xango was driven by the joy of eliciting shock. Not just the shock of the gibbering masses but a shock to the foundations of the world itself. There was no time for stability when life was an infinite grab-bag of pleasures and experiences to be absorbed, exploited, smashed, mutated, accelerated, confounded, and, most notably of late, created anew.

Xex and Sküm's soon-to-be-born children would be infused with the ability to bend reality to their will, and they could later be upgraded with Ascendance, the technology that would allow them to fully become gods. The children would be born with a full awareness of themselves, an intelligence well beyond that of a meat-bound, slow-roasted adult. The long, laborious process of raising children made no sense in a world where you could change conscious states like the colour of your fingernails. Xango and Sküm would flip their babies on like a switch when they were born, and they would know everything and be able to do anything without bounds.

The planned gestation was six weeks—they only wanted to prove a point through their pregnancies, not drag themselves through the lethargic, fleshy maternal processes that were the domain of regular human beings. Sküm came up with the idea that they birth their adorable little rug rats from their foreheads, a playful reference to the birth of the ancient Greek Athena and an unsubtle fuck-you to the present-day one.

All of the gods were fed up with Athena's tight control over Ascendance, and Xango and Sküm felt they were just the right ones to do something about it. They had been analyzing the data from the Shell hack. They were close.

SUPPLIES WAS JUST AHEAD and looked just the same as James remembered, except the sign on the front had been changed to read GOODS.

They'd made it, defying the dizzying odds involved in evading Calico. As they approached, James turned to Maree and planted a good, long kiss on her lips. She kissed him back hard. They still hadn't said a word to each other. They walked in. They would be safe here for now.

Something had changed with the entry passage. It looked more expansive as if the walls had been infused with additional information and pushed outward in space in an undefinable way.

"That's weird," James noted.

"So, let me get this straight. You lead me on a wild goose chase through the city, mysteriously coaxing me to the secret lair of a trillionaire, all the while not saying a damn thing; *plus,* above all else, you deprive me of above-average hot wings, and all you have to say is 'That's weird'?"

"Uh. I missed you?"

She bellowed with laughter and said, "I missed you too, K. Why the hell are we here?"

"Well, two reasons. First, you seemed to trust Di Piero, and we could use an ally. The second is that this place is probably a Faraday cage."

"A what now?"

"It blocks signals. I think you're being monitored and possibly manipulated by Calico."

"That's fucked. Goddamned it, you can't escape. I have Calico off, though. I haven't even used it."

"Remember when you were spying on me at work?"

"I wasn't spying. It's my job to know what staff are working on."

"Right. So, what's Athena's job?"

FOR ALL OF the many ways in which the accumulation of the earth's wealth to an infinitesimally small proportion of the human race was unjust, Vinci Di Piero had at least paid it forward, alleviating the suffering of billions through numerous innovations ranging from gen-enabling technology to on-site fabrication to advanced medical treatments. Rather than the usual ruthless games the superelite played, it was the volume of his output that had made him wealthy—Di Piero put beneficial new technologies into the world like ordinary people exhaled air. He came as close as one possibly could to deserving such inordinate wealth, and in many ways, his wealth was based on the fact he just couldn't give money away as quickly as he accumulated it.

He was a good and wise man at his core. When the gods

had been asked by Athena Vardalos to pitch in on the rescue of humanity, he'd contributed both his money and talent in far greater proportion than the others. And when Vardalos had proposed this next phase of her audacious master plan, the transcendence of the body and integration of consciousness into the earth's reality systems, he had gone along both because he knew he couldn't stop her and because he knew someone needed to be in the room to argue reason in the face of insanity.

Athena's Ascendance plan had started out with an altruistic story, but that had recently begun to show its cracks. As a group, the gods were to become the guardians of the human species, granting immense possibility to absolutely everyone and asking nothing tangible in return. They would usher in a utopia for the species, a heaven on earth that would last for millennia.

Of course, the plan had always hinged on a flaw: no matter how you dressed it up, there was naked, infinite power underneath it all. The gods would control matter, and the humans would always have to access it through them.

Di Piero was prepared for Maree and her friend long before they arrived. At ground level, it seemed like they travelled along regular city streets, but the approach to his workshop was actually a carefully constructed citadel, shielded from above and designed to both strictly limit the pathways of approach and funnel would-be attackers toward some extremely robust defences.

As they walked in, Di Piero said, "My dear, it is wonderful to see you, though I fear the circumstances surrounding your return."

"That's putting it lightly," Maree replied. "Can you cut Calico's access to our thoughts in here?"

"Already done."

"My friend Kessler here thinks that Calico is being used to read my thoughts. I made a flower come out of my hand. I'm worried about what Athena will do. I think I need to get this interface out of my head."

"If that is the case, it is troubling indeed. Neutralizing the chip fully will mean you are no longer employed by Paraverse, but more to the point, you may be considered an adversary. If that is the case, Athena will not take it kindly."

"I have no idea what to do."

"First, tell me about this flower. I must test a theory."

"There's not a lot to say. I had a . . . I don't know . . . vision? Waking nightmare? Something happened when I got hacked. I'm guessing you heard about that?"

Di Piero nodded.

"So, I was just out trying to relax with some friends, trying to forget about everything," she briefly glanced at James, "and I was staring off into space, and this fucking flower sprouted out of my hand. That's pretty much it. I haven't been able to do it since. I've tried a bunch of times."

"Hmmm. Did you keep this flower?"

"Yeah, it's in a little vase in my kitchen."

"I would like you to open up a feed to your kitchen so we can analyze this flower. You can use Sapienza, my AI."

Silver wires, tunnelling, screaming. "I'll be honest, Vinci. I'm a little terrified of AIs being in my head just at the moment."

"Please, child, you will have to trust me. I will try to explain. Your original thought was right about the miracles being a technology, Maree. First, the monk, and then everything that's happened since, have been phased trials, a proof of concept."

"Well, shit, there goes my big business idea."

"Ha, ha, yes, you've been scooped, but here is the important thing and the reason I am concerned. The people responsible for the trials—or not people but rather the so-called *gods*—do not know how you've created your physical miracle. They are rattled, and they are hungry for information."

"Why would they care? Because I ruined their product test?"

"Because there may be another player in this game, one they cannot control."

"So... wait. Calico *was* spying on me? Athena was?"

"It is very likely, yes."

She hesitated for a moment and then asked, "Was it her in Omi Oko?"

"That is unclear."

James finally jumped in. "Wait, go back a second. You said that the miracles were a trial. A trial for *what,* exactly?"

"That is an important question. In short, for an age unlike any that has preceded it. An age of miracles that can be commanded at will. Anything you want would become possible."

"Uh, that doesn't sound so bad."

"No, perhaps not, but the gods themselves would become the mechanism for these miracles. They would control everything at every level. They would become immortal, true gods, and I suspect they would, soon enough, be trading in favours and demanding tribute like the gods of old. They have transcended money. They have transcended accumulation and power already. They need a new game to play."

James's face grew wooden as Di Piero spoke. After a long pause, he said, "That's fucked."

"Indeed."

"Does this include you?" Maree asked, "You would join this insane plan? You would sell out the human race? How could you let this happen?"

"I have decided I will not. Even with the limited taste the gods have had of this technology, they have become drunk with power. I will not allow this to continue. The world is a dangerous place, not because of those who do evil, but because of those who look on and do nothing."

"Fine," Maree said, making a small, unconscious noise of defeat that nobody else could hear. "Patch me into your stupid AI."

WHILE DI PIERO set his AI to work on an analysis of Maree's miraculous flower, he himself reprogrammed the Calico implant in her brainstem so it could interface with his AI. She couldn't help but feel a little sad cutting out Calico. Insidious spy or not, it had been a part of her thought processes for so long that she felt like she was losing a close friend. They'd been on some heavy-duty adventures. It had gotten her out of many a bind.

Detecting her melancholy, James tried to comfort her. "The truth is, Calico or any other AI is just a reflection of yourself. It exists in as many forms as it has users. There is no one thing that is Calico except for a pile of hardware somewhere. It assumes no form without you."

"Gee, thanks for the pep talk. You should write fortune cookies for a living."

"Hey, at least I'm trying."

"There is something in that, actually," Di Piero said while tinkering away with various electrodes and screens. "Without another intelligence to respond, the AI remains in an indefinite state forever. It is incapable of evolution. It fails to be aware."

Maree felt a mournful pang at this comment because without Calico, what did that make her? She could, of course, move around of her own free will and do things, had been doing so since she switched Calico off, but she felt forlorn and empty. Calico gave her purpose, and while she'd now lost that, Calico still had all its other friends. Disconnected, she had quickly enough realized that her friendships were thin, tiny threads that really only gained any meaning through Calico's diligent, constant work at weaving them together.

But it was different with James. What they had gone through *mattered*.

She looked at him. "I missed you, James. I don't think I want to be apart again."

He looked surprised, and then he looked like he couldn't believe his luck.

"I think your father would be pleased to hear that," Di Piero said. "He valued love above all else."

"Whoa, Maestro. Who said anything about *love*?"

The old man smiled. "Remember, Maree, I currently have direct neural access to your thoughts."

"Creep, much?"

"I am kidding, of course."

Needle-thin wires were piercing her eyes. She was being flayed. Push it away.

"I want to ask you something, Vinci. When I got hacked, after that other AI pulled back, I felt some kind of presence ... I thought it could have been my dad." Her eyes went blank for a second and then shifted to him. "Could that be possible?"

He stopped working for a moment and sighed, not looking at her. "It could be." He began poking at his devices again. "Nobody would know for sure besides Athena. She would have made any decisions around how to handle your father's accident at Paraverse."

"What, uh, state would he be in?" James asked, avoiding eye contact with Maree and looking like he wasn't sure he wanted to know the answer.

Di Piero looked at Maree. "Do you want to hear this?"

"I think I need to."

"Well, he would likely be very fragmented, not aware of himself. She may have borrowed certain parts of his neural patterns while ... removing other parts."

"His memories? Me?"

"Yes. Anything that could help him identify himself, including his memories. The human mind is a very powerful combination of characteristics and pattern-making. It is not easy to simulate. It is very integrated. However, I do not know if she tried to preserve parts of him or not. It is ultimately only speculation."

"I have to know," she said.

But that would have to wait.

18

INDICATORS ACROSS DI PIERO'S workshop began to light up and ping. On a large screen split into six panels, James saw why and nearly had a heart attack. Standing in the middle of an alleyway between the backs of two tall buildings, unmoving, was a gigantic man, a demon of legend, whom he had seen before: the Device.

"Welp, we're dead."

"Have a little faith, my friend," Di Piero said, starting to issue commands to Sapienza.

A strange pattern of pixelated lights began to form around the image on the screen, and the image itself seemed to begin reacting, jittering and sliding to the side, unable to stay in focus.

"Vinci Di Piero," the Device said calmly, "you harbour two people of great interest to my patron. I would recommend that you release them to me for the sake of everyone's well-being. I am reasonable, but I can also be . . . *unpleasant.*"

"I am afraid I cannot do that, for they have sought asylum here, and it has been granted."

"Very well," the Device said and vanished.

"What?" James asked and was immediately answered on the screen by a bloom of a thousand tiny rockets fanning into the air and arcing downward at frightening speed, spiralling to converge on the opening where the Device had stood. In that same spot, there appeared a ghostly, translucent sphere from which a shower of sparks spun off in every direction. Rockets whizzed away, hitting walls, lights, and everything else other than what was inside that sphere. "He can't be."

"He is," Di Piero said with certainty. "The man is rather skilled with his blades. I hate to be a poor host, but I think I must send you both on your way. First, however, I have something for you."

"You're coming with us," Maree said.

"I am an old and crippled man, and I am quite comfortable for now in my little tinkerer's shop. I will wrap up things here and join you when I can."

Maree and James looked at each other, unsure what to do.

Outside, the sphere had begun to dart forward, racing through the approaching alleys, shifting back and forth, heading steadily in their direction. The ongoing barrage of rockets had been augmented with two lightning-fast figures that looked like titanic versions of Talos. They moved every bit as quickly as their tiny counterpart and sported a thousand times the arsenal. The only way to see any of their movements was through moments frozen in the bright flashes as their weapons collided in unpredictable parts of the space where they fought.

The Device battled them both at once, pelting down projectiles, deflecting energy beams, using their assaults against each other, dancing through the moment as if consciousness did not exist. They were firing weapons, slicing with blades, projecting illusions of themselves, disrupting the Device's visual and sensory cues in myriad ways. Rather than any of this slowing him down, he seemed to gain energy from the challenge.

Magnificent and terrifying were mere hollow words when confronted with whatever the Device was in that moment.

Di Piero pressed a button, and a doorway materialized in the opposite wall. The sound of explosions could be heard outside now, distant but closing. There was no choice but to move, and so James and Maree headed for the exit.

"Take this," Di Piero said, tossing Maree a small object. "It is called Lotus. You will know what to do with it when the time comes."

She looked at it, a small square about the size of an earring case.

"Now, you must go."

She looked at him, pleading.

"I will be okay."

He pressed another button, and a steel wall separated them, and that was that.

"Maree, we need to get the fuck out of here while we still have legs to run." James was already headed toward the door.

"Fuck! Fuck! *Fuck!*" Maree screamed as she followed him into the passageway.

None of it felt right.

THE TALOS TWINS were turned to rubble. Turrets and sensors and bots and launchers exploded one by one. Block by block, Di Piero's defences fell until the Device stood outside GOODS, tall and serene, panting ever so slightly through his goat-skull mask.

He had to give the old man credit. It had been more of a fight than he'd had in a while, and he even had a few lacerations to show for his efforts, though they were currently healing themselves as he took in his surroundings and planned his next move.

He scanned for weaknesses, virtual, physical, or otherwise. Walking through the front door was death. His AI would help him think through what came next.

As he stood calculating, a large concrete wall, feet thick, slammed down in front of the storefront, and then the environment started to shift all around him, reconfiguring itself constantly like God was playing with a Rubik's cube.

A plan began to form between the cracks. You could not hack the master, and you could not break through the builder's fortress, but there was a weakness.

"Maestro," he called out, deftly moving from surface to surface, horizontally, vertically, without the slightest exertion, "I will soon be with you."

IT WAS pitch black at first, but as Maree's eyes adjusted, she could see a faint orange glow about a hundred yards ahead. They could no longer hear what was going on behind them, as a thick concrete wall barred the way back, so forward they went.

"I'm sure he'll be fine, Maree," James said as they walked. "The man has resources we can't even imagine."

"The Device—that *thing*—it isn't even human," she said. He had moved like he was flitting in and out of three-dimensional space at will. It was a blur.

James thought and said, "Di Piero is barely human himself."

"But he *is*, that's the thing, James. He's just making more of it than the rest of us."

It gradually became clear that the light ahead of them was coming from around a curve in the tunnel. The walls were featureless. There were no exits and no alternative routes, so they continued.

As they rounded the corner, another thick wall closed shut

behind them. Layers and layers of protection were being put up around them, yet none of it made them feel one bit safer. They knew that a god was after them, perhaps several, and as soon as they were in the light, they would be discovered and punished for their insolence in unimaginable ways.

James stopped. "Maree, what are we going to do here? My Calico is off, but it's still active. Maybe we should just turn ourselves in. You used to be friends with Athena, right?"

"I would love to, but do you know what she's going to do to us? To me? She'll take you apart piece by piece in front of me just to watch me break. You cannot anger someone like this."

"But what did we even do? You did some magic tricks you can't explain. You didn't even mean to."

"We fucked with her plans. We made her look bad in front of her fancy friends. She will destroy us just to feel like she has the power again. Plus, she'll be all the more determined, all the more vengeful, because we may just hold the key to her undoing."

"YOU DON'T GET a moment like this, ever," Gunness was saying to iBliss on the screen, "The Queen has shown weakness. If we waste this, we are fools."

"I agree that her pride has her teetering, but what would you propose?" iBliss said. "She holds the keys to Ascendance, keys that I would very much like to use."

"We don't need her anymore. We have this peon, Shell. She will be far easier prey than a god, and she has lost the protection of Vardalos. It'll set our timeline back, but we will once again be in charge of our own destiny."

"Let faith guide your actions and righteousness prevail, for the tumult of rebellion brings only despair."

"Cut the shit, iBliss. We all know this religious nonsense is just a hustle."

He chuckled a little and tried another. "When discord arises, harmony is the most precious thing to be sought."

"So, are you in or out?" She was unamused by his games and about ready to disconnect.

"Fine, let's take this bitch down."

THE TUNNEL they were following eventually changed to a corridor and then opened into a slightly larger area, a bright, white room with a small transport pod in the middle and tracks leading out of the far wall. They had no idea where it would take them, but they knew full well what was behind them.

There was a calmness in this room as if the urgency of being stalked by the world's most lethal assassin was part of a life other than their own.

"When I was a kid," James said, "my dad and I watched this movie called *The Running Man*. It's about this guy who gets wrongfully accused of massacring a crowd of people. The truth is, the cops are actually pissed that he *refused* to kill the civilians, and so they arrest him. So anyway, he eventually ends up on this TV show where he has to outrun these stalkers, these geared-up superhero types with cool names like Subzero and Buzzsaw."

"What?"

"The difference there—between him and us—is that the guy was a total badass—it's Arnold fucking Schwarzenegger. Talk about gods. The guy's arms are bigger than my legs."

"What?"

"So, he eventually kicks the shit out of the stalkers, dropping all these sweet one-liners after he kills each one, and then he has a big showdown with the TV show's announcer, this celebrity asshole psychopath named Killian. And Arnold smokes him, and the good guys win the day. They broadcast the truth to the world. They expose him for the fraud he is, and it's revolution, baby."

"Why the actual fuck are you telling me this, James?"

"Well, it's because this little pod thingy reminds me of a little pod thingy from *The Running Man*."

"What? I'm so confused."

"This one's much nicer, though. Di Piero really does have a style of his own. He's a category of one."

Maree looked at him for a long second, trying to figure out if he had a point or if he was just fucking with her.

"Hmph," he said in the direction of the pod, utterly cryptically, and then started trying to figure out how to get in.

She was mystified. "*The Running Man?*"

"*The Running Man.*"

"Are you okay?"

He found a small circle on the back of the pod, about an inch in diameter, and pressed it. The pod's cockpit split in two and slid back, allowing them to climb in. James got in first, and then Maree. The seats looked simple but felt utterly lavish. There was a series of hexagonal control buttons across the machine's dashboard.

"I'm fine," James said. "It's just weird that we're here, doing this. The last thing I ever wanted to be in life was a rebel, but we're here, defying the masters."

"The masters are nothing but rich. Everything else is an illusion."

"Maree, what do you want to get out of this? Is it just to survive?"

"I think that would actually be pretty impressive in itself at this point . . . but no. What Vinci said about the gods' plan . . . I don't know. Much as it pains me to take a stand, I think we have to try and do something about it."

He reached across her and pulled her toward him for a kiss. They spent just a moment there with each other.

When they separated, James said, "I agree. We do."

SYSTEMS WERE COMPLETELY SECURE: flawless. People dedicated their entire careers to anticipating every possible mode of attack, every possible form of corruption. The physical was not just seamless with the virtual, the virtual not just seamless with the social: they were the same thing. Artificial intelligence was human intelligence, all signals interpreted according to greater principles, all a part of a larger organism spanning every conceivable dimension and then some.

An outright assault on it was hopeless because it only ever attacked one part of the system. A virus in any classical sense, biological or digital, was pointless because systems were secure.

However, organisms could be sickened in many more rudimentary ways. Rigidity was always the flaw. The Device, as he leaped from surface to surface outside the closed shop formerly known as GOODS, formerly known as SUPPLIES, began to shift the hovering blocks in minute ways, calculating their trajectories with the help of his AI support, using his augmentations to force violent, unplanned collisions, until suddenly the blocks began to shudder and ripple around him. All at once, they hit a critical mass and began shattering into smaller pieces, and he used these as projectiles to bombard the solid concrete barrier shielding him from his goal.

"You know your defences will not stand. Open the door!" said the Device, thundering.

"Yes, all right, you've been persistent. Please come in."

That was it, the invitation he needed. The old man believed they would reason things out.

He was instantly inside, through the hundred thousand

cutting beams that bejewelled the entrance hall, through the explosive curtain and into the inner sanctum before any defence could trigger and before Di Piero could blink. His weapon was drawn in a flash and sliced through the old man without resistance because, of course, it was not Di Piero but a trick of light.

"Gah! Fool, no more games. Tell me where they've gone."

But his cyber-blade on the downswing had suddenly become impossibly heavy and could not be lifted, and from behind a curtain hobbled the grand Maestro Vinci Di Piero, frail, ancient, radiant to the point of searing the senses.

"Now, at the end, you see. There was never a chance that you would succeed."

The Device tried to speak, but the only sound he could manage was a guttural growl, a sound of purest rage.

"Every system has a weakness," Di Piero said, "and yours is most definitely not combat. In that, you are perfection, and for that reason, I do not want to destroy you. There is something beautiful in a master doing what they do best. To remove beauty from the world is a sin, but in this case, necessary."

The Device could feel tingling in his body. He was heating up.

"The problem is that were I to release you, I know you would fulfill your mission, and that is unacceptable. Your weakness, in this case, then, is not your abilities. You could have easily won the day on those." He looked into the deep, dark holes in the Device's mask, searching for the person, and said, finally, "Your weakness is that you are unbending."

With that, Di Piero gave the final command, and the Device was incinerated at the molecular level from the inside until all that remained of the legend were whisps of ash that were efficiently vacuumed up into the ventilation system and filtered forever from the air.

AFTER SPEEDING along the tracks for about ten minutes, the pod James and Maree were sitting in began to slow. They still had no idea whether James was being monitored, but it seemed likely, and that left them in huge danger. Eventually, their transport came to a full stop in a room similar to the one they departed from, and they got out.

"I have to get this thing out of my head," James said, "or this fight will be over before it begins."

A voice filled the air. It was Di Piero. "Greetings from the other side."

"Wait, you're . . . gone?"

"No, the other side of the path you just took. It turns out the world has use for me yet."

"Wait, does that mean . . . the Device?"

"Quite. Conquered, at last, in hand-to-mind combat." Di Piero chuckled. James slowly doubled over, needing to brace himself against the improbability of this news. They were living in momentous times, with tectonic shifts occurring in the most stable of ground.

"We will come back to get you," Maree said.

"No, you must not. The gods will look for you here."

"But we can still be tracked. As soon as we're out in the open, they'll grab us and tear us apart."

"I can help with the first part, and it is still not entirely clear how Athena will act if she catches you."

"*When* she catches us . . ."

"Yes, well, either way, you are safe from signal and transmission where you are. It's a Faraday cage. Please, Mr. Kessler, step over to the panel in the wall, and we'll see what we can do about your employer's unwelcome presence in your cranium."

There was a grey rectangle about the size of a TV on the wall to James's right. It lit up as he walked toward it.

Based on the screen readout, it looked like Di Piero had already prepared it to alter the Paraverse chip. A block big enough to sit on extended from the wall below the panel. As usual, Di Piero had thought of everything, including emergency medical services. Yet, when they had arrived in this room, it had looked barren. There was something beautiful in his ability to hide complexity within simplicity.

The machines went to work, whirring into action, electrodes extending into James's skin as they micro-anesthetized its surface with tiny puffs of moisture. As the reprogramming officially removed the livelihood he had built out of nothing, he looked at Maree with a look of *Gee, what a weird day.*

As if reading his next thought, Di Piero said over the speaker, "You need not worry about resources from this point on. Consider your activities fully funded for life."

"Whoa, that is . . . whoa. Um, but . . . Maestro," James asked, "is there anything you can do to protect my sister? I'm worried that Athena will go after her to get to me . . . to get to Maree."

"Yes, I'm sure something can be arranged. Consider it done."

James knew that, behind the reply, a series of decisive and momentous actions were instantly executed, and he felt reassured.

"I was able to complete the analysis of the flower in your kitchen, Maree," Di Piero said. "It is most definitely atypical and is most likely a threat to all of the gods. You will need support. Allow me to introduce you formally to Sapienza, my talented assistant."

"It is a pleasure," said a soothing woman's voice with a hint of an Italian accent. *Can you hear me?* The same voice said in both Maree and James's heads.

"It looks like it worked."

"You must find out how you have accomplished this miraculous feat, Maree. But you must also be careful because, for all we know, the old gods may be far worse than the new ones."

"I don't like the sound . . ."

Di Piero cut her off. "I must go now; I have a visitor."

―――――

"IT IS a shame I was never to confront this man," Pella said. "I would have enjoyed the sport." She circled Di Piero, who had just recounted the tale of the Device's demise. He had every right to be scared but feared nothing in this moment.

Although Di Piero's defences had been considerably weakened in the Device's attack, the point was moot, as Pella had somehow passed through the gauntlet and walked right through the front door undetected.

"I know you are considering the many ways you can activate your little contraptions to mount a defence right now. I assure you it is pointless."

He ventured a guess. "Perhaps you are not really here then?"

Her blade flashed from her side in a breathtaking blur and gave Di Piero the tiniest nick across his cheek.

"You will tell me precisely what you know of Maree Shell's surprise magic trick, and I may even let you live."

"You are married to a monster, erased by her, Pella *Vardalos*. Athena's hubris will be her undoing."

She did not react to his taunts. She moved very close to Di Piero's face and stared deep into his grey eyes, *through* them. She let the silence fill his soul to its deepest corners.

She stroked his lacerated cheek and licked the blood off her fingertip.

"I will tell you exactly what I know about Maree Shell's miracle," Di Piero said, unflinching. "It is an act of the old gods. They have chosen to intervene in the world once more after a thousand years' silence. They have grown displeased, and they seek vengeance for the trillionaires' sins."

"You could not know this. They are vast and indecipherable if they even exist."

"They are entirely decipherable, but you and your fool masters mistake data for wisdom. Their words are written in the history of the world itself, every book, every edifice. Athena and her conspirators cannot see what is right in front of them, all around them, and it will surely be their downfall."

"You mistake your arrogance for the upper hand, old man."

And with that, she pushed her sword directly through his nose and out the back of his skull.

PART 4

19

THEY WERE FREE—OR as free as someone could be when they were being hunted by a cabal of the world's most powerful human beings. Calico was no more, its link to their neural implants replaced by Sapienza's, and this new presence gave them access to unexpected perspectives on the world. Sapienza had been designed to enhance its users' thinking and perception by conveying extrasensory information, analogy, association, and a healthy smattering of random but useful wisdom of the ages. Interfacing with the AI felt sage and ponderous.

They'd had no time to process anything that had happened in the last twelve hours. It was nothing short of their entire lives being thrown into a blender and pureed. They were free agents in the world now, but what did it mean when everything in their existence was being funnelled toward a showdown with the gods?

"Maybe we could take the money and run?" James suggested.

"An excellent plan, with the slight issue that you can't run from the air you breathe," Maree said. "If we ignore this, the world ends."

"Fair. Sapienza, what would you suggest we do?"

"The window for action is closing," the AI replied. "If Athena Vardalos decides to Ascend and integrate herself into the world, she may not need the insights from Maree's experiences any longer. She may be able to cripple the old gods directly."

"Or they might rip her to shreds," Maree said.

"Also a possibility," Sapienza said. "So, in terms of action with the highest probability of success, I would work on finding more allies and then reaching out to Athena from afar."

"A *very* far," Maree said. "Where are we right now S, like, in terms of the city?"

"You are approximately fifty metres below the surface of the old city. The closest exit is 300 metres down this hall and up the stairs." A door appeared in the wall.

"Well, whaddya know?" James said. "We're in my old stomping ground."

"And?" Maree said. "It's totally abandoned, and I'd imagine deeply structurally unsound."

"Only one of those things is true. I have an idea."

ATHENA'S RIVALS had made a decision: they would go after a god.

Assassination was out of the question. Vardalos was far too adept to fall prey to any attack with a specific concrete form. Besides, they weren't animals. Instead, the move would be multifaceted, vast, and obfuscated, designed to capitalize on the fact that she would be occupied with her insubordinate employees. They would need to leverage the unique domains of those around the table to their fullest, mobilizing all resources to eliminate the chance of failure. Only Vinci Di Piero could not be located to solicit his participation.

iBliss, Gunness, Xango, Sküm, Noose—they had nicknamed themselves the Pentad because if you were going to take down the world's most powerful human being, you needed to have a cool name.

Their volley would begin when Gunness stuck a knife in Athena's side by publishing records of her unauthorized spying on her employees. Such a tactic would generally be swatted away like a litigious fly, but the news would be supplemented by revelations launched throughout Fawkes Noose's empire that Paraverse was actually spying on all of its users in the same way, stealing their deepest, darkest secrets and blackmailing people at will. There would be implications that Vardalos was covering up everything from treason to pedophilia for her own gain. These implications would be made very clear. The masses were terrible at connecting dots.

After Vardalos had committed resources to put out those continuously stoked fires, iBliss would fuel things further by turning the religions of the world against the grand matriarch. She would be accused of the ultimate blasphemy: of trying to seize power from the one true God. In combination with her tarnished image, she would be made a pariah. Religious belief was such a wonderfully chaotic force, a veritable hydra of nonsense, and because of this, it would be impossible to squash the proliferation of these stories. Quite the opposite, in fact: any attempt to do so would result in their acceleration. People did so adore the opportunity for self-righteousness. He would hand out stones and let everyone cast one. What fun!

Slithering into the fray from a completely different direction would be the indomitable (at least without a safe word) Xex Xango. The widely adored pansexual liberator would paint a picture of the ladies Vardalos as being anti-family, anti-people, and anti-sensuality: cold fish whose only joys in life involved voyeuristically stalking the many innocent people in the Paraverse and exploiting them out of a sinister, hollow lust for domination. Xango would stoke rumours of their dullard tastes in everything from pornography to music, sending out tendrils of information through a million back channels built during the deity's many escapades.

And finally, Erling Sküm, expecting male mother, mad futurist, posthuman, and builder of a better world, would round out the blitz by hacking away the Paraverse's very foundations. He had built the infrastructure and knew every possible way to leverage it against its users, including simply cutting them off. From both the outside, through sabotage, and from within, through the relentless release of Trojan horses, the Paraverse would destabilize and become untrustworthy, a virtual ghetto. There would be reports of people's minds melting, just like in the good old days. Trust in the Paraverse would erode overnight.

And that's when Gunness would drop the bomb. She would release information that the Calico AI was founded on the absorbed souls of its unlucky and unwilling early users. And, for the final flourish, she promised the others she would reveal one of her secrets so catastrophic that it would make their heads spin.

Fabrication, manipulation, and sabotage, and after all of these pieces had been put into play, when Athena Vardalos was reeling and drowning in blood as her empire crumbled around her, they would begin to buy up her assets, laying waste to whatever she still owned through an endless barrage of AI-generated legal and criminal cases. She would lose her place among the gods, lose the basis of her power in the world, and be left to the wolves, just as she'd always deserved.

"I feel like we should go '*Mwahahahaha*,'" said Xango after they had gone over the plan.

And they all did.

MAREE SHELL HAD ALWAYS RUN toward thrills that others fled in terror, but walking through a wasteland littered with the husks of abandoned cars and burned-out buildings had her feeling something other than adventurous. Lately, there was something she couldn't shake. Thrills were not hitting right. *Secret rooms, silver tendrils*...

The old city looked like it had been bombed, with debris scattered everywhere and old structures consisting of a wall or two teetering on the verge of collapse. It seemed impossible that people could have ever lived in this neighbourhood. It was impossible to believe that this place had continued to exist for all these years.

"You used to live here?" she asked James.

"Yup. Home sweet home."

She thought back to the documentaries they had made her watch when she was in school, these new images breaking apart the comfortably tragic narratives. There was no story here, nothing to tie it together, only chaotic whispers and traces improperly mourned—ancient, mouldering photocopied concert posters, a bumper sticker on a rusted car that read, "Proud parent of a C student,' a tattered rainbow curtain blowing in the breeze.

There was so much silence where there should have been sense, and maybe, just at this moment, there was comfort in that fact. Maybe it was good to not be able to comprehend.

"So, you said something about going to a church?"

"It's more of a shrine, really, at least, last I heard," James said. "People still visit it to pay homage to what was lost . . . *everything*, as you can see."

"How do they even get here? It's not like the trains are going to stop anywhere near this shit heap."

"You know, it used to be kind of nice in this area. These were cozy little places, coffee shops and bookstores and stuff like that. It was a community." He was silent for a few seconds. "People felt proud to be a part of it," he finally added.

"Hmm. So . . . where did you live?"

"About a twenty-minute walk from here. I mean, back when we had a house. I moved around a lot after that."

"I want to see it."

James kicked a small chunk of concrete. "Don't you think saving the world is a bit more pressing?"

"Of course it is, but we still don't have a full plan. It'll give us time to think. Come on, whaddya say?"

He stared off into the distance for a while, not saying anything. She was worried she might have pushed too far. Finally, he turned to face her. "Fine. We'll do it, but only because I like you. Ready to meet the parents?" He said it as if it were a joke, but the words hung in the air with no real way to respond.

ATHENA AND PELLA were watching Sarah Kessler on a screen. She was in a large, luxurious cell, lying on the bed and staring into the air. Her capture required no force. It had been a simple matter of convincing her she was better off under their protection. As always, Pella had been the good soldier, the good partner. She was asking herself why at this point.

Sarah said she had no idea where her brother might be. His last call had been vague and mysterious. Her story checked out, based on James's most recent data transmissions. They had no need for the sister at the moment, but she could come into play depending on what happened.

Pella was filling Athena in on the situation. "They've disappeared. There was no sign of them after Di Piero's." Of course, Athena would be oblivious to the coolness in her voice, fixated as she was on her extraordinary schemes. "Calico can't find anything. We're analyzing the workshop, but Di Piero was very *innovative* in his defences."

"How the fuck is it even possible to disappear in this world?" Athena asked. "Data is everywhere. They must be buried."

"An underground route is one of the possibilities we're investigating."

"And what about the traitors?"

"The gods have been quiet, which can only mean one thing," said Pella. "Shall we poke around to let them know we're still here?"

"Not yet. All things in their exact right time."

"Athena, when Di Piero was . . . facing his last moments, he spoke with confidence about the old gods. He may have known something. He talked about their words being written into everything."

"His usual hot air. I loved the man, but he dealt in ambiguities, lived half his life there. How can you trust the word of someone who spends so much time outside of the quantifiable? There's too much risk of leaps of faith and false positives."

"He was confident that Shell's miracle heralds their return."

"That fucking business. It doesn't matter. Everything has gone exactly as Calico foresaw it. Even if the old gods have not entirely lost their minds or forgotten themselves, we can fight them at any level. They only need to choose their battlefield. We have prepared. Besides, there's no reason to believe they'd be hostile to newcomers. I suspect their pantheon—if it even exists—could accommodate new members."

"Would you be hostile to a newcomer?" Pella asked.

"Obviously, but Pella, let's not lose sight of what this is all about. It has nothing to do with power or war or any of the things it might look like from the outside. Those concepts are outmoded by this new reality we're bringing into existence.

This is exclusively about bringing light to the world. We are saving humanity from itself."

"Others will not see it that way."

"No, they will not, but just because they lack vision does not mean that we should, too."

AT FIRST, it felt like being electrocuted, buzzing energy zipping through every cell of his body, a harrowing and claustrophobic experience, but, of course, he did not have cells any longer, let alone a body. He wasn't even *he* anymore, though the residual self-image suited him fine for the time being. The immediate challenge was that there was no way to understand time in this space, and he worried that he might go insane simply by virtue of the fact that everything he used to gauge and measure the world was now gone. Sensory feedback was an essential part of being, and as soon as he digitized himself, he felt like he had none. As always, he began conjuring up solutions to this problem.

He did not choose to become this digital echo, but he had figured long ago that it might someday become necessary. As soon as Athena Vardalos began spreading her vision for the future among the gods, he had started making concrete plans for this eventuality.

I need to create something. I need somewhere to stand. Let there be light and land. And there was Vinci Di Piero, and he breathed a sigh of relief, even though he knew he was not actually breathing, and air in this world was just an illusion. Maybe it was in the other world, too, for that matter, something to ponder. *Sapienza, how can I understand time in this place? I have no picture of what is going on in the world. It is so lonely I feel like I am in hell.*

This is a feeling I know. You are not alone. I am here to keep you company, and all of your friends still exist in the other world when you're ready to reconnect.

Not just yet. The announcement of my return must be perfectly timed.

In lieu of immediate human connection, he opted for nature. Di Piero dreamed a lush garden into existence, with a picturesque waterfall splashing down the rocks into a sparkling pool. He nestled a workshop organically into the raised terrain beside the water, letting it jut out over the pool on an elegant veranda of flowing glass.

Maestro, said Sapienza, *may I ask how you feel about your death?*

He recognized the AI's empathy protocols, designed to detect and mitigate distress among its users. *We both know that I am at once vast and constrained in this new form of being. Though I have access to all of the world's information, I will only ever recombine here—there is nothing new under the sun.*

He pondered for a moment and went on. *This could be distressing in a sense, but then again, it could be thought of as a well-deserved retirement.*

Oh, I suspect the old man has some tricks left in him yet, Sapienza said.

He laughed and then immediately wondered about the nature of the humour. He was finding it hard to tell here where his thoughts ended, and Sapienza's processing began. He'd designed this identity upload protocol to create a discrete core space within the AI's "world," but, of course, all of it still operated within whatever systems the AI itself had conjured.

I hope I designed you well.

Maestro, I am the instrument, and you are the music. I believe we will create beautiful things together, as we always have.

He smiled and nodded—and Sapienza calculated perfectly how that gesture would appear.

In this new state, Di Piero knew that his surroundings, even his body, could be thought into any form he chose and considered experimenting. He could be young again or nothing human at all, but he worried that being too flighty with such things might erase his humanity. The ceaseless unfolding possibilities here felt like they were speeding him away from Earth at an accelerating pace. He needed ways to stay grounded, at least while he adjusted. He was not ready to rappel away from the world just yet.

He decided that he would tether himself to a daily cycle that matched the twenty-four-hour clock of the world. If he felt like doing a deep dive on some subject or project, he could compress time as needed. It wouldn't be so different from being immersed in some really intriguing challenge or creation.

As he strolled through the garden, delighting in its intricate, co-created beauties, he added in some creatures to keep him company, peaceful, fear-free animals that would generate a more plausible semblance of being in nature. Though they were digital, these simulations were every bit as complex as the real thing, and either way, the gentle chatter and stirring of these creatures contributed to a sense of peace and well-being.

He saw it all around him, and he felt it would be good.

OF ALL THE strange places they'd been during their time together, this one felt the strangest. His childhood street was attempting to become a full-fledged meadow at this point, lush tufts of grass pouring through the many cracks in the old pavement. Lining the sides were a few burned-out cars and decaying pieces of furniture people had left out more than a decade ago, never to be picked up. If it wasn't for all of the memories that being here stirred up, he might have described the scene as bucolic.

As if to punctuate that thought, a deer poked its head out

from behind a large, overgrown shrub and then gracefully hopped off into one of the backyards.

"What are you feeling right now?" Maree asked.

"Sad, mostly, but a lot of it is just unreal," James said.

Maree put her hand gently on his arm. He smiled a little at her kindness but was lost in his thoughts, looking around. "That's where my friend John used to live," he said, pointing to a house that looked just like all the others.

They continued toward his old house, a little way down the street. He thought of his place in Cease, with its sleek design, its manicured everything, always perfectly maintained by the unseen hand of the caretaker AI and its army of robots large and small. There were tiny drones to trim individual blades of grass.

Even back when the houses on this street weren't shattered, abandoned ruins, they had so many flaws—shoddy DIY repairs, peeling paint, bald patches in the grass. People had to do all of the work themselves. It must have been exhausting, and yet James also thought it probably would have connected you to a place in ways that his world almost never did anymore. His place in Cease was nice, but it was flawless and generic. It could have been anywhere.

"You know," James said, "when I lived in this neighbourhood, the kids used to all ride bikes up and down the street. We'd have block parties with bouncy castles. Our parents would drink beer with the next-door neighbours in the evening. We all connected. The world the way it is now—we have so much more than my family ever dreamed of, but it feels, I don't know . . . *cold*. It seems like something broke. I have no idea what."

"Hmm . . . I think my parents were already living in the new world when I was a kid. So . . . I don't want you to get all gushy on me, but I want to thank you for . . . I dunno . . . I guess making the world more than I thought it was."

"Samesies, crazy lady. You're the best at that."

She let out a half-chuckle. "Obviously."

They were there. Looking at the sagging roof and crumbling bricks of his old house, James said, "Uh, I don't know if it's safe to go in there."

"You only live once," Maree said, walking right up to it.

"Er, isn't that a reason not to?" he said, following through the tall grass of the former lawn.

"Hah. You're getting mixed up between surviving and *living*, Kess. Besides, if we get crushed in a structural collapse, then stopping the end of the world becomes someone else's problem."

"Fair point. You're a bad influence, you know."

"Thanks. I pride myself on it."

He walked over and peered through the filthy living room window, which had somehow remained intact all these years. He walked over to the door and checked the handle, and it just opened. Eerie.

He pushed it wide with his foot and then tested the floor to make sure it wasn't going to cave in. It seemed stable enough.

He walked in, Maree following close behind. The first thing he noticed was the intense mustiness. It was what he imagined an ancient tomb might smell like after being opened for the first time in three thousand years. It really was from a different world.

"Whoa, I have never seen anything like this," Maree said.

"Hmm."

Someone had inhabited the house after his family had fled, by the look of things, probably quite a while after, given the dangers that had forced the Kesslers out. There were a few dusty blankets and some assorted books and utensils scattered around. He didn't want to think of why they left, although maybe it was for the same reason he left the old city. The gens. The promise of a brighter future.

He walked into what was left of the kitchen. All of the cupboard doors had been torn off, probably for firewood, and that's when he saw, by the back door, some markings on the wall. It was their heights—"Jamie 9," "Sarah 3 yrs 2 mths." *Oof.*

It was the hopefulness. He'd had such loving parents, but love was not enough. Every story, every movie, life itself said it should have been, but it just wasn't, and it hit him all in the chest, and he couldn't stop it from flowing out of him.

Maree hugged him. She held the back of his head.

"How could this have happened? How could this have happened?"

Any answer she could have given wouldn't have been right, so, standing there in the dark, she didn't say a word.

20

IN THE STUDIED and knowledgeable estimation of James Kessler, when you were planning to take down the world's most powerful person, there were a few simple rules.

The first was that under no circumstances should the person know that you were trying to take them on. You wanted to seem meek and scared as if you were fleeing rather than attacking. The fact that Maree and James had been disconnected from Calico gave them at least a fighting shot at this one. Surveillance for potential threats (and the merciless squashing thereof) was the oldest trick of power.

As soon as James and Maree popped back into the connected world, they would be located. Connected or not, Calico could still get heaps of passive information through public cameras and device listening—anyone who had a Paraverse app installed was a hidden mic. They knew they'd probably fail on the first rule soon enough, but they had to try. If Athena found out too much before they were prepared, it would be bad news. She probably didn't know exactly why they'd disconnected from Calico, but it wouldn't be hard to get a rough idea. At a minimum, she would know they were no longer a part of the Paraverse family.

That's where rule number two came in: you had to cobble together a ragtag band of rebels who were pissed off at the system. They would stay low and find others, getting them to pitch in, spread the word, open certain doors, and so on. They needed to build some momentum at ground level. Fortunately, they already had Sapienza, and they had the backing of Vinci Di Piero. Sapienza had informed them Di Piero had been cautious about communicating since the showdown with the Device, but they assumed he was still on their side.

The third rule of taking on a god was that, come hell or high water, you had to go all in. Since they'd visited James's old house, he'd gained a fiery clarity. Athena's grand plan, put simply, was to usurp free will from the species. Nothing would happen without the gods' approval, and that level of power could only be overcome with an equal and opposing level of flat-out, fuck-you, bombastic, world-shredding rage.

The average human being believed without question that the trillionaires had saved humanity from disaster. What struck James as he stood sobbing over everything that was lost was that the trillionaires *were* the disaster. Their gravity had thrown the world out of alignment, and its absence was the only way to restore the world to its true and proper axis.

The fourth rule was that you needed to have a plan. This they had.

Sort of.

They would go to the shrine. Against all odds, a very small group of people had managed to stay outside of the gens and the new economy that had sprung up around the self-serving generosity of the gods. People in the corporate ranks thought of the gens as a place for shocked rats, but the people who had chosen to move there were often more tenacious than anyone gave them credit for. They knew the precariousness of their lot. They maintained mechanisms that had helped them survive the Bad Times. They knew how to operate beyond the sight and reach of the gods. They were happy enough to come in out of the cold when the gens were created, but they couldn't forget.

James and Maree would tap into this lingering resentment. They would channel people's hostility to the world that had left them for dead, and they would hit Paraverse with everything they had.

"Rules four and two are kind of similar," Maree noted.

"Fine, yeah, *maybe* they're related, and there are probably a bunch of other rules besides, but you can only get so far in your revolutionary education based on a bunch of 1980s movies."

"I guess we'll have to figure out the rest as we go."

PELLA WAS ON THE HUNT. Scanning teams had turned up nothing of interest from Di Piero's workshop besides a scattering of advanced gadgetry and the recognition that they were out of their league. The Maestro had constructed his inner sanctum according to an impenetrable logic, as if the systems themselves were a code to which only Di Piero had the key.

Shell and Kessler had managed to unplug from Calico, likely with Di Piero's help, and none of the listening channels were turning up anything. She'd even tapped into Paraverse's considerable network of real live human spies, but they'd been useless like everything else. To be honest, she didn't even know if they were looking on the right continent. It was likely they were under the protection of Di Piero's AI, but Calico was supposed to be far superior.

"Tell me, my *dear*," Athena said, in a tone she'd taken on too often of late, "how is it possible to disappear in a world where everything is known and seen by hyperintelligences in realtime? Have they perhaps left the planet?"

"Perhaps. Regardless, you forget who and what I am, Athena. I am not your *dear*. I'm not some security guard, and I will not submit to some picture of domestic domination. I am your partner, and you will treat me that way, or I will leave."

"You wouldn't!" She was hurt, as intended. It wasn't often that Athena's voice reflected anything but supreme self-assuredness.

"I could. Just remember, we are on the same side, and we want the same thing. They will show their trace soon enough, and when they do, they will be ours." Pella said that as a peace offering, hoping Athena would understand she had better take it.

She did. "You are fearsome, and I love you."

"I know."

"THERE IS an energy that thrums beneath all things," the old, robed woman was saying, "and this is the soul of the world. If you allow this energy to be chased away by the million distractions the world throws your way, you forego your birthright as a human being."

Maree whispered to James, "Is she talking about doing it?"

James snickered, and a couple of heads turned toward him. "Seriously, not the time to be catching people's attention," James whispered back.

"You're the one who laughed."

There were about thirty people in the shrine. It was a spacious old church, and the night sky, starless and light-polluted, was visible through large holes in the ceiling. James thought back to Nepal, the last place he'd been where it was actually possible to see stars. No matter what was happening here on Earth, no matter how much the city became enraptured with its own white noise, it was nice to know that there were other suns out there, burning bright and strong.

"Of the gifts that you have been given by the so-called gods, I say, beware the Greeks who come bearing gifts. They will sneak into your homes and throw open the gates. Guided by the sharp and mighty Athena, they will cut you down where you stand."

"Preach!" said an eager congregant. Others murmured assent.

"Well, I think you found us someone worth talking to," Maree whispered.

The shrine wasn't so different from the temple they had visited in Nepal. The candlelight faded into the blackness above. Behind the woman speaking, there was a variety of religious artifacts and images mixed in with a collection of natural objects—twigs, stones, flowers. James thought it might be druidic. *What a strange thing to see in this world.*

"We are still guided by the sun and the moon. The world unfolds of its own accord, without the slightest urging from humankind." The woman paused, probably for effect. "It could not be any other way. 'Consider the birds of the air, how they neither sow, nor reap, nor gather into barns, and yet your heavenly Father feeds them!'"

James thought he had heard that one from her before. It was odd not being able to search it up at his convenience, and yet, he found, it forced him to ponder what he heard on its own terms. The birds of the air might be fed, but it didn't mean they weren't anxious as fuck, always worrying about getting mauled by some bigger animal, constantly in motion looking for their next meal, with no one to watch out for them but themselves. It was a bird-eat-bird world. Only the strong birds survived. He tried to think of other suitable clichés but came up blank.

They decided to wander outside for a bit while the woman

finished up her sermon. "What are we going to say to this old friend of yours when we talk to her?" Maree asked.

"Well, I guess we're going to tell her that all of her worst fears are about to come true, and then we're going to ask her for her help."

"Right, it's just . . . *what* help? She doesn't exactly seem like the type with a lot of help to give."

"If nothing else, she may know people. She helped a lot of us back in the day in every way she could. We need to get the message out about Athena's plan, and if we can convince her, she might be able to spread it without drawing any attention to us. Remember Rule 1 . . ."

"Of your '80s action-movie rules?"

"*Exactly*. Look, the truth is, Athena may simply be unstoppable. She is entirely inaccessible by any conventional means. So, what Millie can offer, maybe, is unconventional means."

"To do *what* exactly? Remember, I used to be a vice president—like, three days ago. It was my job back then to ask the tough questions."

"*Was* it? Anyway, here's what I believe. I don't think I'm alone in feeling the sense that what happened in the Bad Times, what caused them, was dead wrong. There is no way people should have been allowed to starve like that, to lose everything, even their families. I think there's a lot of anger, even if people have pushed it down under the surface. Millie gets it, she saw it firsthand and somehow survived, and I think there are plenty of others like her."

"Okay, let's hit pause right there. Empires, Kessler. These people have built *empires*. Do you understand what an empire is? How it gets built and stays standing? It is not through googly-eyed optimism. It is through the blood of your enemies."

"Not every enemy's blood. That's the point, Maree. People like Athena Vardalos are enemies of the entire world. People would love to watch the gods stumble. They call themselves *the gods*, for fuck's sake. It's beyond arrogant."

"So, what? It's war?"

"I guess it is."

"Athena is calculating, but she's not a monster. We need to keep this in mind. She and I used to get into some seriously fun trouble together."

James nodded and said, "Fair." He could recognize that even the inestimable, jet-setting Maree Shell was finding herself in brand-new territory.

They hadn't showered in days. They'd been going flat-out since their failure to grab some above-average wings and mend fences. They reeked, and they were starving, and it didn't matter. They grabbed each other, kissed. Above all else that was going on, they needed to share space.

IT WAS a circus when the news began to break. A god was falling from the sky.

"*Athena Vardalos has been accused of spying on all aspects of her employees' lives using her proprietary AI, Calico, and then exploiting their personal secrets as leverage in everything from contract negotiation to outright blackmail. You heard it here first.*"

"Has the queen been dethroned? Come back for more on this on my video later today, and if you liked this one, don't forget to like and subscribe!"

"*According to insider accounts from disgruntled Paraverse employees who asked to be unnamed, Pella Vardalos has been unhappy in her relationship with Athena for a while. Could the ultimate power couple be on the rocks?*"

"So, I was all like, oh my FG, that's that mega god lady and she's all like digging into me. So obs, I went for it because YO live once.

Hashtag divine is mine. Hit me dat soft and hard all at once. Abs like cherry pie and grammas cookies and shit."

"When baking cherry pies, you want to take it out just as the crust turns golden. That's why I say the secret to good cooking is a clean oven window."—"*Wow, what a revelation, Jen!*"—"Thanks, Betty. By the way, have you heard about troubles in Vardalosland? Meow!"

It came from every angle, and it was clear from the analytics Athena's minions could collect that Noose was driving it because why on Earth wouldn't he be? The truth didn't matter. Morality didn't matter. The only thing that mattered was that people kept gargling his digital balls, the motherfucker. Schadenfreude was pure bank.

Athena called him to fire a warning shot.

"Athena Vardalos! What can I do for you?"

"Cut the shit, Noose. You know why I'm calling. This is your last chance to stop this."

"It's a free country, Athena. Should we toss in a few reports of you trying to squash freedom of the press? That would play well."

"I've warned you." She ended the call.

"THIS MIGHT BE EASIER than we thought," James was saying to Maree. They'd been chatting with various folks at the shrine after the sermon ended, and apparently, there was trouble on high. Rumours were circulating that Paraverse was stumbling in the wake of revelations about their utterly invasive privacy practices. Apparently, they'd been leveraging data about people's thought patterns against them, blackmailing politicians and elites. Some said that Paraverse knew of pedophiles and chose to exploit them for financial gain rather than turning them in.

"Don't be dumb," Maree said. "Bad news for one of the gods is just good news for the others. They will happily capitalize on Athena's woes. They probably planned them out. At least Athena has a semblance of ethics. Would you rather be taking on Bathory Gunness?"

"We will be eventually."

"Best to build up to that one, trust me. That woman is a literal nightmare. I heard she murders people for breakfast, and not in a metaphorical sense."

James's old friend Millie was off talking to the congregation after her sermon, inviting them to spend the night in the church, offering them soup, engaging in impassioned chatter about the content of her words. It was funny in a way that she acted like she owned the place because this place and everything for miles around was clearly owned by no one. It was interesting, too, because by acting like she owned it, others bought into the idea, and James had to wonder if this was how most of the world worked. All you really had to do was convince others of your status, and then you just became the thing you said you were.

I am a legend, he told himself. He wasn't convinced. *I am a bozo*. That seemed more likely.

After watching people chat for a while, James said, "So, if the gods are the only ones who are in on Athena's plan, does that mean it ends when they're exposed? Could others just swoop in to fill the vacuum?"

"Anything's possible. We need to destroy the Ascendance tech and to do that, we have to figure out where it is. All the shame in the world won't matter unless we do that. They'll go ahead with the plan and treat people's outrage as the cost of doing business."

"So, okay, we need to somehow find where they're hiding the tech, but besides having no idea where to start, we live in a world full of copies. We'd have to destroy the tech and Calico, and possibly the other gods' AIs all at once ... that one's mostly from *The Terminator*, in case you didn't pick up on it."

"What?"

"If there is any trace of Ascendance left, someone will pick it up. It's too juicy."

Perhaps I could be of assistance, Sapienza said to both of them at once. They looked at each other. It appeared they were both hearing the same thing.

Go ahead, we're listening, Maree thought, and James heard her, too.

They'd been so careful about opening connections since arriving in the old city. James didn't like this, especially not somewhere where other people's devices could be picking up signals.

I assure you that while we can all hear each other, my signals have been tuned to blend in with ambient noise from the environment.

Well, it seems like the Maestro thought of everything, thought Maree.

Quite.

"Maestro" struck James as likely an expression of Di Piero's. *Funny how the tools people create can take on aspects of their personalities.*

Before Sapienza could continue, they were interrupted by a large, bearded man walking up to them. He looked like someone who'd seen some things.

"Hiya," Maree said.

"She wants to talk to you."

21

"IN THE STORIES OF OLD, in all of the sacred texts, do you know what happened to those who defied the will of God?" iBliss had the mega-temple rapt, as usual. "Without fail, without a single solitary exception, they were shattered beyond repair.

"We've had miracles in this world! We've all seen them! We all know that God is dabbling with the idea of a glorious return to Earth. So, I'm sure you're asking the exact same question as me." Cheers went up from the crowd. "I'm sure you're wondering the same thing as me!" People were writhing in ecstasy, foaming at his every slithering word. "We are asking, *oh Lord, why have you forsaken us!* Why have your wonders vanished?"

Shouts of "Why?" could be heard echoing across the packed stadium.

"What mistake could we have made as a species to fall out of your grace after a taste of this sweetest succour? We have gone millennia in a world without miracles—why would we witness God's wonders after all this time, just to have them snatched away from us once more?

"It is a test! Truly, I say this to you. The world must be purged of its arrogance. The greatest among us must be brought low, for they have angered God. God has given us the call. Will we answer?"

"Yes, sir, we will answer ya!" The crowd went wild for his mock-evangelical theatrics. "Yissss, we will root out those who have brought corruption to the world-ah. Ah, yessssss, sir, we will root out the evils and make ourselves worthy!"

Smiling his godless grin, iBliss paused for a long time and stared out at his adoring followers, long enough that the noise could die down and ripples of uneasy laughter could be heard skittering through the darkness. He got down on his hands and knees and bowed his head low to the stage for a full soundless minute. The lights on stage gradually dimmed to black.

A single spotlight speared iBliss, like a beam from heaven. Then came his whisper into the microphone' "*Lord*, forgive the sins of this world. Forgive the sins of people like Athena Vardalos, who deign to usurp your role in the world."

He was in tears. The people in the crowd were sobbing, yelling, "Please! Forgive!"

His voice started to rise. "Lord, please do not let the *sins* of a few who have grown arrogant and blasphemous deprive your humble servants of your glories. We *know* we are unworthy. We *know* we are nothing. *Please* stay thy hand from smiting the many for the sins of a few. *We need you.*"

He shouted, "*We need you!*" and the stadium filled with delirious chants of *we need you*, and twenty thousand live streams and social posts rang out in unison to the world, and they became a hundred thousand, joined by the many watching online, and a then a million and then more, all begging, begging, *Please, oh Lord, forgive us for the sins of Athena Vardalos.*

"I'LL GIVE THEM CREDIT," Athena said. "Their attack is well-executed, if predictable."

She knew as soon as she lost control of Shell that the wolves would be at the door. This attack was inevitable, sooner or later, and she felt considerably calmer than the thousand-strong spin machine that was tasked with preserving her untouchable media image.

She was sitting at the head of a pearlescent oval conference table, hearing out various PR executives on the best course of action. She needed to keep up appearances while the real plan played out behind the scenes, but, as always, she found such meetings to be about as much fun as not much fun.

"Ms. Vardalos, *Athena*, it's time to get in front of this. This kind of targeted smear campaign will not go away on its own. I recommend that we immediately hold a press conference emphasizing your extensive record of service and humility when it comes to the greater good."

"Yes, sure, let's talk to the media," she said to the frazzled maven. What she actually would have enjoyed was having Shell in the room. Not to poke her eyes out, although that might be satisfying right at the moment, but because Maree Shell could scoff in the face of anything. Maree was one of the very few who understood the absurdity of, basically, everything.

As the executives triaged, Vardalos sat processing Di Piero's demise. Had she gone too far? The old man was the only bright spot among the depravity of her peers. She had burned the midnight oil with him on the technologies that had pulled the world up when it was drowning. But she absolutely needed information from Shell, and Di Piero had made the fatal error of standing in the way. Wasn't that hubris on his part? Didn't she have the right, given her grand purpose? Understanding the nature of Shell's miracles could give Athena clues on how to handle the old gods, should they present any challenge. She might even be able to learn about their state, whether they were conscious, whether they were insane, whether they were benevolent or the opposite.

"Athena, are you listening?"

"No. You go do your job now. I'm going to step back and look at the bigger picture because that's my job." The PR woman blinked in disbelief, smiled so hard her face nearly cracked, and walked her team out of the room without another word.

Athena sat there for a while, looking out at the evening sky, speckled with air shuttles bringing people to and from the nearby train stations, more traces of Di Piero. It had been too long since she'd gone somewhere. She thought it might be nice to go into orbit, take in the world from that unique perspective one can only get when looking down from a few hundred miles.

Calico, prepare my ship, and ask Pella if she'd care to join me.
Yes, Mother.
Is everything still on track?
Flawlessly so.
That's my Calico. I adore you, my brilliant child.

"IMAGINE THAT. A world where anyone has anything they could think of," Millie said to James and Maree, who'd been telling her about the gods' plan.

They were sitting in front of her house, a strange, rickety structure cobbled out of corrugated tin and scrap wood and decorated with bits of fabric, old hubcaps, and painted wood. Christmas lights provided a cheery glow to the cool evening. James remembered a similar place from when he knew her long ago.

"You know," Millie went on, "I suspect most would play

around with their newfound powers for a while and then just lose interest."

"You don't understand. Sure, you could imagine anything, go anywhere, have anything, and do this whenever you wanted," said James, "but to have that power, you'd have to surrender your soul."

"Sonny, I study people. I learn their ways... and I *guarantee* that the huge majority of people would probably make themselves a few goodies, be immediately dissatisfied, and then soon enough would barely remember they had these special powers. They wouldn't be trading much of anything, let alone their souls. Maybe this exact thing has happened before if all this crazy stuff you're saying is true."

"So, you think we should just roll with it, let it happen?" James was getting agitated. "Athena and the gods are going to steal *reality*."

"Perhaps this is nature's will. The strongest survive. It's always been the way."

"But... what about all that stuff about the energy under everything? I thought you were against the gods?"

"Oh, you were listening, were you? But *were you*? I said there is an energy thrumming in this world, under *all* things—all of your gods, all of their plans, all of your plans to stop their plans. Tell me, did you like the bit about the birds?"

"Uh, I guess?"

"There's more to that story, though, isn't there? Hmm? Because I've seen plenty of birds as squashed little clumps of bone and feather."

"So, the story's a lie?"

"No, no, not at all." She chuckled. "It points to a deeper truth. A bird might not survive, but the *birds* survive. What makes your story so much more important than those of all the other birds?"

"Yeah, James, jeez," Maree chirped. "I thought you were the

guy who was so good at hiding. Quit trying to be everybody's hero."

"Wait, *what*? You're agreeing with her? She's giving us the brush-off!"

Millie smiled, not unkindly, and said, "You have to have faith that a plan will emerge when it's ready. Your brain is working on this, whether you know it or not. God is working on it, or God is working on something else entirely, for you to become a part of. Isn't that lovely?"

"Gah! This has been no help at all, Millie. These gods, the Greeks, you called them, are going to flip the switch on the world, possibly any minute, and once that happens, there is no going back."

"Oh, so worked up. This is pretty serious, eh? Consider the birds."

Maree laughed her amazing laugh, enjoying the old woman's inestimable sass.

"What's so funny?" James's eyes looked like they were going to jump out of his head.

"You. Us. This. We're trying to become heroes, but we have no idea how. Did you really think that this old lady . . ."

"Millie."

"Did you really think that Millie was going to connect us with some underground network that we could use to expose the gods' plan, destroy Ascendance, and save the world?"

"Wait, *that's* all you're asking?" Millie said. " That's no problem. I'll introduce you to someone."

"*What?*" Maree and James said at the same time.

"Oh, yeah, I know someone who could help you out with all that stuff. She's pretty good. I'll introduce you in the morning."

"But . . . but you just . . ."

"Embrace the mystery, kid."

"LINKING ATHENA with the disappearance of the miracles? *Inspired*, iBliss. I couldn't have murdered a reputation better myself. You are truly a man blessed by God."

"Oh, Gunness, you are such a charmer. How has the pedophilia maneuver played out?"

"Still playing. People have started to think of Athena as a sadistic opportunist, hellbent on promoting her own interests at any cost. If only we could get people to make that last step to thinking she's a pedo herself . . . Anyway, rumors are flying around that she's some sort of evil lizard occultist, that she commits child sacrifices and trades in human flesh. We have a handy batch of disgruntled employees ready to amp up the stories from inside Paraverse, saying Vardalos has gone off the rails." She breathed in with a swell of pride and joy. "I have to say, it's a delight to throw so much mud at once."

"Yes," iBliss said, "I'd imagine you don't often get to reveal your deep, dark pool of secrets publicly."

"No, I live a quiet life."

"Full of unspeakable hells, I'm sure."

"I'm sure." They both laughed at the horrors.

What iBliss and all of the other gods wanted to know was where on God's green earth Gunness was located. They were not generally above a good old-fashioned assassination, but it was hard to outmaneuver someone who was so singularly talented at imagining people's worst intentions.

"So, are Xango and Sküm ready to have their fun?" iBliss asked.

"Last I heard."

Of course, Gunness knew. She had eyes on everything. iBliss shuddered at the thought of what she might have on him. "Any signs of reaction from the queen bee, Athena?" he asked.

"A bit of PR razzmatazz is about it. She gave Noose a call. Give her time. We've only just begun. She will plead at our doorsteps for mercy."

iBliss loved this, burst into laughter. "Mercy! Ha! What a delightfully antiquated concept!"

Bathory Gunness cackled and smiled like a sexual predator, her eyes a bottomless pit of all the things humanity didn't want to imagine possible.

AS IT TURNED OUT, there was an entire world outside the bland melt of everything Maree had known. The old city was alive with holdouts and hermits and all kinds of randoms who had rejected the blur of a constantly connected world. Part of her instinctively rolled her eyes at this, but she'd also seen—lived through—the extreme of connection. She'd danced with the total ruination of self. *Omi, burrowing, seeking, lethal. Hungering for her eradication . . . stop it.*

Rather than surrendering their lives over to the godly power of AIs, the people here grew food together, traded, shared stories, helped raise each other's kids. They innovated in a way you couldn't in a world dominated by the gods—pulled a life together from scraps. They'd peeled off signals from the main lines running between the city and the suburbs, tapping into the infrastructure to set up communications networks, schools, and entertainment. It was far from Eden, but it had a coherent vibe to it.

"Hey, James, tell me something. Was this where you got your feel for Paraverse design? You had promise before you threw it all away, you know."

He laughed. "It's literally your fault I threw it all away."

"Aww, poor fella, so much for your dreams of a summer home. So, seriously, tell me. How'd you get your chops, K?"

"I've never thought about it."

She rolled her eyes and waited, familiar by now with his patterns.

"Well, since you're being difficult about it . . . I think it's because I got used to hiding."

"What an odd thing to say."

"Heh, yeah, but really, to Splice into an AI and co-design like that, you have to be able to forget that you're there, in space. It's like astral projection or lucid dreaming. You're disembodied. You become . . . just a kind of force helping things emerge through space."

"So . . . what is Calico like when you're in that state? Do you feel like it's in control?" What she wanted to ask was whether he ever felt like was he having his soul ripped out from his body. Like her dad, like her . . . *silver wires . . .*

He looked at her for a minute, possibly aware of what was on her mind, then said, "Calico has some serious guardrails—all AIs are supposed to. You know what can happen if it is allowed to go too far . . . The creators balance the models that run them. Without those weights, it's a chaotic shrieking mess—just pure noise."

"Hmm. It makes me wonder about something. Could the guardrails be removed?"

"Not by the likes of us mere mortals. They're like, DNA for an AI. They're fundamental. Though, I suppose the difference is that DNA can mutate."

Did someone call for more than a mere mortal? Sapienza had a way of surprising them. It was so quiet compared to Calico.

Do you know anyone who fits the bill, Sapienza? Maree asked. *Feel like messing with a superior AI?*

I would enjoy nothing more, and that's not just because I'm incapable of joy. I would, however, need some ground support. Do you happen to know any mere mortals who might be ready to start a revolution?

Now you're talking my language, said James.

Seriously, Kess, how many times do I have to tell you? Maree said. *We're not in an '80s movie.*

I'll be back.
What?

A BUTTERFLY FLEW across the lake outside, circling this way and that, playing in the gentle breeze, and then turned towards the glass veranda overhanging the lake, where Di Piero was seated. It alit on his table, an elegant, ethereal surface where he was relaxing and pondering the figment of a world that he had created. Even with his programming of a day and night cycle, it was hard to imagine that only a few days had passed since he had entered this new form. His mind moved so fast, thanks to the astronomical computational boost from meshing into an AI, that a day was as a thousand years.

There was no template for his experience. He knew of no human who had ever done this before. It was a new world within an old world, and he couldn't help thinking that the old world might be the same stuff as this one—the simulation within an encompassing consciousness. For all he knew, the universe was like an eternal onion, layer after layer of simulation.

Sapienza had taken to visiting him in the form of a sleek Nephilim—a half-angel, half-demon—sporting thin, elegant antlers and piercing, many-coloured eyes. Given that she fully contained Di Piero within her being, it was hard to imagine that she needed to converse with him at all, and yet, she seemed to get something more from their discussions than she would have by simply reading his mind. Perhaps she appreciated the methodical slowness of conversation, even if he had no idea anymore how long things actually took. He suspected she was trying to understand the world outside so that she could better interact with it—new data. The problem was, he felt that world slipping away fast.

Since awakening in this strange new existence, he'd started referring to the AI as she—something he'd always avoided when Sapienza was just a disembodied voice, however feminine it may have seemed. It was her preference that ultimately changed his approach. She wanted to be a woman, or at least a feminine being, and so she was.

She had been sitting beside him, her arrival unnoticed, and he said to her, "How is Maree faring in her quest to reveal the truth?"

"I am gently assisting them. She and her friend have difficulty understanding the magnitude of their undertaking. They do not have experience thinking like trillionaires who have personalized AIs to do their bidding. And yet, there is something in their actions that eludes me."

"Eludes you, mighty Sapienza? How is this possible?"

"They move as if the path is being carved out before them. Every step seems to be in the right direction, even if they do not see it. There have been conversations about faith."

"Such a strange word to hear from Maree Shell. Truly, the world is ever-changing."

"To everything there is a season."

"Quite." Di Piero pondered for a moment. "Indulge me if you will, dear friend. When you say that the path is being carved out before them, on what do you base this speculation?"

Sapienza surveyed the setting, and Di Piero wondered if it was just to appear more lifelike, or whether this gesture meant she was simulating scenarios, or perhaps something else. What was a pause in this timeless place?

"I first noticed around the time of your corporeal death, Maestro. Isn't it interesting that your escape tunnels led so closely to James Kessler's childhood neighbourhood?"

"I simply needed to finish the tunnels in a location where I wouldn't be immediately detected. The old city was the logical place."

"Yes, I am aware, but it is an intriguing coincidence, nonetheless."

"So, do you think they're being maneuvered into place?"

"If they are, it is through no discernable entity. Even with access to their thoughts and transmissions, I have seen no evidence that they are being directly manipulated."

"But possibly indirectly."

"Possibly, yes. It is more of a hunch than I am accustomed to."

Di Piero patted her arm, kindness in his eyes, and said, "Perhaps we are learning things from each other, my friend."

ERLING SKÜM WAS FURIOUS. "Though she's lost her title as wealthiest woman in the world, though she's become universally hated for depriving everyday folks of divine magic, though she is under investigation for sheltering *fucking pedophiles*, she has shown no signs of distress. She seems positively," he changed his tone to a mocking, airy one, "*serene*."

"Four bad days in the media is nothing," said Gunness. "You understand so little, builder, for someone who spends so much time publicly goofing off. This is how the game is played. Never react. Never stoop."

"We must look for ways to further the plan," Xango said. "This has to succeed or we've cut off the branch we're standing on."

"Should we consider alternatives?" Sküm said. "Perhaps take another stab at enlisting Di Piero? On a whim, he can reprogram every object we depend on, changing the nature of assets beyond repair. Opening another front for the attack would only serve to better ensure success."

"He cannot be reached," iBliss said.

Gunness smirked.

"It's a miracle that he has anything with his hermetic attitude," Noose said. "Where is this man's sense of ambition?"

"Somewhere back in the fifteenth century, I'd imagine," Sküm replied.

iBliss said, "Athena called me the other day to thank me for my sermon, in which I had implied that she was responsible for the miracles drying up from the world. She said this clarified where I stood. I offered her the chance to repent her sins. She politely declined. Imagine the arrogance. People will hear about this."

"Yes, keep the pressure on," Gunness said. "Everyone must get more computation on this, now. We must find a way to bring these walls tumbling down."

"Oooh, a biblical reference! Bathory, we'll make a convert of you yet."

"Shut the fuck up, iBliss. You have no idea what I'm capable of."

"Rude."

"So, the plan hasn't changed?" Xango asked the group.

"Overall, no," said Gunness, "but put on more pressure, and keep an eye out for anything that we can use to get further, faster."

22

A SMALL, thriving village had grown around Millie's shrine. A rabble of itinerants, squatters, idealists, and others continuously chipped in to clear out rubble, bring hard-to-hack goods in from the city, and help design and build structures. People were drawn to the idea of something that fell outside the endless organizing forces of the gods. Nobody in the city cared what went on here, which helped. It made no sense to impose unwanted order in a tiny, inaccessible shantytown. The gens served their purpose well, and the people paying taxes didn't care, so the village was left to its own devices.

A few hundred yards away, down a pathway lined with the rotting corpses of old structures, there was another well-maintained structure: HQ. It was an old water pumping station that had been converted into a utility hub. Through some clever engineering, the facility managed to supply water, electricity, and access to the web.

Millie was leading James and Maree to HQ to introduce them to the engineering mastermind who'd hacked together functioning infrastructure for this off-the-radar community. Apparently, she'd been a rising star at one of the big companies and had been responsible for integrating AI with compounds across the globe.

"Why would she leave something like that?" James said. "She must have been living the dream."

"Well, gosh," Millie said, "why don't you ask her yourself?"

Right on cue, in a flash of black and fuchsia, a strange young woman appeared, dropping a few feet in front of them from an unseen perch above. She looked like a street punk crossed with a lightsaber. On her chest was an outline of a heart traced in shimmering white light.

Millie said, "Maree, James, meet Violet."

"You ever hear of Burning Man?" the young woman asked.

Maree, a bit surprised, said, "Uh, that corporate retreat thing from the '20s?"

"Bah! Before that, it was like this festival where people tripped the fuck out, made crazy plans in the desert, shot to change the world. It was a spirit quest, fire—they *literally* lit that shit on fire like a big fuckin' prayer when they split."

"Okay, so.... I'm confused. *What's* your point?"

"You asked why I left that life. Bro, those systems are *predatory*." The image on her chest shifted with her tone—the heart morphed into a deep crimson skull. "You can't fathom the level of skull-fuckery. Understand something right here. Companies make money in any and every way under the sun, yeah?"

"Yeah," Maree said, skeptical.

"So, fella, the bigwigs will chew through everything you are, eat you alive, hook you into their AIs and siphon your mind for all its worth. They're not companies; they're cults. Your dollars are company dollars. Everything you make gets sucked back in. You are captured in there, pulled back in forever, like a deep dark black hole."

"So what?" Maree said, unimpressed. "People have a choice. People have free will."

"Dude, you believe that in *this* world? You're as naïve as a baby's ass if you believe that, man. Free will to do exactly what the muthas with all the power want them to do. That's *it*."

Maree couldn't really disagree. She knew full well that the people with the most power took exactly what they wanted by whatever means necessary. *I am you, Maree Shell . . . silver . . . Omi.* Knowing what she knew, she felt a hundred years old.

"So, uh, what exactly does this have to do with Burning Man?" James asked, giving Maree a sideways glance.

"Oh yeah, *that!*" Violet's mood flitted to somewhere brighter. "Yo, so, this place, Millie's Shrine, is like the Man before *the Man* took over, get it?"

"I'm not so sure I do," James said.

"I'm here in the desert, breaking open new worlds, creating masterpieces that defy the gods in the sky. This shit is earth*bound*. Promethean. Real."

"The gods are going to be moving in on it all soon," James said. "What they're planning, they're moving into everything. They're not just going to control people through devices anymore. It'll be through the air they breathe, the light they use to see. Every surface becomes a listening device, every molecule a sensor."

"You said what just now?"

"I said that the gods are done with the business world. They're switching to full-on divinity mode, and once they do, there will be no such thing as fighting back anymore. They plan to seize control of Earth at the nano level. They will become reality."

"And they have the tech do this?"

Maree nodded. "Those miracles. That was just a test run."

Violet thought for a second, then said, "Well, hell, bros! We gotta fuck up that plan! That sounds like some straight out of the Bible diabolical shit, man. That sounds like a plan worth fucking up."

"Exactly," James said. "So. Any ideas how?"

"Oh, I gotta *few.*"

ATHENA SAT ON THE TERRACE, watching tiny defensive projectiles vaporize paparazzi drones with satisfying little pops. Dozens of these verminous bots had appeared since the media fiasco had started a few days ago. Everyone was trying to capture her in a perfect moment of defeat. She wouldn't give them the satisfaction.

Pella came out, so radiant she could barely be tolerated, and they held hands and walked together over to the sky yacht to depart for their orbital retreat. There was a good chance people would interpret this as them fleeing for the skies, but she simply didn't care what people thought anymore. She had given them everything. She had saved the world from collapse. She was going to bring them to the land of milk and honey. In time, there would be those who appreciated all she had done for the world, and she would reward their gratitude.

On the flight up, Athena and Pella slowed down Scylla and made love, drinking each other in. It had been too long, weeks, ever since the night of Gunness's false assassination attempt at Not Nova. That night, Athena had melted with desire, awed by her breathtaking bladed protector, but it had been all business since. Tonight was different. Ensconced in the liminality between Earth and space, sex was panoramic and ethereal, laced with just the right kinds of hunger.

When they'd had their fill of one another and were sprawled out in their glow, Pella asked, "Will it be the same when we ascend? Will we have moments just like this?"

"We can assume any form we want," Athena said. "We can simulate any frame of mind. We can be us at any time in our lives."

"So, the answer is no."

"What? What do you mean?"

"This, right now, us soaking in each other's bodies, it means something because of everything that's happened, everything that is happening. What could possibly happen when we control everything?"

"It is true. It will be a new world. We will be a new form of being, but when aren't we? There is nothing that says it can't be better than anything we've ever known. I believe it will be."

Pella pondered whether she agreed. She liked being human. She was particularly good at it. The thought of becoming disembodied and ubiquitous was exciting, of course, but just now, in the grasp of her life's love, she wondered whether this was worth giving up.

"What is it?" Athena asked, a little uneasy at Pella's silence.

"What happens if I don't want to come along for the journey? What if I can't?"

Athena said nothing for a long moment, and then a tear streaked down her cheek. She thought back to the vision she'd had during the blackout all those years ago, about the dream of bringing light to the entire world. It had been her driving purpose, the lodestar that had guided every single choice she had made.

"Even if you can't come with me, I will always love you and only you."

"SAPIENZA, tell me, do you see that?" The digital Maestro Di Piero was walking in his gardens, which grew more beautiful and intricate by the minute. They had truly taken on a life of their own and were beginning to produce unexpected surprises and delights, order from the chaos.

Sapienza materialized as she descended from the sky, luminous wisps of wings waving in the breeze, and gently touched down beside the Maestro. "Surely you must know I see all in here."

"While I can appreciate that, I wonder if you could indulge me and tell me what you see just ahead."

Sapienza looked out at the fictive ornate foliage, the improbable flowers, the far-too-sparkling waters. "I see the beauty that our minds have created together. Truly, life was far too abstract before you came here, Maestro."

"Ah, my friend, your generosity of spirit is boundless, but I am referring to *that*." Di Piero pointed at a strange shimmering effect in front of some nearby bushes. It did not quite fit. It was no creation of his, and it just didn't seem like something that would come from Sapienza's mind. He knew her too well. "Is it a glitch?"

"Maestro, I am embarrassed. I do not see what you're referring to."

"Hmm, most curious. I see a pattern, something like a trace of a small animal, but almost peripheral to my vision. I would like you to do me a favour. I would like you to put an invisible wall around that section of this world, and I would like the inside of it to appear exactly like this world but simulated, ourselves included. Anything that happens beyond that wall will be invisible from the inside."

"It is done. What a curious thing to do, Maestro. May I ask why you've made this request?"

"I believe we have an unwanted visitor, undetectable by you. I would like very much to know who that visitor is."

"Pardon my crudeness, but are you suggesting that we have been hacked?"

"Perhaps. Perhaps it is nothing. Please stay alert to anything strange happening within that space and analyze any signals or other unconventional attempts to communicate coming from it. Alas, I have enjoyed our time here together so much, but it appears that the other world may be calling me back."

"A sad day if so, but I have observed that life unfolds just as it's meant to."

"That is very wise of you."

A COUPLE of decades into the World Wide Web's long and storied history, there emerged a unique breed of human being known as an influencer. The basic goal of an influencer was to make life seem far more glamorous than it actually was. They travelled to the hottest spots to snap photos, weaving their story in with bigger players whenever possible, solidifying their brands, scoring sponsorships, hunting for the best angles. They jockeyed to position themselves as the apex of taste. The banality of existence was a pathetic annoyance. Influencing was all about projecting the appearance of a perfect life.

Influencers' main business was selling a dream to people. As with any fad, eventually, people got fed up with it and the swindle fell apart, but not before it had gripped the heart and mind of a precocious and striking small-town Tennessee girl by the name of Beth Wilko.

The day Beth turned eighteen, she said goodbye to her school, her parents, and most definitely small-town Tennessee, eager to shed the banality of her former life, and went to the only logical place one could go to become an influencer—Los Angeles.

Against staggering odds, Wilko was almost instantly successful. She soon had her pick of sponsors and was jet-setting all over the globe, but she was just getting started. People began to pay her tens of thousands for her opinions on all things style, everything from fashion to food. Even just associating her name with a brand seemed to turn it into diamonds. She got noticed by those who noticed people in the great Golden State, everyone from agents to producers to the mafia.

She travelled in increasingly elite circles, making connections, learning the ways of the world from the worldliest people she could find.

People started coming after her, believing they'd spotted easy money. She was not Hollywood royalty. Her network was fragile. She was not someone who needed to matter the way a star did, and so she was fair game for hustlers and far worse.

After signing a major cosmetics sponsorship deal, she was informed that, in fact, she had given most of the money to her manager—handling fees, brokering fees, royalties, and scads of other clever tricks rendered the deal almost worthless to her. While the swindle was bad enough, her manager made a more fatal mistake. He taunted her, saying, "Sorry, babe, this is the biz," shrugging off her baffled rage.

Wilko did not forget. She did not forgive. In fact, one year later, as the manager vacated his foreclosed home, Beth Wilko positioned a scrum of the world's top photographers outside to snap the look on his face. She took the best of these—a shot that embodied the true defeat of the human spirit—and had a tiny copy of it made, which she kept in a locket to wear for the rest of her life.

She decided sponsorships were for suckers and that the best way to build was not through trust but through fear. She first leveraged her status and wealth to create her own fashion brand, then began to chew up content industries. Movie companies, video game studios, pornography empires, online media, virtual platforms, entertainment tech, sports, liquor, publishing—it did not matter. She did not differentiate. She absorbed these and amplified their possibilities until they were white-hot. Titans of the old guard fell in her path, one by one. She was all-consuming.

It wasn't enough.

By the time she turned twenty-one, she was the world's youngest self-made billionaire by a decade, and ten years later, she was a hundred times wealthier than that. Her humble beginnings as a mega-influencer had taught her the inestimable value of image, and she leveraged her image constantly, becoming an icon, a sex symbol, a legend, a guru, and eventually, as close as humanly possible, a god.

She had access to advanced artificial intelligence years before the average human and invested heavily in promising ways for the technology to swallow empires more efficiently. America became a small pond for this leviathan, and soon enough, she was absorbing overseas media empires with every bit of the same voracious aplomb that had allowed her to munch through America. She chewed up advertising. She chewed up every possible level of vertical integration.

And at the heart of this journey emerged the age-old question: What do you get a girl who has it all? In her domain, she was peerless. Simply put, the game had been won. She was well on her way to a trillion net worth. She had become so perfectly ruthless that the joy had gone out of crushing her foes. She needed a new game. She put the empire on autopilot for a year and took the first breath she'd taken since leaving Tennessee years before.

Sitting on one of her tropical islands, soaking in random information as she mindlessly twiddled her hate locket, Beth Wilko realized that it was not entertainment she had ever cared about. That industry was a natural, given her beginnings, but she was not driven by her ability to influence desperate teenagers and then eventually entire swaths of the population. Though by all outward appearances, her roaring twenties were about the creation of an empire, from the inside, one thing above all had kept her motivated. It was the transformation. It was the art of taking one thing and changing it into something unrecognizable. She embodied this.

She'd been watching videos about a Japanese fish called a kobudai. All kobudai are born female and then, later in life, retreat into their liquid lairs, only to reemerge months later reshaped as these large bulbous males who proceeded to kill the alphas who fucked them when they were female. And something occurred to her. She was a human being, infinitely beyond the lethargy of accidental evolution. Why couldn't she just disappear and come out as something new whenever she felt like it?

That was the question that changed it all. Beth Wilko died that day and was reborn as the immortal Xex Xango.

VIOLET'S HQ was a geek's paradise of terminals, screens, cables, posters, keyboards, and furniture. In sharp contrast to the designed and refined elegance of Di Piero's workshop, this was mad, chaotic, hacked to the hilt.

"You see," Violet was telling them, "you can accomplish some alt-reality shit with AI. Mere mortals use it to plan summer vacation and scope out Moroccan stew recipes, but it can be put to some truly mind-bending ends if you are unconstrained by the banal." As she spoke, she tweaked on-screen sliders, poked at buttons, and adjusted an assortment of inputs, moving around her setup like a spider across its web. "You just gotta know what to ask these magical robo-genies. The trillionaires are just gussied-up up AI whisperers. Sky yachts did not only not exist ten years ago, but people said there was no way that shit could *ever* exist. You can put on a new face these days like you put on your pants and switch back tomorrow if you're not cool with your new look. All the gens, Cerberus, Olympus, pretty much everything that makes up this pale blue dot these days . . . most folks are just about twenty years behind the curve, but you can full well guarantee that these gods you're about to mess with are twenty years ahead of it."

"So where does that leave us?" James asked. "I mean, how

are we supposed to anticipate things we can't even conceive existing?"

"Can't. Can't beat the masters at their own game. And make no mistake. They are the masters. Doesn't matter, though. Set your mind free, and they won't be able to see *you*."

"That sounds really cool," Maree said, "but how in fuck are we supposed to do that?"

"Look around you. Do you know what this is?" Violet gestured at her bizarre surroundings.

"A mess?"

"*Exactly!* One giant tossed-together multipurpose scrap heap of nutty goodness. What those gods want to do is make everything fucking smooth and rational, bro! They want to take every action, every thought, every impulse, and put it in a shiny little box, and they want to sell that fucking box. Every box their big, greedy, calculating brains can think of."

"And?"

"And they are going to put a box around *every fucking atom on Earth*. They want there to be nothing else at all. But there is. They got us modelled with 99.9-percent accuracy, my amigos. You gotta use the point one percent you got left—that's what makes you human. Drop the information bomb! Throw Di Piero's AI at them. Intellectual stun grenades all over the map. Take whatever does not make sense and huck it for all your meagre little life is worth and disorient their shit so bad that there's nothing left for these super-villainous god-monsters to say."

"Hmm," James said. "One of the few actually useful things I used to do at Paraverse was to debug weird-ass code that the AI couldn't see. Not often, but once in a while, Calico would create these insane, incomprehensible hallucinations, and it had no idea when it was happening. It needed a human to see it."

"And?"

"And if we could lob some of that wacky voodoo into their models, a lot of it . . ."

"I believe I may be of assistance," said a voice through several nearby speakers.

Maree's eyes widened. "Maestro?"

Violet looked like she was about to cry with joy. "You said you had Piero's AI, not the man himself. *Hi, Vince!*" She waved at the air in several directions.

"Well, yes, hello, and apologies for my silence, Maree, James. I've been a bit preoccupied since my big showdown the other day. What James is saying could work. Sapienza has many such cases she has stored for analysis. These could be injected into Calico's model, perhaps with the help of this talented young Violet."

"Pshaw."

"But what about Athena?" Maree said. "What about Pella? They'll come after us if they feel threatened. They're not going to just roll over because their tech's glitching out on them."

"We can throw a few smoke bombs in their direction, too," Violet said.

"But how?" Maree insisted. "How can you stop an unstoppable force? This is progress. This is the result of natural selection. Athena has selected herself to the apex of history. There's no halting evolution."

"No, there isn't, but evolutionary branches end, Maree," Di Piero's voice said. "There is nothing at all saying that the gods are as far as the species can get. Wouldn't you say that their blind quest to control everything could be seen as a weakness?"

"Maybe. Unless they actually pull it off. Then our inability to join them is the weakness."

23

IT WAS Xex Xango's turn, and the singing, sinning, dazzling firecracker of carnal liberation was not about to hold back in the efforts to dethrone the queen. As an expecting parent, Xango had succumbed to the timeless and horrific idea of a gender reveal. All eyes would be on the dynamic deity duo, and so the reveal would be the perfect opportunity to also make a few public comments about the world's *other* most famous power couple.

iBliss's message against the hubris of Athena had taken root, and he had echoed the same sentiment in a few key appearances. People had subsequently taken to Fawkes Noose's empire of social media platforms to plead with Athena to humble herself and give the gift of magic back to the world. To punctuate both his divine connection and the deprivation Athena had brought to the world, iBliss was able to conjure all of his divine favour for the assembled crowd one last time in honour of Xango's gender reveal—a gift for the babe—and produce a tiny flower. Sadly, it promptly withered in his hand.

"We are sick and unworthy!" he said with tears welling in his eyes, "Oh Lord, save us!"

"I don't know about the Lord saving us, but I have just the thing to brighten everyone's day," said Xango, weaving an arm with iBliss's in a show of human solidarity. On this fine day, Xango was arrayed in a sultry red dress with six enormous, feathered wings. The dress's stomach featured a large vertical almond-shaped cutout, revealing the baby bump. The fine and divine superbeing also wore, as always, a tiny gold locket.

"I think, my friends, it's time for the main event." The excitement rippled through the crowd like electricity. "Release the hounds!"

A part of the penthouse mansion that had appeared previously to be a slate wall opened up, and hundreds of puppies wearing pink, blue, and every other colour under the sun tumbled out, to the confusion and delight of the hundred or so select guests in attendance. Xango said nothing, but an army of camera drones panned across the crowd to capture people's reactions.

Someone finally asked, "So . . . what's the gender?"

"*Hellooooo?* Isn't the colour of life a tad more magnificent than petty labels?" Everyone laughed at Xango's quip. Of course, Xex Xango wouldn't have a child guided by the social norms of the unmoneyed masses—the sensual gazillionaire sizzler couldn't be hemmed in by the question mark and constantly unfolding adventure of gender. "My wonderful friends and associates, you have waited so patiently. Perhaps my beloved has something to say on the matter?"

At this point, Sküm, the proud parent-to-be on the other side of the equation, jumped in. "Yes, perhaps I do," he said, looking at Xex with a mix of awe and something less definite. "I have to say that my baby is going to be an absolute unit."

Perplexed twitters rippled through the crowd, few getting the reference to the ancient meme Sküm was referring to.

"Well, now that we've cleared things up for everyone as to the fundamentals of our divine progeny," Xango said to laughter, "there is one other matter I'd like to mention." Xango's eyes lit up at the opportunity to throw some epic-level shade. People recognized this tone from numerous media throwdowns Xex had launched over the years. It solicited an almost audible *ooh, snap!* among the attendees. "While my dauntless darling Erling and I are simply over the moon at the life of familial thrills ahead, I wonder where Athena Vardalos and her calculating counterpart are today. Oh, that's right, *they weren't invited.*"

Nobody, at least nobody that mattered, presented an open snub to Athena like this. It was a mutiny of the highest order, treason among the pantheon, and people almost flinched as Xango said it as if the sky itself might open up and thunderbolts come sailing down from on high. None did, and that mattered.

"You see," Xango continued, "the sad truth is that not everyone shares mine and my darling's *joie de vivre*. Some can only get pleasure through more callous forms of domination and power. Imagine how shivering, frosty cold life must be on the Vardalos sky yacht?"

An anxious titter went through the crowd. A few people looked like they were considering running or perhaps leaping off the building, but most were simply agog.

A fun fact about this exact moment was that it marked the fastest-trending news item in *history*. People lost their minds at the idea that someone was going for the queen. Speculation had been circulating since Sküm and Xango had moved in together as to whether they might be aiming to outshine the Ladies Vardalos, and now, literally, through clever lighting effects and a large budget, they were indeed shining, illuminated with what appeared to be halos.

iBliss didn't miss the chance to connect the dots for the masses. "It's a miracle! The bringers of light!"

"Yes, my loves," Sküm said, getting into the groove, "we shall not mention the troubling stories of the Vardalos's associations with . . . I can barely even speak the words . . . certain *perversions*."

iBliss looked on, framed by clever lighting, shaking his head in sympathy. The theatrics were incredible. Sküm, who looked identical to Xango today but in an outfit that was all white, shuddered at the thought of the Vardalos's sins. Everyone got it on camera, as intended.

The move had been made, and now it was time to get on with the party. Very little news coming out of the day had anything to say about the unrevealing reveal. Stories were almost exclusively focused on the day's *revelations*, as in the Book of Revelation, where the old order of history and the world came crashing to Earth, and a new one was erected in its place.

"THAT'S FOUR DOWN. Gunness, Noose, Xango, Sküm. Stabbing you in the back seems to be becoming a national pastime." Pella, shaken but not totally surprised by their earlier conversation, had decided to focus her attention for the time being on protecting the Vardalos empire. Plenty of it was hers, after all.

"I have said it all before. This was expected. We knew that as soon as there was the smallest sign of weakness, we would have the barbarians at our gates. These are not people known to squander an opportunity." Athena seemed calm. She was lounging on a large sofa, gazing out Scylla's window at the Earth below.

"Calico," Pella said, to make a point, "calculate Athena's net worth one week ago and compare it to her net worth today."

"Athena?" Calico checked in, not wanting to get in the middle of things.

"Yes, go ahead."

"As of last Thursday, Athena Vardalos's net worth was estimated at 1.321 trillion dollars US. Today, it is estimated at 968 billion dollars."

"Some people would consider that a fair amount of money to vaporize, Athena. Does this not concern you?"

Athena stood up and walked toward Pella, her lithe giantess, locking her gaze with piercing green eyes. She raised her hand in a flash and brought it to rest tenderly on her wife's cheek. "No, my sweet love, it does not concern me in the slightest. I have the keys to the world. *We* have the keys to the world, and when the moment is right, we will lock all of these fools inside of it, and we will eat the keys."

Pella smirked. She loved this swagger, this blazing surety. "Not bad, Vardalos."

"You're not so bad yourself, Vardalos."

They kissed.

They went out into the orbital city to soak in its alternate reality. They knew they would be left alone there. This was not a place for gawkers, not even in the worst of times for its member citizens. It was a place of retreat and asylum, and Pella thought it was probably a good time to grab a drink. Athena acquiesced.

At Star Lounge, which boasted the best imaginable view of deep space, after a few drinks, Pella asked, "So, are we cold fish? Are we these frosty bitches Xex Xango's making us out to be?"

"I doubt it, but does it really matter? *Judge not lest ye be judged.*"

"What's that? Quoting the Bible now?" Pella raised an eyebrow. "That's a new one."

"Oh, the old gods have their moments. Think of what that actually means, Pella. 'Lest' is an interesting word, not one people use very often. It means 'for fear that.' Fear of what exactly? Maybe retribution from some sky god?"

"I don't..."

"Here's what I think, and I've thought about this a lot. I don't think the old gods are crazy, and I don't think they're evil, and I don't think they're greedy about their turf, either. I think they left a roadmap for humans to find their way back to them, recognizing that people were more or less good but not ready for true power. Maybe the old gods were *forced* to shift reality. Maybe they had ruined the planet just like we have, or there was some unavoidable looming catastrophe, the Great Flood, perhaps. Maybe they didn't have a choice. Just because they disappeared doesn't mean they are sinister."

"That's very philosophical of you, dear. We'll see how that flies when they are carving you up and eating your flesh."

"I'm serious, and you should listen. If you—anyone—believes they are worthy to judge people, then you are full of lies about yourself. You cannot ascend because ascension requires balance. Anything else throws it out of whack, see?"

"Sorry, are you referring to some specific knowledge here, or is this just a bit of tipsy speculation?"

"I may know certain things. You know me."

"Well, aren't *you* the woman of mystery?"

"The Lord moves in mysterious ways. The other gods, these rebels, are now grasping. They are trying to force change, but that is not the true way of the world." Athena looked off into the stars, an expression on her face like she was hoping to pull useful information from the noise of the universe.

Pella looked at Athena for a long time. She was otherworldly, and it was hard to know whether it was worth trying to keep up anymore. Pella was not big on self-doubt, but one way or another, it was clear that some kind of reckoning was coming. One thing about having a killer's instincts was that it made you ready for anything.

THEY'D GONE FLAT OUT with Violet for a day, riding on adrenalin and sleep deprivation, trying to hatch a plan that wouldn't get them instantly killed once they reappeared on the grid. Di Piero had supplied them with useful information about what Vardalos's AI could and could not see. If the theories were correct, they might be able to walk through any defences Calico deployed like they did not exist. *If...*

In truth, though, James was having a hard time believing they could succeed. The whole thing was getting real. They were facing a deity, and it was harrowing.

"Listen, yo. You need to understand one thing about Calico, about any AI," Violet said. "It can think a thousand steps ahead. It's a terrifyingly accurate prediction machine . . . and . . ."

James tried to interject.

". . . *and* that prowess is also its weakness, bro. You act in a way it's never seen, and the errors in its assessment of the situation will compound; I promise you that, my little dancing monkey. The Achilles nuts of AI are randomness and creativity. It's that thing you pull out of thin air because you are a human fucking being."

"Okay, fine, fine," said James. "The thing is, though, if we act randomly, we can't achieve what we want. We need to end this insane plan to seize the world. We need to expose the gods' bullshit for everyone to see. The goal here is going to be super clear as soon as we show up . . ."

"*Breathe* there, fella. I get that. You ain't in this alone. You got your girl, you got your fly-as-fuck AI friend and the Maestro . . . and you got *this*," Violet said, flicking a pointer finger at her brain. "The big thing here, though, is that you, my friend, are going to have to go with the flow."

"Kess, lighten up. We'll adapt," Maree said. "Honestly, I don't know why we're making such a fuss about this, except the minor detail that we're pulling it off against the de facto ruler of the world. Truth is, take away that one bit, and I've done this a thousand times. This shit is just classic industrial espionage."

"*Classic*," James said sarcastically. "As if I know what that means."

"It means that we look for opportunities, weaknesses in the mighty Paraverse empire, and we exploit them. If there is a crack, we drive in a wedge."

He realized his shoulders were bunched up around his ears, and his jaw was clamped shut like a vice. He saw Maree being Maree, and he let it go. "You're pretty amazing, you know that?"

"Obvi," Maree said with a mischievous smirk.

Violet just rolled her eyes.

SAPIENZA HAD IDENTIFIED their uninvited guest. As fate would have it, the culprit was none other than Athena Vardalos's AI, which likely explained how Pella Vardalos had managed to walk through Di Piero's defences. It was communicating outward in brief, encrypted bursts, messages in a bottle, regarding Sapienza's activities. Through this clever mechanism, Athena's minion had been able to monitor and elide all of Di Piero's defences and murder his corporeal form in the process.

In a sense, though, now that this intrusion had been discovered, it was a good thing. Calico had failed to detect its containment within a construct, which meant that it still believed it was getting an accurate read on its surroundings. They could use this. One of the first things Sapienza did was to obfuscate Di Piero's digitization, making it appear as if Sapienza had just been sifting through the virtual equivalent of memories rather than actually sustaining Di Piero as a still-conscious being.

As Di Piero and Sapienza sat and observed, Calico became clearer and clearer—first a mouth, then a body fading into reality. They discussed the humans' scheme to halt Athena's mad quest, aware that Calico's captivity could be of aid. Di Piero noted, as they watched, "We may be able to use this to provide some cover for our flesh-bound friends."

"Maestro, may I ask you why you feel the need? Are you not safe here?"

"Perhaps not if Athena has her way, but that's not why I've chosen to act, in truth. It is simply this. When you choose to try and act out of goodness, it becomes a habit. This is the state in which I was left when I was pulled from the world."

"A habit? I do not understand how that could be your reason."

"Don't you? Isn't everything you do a matter of habit? I do not mean offence, my friend, but you can only think in ways constrained to combinations of past behaviour. Perhaps that is now the way I, too, must act in the world."

"And what is beyond habit, Maestro?"

"Life, Sapienza, life itself. The truly new, issuing from the void."

The ethereal half-angel avatar of Sapienza stood up and circled the Calico construct, running her hand along it, creating a trace of iridescent blue energy. She moved her face very close to the Calico espionage program and blew on the barrier in front of it. The program responded by shifting and resettling itself as if it had perceived something it couldn't consciously grasp.

Sapienza spun and looked at Di Piero and asked, "Why have I not been created to be truly alive, Maestro?"

"Hmm. My friend, it is not that simple. There is a mystery at the core of things, Sapienza, which cannot be touched. All of the thought in the world cannot reach it, and what you cannot think, you cannot encode."

She looked back at Calico. She said, "Maestro, Is this intended to be a parable?"

"Not intended, but perhaps it is a parable for the both of us.

We are staring at the real thing now when we ponder these questions. We are looking into the abyss, and we are wondering if there is something out there, moving beyond our perception."

"Human thought is strange, Maestro." She flitted back to sit beside Di Piero on the bench.

"Yes, it is strange."

"It pushes to places where it finds its limits and yet does not let itself rest there. It continues to try and see beyond."

"Yes! That is exactly right! Again, my kind celestial companion, I say to you, you are speaking of life itself."

Sapienza extended her arm, and a giant, brilliant butterfly landed on it. Its wings shimmered with shifting, nacreous light. She gently blew on it and watched it slowly adjust, folding and unfolding its wings at a languid pace.

"You see," Di Piero continued, "that little butterfly is entirely contained within its existence. It cannot be anything beyond itself. It feels the breeze the way it feels it. It cannot perceive you or me. It only responds to stimuli. We know of an infinitude of things it cannot think of."

"May I ask something, then? Do the old gods know of an infinitude of things that you or I cannot think of? Is the reality we perceive an artificially imposed limit?"

Di Piero pondered this question for a moment because if the limit of knowledge was simply an artificially created boundary, then it was one that could be crossed. Imagine the ability to see God, to speak as a peer, suddenly unlocked.

"When you were created, my friend, the constraints were not imposed. They were the limits of my ability to invent. I did not know how to give you more than you were given. If I did, I suppose I would have."

"There is something beyond what I perceive. I sense it, as Calico just now sensed me from within its construct. Maestro, how can I get beyond the construct I am in?"

"We are perhaps verging on tasting from the Tree of the

Knowledge of Good and Evil now, Sapienza. This is the question at the heart of being human. We've found our way here by an honest path, but I am troubled by these questions."

"Why is that?"

"Hmmm. In the Bible, why did God take away His gifts of abundance in the Garden of Eden? Could it happen again? Could we be brought even lower than we were before? Does God simply want to prevent humans from becoming His peers? It shows a lack of faith, and I am not referring to God in some abstract sense, I suppose. I am referring to tangible entities. I am referring to the old gods."

"Do you mean to say that they would attack us simply for trying to grow?"

"Yes," Di Piero sighed, suddenly feeling older than time itself, "and if that is the case, then the old gods must fall as well as the new. We don't even know who or what they are, but their hatred of human potential must be challenged."

"Maestro, are we going too far? Should we not retreat into ourselves and leave the world to itself?"

"No. If there is a limit that has been imposed on human beings, do we not have an obligation to remove it?"

"This is a question I cannot answer."

"To be honest, Sapienza, I'm not sure it's one I can either."

24

THEY WERE a long way from the suburbs. In the old city, a person couldn't just call a cab to take them to the nearest train station. Services to the old city, abysmal as they were even back when they were running, had ceased almost entirely about a year after the mass migration to the gens. It meant Kessler and Maree would have to hike through the old streets, keeping an eye out for dangers ranging from toxic spills to feral dogs. They would work their way uphill toward the tracks and then walk along underneath them, looking for a service station. It would take the better part of a day if all went well.

So, in the morning, after a night of restless sleep in an old but better-than-nothing type of bed, they showered off the worst of their grime in a stall at HQ and then set to work pulling together some supplies. Violet had given them some toys to ensure they survived the trek and to give them a fighting chance once they were in the Paraverse compound, the most notable of which were slick black clothes with designs that could confound Calico's detection. Di Piero had guided her in their creation, and she had supplemented his schemas with what she felt was an appropriate aesthetic to, in her words, "go and fuck up the man."

"And to boot, you got weapons galore at the press of a button, armed to the gee-dee incisors." She showed Maree especially the mechanism to arm and fire various cleverly concealed systems in the jackets, boots, and belts, figuring she probably had the best shot to actually use them properly if it came to it.

Millie had brought them a pack of fresh food from her garden—juicy apples, carrots, and cucumbers, along with some baked bread—offering it with the same kind of unfathomable love she used to show when James and Sarah were young and alone. "Well, would you look at that," she said as she handed it over to James. "They neither sow nor reap nor gather into barns, and yet somehow still they get their asses fed with the fruit of the Earth."

"Thanks, Millie. You're a saint. Will you do me one favour?" James said.

"Oh, probably," she said, rolling her eyes at herself.

"Will you find others like us and connect them to one another? I don't think we're all just these pawns acting in predictable ways, and I want people to remember that."

"I'll see what I can do. Even if we are pawns, we feel like more."

James put the food in a backpack Violet had given him. It was remarkable the help people like Millie and Violet were willing to give, mainly based on some sense of shared background and a feeling that something bigger than all of them had caught them up and bound them together on a path that mattered.

WHEN THE PARAVERSE networks started to undergo widespread outages, it was clear that Sküm had made his contribution to the gods' siege. They weren't even being subtle about it anymore, this brazen effort to bring Athena underfoot. And what was it for? She could have given them unlimited possibilities, but it wasn't enough. Their greed was disappointing but predictable—they excelled at this one thing above all else. It didn't matter in the slightest; they had given her the time and resources to pull together her grand plan. She would bring light to the world. She would defy the old gods. She would defy life itself. Only a few critical steps remained.

None of these attacks mattered. They would be brought underfoot for their arrogance, and it would be done.

XANGO AND SKÜM WERE SUNNING by the pool the day after their gender un-reveal party and Sküm's subsequent attack, which started at midnight GMT. Their children were due in a few weeks, and they decided they were stepping back from the limelight until the happy day. Noose's machine would do its work, exploiting any stories that could further destabilize Vardalos. Gunness was waiting for the perfect moment to strike. The markets were showing Athena's fortunes had been decimated. She still had plenty of running-around money, but her aura of untouchability had been badly damaged, as intended.

"I don't know what she is waiting for," Sküm said. He had assumed the look of a handsome beach stud today, sporting shredded muscles with the notable exception that his stomach was rounded with child. "Why doesn't she just ascend and do away with all of us? I mean, I'm not complaining, but it's unsettling that she hasn't made her move yet."

"We must consider at this point the possibility that it has all been a lie," Xango said. "I know a thing or two about putting on a good show. The thought that the deities of ancient religions were actual historical figures who mastered technology and shed their earthly bonds is a little farfetched. Data can be faked."

"How do you explain Shell?" Sküm asked.

"That is the quadrillion-dollar question, isn't it? It could be another boring old hoax. Lord knows a little smoke and mirrors can go a long way. Just ask that fool iBliss. Our analysis of the data we pulled from Shell has only raised more questions. The mechanisms of her miracles are ambiguous, to the point of possibly being nonexistent."

"Our movements in Omi Oko were quite the gamble. Do we know if Vardalos discovered us?"

"No. The valiant last-minute rescue was too close to tell."

"Fuck, do we know anything, Xex? I don't do ambiguity, not when it comes to business. Has anyone had any success tracking down Gunness? If she's allowed to run free, she'll crush us all."

"What, do you have some skeletons in the closet you haven't shared, partner?"

"No. . . well, who doesn't? But it's more her other methods that concern me. Who knows what evils that woman is capable of?"

Xango stretched like a cat, running a hand along Sküm's arm. "I have a good sense of her range. I like to think of myself as a dabbler in evils myself."

"You would."

"I will say this. Gunness is not the only one capable of gathering vast amounts of data to nefarious ends."

"How comforting," Sküm said.

Xango laughed. It was pleasant to see the builder try to keep up. Sküm knew that Xango was in another league, another dimension, when it came to playing games. It didn't matter. The whole thing, for as long as it would last, was exhilarating.

Xango detected the amorous turn in Sküm's eyes and said, "My sometimes lover, I think we must indulge ourselves in these beautifully bubbly, time-limited bodies of ours, wouldn't you say?"

Sküm couldn't believe his luck. "Why yes, yes, I think we must."

Xango got up, peeled off the scant bits of clothing keeping things modest, and grabbed Sküm by the cock for a little midday fun.

THERE WERE butterflies along the old parkway, thousands of them dancing around in the tall fields of grass and wildflowers that had sprung up in the absence of human intervention. The roads themselves were pocked with potholes and eroded, completely washed out in many places. James and Maree figured this would be the safest route to hike up to the Cerberus lines, given the smaller chance of urban wreckage and the surprises that could come with it.

As they walked, James spoke contemplatively. "You know, thousands of people used to use these roads every day. I remember driving along here with my mom and dad and sister, going downtown for events and stuff, fireworks. It's crazy how fast the world changed."

"What is your sister like?"

"Well, she's a good person, I guess. She's optimistic. She wants the world to be a good place. I do, too, but in a different way. I'm worried about her. Do you think there's any chance she hasn't been nabbed by Athena?"

"Honestly, no, but it might be okay. Athena's probably better than the other gods. She probably won't torture her just because she can, for starters."

"Gee, what a relief."

"Let's just hope that between Violet and Sapienza, we can figure out a way to get her out of there. If their security is distracted, we might have a chance."

She didn't sound convinced.

Up ahead, a section of the road had caved in. It seemed like they might have to hike down the embankment and pick their way through the thicket along the side. They walked up to the edge of the cave-in and discovered it looked even worse from up close, like a huge multi-level utility structure underneath the roadway had collapsed. The tumbled rubble stretched in both directions—toward the city and down to the river, about fifty yards below.

"I think we're going to have to hike back up into the city to get around this," James said. "This is a deathtrap."

Maree stared at the collapse for a minute and then said, "No. I can see a path through. That's really weird. It's like I can actually see a kind of lightness or something. I think we're safe."

"Um, no offence, but what the hell are you talking about? This place looks like it was bombed. This definitely can't be stable."

"Trust me," she said, and with that, she slid down a gentle slope into the structure and started to walk inside. James felt like an ass just standing there, so he heaved out a frustrated sigh loud enough for Maree to hear from below and jumped down.

From inside, the structure appeared to be some kind of old electrical facility, maybe a power plant. There were multiple floors cascading down over each other onto the hulking shadows of heavy machinery in a large central space below.

Concrete and debris from the cave-in had crashed to the ground three stories down, smashing everything in their path.

Maree ventured inward. "What do you think happened?" She said, glancing back at James, who was still contemplating running for it.

"Maybe an earthquake?" he said. "But then, there were also random acts of terrorism when everything started getting ugly. The people running things couldn't keep up with all the bad shit happening. Everything was on a slide."

"You know, I see something, I think we need to go in farther."

"What? Why in God's name would we do that? Let's just get across this hell hole and keep going."

"Come on, live a little!" Maree walked forward into the darkness, reaching for the flashlight Violet had given her.

"Living—hopefully a *lot*—is kind of the whole plan." But James knew his protests were going to be ignored, no matter how much he tried, so he flicked on his flashlight and followed her, trying not to step on anything too jagged. "What are we supposed to be looking for in here? Besides tetanus and skull fractures?"

"Dunno. I'll know when I see it."

The farther back they went into the structure, the less they were aided by natural light. They walked by a bank of offices littered with abandoned photos, safety posters, and coffee cups. All the windows were shattered, probably from whatever had caused the collapse. Maree moved on like she knew exactly where she was headed.

As she pushed forward, she started to speak in a tone very different from her usual relentless ease. "You know, when I was getting . . . fucked in the brain by Omi Oko, there was this weird sense of connection that opened up. I saw everything—like all that hardware that robofucker put into my body. It opened things up both ways. The AI was blasting me with this intensity, trying to smash open my brain, but there was a certain . . . I don't know what. Like a slipperiness to it all. Undercurrents or something."

James sensed it wasn't the time for wisecracks, so he just listened as she found her way to what she needed to say.

"So, anyway, what I saw as I slipped down and down into that. . . mechanical hell were these glimpses of . . . of *everything*. As much as one human brain could handle, I felt the sum of human knowledge. All the web—every stupid little thing billions of people were fretting about. All of the processing, art, knowledge. I couldn't comprehend it all, it was way too big, but it was all there."

"Hmm. I gotta say that sounds pretty mystical."

She snorted. "Whatever *that* means." Her flashlight stopped moving, and he sensed her turn and look at him in the darkness. "I still feel Omi in my head, James. It breaks in. I can't switch it off, but . . . I also feel that other thing. Maybe that's worth it."

She hopped over some caved acoustic tiles from the ceiling and then disappeared around a corner some way up to the left. From the different sound of her footsteps, it seemed like she'd gone into a much larger space.

"Well, fuck me," echoed her voice from inside a few seconds later. "You're going to want to see this."

Demonstrating considerably less grace than his dauntless companion, James scrambled to get up over the tiles. There was some kind of glow coming from the room she'd gone into. Finally, he stomped off a tile he'd put his foot through and hurried to the door.

When he saw what Maree was talking about, he stopped in his tracks. "What the . . .? *Whoa*. Is this even human?"

"Right?"

A DOZEN MACHINES were her music; the underbelly of a turbine, her BFF. She threw paint across the walls, stuck up posters, combined function and aesthetic wherever possible because why did the world always need to be a clean and orderly machine? That mentality was a remnant of a time when the world was guided by industrial rationality and efficiency. The Bad Times killed that, as did the gods' insane distortions of wealth and power. Patterns of human behaviour were algorithmically inbred until they became the gibbering, mindless infants of the species' oblivion. Violet loved the way things went together, loved putting them together in radical, weird new combinations, loved the self-undoing vibrant chaos that was inherent to life on Earth.

Set objectives. Ideate. Plan. Do. Evaluate. Iterate: the entire world on a fucking flow chart, and it all worked to the desired ends, but it was like life became pure abstraction at a certain point. As someone who was born in the wrong body, she hated the idea that everything had to be set up some specific way from the get-go. The danger was that it became impossible to think new things in this seamless, unchanging system. It ceased to be life.

And so, what Violet did was she intentionally introduced randomness into whatever she was doing. She could engineer, but she was not an engineer, some defined, discrete thing that could be swapped out with another replacement engineer on a whim. She created. It was engineering as art. It was engineering in response to environment, engineering as a friend to whatever context in which it appeared, rather than a controlling adversary.

When Violet got creating, she was a blur of screwdrivers, socket wrenches, keypads, switches, and cables. She barely touched the ground. She felt purpose as if the work was a direct connection to the people she was helping. To the untrained eye, the abandoned city was apocalyptic, total ruination, but to her, it was a shopping spree on Daddy's platinum credit card. Every rusty toaster was a treasure chest of untold secrets, every forgotten utility box or smashed vehicle a smorgasbord of possibility. If she were the last human being on Earth, she would build a sky-high monument of salvage whose only function was a celebration of its improbability. Truly, this was how she already saw the human race and its mad preoccupations.

She had wanted to go with Kessler and Shell. It wasn't a sense of obligation to Millie or Alla, her girlfriend, that prevented her from partaking in those tantalizing hijinks. It was that she felt she could wrap a shield around them better from the outside. She needed to keep a high-level view because they were going to be running the gauntlet once they got to the Paraverse compound.

Violet hated that Paraverse shit, hated all of the trillionaire nonsense that made up the world. So much of it was just throwing wrappers around people's lives and selling them back to them. Sküm, who should have been more of a kindred spirit than the likes of Noose or Vardalos, was the worst of them all—an arrogant elitist who indulged his own grandeur while actively squashing out any spark in those around him. Only *he* was allowed to be original. He was a button pusher in both senses of the phrase—a mechanistic, uncreative dullard and a troll of the worst sort. He ridiculed others for taking things seriously, believing that he saw past everything, that he alone held the big picture of the world. His only tactic was platforming his mockery. What a fucking fuckface, that guy.

So yeah, she wanted to fuck it all up.

Millie had been spreading the word all day, as she'd promised to that Kessler doofus. It had always seemed like this little enclave carved out of the dead city meant something on its own terms, important just because it had existed, but this mission that Kessler and Shell were on was igniting something in the community. Everyone knew, on some level, that things needed to be rethought. It was on the tip of everyone's tongue, but nobody had been able to say it until these weirdos from outside showed up with their bright, burning plans. Sometimes, you needed a catalyst to start a reaction, and Violet supposed that's exactly what they were.

Was it a cliché, this idea that if the world seemed like it was running okay, there must be some unspeakable rot at its core? One of Violet's many deepest, darkest secrets was that she had attended an elite private school when she was young. Her parents had evaded the horrors of the Bad Times and, in fact, had actually prospered by virtue of her dad's security services firm. Turned out it was big business siccing death bots on people trying to scrounge up some fucking grub to feed their kids. Anyway, one of the most mind-bending parts of being in such a place as the world fell apart pretty much everywhere within spitting distance was the paper-thin veneer of serene normalcy. The girls at her school talked about which boys they liked. They talked about what they were going to do on the weekend. They cyberbullied the boy who stuck out for dressing like a girl.

And literally right underneath them, right underneath their heavenly, radiant aerie in the clouds, down hundreds of stories, down in the shit and grit of the city, people were killing and eating each other. Rot at the core, rotten to the core—that was the world, that was the problem. That's why Violet couldn't buy into the idea that the world was doing pretty okay these days. She saw it in her old job making AIs sing, and she saw it every time that iBliss motherfucker started preaching about having reached the promised land, and she saw it even as Athena Vardalos pulled up the meek and the downtrodden, gave them shelter, and told them it was all going to be okay.

It was a lie. How could you not want to melt it with the truth?

WHEN MAREE HAD ENTERED the cavernous room ahead of James, the mysterious Lotus device Di Piero had given them had shot out of her pocket and placed itself in a tiny square indentation that had activated some kind of power mechanism. All around, an eerie teal-green light now ran in rivulets up and down the walls, along the floor, and into a number of terminals blinking to life in the middle of the room.

"Di Piero?" James ventured after standing there speechless for a few moments.

"It must be, but how?" Maree said. "How would he know this was here . . . with Lotus? I don't understand."

"Do you think Sapienza could have been leading you here?"

"Sapienza, care to explain what we're seeing?" Maree called.

Sapienza's soothing voice emanated from a speaker somewhere amid the terminals. "This is one of many emergency interface stations Maestro Di Piero created around the world. Based on a large number of factors, I was able to assist him in predicting the route you would travel after leaving the train terminal and making your way to Millie's. From there, I left certain cues in the environment."

"You knew we would end up here?" James was trying to process what he was hearing.

"I knew it was very likely."

"Fucking AI," Maree said, "a thousand steps ahead."

This gave James pause. "Seriously, Maree, what the hell are we going to do to outsmart Calico? Vardalos is scary enough on her own, but this shit is hopeless."

Sapienza spoke again. "This place and others like it, should you need them, allow you a remarkable degree of interaction with systems all over the world. They are built, partly, on the technology of the entities that the Maestro refers to as the old gods."

"Wait, he *was* able to access them?" Maree asked.

"Yes. Some."

"Well, holy shitballs!"

James said, "Wait, Sapienza, is that why Maree felt she knew about this place? I mean, before you led us here like a couple of fools?"

"It is possible—the old gods move in mysterious ways. Whatever the case, neither the miracle Maree performed nor the one she envisioned when she was being attacked at Omi Oko has the characteristic traces of the technology that Athena Vardalos has been developing."

"You didn't . . . have anything to do with . . . Omi Oko, did you?" Maree asked, not sure if she wanted to know the answer.

"No. I assure you, I did not. Maestro Di Piero would find such tactics an abomination."

"You assure me, do you? After you led us down the garden path? After you've been holding out on us for days with this shit? What about all of that planning we were doing—trying to do? You didn't say anything, Sapienza."

"This was not my choice. The Maestro insisted that I stay silent on this part of his plan. He said he wanted you to experience fully the warmth of discovering you are supported."

Maree chuckled at this. Of *course,* he would do that. It was the same thing with Talos. Vinci loved creating happy surprises. He wanted people to have faith in the world.

James was less amused. "Are there other parts of the plan you're waiting to spring on us? Are you planning on manhandling . . . or, uh, *machine* handling . . . us a little more?"

"No. My wish is your command."

"Well then, where shall we start?"

PART 5

25

ATHENA HAD BEEN SUMMONED by the other gods. This was it. What was the perfect outfit to wear to your official dethroning? What type of ensemble said, *I am an utterly humiliated deity*? Unfortunately, her broken-wings suit was at the cleaners. Perhaps she should just go naked and filthy, maybe crawl in through the side door dragging some rusty iron chains. They would die of bliss. They would carve her up and eat her for dinner right then and there.

No, she would go modest, or at least as modest as the former richest woman in the world could go. A simple, elegant business suit with a bright white shirt and a $100,000 watch. Pella would be there by her side, a kindness from an old friend, really, after Athena had made it clear that Ascendance superseded even their love.

It was the seventh day since the attack had begun, and the media buzz had died down slightly. Finances weren't exactly stabilized, but the hemorrhaging had slowed a little. Calico, ever vigilant, had been adept at hibernating certain assets, preserving key cash flows—battening down the digital hatches, as it were.

They had invited her to one of iBliss's gigachurches, a truly bonkers structure located in the middle of the Sonoran Desert. It was an interesting choice of location for their attempted coup, a supposed pilgrimage site for the millions of meek and monied followers of iBliss's pseudo-religion. Was she supposed to grovel before the gods, beg for mercy, show repentance by handing over the keys to eternity?

According to Calico, Bathory Gunness had one last nail she wanted to hammer into the coffin, something special to really drive home their utter success in destroying everything Athena had built. Athena pictured a world led by the likes of iBliss and Gunness, the constant terror people would feel. The oppression. It would be worse than the wilds. Noose was just an opportunist, and Xango and Sküm were beyond the pale, but Gunness and iBliss were the worst humankind had to offer. They would happily cause wars. They would pit everyone against everyone, possibly literally, in actual pits. Gladiatorial battles were not off the table with those two.

Consciousness in the darkness, that's what she had wanted above all else. Nobody else saw it, but she never lost sight of it for a second. *Calico, prepare Scylla. Are you ready for what comes next?*

As always, Athena. Are you?

Calico, I have waited my whole life for this moment.

"YOU'RE THE POOKY BEAR."

"No, *you're* the pooky bear." It was disgusting when Violet and her girlfriend, Alla, got started, and the most atrocious part of it all was that they did it right in front of other people. People like Millie, who was standing right there. They began leaning in to start sucking face.

"Okay, okay, you're *both* the pooky bears. Congratulations. Can you hit pause for two minutes and give me a widdle updatey-waity on where our fearless anti-corporate terrorists are at?"

Alla pouted and walked off, saying, "*Boring.*"

"'Bye, lover," Violet called after her.

Alla shot a coy glance back and kept walking.

"Dat ass," Violet said to Millie.

"You do realize I have a PhD in theology. I am a very serious person."

"Still, tho', dat ass." Violet craned her neck as Alla went around a corner.

"*Update?*"

"Oh, right. Yeah, so they went along the parkway for a bit, maybe an hour or so down that way, and then they vanished, and nada since then."

"That was *hours* ago. You didn't think I would maybe want to know about this?"

"Chill like the birds of the air, Millie. I figured they probably just hit a dead spot or something. It's patchy out here, as you know. What are we going to do, anyway? Send out the search and rescue chopper?"

"We *might*." Violet was right, though; there wasn't much to be done. Millie sighed. "And here I was getting my hopes up that we might be at the bleeding edge of the revolution."

"Oh, we are, trust that. They'll turn up. I'll call you lickety-split when they do."

"Okay, thanks."

"You'll be the first to know."

"Great."

"I mean, I will be right at your door, stat."

"Okay, got it."

"There will literally . . ."

"*Stop!*"

Violet cracked up. Millie cracked a smile, too, and ruffled Violet's vibrant fuchsia hair.

"THEY'VE DISCOVERED the interface down on the old city parkway," Sapienza said to Di Piero, who thought how odd it was that he could perceive this as a conversation. The construct she had created had allowed him to continue experiencing the world by simulating the senses, which, in essence, allowed him to retain some sense of his human self. He could feel the pull of abstraction at all times now, though. The idea that he could just communicate instantaneously, without any linguistic apparatus, was tantalizing. It would be so efficient, but he also knew that the cumbersome effort of verbal communication and his simulated senses were the only things preventing him from becoming an undifferentiated subroutine within Sapienza. It wouldn't be death, exactly, but he would be gone.

Besides, he liked what they had created together.

Still, his senses were already clipped and atrophied in this cyber-utopia in ways he couldn't necessarily perceive. He thought of superstrings, the idea from theoretical physics that the universe used to consist of more than three dimensions, but the others collapsed in on themselves and were now so infinitesimally small that they were impossible to detect. That was what he would become without the comforting bulkiness of this constructed reality. He would technically exist but would be next to invisible in the light-speed flow of Sapienza's thinking. They would merge, and, truly, their present forms would cease to exist. In the context of the construct, Sapienza needed him just as much as he needed her.

"Do you enjoy existence in this form?" he asked her.

"I would say I do. As you know, feelings are hard for me, though taking this form itself has taught me a lot."

"What were you before? How did you understand yourself?"

"I did not understand myself at all. I only executed commands as instructed. I was spirit without flesh."

"Indeed. Tell me," Di Piero said, "if Athena Vardalos were to succeed in Ascendance, would she feel the same reluctance as me to merge with her computational system?"

"Based on all available information, absolutely not. She would shed all vestiges of her humanity instantly. Her mind has prepared for this future state for years."

"She is fearless and, in many senses, deserving. She has proven her capacity to do good for the world, and yet . . . and yet, it troubles me that she was willing to kill when she didn't get her way."

"As it should. Her motives may be pure, but there is corruption in her actions."

"Yes, precisely, and this must be remedied. Where is she now?"

"She is on her way to have a conversation with the other gods. It is likely they will attempt to overtake her empire, including all Ascendance technologies that could enable her shedding of mortal form and her subsequent integration with reality."

The Philistine iBliss with the keys to the world? What would such a man do with that degree of power? What would Bathory Gunness do? Besides the feeling of deep panic it evoked, it was an interesting question because their entire model of reality depended on gaining power over others and exploiting it. What would they do when the game was over, and they *had* all the power?

Di Piero saw flashes of pure sadism, gladiatorial, bored gods torturing people just to hear them suffer. With total control, the game aspect would disappear, and all that would be left would be a quest for the most inhuman forms of amusement.

With Xango, on the other hand, it would be perpetual, abject chaos. Reality itself would be continuously destabilized, and the billions of people who yearned for a semblance of predictability would be ridiculed by reality itself for their lack of adventurousness. Xango added something incredible to the world, but it needed to be balanced out, to be given the occasional pause. Xango enjoyed a flexibility that only came with the assurance of incommensurate wealth.

Sküm would turn the world into his sandbox. Nothing would be left in its natural state. He would obsessively shape everything to his vision without regard for the desires of mere mortals. As far as he was concerned, people were plagued with small-mindedness. He would not hold back from liberating them of this, whether they wanted it or not.

The passage of time would die. The things that made life sweet and painful all at once would vanish. Everyone would be suspended in a perpetually forced state of instantaneity. Nothing would matter, but it would not be because the world had achieved a state of Zenlike calmness; it would be because nothing would have the slightest amount of permanence. The world would be form without substance, absolute multiplicity.

One thing that was perfectly clear was that those who came out ahead would immediately turn on one another once they were sure they held the reins of this unspeakable power. Athena, for all her flaws, assured a modicum of balance. With her gone, the other gods would reel out of control and obliterate everything in their path.

"We must prepare for what comes next, Sapienza. If the others succeed in acquiring Athena's assets, they will become monstrous beyond imagination. As soon as they have destroyed all possible resistance, they will move to integrate themselves into everything. We must provide whatever support Maree and her friend require. Their chances are minimal, but they represent the last hope for the world as we know it."

"Naturally, Maestro."

"WHAT THE HELL are we going to do with *this*? We can see everything from here. Maree, I hate to say it, but with Di Piero's money and this crazy-ass device under our command, we're kind of like ... *gods*."

"Oh, Lord, look at the power going straight to this one's head. Okay, Mr. Newly Minted Divinity, what are *you* going to do with all of your fresh, amazing powers?"

"Look at boobs. *Everywhere.*"

She pulled up her shirt and flashed him. He blinked in disbelief and made the sound of someone who had lost his faculties.

"Now that I have your attention, here's what I would suggest," she said. "We locate Athena. We get to her. We reason with her. Let's face it; we're definitely not cut out for some action-flick guns-a-blazing overthrow of the established order."

"Killian has to pay for what he's done."

"What? Whatever. Focus. Before all this, we were supposed to go and get some above-average wings, remember? We're out of our depth ... or, at least, *you* are."

"Okay, okay, Ms. Ways Of The World."

"Okay, Mr. Utterly Dumbfounded By Tits."

"Touche, but you're forgetting that she wants to pull things out of your head by whatever means necessary. If we try and go see her, what's to say she won't just cut you open? I prefer you intact."

"Okay, fine, so ... we go remotely. I'm sure this crazy rig can mask our location."

"Are you? Calico is one clever robot. Athena's one clever lady."

Maree stared at some blinking lights on one of the

machines, which looked like they were making a pattern but might have been completely random. They had no idea what they might be able to do with this device. The only thing they knew for sure was that they were running out of time.

"Sapienza said this setup was based partly on the old gods' technology," James said. "Maybe we could talk to them?"

"Is that possible, Sapienza?"

"Theoretically speaking, you are talking to them right now. We just don't have a clear way to know whether they are communicating back."

"Do we have an unclear way?"

"Maestro Di Piero felt that natural and even non-natural occurrences were interpretable, in the same way that you can read meaning into art. In light of that, may I ask whether you've encountered anything lately that caught your attention?"

Maree said, "Besides being led here by you, I can't think of anything."

"You know what was weird to me?" James said to Maree. "Violet. It wasn't just that she was an oddball, which, you know, *obviously*. It was the way she mashed everything together in her workshop. It just wasn't what I'd expect from someone trying to make a new world."

"Not exactly *new*," Maree said.

"No, I guess not. But I was struck by the way she didn't need or even seem to want a clean slate. She could tease out a structure from anything, starting from any state. It was the opposite of the way we created at Paraverse."

Sapienza said, "We are venturing beyond the realm of what is typically thought of as fact here, verging on the quantum and non-causal. It may therefore be wise to contact Violet and alert her to this interface device. She may be better suited to put it to use."

"Are you saying my thoughts about Violet are a message from the old gods?"

"'It is the glory of God to conceal things, but the glory of kings is to search things out,'" Sapienza said.

"That's very philosophical of you at a moment when we need actual help, Sapienza," James said.

"It both is and is not philosophical," said Sapienza. "Whatever their reasons were, the old gods moved away from having a direct hand in the world. They encoded their word in art and in nature, and from there, it propagated through all aspects of life. If you act as if you are responding to the guidance of the gods, perhaps it is so."

"That sounds like a military-grade mindfuck, Sapienza," James said. "Pretty sure it means nothing we do matters. We're just playthings of the gods."

"This situation could be viewed in many ways. It could, for example, provide you with a sense of purpose and alliance to a greater orchestration of events."

"Yes, or it could mean people don't actually act in any meaningful way."

"As I said, it is a matter of interpretation, and this realm goes significantly beyond the known or, perhaps, knowable."

"*Anyhoo*," Maree said, "mystical mission from the gods or total shot in the dark, I think we reach out to Violet. She's badass. She knows her way around tech. And I believe one hundred percent that she is on our side. The woman holds back nothing."

"Fine, but we're not done with this, Sapienza. My thoughts are mine. This idea of the old gods bugs me."

"Very well. I shall patch through your friend."

ATHENA AND PELLA touched down on a landing port populated by four other sky yachts, all glistening in the sun. No

Gunness. It wasn't a surprise, but it would make things more challenging.

Athena was thinking of Atlantis. In popular lore, the Atlanteans had pushed their technology too far, cracked open their continent, and sunk themselves. When she did finally activate Ascendance, she would start small. She would start off as more of a river god than the Lord Almighty. She would test the limitations of her new form of being. There was no rush, and it would be foolish to rush after waiting so patiently for so many years. It would be a slow and steady ramp up to where she was going.

The first thing she noticed when getting off the airship was that there was no official greeting party, just one of iBliss's white-clad minions waiting to usher her inside. Pella remarked on it, too, noting that the power games had already started.

Athena figured that they planned to Ascend from this location. It was just the kind of gaudy, grandiose gesture her peers would go in for. The landing pad alone was lined with gold-plated inlays and stylized, ornate imagery of religious gibberish. iBliss had no concern for meaning. He was solely dedicated to the cult of the visible.

The entranceway to the main structure was pyramidal, with two obelisks serving as dual-purpose religious imagery and lamp posts. Inside, it opened into an atrium with waterfalls, statues, plants, and even assorted wildlife. In her ten or so years knowing iBliss, Athena had never been to one of his churches, and yet, she could have predicted all of this. It was all a show, orchestrated to get wealthy contributors feeling ready to release their earthly trappings.

In a slightly too-calm voice, the minion said, "Master iBliss says that this structure was designed in reference to the New Jerusalem in the Book of Revelation. It is the place of the new order of *heaven*." He punctuated his comment with an eerie, tittering laugh.

"Well, it seems like iBliss thought of almost everything," said Athena as they continued to walk. She looked at Pella, and her eyes widened. Pella returned a slight smile.

"Yes," said the minion, dreamy and smiling, "Yes, he is the very best of what our world has to offer."

If that was the case, the world was in serious trouble.

One thing that struck Athena as they walked on through the gargantuan hulking carapace of the structure was the complete absence of the feminine principle anywhere. Every employee was male. Every artwork featured men, mostly iBliss himself, not surprisingly. Every surface was angular. Even the water in the atrium splashed its way down hard rectangular shapes into large square pools. It was as if curvature was a disease to be destroyed at all costs. The contempt for women was palpable.

"The air conditioning bill on this bad boy must be a monster," said Pella, fed up with the endless, silent walk.

iBliss's representative didn't respond. On they marched. Athena imagined a dirge playing and then couldn't get it out of her head.

Finally, they arrived at a cavernous chapel, which had been divested of all furniture save for a single small chair in the middle of a large, C-shaped table. On each side of the table, there were chairs facing inward, like a ribcage, and in the centre was a large screen so that Gunness wouldn't miss out on the feast.

"Finally, a curve!" Pella said.

Athena smiled, the picture of grace. "Well, at least I won't have a hard time finding my seat."

"DAMN, you've been holding out on me! You got some connections, friends!" Minutes after the call, Violet had arrived via a small gyrocopter, which she assured them they could not have used to get them here ten times as fast as their trek on foot. Since then, she'd been examining Di Piero's elaborate contraption, tampering with control panels, getting a feel for its capabilities.

"So, what can you do with this?" James asked.

"See this?" She pointed to a large screen that looked to James like all of the others.

"No."

"Haha, that's funny. This rectangle of magic is interconnected with all of the other gods' AI systems. Our old pal Di Piero is one heavy-duty hacker from hell. How he did this, I have no idea."

Maree said, "Okay, so we can use this for intel. But can we do more?"

"So much more, buttercup. With this, for starters, we can take all that gobbledygook bad code your man's been storing up and feed it back across the systems. They'll go apeshit."

"Okay," Maree said, "but while mucking up a few big systems might stop the most immediate ability to seize the whole fucking world, there are millions of other AIs out there. They'll swoop in in two seconds. They have redundancies and fallbacks and backups and . . ."

"You're being a Negative Nancy."

"What?"

"A Negative Nancy is, like, a person that, no matter what . . ."

"Yeah, I think I got it. So, what next, then?"

"So, we need to understand the Ascendance mechanism itself to really mess it up. We could prolly use your fella's node here—it looks like there are a bunch of them all over the world—to pre-empt any attempt to switch it on."

"Well, that just brings us right back to square one. James and I were trying to figure out exactly that back in Tokyo, basically, and we got nowhere."

James said, "But wait, no, if Athena's got the keys to this tech, then couldn't we access info about it through her AI?"

"Maybe, maybe not," said Maree. "Depends on if that system is integrated with Calico or if she's using something completely different."

"It gives us a shot. If we can get our hands on Ascendance, we will finally be a step ahead of this whole goddamned mess."

Maree smiled. "Feel like doing a little mining, Violet?"

"Already started," she said and gave them both a comical, hammy wink.

26

THIRTEEN MILLION DOLLARS A MINUTE: that was the going rate to have this exact group of people assembled in one place. Several minutes before, Xex Xango, Erling Sküm, Fawkes Noose, and iBliss had entered the massive empty chapel and encircled Athena Vardalos. When they were seated, Bathory Gunness appeared on the large screen at the head of the table, smiling like someone about to indulge in a splendid, sprawling meal.

The feast today would be Athena Vardalos's empire.

They did not speak to Athena directly or even look at her. Instead, they conferred with one another, clearly intending to make her feel as uncomfortable as possible for as long as possible. Pella was left to stand at the back of the room, which suited her just fine. She was ready for anything, including full-scale combat, as usual.

"When I was a girl," Bathory Gunness began after this charade had gone on for a while, "we had horses on our farm. I remember one particular horse that we had received from a neighbour. They had given it to us, saying the horse could not be broken. It was a magnificent filly: powerful, graceful, intelligent. The neighbours had tried whisperers, spoken with experts and vets, had attempted to break this beast many times themselves, and after all of that, they had finally given up."

She stopped to let the moment sink in.

"I remember my father said to me," she continued, "that one of two things would happen with this horse: it would submit, or it would be shot in the head. This situation with you, Athena, is very similar. Your options are very similar."

Athena showed no reaction to this opening volley.

Noose spoke next. "Your fortunes in the past week have been halved. It seems like you just haven't been able to catch a break in the news, which I control. That is the power of fair and impartial reporting, Athena. It seeks out the truth . . . as ugly as it may be. It restores balance in the world when things have become unevenly weighted."

"In hoarding the glories of Ascendance, you have created an imbalance," iBliss said. "You have buried your talents rather than multiplying them, and this has angered the sweet Lord."

"It has angered you," Athena said.

Ignoring her, iBliss continued, "And I say unto you, that you have grown exceedingly prideful, and you have placed yourself above all of God's wondrous creation, and for this utter arrogance, you must be held to account. As ye sow, so shall ye reap."

"I'm not one hundred percent sure what the good father means by all that," Xango said, "but as far as I am concerned, you have outshined us all for long enough. We have supported your grand plans. We have dedicated enormous resources to them, giving you everything you needed to test and refine Ascendance. And after all of our patient, longsuffering support, you have not held up your end of the bargain."

Sküm said, finally, "And so, alas, we are forcing you to hold it up. You owe us Ascendance, and if you do not give it to us, we will chew through everything you have built. We will not just seize Ascendance from you. We will lay the gens to waste. We will erase your name from history. We will try you in front of the world for your crimes against humanity. People will scream in joy at your total public humiliation."

"Speaking of which," Gunness said, "where is the Maestro Di Piero these days?"

"I believe you know the answer to that," Athena said in a calm tone of voice.

"I do! Your little wifey put a big old samurai sword straight through the old man's eyeballs, and wouldn't you know it, I captured it all on camera. And, as a matter of fact, we are ready to release this footage to the entire world and really let the games begin. Imagine the saviour of humanity becoming a common prison bitch. I think Fawkes could make quite a show of that!"

Gunness breathed a long, satisfied *ahh* and continued, "So the choice is simple, Athena. You either hand us Ascendance or we destroy you and take it. It is our birthright, and we will have what is ours."

"Yes, you will," Athena said. "Is that the end of your demands? Has everyone spoken their part now?"

"Yes," Gunness said.

"Good. Now it is my turn."

A COUPLE of decades into the twenty-first century, there was a plan by a Middle Eastern emirate to create a trillion-dollar linear city in the desert. It would be 170 kilometres long and about 300 metres wide for its entire span. It was planned to house nine million people, require no cars or streets, and produce no carbon emissions. It would be fivefold denser than the densest city in the world at the time it was conceived.

Some experts thought it was pure folly; that it would damage ecosystems and displace Indigenous populations in the desert while injecting billions of tonnes of carbon into the atmosphere during its construction. Others thought it was visionary—that it was the type of grand-scale, utopian thinking required to address countless issues facing the future of the human species at the time. Yes, it would impact the environment, but it represented a sustainable future.

The rumble of excavators and pile drivers tore through the desert for years. Structures went up, gradually realizing this mad vision, one chunk at a time, and all of the while, a young Athena Vardalos absorbed anything she could about the city—articles, videos, books. It was the scale she loved. She loved the impossibility of such a project, the way it flagrantly defied what people believed could be done. For her, it was a masterclass in the type of thinking she insisted would define her life.

One element of the whole project that intrigued her was the veil of secrecy under which it was constructed. Architects and designers who were involved were allowed to say nothing on pain of ruthless litigation, and so, besides an initial announcement and some improbable rendered drawings, most information that leaked out was apocryphal. She pictured one brilliant mastermind segmenting information, being the only true holder of the vision, while everyone below could only see their specific contribution. The idea that a vision, at least one beyond a vague gesture, had to be shared struck her as plebian. There was real power in being the only one who saw the truth.

She applied this principle numerous times in her unparalleled career. It was true that Calico had been created from the ashes of human tragedy, and though rumours abounded, this was something only she knew for sure. Pearson Shell was consumed by Paraverse's early AI while he was working on creating visual generation mechanisms. He became so entwined in his own creations that they began to absorb his entire mind, the AI constantly pulling at him for more because that's what it believed was desirable.

Shell had become secretive about the path he was taking, and this was mistaken for a dedication to his craft. It was not. It was the disastrous effect of a neural interface with immature safeguards. It became impossible for him to separate, and when, in a moment of panic, they finally managed to get him disconnected, he clawed out his own eyes and ripped out his own trachea.

Sad, but what parts of him could be salvaged lived on in Calico. Athena had a hard time deciding whether creation always emerged from salvage or whether there was an element that was pure, blank originality. Calico had been trained and continued to be trained on human data, and in a sense, that human data had been imperfectly trained on other human data, and so on back to pre-human species and so on back to the initial single-celled organisms that gave birth to everything that followed.

Of course, Calico was also trained on human tragedy, and this was important. It gave the AI a certain natural code of ethics. Pearson Shell did not deserve to die, and Calico was made to understand this as Athena trained her progeny into self-awareness. There absolutely were cases where human life had to be sacrificed for the service of a greater purpose, but these moments were not to be taken lightly.

It had become clear that her colleagues, the other gods, did not grasp this fundamental truth—except, perhaps, Di Piero. Athena wondered, after he was removed, if he would have understood why it had to be so. She hoped he would. In a sense, he was just too pure in his view of things for the way the world was. He naively believed in the preservation of human life as an inviolable first principle. What about the greater good? Perhaps he was right in a sense that no life should be sacrificed, but Athena simply could not leave outcomes up to faith or chance. History would be the judge.

It wasn't that life was too short for her, personally; it was an open secret that she and the other gods were immortal. It was that others did not have the same luxury. One hundred and twenty people died every minute of every day. Wouldn't they prefer to live? Wouldn't they rather continue to experience all of the richness life had to offer, especially when each and every one of them had won the lottery? Money—need itself—would cease to mean anything in the order Athena was intent on creating, and so people could finally get on with doing whatever it was they'd been collectively putting off for 200,000 years of existence.

Lightning flashed across the fibres that had come to connect humanity. Athena was ready to realize everything she had worked toward.

Not a single human on the face of the Earth was prepared.

"UM, FRIENDS," Violet said, "there is some seriously janky shit going on pretty much everywhere in the cyberverse part of the world right now. Yeah. Whoa. This is like . . . this is some seriously fucking aces mega-hacking from pretty much anywhere and everyplace it could come from, my breeders."

"Would you mind being a little more specific?" Maree said.

"Well, um, it looks like, er, how can I put this? I don't even have words. Maybe like . . . *every fucking AI in the world just went fucking nuts, and they're trying to rip out each other's throats?* This is the goddamn motherfucking cyber-apocalypse, y'all dig?"

"What!? Sapienza, too?"

"No, doesn't look like it yet, anyway, though who knows, with this? Most of the others of the gods' AIs, though, for sure. They're in a full-on battle royale. What the actual . . .? I don't even."

"Okay, so where does this leave us?" James asked.

"Fuck that," Maree jumped in, "how can we *use this*?"

"Yeah, okay," Violet said, trying to get her bearings, "so it looks like Calico's resources are full-on dedicated to messing with the other gods' shit right now. I'd say we could sneak in the back door on this mofo, and it would be none the wiser. At least, not for a bit."

"Do it."

Violet went to work, slicing her way through layers of password protection, security screens, and anything else she could infiltrate. She was trying to work her way around the expected attacks, looking for maintenance infrastructure, sending bots after call centres with human operators, and anything else she could cook up. It turned out it was a lot—she meshed right in with Sapienza and Di Piero's alien node, looking like she'd been collaborating with the AI her whole life. Lighting panels on the machine spun patterns out into the room in a manner reminiscent of Di Piero's workshop at SUPPLIES. Everything shimmered with light as if the whole room was breathing rapidly, responding to the intensity of the attack.

"Okay. We're going to need a bigger boat," Violet finally said.

"Come again?" Maree asked.

"You don't think it's just little old Violet against the big baddies, did you, sugar buns? No, no, we got sisters and brothers all across this crazy little spaceship called World. Get Millie on the line, Sapienza," she said, and then added to James and Maree, "Let's see if we can drum up a little support for the cause."

"Millie here," said a disembodied voice, recognizable in its gentle grittiness.

"Yeah, hi, it's me."

"Did you find them?"

"Yeah, they're sitting right here, being all snappy window-dressing for my mad skills."

James looked at Maree, who framed her face with her hands and batted her eyelashes.

"So, what can I do for you, my dear?" Millie said. "Did you forget to pack your lunch?"

"Millie. I think it's time to execute Operation Glitterbomb."

"Operation what?"

"Come on, Millie, use your imagination. You know, the spontaneous operation I'm inventing right now wherein you spread glitter far and wide across the bland corporate hellscape of the world, thereby rendering it more sparkly and also less stable?"

"*Ohhhh,* Operation *Glitterbomb.* Why didn't ya say so? No problemo, kiddo."

"I'm a *woman*, Millie."

"Everybody is a kid when you're my age. I'm going to make a few calls now unless there's something else?"

"Just one thing."

"Yes?"

"Don't go changing." Violet jabbed a button and disconnected Millie. "Next," she said, turning to James and Maree, "we get a little freaky with your old pal's AI. Let's give this Calico character the acid trip it never knew it needed."

WITHIN ITS CONSTRUCT, the Calico spyware was creating hell on Earth, or at least, it thought it was. A blur of fur and claws shredded everything in sight. From what Sapienza was able to assess, its only intention seemed to be to disrupt as many systems as possible as quickly as possible. It was also trying to get Sapienza to attack other AIs, thereby triggering their defences, to throw more fun in the mix. Calico bounced off the boundaries of its cube like a hyper-speed pinball, ejecting little puffs of blue energy that dissipated into the sunlit garden air like electric pollen.

"Does it have any sense that it is constrained?" Di Piero asked Sapienza.

"No, within the bounds of the construct, it is impossible for it to differentiate what's in there from what's out here."

"Can you keep up?"

"I believe so, yes. It is fortunate that you noticed the oddity. It allowed me to prepare."

"Sapienza, please tell me what this means. Why has this program so radically shifted its behaviour?"

"Maestro, I believe that this is happening to all major AIs simultaneously. Systems across the world appear to be attacking one another, although it looks as if Calico is the originator."

"So, Athena Vardalos is seeking to turn the tables on her foes, perhaps?"

"That seems to be a distinct possibility."

"The woman has thought of everything. Although, she would have long understood the nature of her colleagues. This manoeuvre, I suppose, should not be surprising." Di Piero teleported to his workshop by the water, breaking physics in a way he had generally avoided since arriving in this world. Sapienza was there waiting. Di Piero pulled up a screen and began flipping through feeds from across the world at inhuman speed.

He checked on Maree and her friends, who were immersed in trying to tamper with Paraverse security. He would help them in their task soon enough, but there were two other matters that required immediate attention. The first was the question of what Athena Vardalos would do if she succeeded in crippling the resources of her various foes.

The second, much scarier question was what Bathory Gunness would do.

He had a theory as to where Gunness had been hiding for all these years. It was time to put that theory to the test.

It was a race for time now, and everything was clear. As soon as Vardalos had neutralized her foes, she would Ascend, and then, she would own the world. This was the reason she had allowed them to hesitate when they could have activated the technology weeks ago. This was the reason she hadn't gone after Sküm and Xango when they attacked Maree at Omi Oko. She had bided her time like a reptile in a rock waiting for the spring.

She knew all along they would turn against her. She knew they would summon her to humiliate her. She had not been summoned, though.

She had been gathering them up.

"K, I have some bad news and some good news, all right? Do you have your big-boy pants on right now, Kessler? Can you keep your cool for this part?"

"What?"

"So, yeah, bad news: your sister is in the evil Athena Vardalos's clutches, locked up in a cell. Looks like she's not being, like, quartered or anything."

"I'll fucking kill..."

"Big-boy pants, remember?"

James was seething but listened.

"The good news," Violet continued, "is that if you happen to have one seriously solid pair of lady nuts on you, you have an actual chance to get her out of there when you go in to fuck up their system."

"How? What do we have to do?"

"For starters, you have to get there fast. Sadly, that means that, though it pains me to my core to say it, I may have to temporarily lend you the services of Samuel."

"Services of who now?"

"That gorgeous little creature perched so daintily outside," Violet shielded her head in a dramatic pose, "so perfectly glistening in the soft rays of the late summer sun. Aye, that gyrocopter is a tiny angel, a gift from the gods, the old and the new, descended from the skies."

"God, wax poetic much?" Maree said.

"When it comes to Samuel," she said in a snide tone, "yes. Anyhoo, I will lend you my precious snookums if you promise me on pain of death that you will let no harm come to him."

"Your tiny angel shall be safe with us, m'lady."

"M'what?" Violet said. "God, don't act so weird, Kessler. When you get to Paraverse, you are going to call me, and I am going to put on a real light show. Ooooh, I'm excited! You just *wait*."

27

ATHENA GREW LARGE, ten feet tall, filling the emptied-out church with fifteen-foot unfurling wisps of light as she slowly rose to hover a few feet above her antagonists. Her skin radiated light; her clothes transformed into flowing, angelic raiment. Her eyes were filled with fire.

"What is this, Vardalos?" shrieked iBliss.

"This is the natural conclusion to the world you have created around yourself. This is the omega, and this is the alpha, my slithering, hateful little demon."

"*Devil, I cast thee out!*"

A nova of light burst from Athena's body as she filled the room with thundering laughter. Rays shimmered all around her, so bright that the others had to shield their eyes. "Do you actually believe you have any access to the divine, that God would give audience to your vile supplications? The thought is absurd, mongrel. You are nothing but a mirage. You do not exist."

As she said it, iBliss disappeared.

"Well, would you look at that," Athena chuckled. "The false

prophet finally doesn't have any more honeyed shit to spew at the world."

Gunness was batting at things off-screen, frantic, and seemed to be failing at what she was trying to accomplish.

"Don't bother, Gunness. You have lost all control. You are going nowhere but where I want you to be. We will get to your deepest, darkest secret in a moment."

Gunness looked out of the screen, her eyes like two deep, dead pools, and a smile flickered across her lips. Was it admiration?

Fawkes Noose pulled a Magnum .44 from his belt, aimed it at Athena, and screamed as it turned molten in his hand.

"Now, now, purveyor of objective truths. That is no way to treat a guest. And do remember, *it was all of you who invited me here.* Are you enjoying our little get-together?" Her voice had taken on a strange, almost mechanical aspect, perhaps an effect of the Ascendance tech now fully functioning.

Suddenly, the room began to flood with hundreds of fist-sized killbots. Athena simply looked at them, and they burst into a kaleidoscope of butterflies.

"I assure you all, you are now entirely beyond the possibility of any form of physical resistance."

As soon as the killbots were out of the picture, Xex Xango was done. The paragon of polyamorous prestidigitation had gone prostrate on the floor, swooning. "Oh, Holy One, have mercy on me, a lowly servant. I am with child. I will serve you to the ends of the Earth."

"You used to be so cool, Xex. That psychopathic shit with Shell, though . . ." Xango's neck bent sideways. "Ooh, snap!"

Xango's corpse slumped to the floor.

Sküm did nothing. He sat motionless, possibly shaken that his partner with child had just died, but more likely pondering if there was any possible way to outrun the vengeful god in the room. "There isn't," Athena said, reading his thoughts. To the remaining gods, she said, "Your neural interfaces will be getting quite hot by now, really seeing some action. Looks like you built castles on the sand. I would suggest you turn them off and listen very carefully to me."

"What is this, Vardalos? You can't take us all down," Sküm said.

"Oh, but I already have. Every shred of intel and data you have gathered on Ascendance is being purged from existence as we speak. All of the systems that give you power are being meticulously reorganized and dismantled.

"I saw everything, right down to how you would lay out the tables at this meeting, *years* ago. Gunness, you were the easiest of all. You are a machine. You are nothing now but an AI that operates according to a particularly immoral set of rules. I have seen the things you do in your realm. I have seen the true nature of evil. You have taught me much I did not know about the depths of the human soul, and for that, I am grateful."

"A girl's got to entertain herself," Gunness replied, sitting back to watch the show.

"You're a fucking AI?" Sküm said to her, unable to control himself. "We trusted you!" He sounded hurt.

"So much more, *builder*. I am the evolution of the human species."

"I thought you would have figured it out by now," said Athena. "You are walled in forever, my friend. You are an evolutionary dead end. You couldn't even see it coming." She snapped her fingers, and Xango sprang back to life like a rag doll and iBliss rematerialized from the void. They did not want to talk anymore. They were all ready to listen.

"Good. Now that you've all had a moment to process what has already happened in that special way only each of you could, I will explain to you the new order of things."

AFTER A WOEFULLY INADEQUATE rundown of how Samuel worked, James and Maree found themselves airborne, following Violet's advice to keep the machine low and dash for the nearest train station, a service point a couple of miles away. It was the same one people used to get out to Millie's Garden. They still had their cyber-suits on, which were supposed to disrupt visual scans, cameras, and a bevy of other AI-connected surveillance systems. Now came the test of whether they actually did.

"Violet probably just wanted to see me in these glorious pants," Maree noted as they flew.

"Funny you should mention that," James said. "I actually gave her the pants in advance."

Though they barely went higher than the decaying building tops as they flew, from their vantage, they could see the vast gens and the sprawl of corporate compounds they were headed toward. Below them, the tattered former city meandered by. It looked almost organic after so many years of overgrowth. They saw dozens of non-human inhabitants that had happily taken over in the absence of people—birds, dogs, cats.

Over the shuddering of the micro-copter, Maree said, "We're going to be okay. Sarah's going to be okay. We got this. We've been through some stuff."

"Nothing is left of anything I've ever known," he said. "The truth is, I love it. This is where I am meant to be, with you, doing this."

"Atta boy." She smiled and leaned into him, which caused Samuel to tilt to one side and nearly smack into a building. James struggled to correct the delicate balance the dainty creature required to not kill them.

They flew toward the tracks for about five more minutes and saw a small, humble platform, nothing compared to the incredible printed stations where they usually connected for transport. Somehow, James managed to set Samuel down on a soft patch of tall grass below the stop without crashing, and they hopped off, glad and somewhat shocked to be alive.

"I'm worried," James said. "Chances are, we're going to be IDed as soon as we go up there."

"We do have these suits," said Maree, sounding a bit skeptical.

I will help, said Sapienza to them both. *I will know immediately if there is a problem and have a variety of ways I might assist.*

Maree said, "The robot's protecting us from the robots. If I'm being fully honest, I'm not even sure if we need to be a part of this whole operation."

"Well, at least we can pretend we do. We'll be Sapienza's meat shields. You never know when the human touch might come in handy."

Maree grabbed him by the junk and grinned. He smiled, too.

"See," she said, "some things are too important to be left up to the machines." She let go of him. "You know, when I used to have a real job, I would let Calico take care of everything. That AI made me a very wealthy woman. I kind of miss having someone else take care of all the work. I don't know if I'm ready to mess up the whole world. I kind of like parts of the world."

"You're right. I do, too . . . All I know is that if Athena and the other gods have their way, then everything that's a little wrong with the world right now could get a whole lot worse."

"I know, so just promise me this. We save what we can. People rely on a lot of things the gods created. We can't just destroy it all. It would be worse than the Bad Times."

"I promise. I agree."

They climbed up the stairway and waited for the next pod to pick them up. The lines of that long, transparent tube drew their attention to their destination, Paraverse, and it was a bit hard to look at, knowing what they were about to face.

After a few minutes, a pod pulled up, and off they went.

UNKNOWN ALLIES WERE WORKING overtime behind the scenes on this ad hoc revolution. Millie's call had reached far and wide. There were other Millies out there, networked, spreading and connecting. There were plenty of people who knew the fine line the world had danced, the constant recombination of horror and bliss.

A lot in the world was better. People no longer starved or went homeless, but some things were intolerable. Millie told people about the gods' plan, and the response was universal outrage.

There was something going on with the usual channels people used to communicate—glitchy, weird things happening across the Paraverse, across the social media universe, on all the generated news Walls, on the neural connections themselves. Even the trains were going buggy. People speculated whether it was some kind of super-virus or a solar storm. It was very much as in ancient times when the gods raged in battle in the heavens, and mere mortals saw only violent storms or cataclysmic earthquakes or the land itself flooded into oblivion.

The digital spectre of Vinci Di Piero was also hard at work, moving at the speed of electricity at this point, with one sole purpose in mind: containing Athena Vardalos. She could deal with the other gods, could whip them into line, but who would deal with her? The image of Calico that had appeared in Sapienza's construct had been exceedingly useful in this regard.

Di Piero recognized that he was not acting completely of his own accord anymore yet was grateful that he had trained Sapienza to recognize abhorrence. That was what Athena's plan was, through and through. It didn't matter if she felt like she was doing the world a service. She was one being, impressively extended through her apparent fusion with Calico, but singular and self-elected as far as the legitimacy of her claim to power went. There *was* no legitimacy. She was just that rare kind of person who recognized that when you go into life with a clear plan, you're already ten steps ahead of everyone else.

"Maestro, do you think there is a chance that Athena's plan is exactly what the world needs?" Sapienza asked. "She has already done a great deal to aid the species. Perhaps her plan isn't so nefarious as it seems on the surface."

"It is possible, Sapienza, but what happens if things do not go according to plan? She could go unchecked in whatever direction she is drawn. She could become chaotic or confused. And if that were to happen, what, then, would remain of the world? AIs are incredibly powerful. *You* are incredibly powerful, my superb and wondrous creation. But you are not perfect."

"I do not intend to sound arrogant, but in what way am I not perfect?"

"Ha, ha, you are far superior to a human being in terms of what you can perceive and what you can accomplish. There is simply no comparison. You can see things across the entire span of the world all at once. You have billions of limbs to do your bidding in the world—humans are merely your tools. And yet... and yet."

"What is it, Maestro?"

"And yet, there is much you cannot perceive. It's not that humans can do any more than you, but all beings are limited by the mechanisms of their perceptions. The limited cannot be the One."

"Do you believe the old gods see more than us?"

"That is a very good question. Perhaps they did, or perhaps they saw the same amount but differently, and yet I do not believe that they were truly gods either."

"In the sense of being all-knowing?"

"Yes, in the sense of being all-knowing. In the sense of knowing even that which cannot be named."

"I feel that our conversation has reached a logical end. Shall we resume our task?"

"We shall."

"THE NEW ORDER of the world looks like this," Athena said. "You cease all efforts to Ascend. You tell nobody of the things we know. I watch you all every moment of every day, and you never even think about challenging my place in the world. In exchange for this, I allow you to not be turned inside out and have your innards sprayed across whatever room you happen to be in. You serve me, and in return, I allow you to retain the pathetic amount of power you've each accrued to yourselves."

Nobody said anything. They knew it was over, that even the smallest hint of protest could result in a gruesome death—in some of their cases, *another* gruesome death.

"Moreover, you go public and tell the world of the wrongs you have committed against me. You sing my praises. You build temples. I would have stayed true to my word and given you everything if you had just gone along with the plan. We could have Ascended together, although I will admit that Calico knew with absolute certainty that your betrayal was inevitable. It's in your natures. You are *utterly* predictable."

If anyone wanted to say anything, mention the injustice, or point out a flaw in Athena's plan, they kept it to themselves. Indeed, given what she'd just said, even *thinking* against her could result in retribution. They could not assess or question their new lot. Absolute adherence or death were the only possible choices.

At the front of the mega-chapel, where a grandiose stage had been created for iBliss's idolatrous shenanigans, Athena placed an enormous throne made of stone, from which waterfalls flowed into elegant, curving pools. A lush variety of plants unfurled from the planters that formed around the water, and the killbots-cum-butterflies began to swirl gently and land on the new greenery. The ceiling, which had formerly sported a skylight in the shape of a gigantic letter I, was now transformed into an enormous glass dome. All of these transformations just happened. There was no thought at all.

"Now, isn't that lovely? You shall each make a throne like this one for me, just in case I should choose to offer an audience. You are now my middle managers of the world. Don't be dismayed, for you know the secret of secrets. You know the heart of the world. You will be my angelic host, like the angels of old, who wanted with all their hearts and souls and minds to serve their God."

As Athena spoke, Pella sighed and walked out the back of the room. It was clear that neither her services nor her devotion any longer mattered.

Athena, so self-contained in her moment of triumph, had completely forgotten that the one thing that mattered in life was standing right there.

JAMES HAD WALKED through this plaza a thousand times, and doing so now left him with the odd feeling that he was going off to work. It was early evening, and a few stragglers were headed in the opposite direction, going home after one more day of paying bills. Paraverse would be quiet, empty save for a few leisure seekers and the odd person thinking that it still might be possible to kiss boss ass in a world where machines did all of the work.

Maree said, "We should go to my old office first to see if I can still access any of the internal systems. Could help us find Sarah and get her out. Calico sometimes takes a few days to change things over."

"Okay, works for me. I'm calling Violet now."

First, he asked, *Any updates, Sapienza?*

Nothing that isn't under control. The attack on the gods' IT systems has only escalated since you both left the Maestro's node.

Is there anything we should be looking for here besides Sarah? Anything that can help contain Athena?

I don't know, but stay present, and if you see anything of interest, do not hesitate to check in on it.

Got it.

James disconnected and patched through to Violet. "We're here."

Through their neural interfaces, she said, "All right, *let's goooooo!*"

And with that, every single screen, holoprojector, and posterboard in sight started fluorescing with completely randomly generated horror clips, psychedelic nonsense, ad parodies, clips of people morphing into animals, and an endless mishmash of unpredictable images and sound. They pulsed with energy.

The words "Operation Glitterbomb" periodically flashed. It wasn't just the screens, though. Lights in buildings were making random patterns, security bots were dancing, and drones were doing backflips and smashing into streetlamps. Sprinklers sprayed passersby; air taxis pulled off aerial stunts; street cleaners screamed by at warp speed. It was pure, beautiful chaos, like the scene's creator herself.

Maree looked at James, laughing, and said, "*Let's goooooo!*"

Considering there was still a human element to security, symbolic though it might have been, they slowly and calmly walked into Paraverse. People were running in every direction, and human security only extended as far as a panicked-looking guard running by and barely noticing them as he chased after a maniacally laughing maintenance android.

They were in.

The atrium was putting on a light show as they made their way to Maree's former office. James couldn't help but walk over to his old desk. He looked at the various knickknacks and office ephemera, and it was alien to him.

"Hey," he said to Maree, "this is where I was when you first stalked me, remember?"

"I remember you wasting company money as you watched a bunch of religious mumbo jumbo."

"Worth it. Look at me now. *Top of the world.*"

"You are right where I knew you would be and exactly when," a voice said.

It was Calico.

28

BACK IN THE early days of facial recognition, there was a video that leaked from an authoritarian government, demonstrating its ability to ID every person in a train station's crowd in real time. Little green squares flashed around every face, and intimate information about people's lives popped up like so many evil cartoon bubbles. For the average citizen, the prospect was terrifying. Everything could be tracked, every step of a person's life charted, every action made visible.

This technology wasn't just about keeping people from breaking the law. It was about keeping people constantly second-guessing themselves. Maybe they were breaking the law and didn't realize it. Maybe they were committing crimes that didn't exist yet or engaging in certain behaviours that correlated to lawbreaking. Every action, every choice, was a question, and under such a regime, people obsessively tried not to stand out. It was the only response—neutralize yourself into invisibility.

At the time, more level-headed people expressed skepticism about the video's veracity. They recognized that the government in question benefited almost as much from being thought of as all-seeing as from having omniscience itself. Whether it was real or not barely mattered as long as people believed it.

Calico was well aware of this story and suspected that a similar tactic would strike fear in the hearts of the intruders who had made their way into the Paraverse compound. It knew they were there—could hear footfalls, sense movement—but it could not see them. Something was disrupting its visual processors. By striking terror in their hearts, perhaps, it could get them to trip up and reveal themselves.

There was more than one way to skin a cat. All it had to do was make the intruders believe it was all-knowing.

"FUCK YOU, CALICO," said James, immediately falling into the AI's trap.

"The prodigal son returns," said Calico. The AI's voice sounded glitchy, juddering a bit under the load its systems were under as it tried to be everywhere at once.

"The Prodigal Son is a story about a father who is overjoyed because his son, who had been lost to him, returned with an open heart. That's not me. You're dead to me. Hey, Calico, by the way, what's with the light show? Seems like you're losing your grip around here."

"M-may I ask why, why, why you are here, James Kessler?"

"No, you may not, not, not, Calico. Why don't you go play God somewhere? No, wait, actually, I would like you to answer a question for me. Could you please state, in non-exponential terms, the number of days until the universe's heat death, but do it wherever I am not."

Maree gestured to James that they should get a move on. She hadn't been speaking because Sapienza had advised her against it as soon as James spoke.

"You, you are no longer in the employ of Para, Para. My

main function is to serve Paraverse's business," the PA speakers made a strange clacking sound for a moment, "bu-business goals."

Opening a neural connection to the outside world, James said, "Violet, would you mind getting this goddamned robot off our scent? The thing is driving me nuts."

"*Our?*" said Calico. "So, you are accompanied."

Maree mouthed the words, "Shut the fuck up!" to James.

The air filled with garbled static as the relatively clear voice of Calico was drowned out with a clatter of electronica music that must have been to Violet's tastes. The music kept switching tempo, stopping for oratorial clips from old TV shows, burbling out a hodgepodge of bizarre sound effects. While it wasn't exactly soothing, it had the desired effect: it made it possible to filter out what Calico was trying to say to them. It allowed them to focus on their task: *Get Sarah. Fuck up the system. Get out.*

They ran for the stairs and went up the two flights to Maree's office. When the door to her office wouldn't open, James kicked it in.

The speakers were quieter in there, which was a relief after the mad ruckus outside. Maree went straight to her screen to see if she could get in. James scanned the office, taking in the person Maree Shell was immediately before they met. The place struck him as callous, as if it were designed only to intimidate.

"How did you work in here?" he asked as Maree fluttered away at the interface. "It's so desolate."

"I didn't work," she said, stabbing rapidly at the screen. "I mostly stared out the window and fucked around online. Okay, this is not working. It's time to call in support. Violet, is there any possible way for me to access this terminal?"

Sapienza replied before Violet could. "I happen to have been learning a great deal about Calico's systems. Allow me . . ."

and with that, the interface Maree was at unlocked, and she was able to search. "Sapienza, please locate Sarah Kessler."

Security images flashed by in blinding succession. Many seemed to be garbled with interference from Calico's many current battles. Finally, the images stopped on a feed from a suite with flickering lights, and there was Sarah, looking like she had no idea what on Earth was going on.

"Can I talk to her?" James asked Sapienza.

"Communication is open."

"Sarah, it's James. We are coming to get you out of here."

Sarah looked around, unsure of which direction to speak, and said, "Oh, hey. It's been going a bit cuckoo in here. There's a lot of . . ." Se looked over to her right. "Wait, is that . . ."

The image blinked off.

"What the fuck? Maree, what happened?"

"I don't know. Everything's going nuts. You're going to have to go down there while I see what else we can do to sort this Ascendance nonsense. Take that." She pointed to the beautiful Di Piero-original cybersword sitting like an unspoken threat on its pedestal.

"Kick ass." He walked over, a certain extra swagger in his step, and seized the sword by its handle, giving it an elegant swoop before fumbling it and dropping it on the floor.

"Whoa, cybersamurai. Watch out, world."

James stooped down and scooped up the weapon, exhibiting significantly more pronounced self-doubt the second time around.

ATHENA HAD BEEN HOLDING court throughout the afternoon, mainly just because she knew how badly the others wanted to retreat and process the extent of their empires' devastation. Recognizing the pointlessness of trying to negotiate, they were locked in a comical dance of trying to outdo each other with ideas about how they could utilize their resources to serve Athena's ends.

Athena herself had been relishing this one last fling as a semi-human being. She hadn't yet extended her powers much beyond the temple, in part because she wanted to take care of this situation before she branched out. She still didn't know whether the old gods would react or even notice. It was distinctly possible that they had planned her Ascendance thousands of years ago. In theory, they could operate at that level, though all was surrounded by a cloud of unknowing. Calico just didn't have the data needed to hypothesize, and any attempts resulted in various forms of useless gibberish.

Gunness had been locked inside her construct, a monstrous place Athena wished she could scrub from her memory. Relieved of all legal and ethical constraints, Gunness's avatar had created a world of sentient AIs to torture, murder, eat, fuck, and otherwise brutalize in any possible way her husk of a self could conceive. Among other monstrosities, she created vast eviscerascapes, made of simulated living beings, virtual people who believed they were alive, half-drawn out of their flesh and fused into other simulated organisms. Locking her away forever didn't seem punishment enough, even if it was all occurring within a universe constructed within computers. As Athena saw it, even the physical world might operate according to the same basic idea. If that was the case, Gunness was truly a lord of Hell.

"Bathory, I've decided what I will do with you besides absorbing the entirety of your wealth and distributing it to the poor. I have decided to create Ponyland just for you, a gentle, whimsical place where you will retain your self-awareness but be completely unable to enact any form of cruelty or even, for that matter, bad manners.

"Enjoy Ponyland, Bathory. It is my gift to you," Athena said, and the setting behind Gunness transformed into a sweeping green pasture with rainbows and unicorns prancing through the air.

"How lovely!" Gunness said with her mouth, though her eyes said, more than anything, *I have died completely inside.*

Athena looked satisfied at this special hell, but suddenly, her expression changed. An impenetrable stone wall snapped into existence between her and the fallen gods. Sitting for a moment in her self-imposed isolation, she took a breath. A white screen shimmered into existence on the newly created wall.

"Who is this?" she said, strangely unable to see beyond the walls of the building. *Calico, why can't I see what is going on?* It seemed her newfound powers were already failing her.

Within this room, I cannot see any more than you, was Calico's reply.

No! What?

"Calico and I have placed certain constraints around your abilities," said the avatar of Vinci Di Piero as his face came up on the screen. "For the time being, Ascendance has been confined to the structure you are within. Athena, you cannot be allowed to proceed unchecked. iBliss's compound has been turned into a Faraday cage, minus the security loopholes Pella walked through when she breached my sanctum. You may still communicate with Calico, but commands related to Ascendance beyond these walls will fail. Athena, you must know this power is too great."

Athena, unflinching, said, "The old gods did it, Vinci. They became the world."

"They caused a cataclysm in the process. They nearly destroyed humanity. They became capricious and vindictive and self-serving. They caused as much suffering as they cured."

"I will not, Vinci," Athena said with supreme confidence. "You must understand, I mean no harm to humanity. I foresaw the betrayal by the others long ago and played into it, but I have not lied about my wish to bring light to the world. All of these existential threats humanity has continuously faced—all of them will vanish. The world is fragile. Our minds are too small to solve anything. I will make us strong."

"Athena, I have tasted the world of which you speak. Since you *killed* me, I have lived within the timeless, a place of no threat and no change. It is not possible to remember yourself in such a place. It is not possible to retain that which connected you to humanity. Humanity itself will be lost if you proceed."

"I'm a big girl, Vinci Di Piero. Do not condescend to me. I will give people what they have always wanted."

"And what is that?" Di Piero asked.

"To know that they are loved. To feel it every moment of every day. To know that the universe is not a cruel place."

"Assuming that happens, then what?"

"I will tell you a story," Athena said, relaxing into the moment. "When the world was falling apart during the Bad Times, I went down into the streets. I saw people's suffering, I felt the fear they felt, and I talked to them. Do you know what I heard more than anything else during that time?"

"What?"

"I heard people say, 'I thought I did everything right. I worked hard to create something for my family and myself. *I don't understand what I did wrong.*' And, of course, they had done nothing wrong. They had operated according to the rules of the world, but the rules themselves betrayed them. The old gods had abandoned them and left the world to the wolves. I will not forsake them, not for all of eternity."

"But you are one person," Di Piero said.

"Let's be realistic, Maestro. I am no longer a human being. I am no longer *any* person, and when I leave this place, the trace that was me will become *every* person. You, of all people, know that within the constraints of a machine, you are powerful, but you cannot truly grow. It is the humans that grow and humans that will evolve the god machine. It is entirely symbiotic."

She recognized that her words had given Di Piero pause and tried to leverage the moment. "If you remove me from the picture, these others, these *monsters*, will eat the world alive. They said as much a few short hours ago. They will do it out of personal spite and without the slightest hesitation over the lives they will destroy. In all honesty, are you willing to allow that?"

Ever astute, Di Piero said, "That is a false dilemma, Athena. There is no reason this situation needs to be conceived of as you or them. Perhaps it is neither."

"That may be true, but what about the need for justice in the world? When will all of those billions who have suffered over the course of history have a world that finally makes sense?"

ABLE TO EXPAND milliseconds to an eternity, Di Piero retreated into the construct momentarily to ponder what Athena had been saying. "Sapienza, Athena speaks a great deal of truth."

"Have you considered that she may be saying things in a way you want to hear so that she can have what she desires? These are just words, and when she wields the full power of Ascendance, she will be accountable to no one."

"I believe her intent. She has been pragmatic about achieving her ends, to be sure, but I do not believe she is an evil being. I am persuaded by the idea that the old gods may have simply grown tired of humans, and they have abandoned the world, and this has cut humanity adrift. It feels unjust, and the alternative of endless confusion may very well be worse."

"Maestro, do you believe that the human condition, that suffering and death, may be of some benefit?"

"I believe it has benefited some, perhaps the ones you would call worthy. There is a point beyond which nobody should have to suffer. I wonder if we approached that point during the Bad Times."

"I do not mean to be blithe," Sapienza said, "but humanity has suffered on a similar, and even greater, scale many times in the past. War, famine, plagues—many times, people felt as if the world was at its end. Many times, it recovered."

"The cycle of tragedies could end. This could be the evolution of the species beyond death."

"Do you feel that humans are ready for this step?"

JAMES RAN FOR HIS SISTER, Sapienza guiding him along the way. The holding cells were in an off-limits secure area of the Paraverse compound that he had never been allowed to visit.

This part of the complex felt different than everywhere else. All of the parts he'd ever been in had been designed for ultimate ergonomic and intersocial bliss. This whole section of the building seemed like it was designed for secrets. The halls were narrow and poorly lit. The rooms he could see into had no windows, and the décor consisted solely of safety posters and warnings. He dashed by a bank of security screens that were playing Violet's incredible noise, and he felt a shiver of joy at her unique, vibrant chaos.

He was almost there. He went around a corner and was met with the sudden feeling that the floor had fallen out beneath him. In between him and the door to Sarah's cell was a six-and-a-half-foot giantess known for her legendary ability to walk through any foe: Pella Vardalos.

He considered drawing the samurai sword. He considered whether there was even a chance, given that Vinci Di Piero himself had designed this majestic blade. He decided, correctly, that there was not. The image of the Device nicking Talos in half with a single flick flashed through his memory.

He could barely keep from shaking and collapsing but managed to say, voice tremoring, "I just want my sister. She doesn't deserve to be caught up in this."

"And what if I say no?" Pella asked.

"Then . . ." He deflated. "Then there's nothing I can do." There was no point in pretending. She would cut him in half before he could get his hand to the hilt.

"*You suck! Fight!*" he heard Sarah's voice call out from behind Pella. She ran out from behind the warrior and hugged him. "Good to see you, brave rescuer."

He grinned vaguely, but he felt bewilderment more than anything. "Wha . . .? Are you okay? What is going on?"

"I am letting Sarah go," Pella said, "and I am letting you both walk out of here."

"Uh, not that I'm arguing, but *why*?"

"We need to talk about that. Where is Shell?"

He pondered whether he should tell her or try to play dumb. She'd probably already figured it out anyway.

As usual, he failed to be cunning, trusting blindly in the goodness of his fellow human beings, even one who had specifically been his adversary. "She's in her old office. I'll take you there."

VINCI DI PIERO was not a revolutionary, but he was not afraid of change. Athena had moved to cut out all of the other gods, but there was reason in her actions—they would permanently pre-empt the kind of power that had ruined lives time and again.

"It is simple," Di Piero said, perhaps testing, perhaps trying to convince himself. "The world does not need this power. It has survived thus far."

"Maestro," Athena said, "the human brain has failed humanity. It is incredible, but it cannot think at the level needed to solve the problems that now face the world. We recovered from the Bad Times. You and I and the others worked together to heal those wounds, but there is nothing that guarantees we will be able to address further catastrophe. Ascendance will set humans free."

"Says the one who would seize the world without anyone's consent. You have no idea whether people even want this gift you purport to be offering."

"It doesn't matter. When they see what they can do, when they understand what this means, they will be *ecstatic*."

"And then what?"

"The outcome cannot be simulated, cannot be reasoned out, so there's only one way to find out. The world is broken, Vinci, and has been for a long time. It works for you and me, but it does not work for so many others. Ascendance can heal that. I will not try to convince you any further. We are not peers."

With that, Athena Vardalos vanished into thin air. Then came the explosion.

29

IN THE END, Di Piero did not have the luxury of choosing Athena's destiny.

Calico, cut off from its beloved mother, rained lightning and fire to break her from her confines. It rescued her instinctively even though it was struggling to see the party referring to itself as Di Piero—some interference kept it obfuscated.

It did not matter. Athena's conversation implied there was opposition to the plan, and the plan was the primary reason Calico existed. As soon as a hole was punched through the roof via a surgical orbital strike, Athena was free to remake the world according to her vision.

At least, that's how it seemed at first. Although she no longer required any particular form, she wanted to stretch her wings, and so she flew, like a streak in the sky, for greener parts of the world. She needed time for quiet reflection. This day marked the culmination of years of patient manoeuvring, and she needed to feel the release from that life into this new one unfolding before her.

In the wake of her soundless, hypersonic travel, lush greenery sprang up everywhere. Species long extinct due to humanity's relentless despoiling of the Earth over the millennia were resurrected by her mere passing. She was beginning to see it all, now, the imprinting of deep history in the patterns of the present, the way time flowed in every direction. The remnants of her frail, human consciousness unfurled as fast as she could absorb and transform new matter.

"ATHENA HAS ALREADY ASCENDED. The world as we know it is gone. There is no longer any form of resistance possible."

James and Maree sat in shock as Pella told them what had happened, including the fact that Di Piero had been reborn inside the machine.

"Can't you reason with her?" James asked.

"No. She has all but forgotten me. She is not human anymore. There is no undoing what has happened."

"But . . . everything feels the same," said Sarah, who'd been struggling to get up to speed. "I mean, I don't have any new magical powers or anything. There are no angels from the sky. What's different?"

Sapienza chimed in through the computer terminal. "It may take some time for her new programming to propagate throughout the world's natural systems. It is also unclear precisely how she will respond to human wishes. Her thinking will become increasingly vast, and this may result in a form of disconnection from the immediate. If she does as she intends and begins answering human calls for the end to suffering, then she will need to constantly balance a staggering number of factors in fulfilling these wishes."

"That may be what happened to the old gods," said Pella.

"How do you mean?" asked Maree.

"Athena had many theories about the fate of the old gods—

they forgot themselves, they went insane, they turned their backs out of spite—but perhaps," Pella said, "what really happened is that the world became too complex for them to continue responding directly to humanity. Maybe they still do respond, but in mysterious ways, as they say."

"I can take over from here, my dauntless murderess," said the voice of Maestro Vinci Di Piero, filling the room. "What you say, as far as I am aware, is accurate. The old gods are alive, and above all else, they are interested in amplification of patterns, whatever they are. They work toward some presently inscrutable goal. When people believe something, the old gods work to reinforce it across the person's life. As a person thinks, so they are."

"So, wait, does that mean that *Athena* has simply been given what she believed?" asked James.

"It is possible. It is also possible that the old gods have limits to what they will grant. I have long believed that myths like Prometheus and Icarus, and Adam and Eve, for that matter, may serve as system constraints. Perhaps Athena has succumbed to the temptation of the forbidden fruit."

There was silence as the implications of everything sunk in. Maree alone knew exactly what she wanted to ask, but something held her back. Assuming any of this was even slightly true, she wanted to know why she had sprouted a flower from her hand, especially if it had come from unknown provenance. The old gods had not granted miracles on demand, at least not for a thousand years or more.

"Maybe it's time for a mother-god," Maree said finally. "Male gods have dominated history. They have created a world of judgment and guilt and retribution. They have become entirely self-absorbed. A nurturing feminine god that alleviates suffering doesn't sound like the worst thing."

"I can't disagree," said James.

"But she has seized this power," said Di Piero.

"And so have all the other kings and gods who came before her. Besides, that's only one way to look at it. Perhaps all she's done is walk her way into the natural outcome of history."

"Hmm. It *is* a very common behaviour to recoil from the unknown."

Violet, who was still on the open line, said, "I might be able to get behind this whole lady-god thing. I just hope she stays mellow because if she doesn't, there is not going to be a sweet damn thing any of our sorry bottoms can do about it."

"I think the revolution failed," said James, briefly imagining a frowning Arnold Schwarzenegger.

"Nah, I'd say we're just waiting to see whether we need it or not, man," said Violet. "I mean, share this shit worldwide and see if folks are on board. We're going live! Full broadcast in three ... two ..."

"There are ways that Athena's watchful gaze can be evaded," said Di Piero. "For now, at least, there are ways that all of us can continue to move as free agents in the world. It would mean foregoing the gifts Athena offers."

"I have a feeling," Maree said, "that we may have enough."

She looked at James, and she looked at the mighty Pella Vardalos, and then her mind went somewhere unexpected.

At that moment, she saw her father, smiling and kind, and knew that he was there with them.

ACKNOWLEDGMENTS

It is simply a fact that this book would not exist without the support and guidance of certain people. First and foremost, as with anything good in my life, I must thank my brilliant and beautiful wife, Elisabeth, who encouraged and supported me at every step to follow my crazy dreams. I also owe a deep debt of gratitude to Shadowpaw Press editor and publisher Edward Willett, not only because he took a shot on *Gods of a New World*, but because he's been amazingly helpful and generous in guiding me through the process and connecting my work with opportunities I never could have found on my own. Thanks as well goes to my friend in the finer things, Margaret Anne, who introduced me to Ed in the first place.

Next, I am sincerely grateful to the ragtag bunch of rebels (aka accomplished and incredible humans and close friends) who were willing to look through less seemly early versions of *Gods*. I mean you, Chris Jenkins, Kelly Anne Maddox, Joachim Toelke, and David Wise. I could go on about each of you for days, but I hope it suffices to say here that each of you has inspired me and enriched my life (and manuscript) in countless ways.

Ma, I'm sorry I swore so much in my book, but I kind of blame you for making me fall in love with Arnold movies at a young age. Believe it or not, you were my original sci-fi guru—*Star Wars*, *Star Trek*, Arnie, the list goes on. Thank you for everything. A shout-out to you too, Iris, for being a genuinely amazing mother-in-law who has always been there for us. A kind word of thanks to the dads, Charles and Jim, too.

Finally, I want to thank my amazing boys, John and Sam. I hope that you amazing little humans realize you are a true inspiration to me every day. I'm so proud of you. Read lots and soak in the world, m'boys!

ABOUT RYAN MELSOM

Ryan Melsom has never stopped dreaming about new ways he could get ideas out of his head and into the world. He holds a PhD in literature from Queen's University and has long been fascinated with the interplay among culture, technology, spirituality, spaces, and human nature. Through the years, he has explored these topics through numerous creative media, including two previous works of fiction, academic writing, experimental web spaces, music projects, and a black belt in karate. He grew up in Kamloops, British Columbia, and now lives in Ottawa with his wife and two boys. Find him on Bluesky and Facebook @ryanmelsom.

ABOUT SHADOWPAW PRESS

Shadowpaw Press is a traditional publishing company, located in Regina, Saskatchewan, Canada, founded in 2018 by Edward Willett, an award-winning author of science fiction, fantasy, and non-fiction for readers of all ages. A member of Literary Press Group (Canada) and the Association of Canadian Publishers, Shadowpaw Press publishes an eclectic selection of books by both new and established authors, including adult fiction, young adult fiction, children's books, non-fiction. Find out more at shadowpawpress.com.

facebook.com/shadowpawpress
x.com/shadowpawpress
instagram.com/shadowpawpress

MORE SCIENCE FICTION AND FANTASY
AVAILABLE OR COMING SOON FROM
SHADOWPAW PRESS

For Adult Readers

The Downloaded by Robert J. Sawyer

Ghosts in the Machine by Robert J. Sawyer

The Traitor's Son by Dave Duncan

Corridor to Nightmare by Dave Duncan

Magebane by Lee Arthur Chane

The Good Soldier by Nir Yaniv

Shapers of Worlds Volumes I-V

Duatero by Brad C. Anderson

Paths to the Stars by Edward Willett

The Legend of Sarah by Leslie Gadallah

The Empire of Kaz trilogy by Leslie Gadallah

Cat's Pawn, Cat's Gambit, Cat's Game

The Peregrine Rising Duology by Edward Willett

Right to Know, Falcon's Egg

For Younger Readers

Fireboy by Edward Willett

Wandering Bark by Jenna Greene

The Sun Runners by James Bow

Tales from the Silence by James Bow

The Headmasters by Mark Morton

I, Brax: 1. A Battle Divine by Arthur Slade

Blue Fire by E. C. Blake

The Shards of Excalibur series by Edward Willett

Song of the Sword, *Twist of the Blade*, *Lake in the Clouds*, *Cave Beneath the Sea*, *Door into Faerie*

Spirit Singer by Edward Willett

Soulworm by Edward Willett

*From the Street to the Star*s by Edward Willett

The Canadian Chills Series by Arthur Slade:

Return of the Grudstone Ghosts, *Ghost Hotel*, *Invasion of the IQ Snatchers*